# BANE OF MALEKITH

METALLIC THUNDER RAGED as the two lines came together, the heavier high elf cavalry smashing through the lighter dark elves despite the other's advantage of slope and momentum. As the two lines came together, Tyrion was shocked to see a familiar face among the dark elf lines.

Fear and hatred warred in his heart. He had been seeking a worthy foe and suddenly he had found one.

'Iltharis! Or Urian or whatever you call yourself! Face me, traitor, and die!' His bellow carried above the sounds of battle, as did the answering laugh.

'Prince Tyrion! This is a not-unexpected pleasure.' Somehow Iltharis's mocking voice carried over the ring of metal on metal. He carried a glowing runeblade in each hand and he used them to cut his way towards Tyrion, slashing through seasoned elf warriors as if they were no more than children.

Blade rang against blade as steed encountered steed.

*More elves from Black Library*

**• TYRION & TECLIS •**
William King
Book 1: BLOOD OF AENARION
Book 2: SWORD OF CALEDOR
Book 3: BANE OF MALEKITH

**• TIME OF LEGENDS: THE WAR OF VENGEANCE •**
Nick Kyme & Chris Wraight
Book 1: THE GREAT BETRAYAL
Book 2: MASTER OF DRAGONS

**• TIME OF LEGENDS: THE SUNDERING •**
Gav Thorpe
Book 1: MALEKITH
Book 2: SHADOW KING
Book 3: CALEDOR

**• ORION •**
Darius Hinks
Book 1: THE VAULTS OF WINTER
Book 2: THE TEARS OF ISHA
Book 3: THE COUNCIL OF BEASTS

DEFENDERS OF ULTHUAN
Graham McNeill

SONS OF ELLYRION
Graham McNeill

GUARDIANS OF THE FOREST
Graham McNeill

A WARHAMMER NOVEL

# BANE OF MALEKITH

A TYRION & TECLIS NOVEL

WILLIAM KING

BLACK LIBRARY

*For John McLintock, Sword Against Evil.*

**A BLACK LIBRARY PUBLICATION**
First published in Great Britain in 2013.
Paperback Edition published in 2014 by
Black Library,
Games Workshop Ltd.,
Willow Road,
Nottingham,
NG7 2WS, UK

10 9 8 7 6 5 4 3 2 1

Cover illustration by Raymond Swanland.
Icon by Nuala Kinrade.



A CIP record for this book
is available from the British Library.

UK ISBN 13: 978 1 84970 766 4
US ISBN 13: 978 1 84970 755 8



Printed and bound by CPI Group (UK) Ltd, Croydon, CR0 4YY.

This is a dark age, a bloody age, an age of daemons and of sorcery. It is an age of battle and death, and of the world's ending. Amidst all of the fire, flame and fury it is a time, too, of mighty heroes, of bold deeds and great courage.

These are bleak times. Across the length and breadth of the Old World, from the heartlands of the human Empire and the knightly palaces of Bretonnia to ice-bound Kislev in the far north, come rumblings of war. In the towering Worlds Edge Mountains, the orc tribes are gathering for another assault. Bandits and renegades harry the wild southern lands of the Border Princes. There are rumours of rat-things, the skaven, emerging from the sewers and swamps across the land. And from the northern wildernesses there is the ever-present threat of Chaos, of daemons and beastmen corrupted by the foul powers of the Dark Gods.

An ancient and proud race, the high elves hail from Ulthuan, a mystical island of rolling plains, rugged mountains and glittering cities. Ruled over by the noble Phoenix King, Finubar, and the Everqueen, Alarielle, Ulthuan is a land steeped in magic, renowned for its mages and fraught with blighted history. Great seafarers, artisans and warriors, the high elves protect their ancestral homeland from enemies near and far. None more so than from their wicked kin, the dark elves, against whom they are locked in a bitter war that has lasted for centuries.

# PROLOGUE

THE WIZARD LOOKED over the gameboard at Death. 'You are not real,' he said.

'Come now, Caledor,' said Death. 'You are in no position to cast aspersions. After all, you are dead.'

The wizard touched the place where his heart should have been. There was no beat. He placed his hand over his mouth. He did not breathe. He touched his wrist. There was no pulse.

A small fragment of knowledge came back to him. He had died a long, long time ago, trying to save the world. He had died slowly, in great pain, while trying to work powerful magic.

Caledor – his name *had* been Caledor once, when he had walked among the living and still had use for such a thing. He had not known that until Death had mentioned it. He could remember almost nothing else about himself, but it was good to have a name once more. It was a beginning, something he could build on.

'Nonetheless,' Caledor said, 'you are not real.'

Death raised a long pale hand and removed his ivory mask. He knuckled the hollow space below his eye and he let out a long patient sigh that seemed to go on forever, as was the nature of even the least of the actions of gods. 'I suppose you are going to argue about the nature of a reality that allows you to be dead and yet be aware of my existence and of your own. You are one of those for whom there is no afterlife, only a negation, a non-being.'

'Not at all,' said Caledor. 'I merely doubt the reality of this whole experience.'

'Living things have been doing that since the world began,' said Death. 'I am surprised that you, of all the elves, should be so unoriginal.'

'Why am I here?' Caledor asked.

'You are here to play the Great Game and decide the fate of the world.'

Caledor considered Death's words as he considered Death himself. The dark god had taken the form of a tall elf, very pale of skin. His nails were black. His teeth were black. His eyes were pools of infinite darkness. He wore robes of spider silk the colour of the black grapes from the vineyards of the furthest south. On those robes, in silver thread, were inscribed the runes of all the names by which the elves knew him: Khaela Mensha Khaine. This was the Reaper of Souls, the Ender of Worlds.

Propped against the side of Death's chair, unscabbarded, was a tall black sword that Caledor had seen before, although it had not then been borne by Death. Hideous runes glittered on its blade. The remnants of the souls it had devoured clung to the naked metal in a scummy crust. It was an evil blighted thing, its aura of matchless malignity noticeable even in this odd place and even while the blade was quiescent. Caledor could not look at it for too long without feeling queasy.

Instead he studied the game. It looked something like chess but was played on a larger and infinitely more complex board. The squares each contained Slann runes pregnant with mystical meaning, symbols that governed the magic of time and space.

It was hard to tell the board's true size. Each square was like a hole in reality that looked out into some other section of creation. The patterns were not like that of a chessboard at all. The squares, the focal points of the action, were not beside each other. They floated in the air at different levels. They were connected by lines, ellipses– the whole mass of squares lay amid concentric circles which had their own mystical significance.

He knew somehow that each square represented a specific place, some of which he had known in life, some of which had been created since his death. This gameboard was a map of a very specific reality. There was an underlying pattern to it that he felt he could grasp if only he was given time.

As above, so below, whispered a small distant part of his

mind. What we change here, we change in the true world. This map not only represents the terrain, in some strange way it *is* the terrain.

The game was already in progress. Pieces that represented kings and queens, wizards, demi-gods and daemons were already in motion. Some of them lay beside the board, removed by the effect of earlier moves. Just as the squares represented real places, the pieces represented real people.

Death's pieces were carved from bone ivory, of course. His own pieces were made of silver and gold. Many more of his than of Death's were gone. It was obvious to even the most cursory inspection that he was losing.

He knew that it was very important that he win. If he failed here, his world fell too and his entire life, his death and the deaths of all his friends would have been in vain.

Despair filled him. He was no player. Not the way Aenarion had been.

Aenarion. That was another name he had once known. Aenarion had been there when he had died. He had died himself shortly thereafter. Looking over at the sword, it came to him where he had seen it before. It had been Aenarion's once, a long time ago, in that different world the gameboard represented. In the world they had died trying to save.

He saw a resemblance in Khaine's features to Aenarion's. Aenarion had been half a god himself. Perhaps they were related. Or perhaps this was something else entirely. He was not sure what, but he knew it was as well to question all of his assumptions here.

'You are considering your move,' Death said.

'No. I am remembering Aenarion,' said Caledor.

Death smiled. 'He was my greatest servant.'

Even lacking all the knowledge that had made him what he was, Caledor sensed the lie in that. 'Aenarion was never your servant.'

'He bore my sword.'

'That still does not mean he served you. It was a tool which he used.'

'Perhaps you are right,' said Death. 'Let me rather say that his aims and mine coincided for a while.'

Caledor did not have the energy to argue. Death picked up the piece that represented Aenarion from where it lay beside the board. It was old now, marked by age, its surface rubbed away in places. It might have been tarnished silver or grubby ivory. It was difficult to tell.

'He was a very great killer,' said Death. 'Even the greater daemons, the firstborn children of Chaos, feared him.'

Looking down at the board, Caledor could see that a couple of his own pieces had similar features to the ones Death wore. One of them was tall, broad-shouldered and golden. Looking at the piece, Caledor saw him as he was in life. He could have been Aenarion reborn, but a smiling, good-natured Aenarion, without the weight of care that had always bowed the broad back of the first Phoenix King.

Tyrion, Caledor thought. That was this piece's name. Tyrion, son of Arathion of the line of Aenarion. Looking at Tyrion's face now, he could see it was twisted with uncharacteristic worry. He was wearing the armour of the druchii, which was not natural for him, for he was an asur, a high elf. It was a distinction that had not existed when Caledor had been alive.

Beside Tyrion was a woman of glorious beauty, whose life too had been touched by the power of a god. The piece that represented this woman's mother had already been removed from the board. She was a pawn promoted, a new Everqueen. This was all part of the pattern, he told himself, and he needed to understand it, as he needed to understand what was happening to him.

Before you can rule others, you must first rule yourself.

It was a law of wizardry and more than wizardry. Another fragment of memory bubbled to the surface of his mind. He remembered Aenarion talking to the young Malekith in the great armed camp at Skaggerak. The child had thrown a tantrum and his father, with a tender patience so different from the attitude he displayed in his dealings with all others, was explaining that law to his young son. Caledor remembered that even at the time he had found it ironic. Aenarion had been incapable of the least restraint, resented anything or anyone that tried to baulk his wishes.

Malekith was there upon the board now, no longer a small, watchful boy but a towering, terrifying armoured figure that reeked of death and ancient dark magic. He had turned out badly then. The thought saddened Caledor because he fondly remembered the child. Still, how could he have turned out differently, with two parents such as Aenarion and Morathi; a more self-centred, doom-torn pair of elves had never lived.

Morathi was still on the board too, as wickedly seductive as ever. She did not appear to have aged in all the long ages since Caledor's death. She was still much as he remembered her: dark-haired, sinuously lovely. Like every other elf who had ever looked upon her, he felt the erotic power of her beauty.

Unlike most of them, he could see exactly how much of it came from sorcery. Spells glittered in the air about her, obscuring her true self. Over the millennia a patina of evil magic had crusted around her. As with the Sword of Khaine, the residue of the souls she had devoured clung to her. In her case, they were the fuel for the spell that kept her alive.

She always had a great gift for magic, Caledor thought. More than that, there was a power in her. That which let her look into hell and the future had other side effects too. He could catch the resonance of her thoughts concerning him.

Do you watch me, old ghost? Do you shiver at the thought of what I do?

Caledor did not shiver. He was no longer capable of it. All he could do was watch, appalled, as she tried to destroy his great work once again. All elves were selfish, but she took it to an extreme. She was prepared to murder a world so that she could live forever.

Had she always been this bad, Caledor wondered, or had the madness slipped on her over the centuries? Did her son realise what she was up to? Perhaps he did, judging by the company he kept now.

Malekith was accompanied by something even worse than his mother, a daemon Caledor had known of in ancient times, a creature responsible for the destruction of half a continent and the killing of countless elves.

N'Kari, it was called. The piece on the board was a huge, four-armed monstrous thing, the sort of daemon that the texts referred to as a Keeper of Secrets. The vision that entered Caledor's mind was of a beautiful elven woman, chained by magic that might have bound a god. Malekith had indeed grown in power if he could do that.

Something told Caledor that this daemon was important, that its presence on the board was one of the reasons why Death was doing so well and he was doing so badly. It should not have been there.

'Are you going to move?' Death asked. 'Need I remind you that we are playing to a time limit, and that you forfeit the game if we do not complete it before the sands of time run out?'

Death indicated the hourglass that sat beside the table. Caledor could not remember it being there before. Perhaps Death's gesture had called it into being.

'I do not like this game,' said Caledor. 'It seems all the rules are stacked in your favour.'

'If you do not like the game, why did you agree to play?'

That was a good question. Why was he sitting here, playing an unbeatable opponent at a game he had no hope of winning?

'I had no choice,' he said at last. 'Nothing that lives does.'

'You had a choice,' said Death. 'You least of all can claim you were forced into this. You started the game when you created the board, wizard.'

Caledor reclaimed another part of his memory. The board was, at least in part, a representation of the vast spell he had woven over six thousand years ago and which had trapped him in this limbo. They were in the place where he had died, at the exact centre of the Vortex.

Contained within that truth was another one, a truth he was not yet prepared to face. It was still too terrible for him to contemplate.

Caledor picked up one of his pieces, the other one that resembled Aenarion. It was made of moon-silver. Teclis, this one was called. He blazed with power, power almost as great as that Caledor had wielded himself once, even though this one had been born into a world of far less magic. Teclis was Tyrion's twin, although physically they were nothing alike.

As he touched the piece he recalled other things. He had spoken to this Teclis before, had reached out to him through the Vortex and through other things. He had spoken to him of magic, the fate of the world, and of secrets long hidden and now become important once more.

He knew then how he could influence events and where. He could sense those who were close to the Vortex and close to the things he had once created. With this one, as with Morathi, there was something else. This one had studied Caledor's work, had deciphered its patterns and held them in his mind. This had set up a resonance of sympathetic magic between them.

'You have touched the piece, do you intend to move it?' Death asked.

Indecisively, Caledor returned the piece to the board. 'No. Not yet.'

'Waste all the time you wish. The sands of time are running out.'

Caledor glanced again at Death and at the powers arrayed against him. A daemon, a dark lord and a would-be divinity. They had all grown stronger over the millennia and he had grown weaker. Even at his mightiest he would have been hard put to stand against any one of them. Now, in order to preserve what he had made, he needed to defeat them all.

It was not a matter of power, he told himself. It was a matter of intelligence and strategy and the ability to think ahead. Even there he was at a disadvantage. Who had ever out-thought Death? Malekith was one of the greatest generals in history. Morathi could see the future.

There was nothing to be gained by complaining. Some things simply had to be done. He gathered the tattered remnants of his once near-immeasurable strength to him and raised the piece that represented Tyrion from the board.

'Come then, Ender of Worlds,' Caledor said, placing Tyrion decisively in his new position. 'Let us play.'

# CHAPTER ONE

All around them the ancient forest burned. Shadows danced like mad ghosts at a daemonic revel. The air reeked of the fiery death of trees older than empires. The shrieks of the dying, the raped and the tortured mingled with the roar of the flames.

Instinct screamed at Tyrion to put as much distance between themselves and those awful sounds as they could while night lasted.

Those were his people being put to the sword. Those screaming voices belonged to asur, high elves. Their blood enemies, the druchii, had come upon them in the night. If he had not rescued Alarielle from the grasp of the dark elf general, the Everqueen herself would be in the hands of her most deadly enemies.

They needed to get out of here now, to flee, so that she

might be spared capture and humiliation by her foes. That was the reason to run.

He glanced across at the Everqueen. He doubted that anyone would have recognised her as the proud and beautiful ruler of Avelorn now. Like him, she was garbed as a druchii soldier. Her face was bruised and her body blood-spattered. Her green eyes held fear and a courage that kept that fear contained, if only just.

Until a few hours ago she had been the pampered ruler of her people. The only fighting she had seen was at tournaments where warriors fought for her favour. Yesterday, he had been one of those warriors, if an ambivalent one, fighting in the great tournament to be her champion.

Today the position seemed to have fallen to him by default. All of the others sworn to her protection were dead, killed by a druchii army which had somehow, impossibly, managed to erupt into the very heart of the forest kingdom of Avelorn without any warning being given.

Other sounds interrupted the shrieks of torment – the blaring of horns and the bellowing of orders. Pursuit was being organised. He needed to get Alarielle to safety. Another chilling thought struck him. If a dark elf army could reach the heart of Avelorn, where else could it reach? Perhaps no place was safe any more.

The Everqueen looked at him, as if frightened by what she read on his face as by the possibility of pursuit.

'You look thoughtful, Prince Tyrion.' He could tell she had wanted to say something else but she was being tactful.

He caught her by the wrist and pulled her along behind

him, his elven eyes following the shadowy path without difficulty. 'I was thinking that Avelorn might not be the only place the Witch King has attacked. In fact, it is very unlikely.'

Alarielle looked troubled. 'Of course,' she said. 'Avelorn is not the centre of the world.'

'Ah but it is, at least as far as the elves are concerned, your serenity,' said Tyrion. 'That's why we must get you as far away from here as possible come dawn.'

He was not sure how long these disguises would hold once the dark elves really started looking. He doubted either he or Alarielle could pass as druchii under even the most cursory of inspections.

As if summoned by that thought, a group of at least a dozen figures emerged out of the gloom, all of them dark elves and all of them female. They were beautiful in a savage sort of way – their garb consisted of leather straps, quivers, scabbards and very little else. Their hair was long and matted. Intricate, evil-looking tattoos marked their skins with shocking runes.

Crimson smeared their pouting lips as if they had been drinking the blood of their victims. Each of them bore two blades, and those bloody blades had seen use. Runes on the blades mirrored the ink on their skins. Into those swords, fell magic had been woven. Strange poisons dripped from their points, venoms capable of killing a warrior over a period of many days, making sure that he died in screaming agony.

Tyrion's heart sank. He had faced these women-warriors

before in the cold dark lands of Naggaroth. These were witch elves, among the deadliest fighters of a deadly breed.

The women blocked their path away from the tournament grounds. Tyrion had no idea what they were doing out here. Perhaps they were already scouring the woods for high elf survivors fleeing the battlefield. He gestured for Alarielle to hold her ground.

The witch elves came closer, half surrounding them in a great semicircle. Tyrion did not like the way their leader looked at him at all. He liked the way she looked at Alarielle even less.

'Hail, brother,' she said. 'You seem to be going the wrong way.'

Her bright, mad eyes studied Tyrion. He smiled easily and said, 'we were just looking for a private place to do some celebrating.'

The witch elf smiled, showing small, sharp teeth. 'Is that so?'

Tyrion reached out and took Alarielle's hand and squeezed it. 'That is so.'

The witch elves moved closer, and it was all that Tyrion could do to keep from drawing his blade. That would give them away as nothing else would. No dark elf bore a sword like Sunfang. The magic of that ancient blade would mark him as a stranger among the druchii.

The leader reached out and stroked Alarielle's cheek. The Everqueen shivered a little at the contact. 'She is certainly a pretty one. I can understand why you would feel that way. On the other hand, now is not the time to be leaving the battlefield.'

'Perhaps you are right,' said Tyrion. 'Perhaps we should head back and report to our units.'

'And what unit would that be, my pretty boy with the so-strange accent?' The witch elf was suspicious. He knew that he did not sound very much like an inhabitant of Naggaroth even when he tried. He was always going to have the accent of Lothern overlaying the mountain twang of Cothique he had picked up as a boy.

'We are with Captain Ichmael,' Tyrion said.

The witch elf laughed, a high-pitched crazed tittering that set cold fingers running up and down Tyrion's spine. She reached out and stroked Tyrion's chin now. Her nails were long and sharp and enamelled black. She tilted her head to one side and her eyes narrowed. 'Captain who?'

Tyrion did not miss the faint gesture she made with her left hand or the response that the other witch elves made. They had begun to circle behind Tyrion and Alarielle and within heartbeats the two of them were surrounded. Somewhere in the witch elf leader's crazed mind a mad suspicion had bloomed.

Tyrion drew Sunfang in one eye-blurring motion. The sword blazed to life, flames flickering along its length. The woman's drug-enhanced reflexes were so quick she almost managed to parry the blow. Sunfang grated along her blade, sparks bursting out as the metal ground together, then buried itself in the witch elf's head with the sound of a butcher's cleaver hitting a hanging carcass.

Tyrion lashed out left then right, taking down two more of the witch elves with as many blows. The rest of them responded with the speed of elite troops and something else…

Surprise did not slow them. Something about the drugs they had taken made them accept the sudden eruption of violence in their midst as if it was a perfectly normal occurrence. Perhaps for them it was. He knew how crazed witch elves could be.

They swarmed towards him, blades stabbing. He danced through a whirlwind of razor-sharp swords, ducking, weaving and slashing. Within a few more heartbeats he had killed three more. Other elves might have turned tail and fled in the face of the carnage that he wrought, but not these ones.

A poisoned dagger flickered towards the Everqueen. Desperately, Tyrion twisted to parry the blade, striking it from the air. As he did so, he felt a stab of pain in his side. One of the witch elves had managed to penetrate his stolen armour. He could only pray that no poison had got into the wound.

Seeing his concern for Alarielle, his foes switched targets, two of them going for her and the rest of them striking at him, knowing that he would be distracted.

There was no way he could protect Alarielle and himself at the same time. If the witch elves were determined to cut her down, they would, and there was nothing he could do about it, short of throwing himself in front of their blades.

'Don't kill her! She is the Everqueen!' Tyrion shouted. It was the only way he could think of to slow them down.

The two witch elves attacking Alarielle paused for a

second. Tyrion took advantage of it to stab one of them through the throat. Her flesh sizzled as Sunfang bit.

Alarielle raised her hands together over her head and spoke a word. There was a flash of greenish light and the witch elves reeled back, momentarily blinded. Tyrion leapt forwards into the blinded mass, blade slashing, leaving only dead and dying in his wake.

'You are hurt, Prince Tyrion,' said the Everqueen. Her voice sounded unnaturally loud in the strange quiet after the combat.

Tyrion's side stung where the witch elf's blade had bit. He took off the chainmail shirt, unlaced his jerkin and inspected the wound. It was nothing, a mere scratch that would not even require stitching.

'I took worse in practice matches when I was a boy.'

The Everqueen looked at him scornfully. 'I doubt you duelled with witch elf blades when you were a youth. There is no need for such bravado.'

She was right, of course. He had seen too much of what happened to those wounded by witch elves to want to take any chances now. He unstoppered the canteen that was part of the gear he had stolen. It smelled of potent alcohol. Trust a druchii to carry that in his water bottle. He poured some out onto the scratch. It burned as if he was being branded by a dark elf torturer. He kept his face calm, not wanting to give the Everqueen the satisfaction of seeing him in pain.

'Let me see it,' Alarielle said. Tyrion wanted to refuse but to do so would have seemed childish, so he stood there while she bent down to look at it.

'You might have been lucky, but I don't like the shadow surrounding the wound. If it gets worse, let me know.'

He looked at the wound again. There *was* a curious blackness around its edges that did not bode well, but there was nothing he could do about it now.

'What will you do, work magic on it?'

'I might have to.' She did not sound at all confident in her ability to do so.

In the distance horns rang out again. They made Tyrion think of hunters with packs of hounds. 'Not now. We had best be going,' he said. 'Run!'

They raced off into the night.

'A NEW DAY at last,' said Tyrion, looking at the red sun as it rose upon the horizon, clearly visible through a gap in the foliage. Birds had begun to sing. The grass was moist with dew. It all seemed strangely normal after the long night of flight and terror.

'Let us hope that it proves to be a happier one than the last,' said the Everqueen. 'I am not sure that I can endure another like yesterday.'

'I'm afraid you're just going to have to, your serenity,' said Tyrion. 'There will be many days like yesterday and worse ahead of us.'

'You're doing nothing to bolster my courage, Prince Tyrion,' said the Everqueen.

'I am trying to be realistic. We don't have an army. We don't have any friends. We only have the two of us to rely upon for our own safety.'

The Everqueen nodded. Her jaw tightened. Her eyes narrowed. She straightened her shoulders and stood a little taller. She was grim but resolute, and for the first time in a long time it seemed to Tyrion that here was someone he could follow.

'Where should we go?' the Everqueen asked. Just when she seemed ready to be a leader, she reminded him she was hardly more than a young girl. It was a strange mix.

'That's a very good question,' said Tyrion. 'We need to go in the direction that Malekith's minions least expect.'

'That's all very well, but it needs to be a direction in which we can eventually find refuge and get help.'

'Indeed. I say that we should strike out east.'

'How do we know that the dark elves are not waiting for us in that direction?'

'We don't – we will just have to take our chances.'

'What I still don't understand is how they managed to get to us. It should have been impossible for a force so large to penetrate so deeply into Avelorn without being spotted.'

'Magic,' said Tyrion. 'It's the only explanation.'

'Even so, I should have been able to sense such magic in the very heart of my domain. I may only have just become Everqueen, but in these lands nothing should be able to happen without me knowing it.'

'I am no sorcerer, but if you've only just inherited the power, perhaps you overlooked something.'

'You're not making me feel any better, Prince Tyrion.'

'I don't think it was a coincidence that the dark elves attacked so soon after your mother's death. I think that we have fallen into a trap that has been in preparation for a very long time. I think that we are very lucky indeed to have escaped it with our lives.'

The Everqueen looked thoughtful. 'The only reason that I am here, that we managed to escape at all, is because of you. I am very grateful for that. Perhaps I misjudged you, Prince Tyrion.'

Tyrion was very surprised to receive that apology. After all, he was the one who had been rude to her over the past few days. 'I do not think you were wrong about me at all, your serenity. And I think that the reason that we are here is that the gods have smiled upon us so far.'

'Then we are the only ones that the gods have smiled upon. I do not think there are many more survivors among our people.'

Tyrion felt cold rage spark within his heart. 'I left a number of friends back there cold upon the ground. The dark elves owe me a great debt, and I intend to collect upon it. But first we must get you to safety. As long as you are alive and free, the Witch King's plan has failed. Let us see that it continues to do so. If this is the only blow that we can strike against our enemies, it will have to do, for now.'

'Yes, Prince Tyrion. Let us do exactly that.' She began to collect some berries from the undergrowth. 'And now let us eat. We will need all of our strength and all of our wits about us if we are going to maintain our freedom.'

'How do you know these are not poisonous?' Tyrion asked.

Her smile was dazzling. 'I grew up here, Prince Tyrion.

There is little I don't know about life in these woods.'

'I am glad one of us has that knowledge,' said Tyrion. 'I suspect it is going to prove necessary.'

# CHAPTER TWO

DEATH LOOKED AT the witch elf piece and smiled. It was removed from the board now but the pawn had done its work. It had infected Prince Tyrion with a poison that would surely kill him before he could perform his purpose. If nothing else, it would slow him down until the pursuit could overtake him.

'A subtle move,' Caledor said.

Death smiled. 'I await your response with interest.'

Caledor focused his power on the square containing Tyrion and the new Everqueen. It was near a waystone. Of course it was. He saw another part of the pattern here.

Somehow his enemies were using the Vortex as part of their plans, or perhaps the mystical structures of the Old Ones that lay beneath. It mattered not at this moment in time. He needed to concentrate on making events run his way.

A vision danced into his mind, of a torn pavilion, a pile of corpses, an army running half out of control. The dead lay everywhere, elves. A huge number were garbed as if for a festival. Far fewer of the corpses wore the iron armour of the dark elves. It saddened Caledor that his own people should have taken to slaughtering each other, as if there were not enough enemies in the world. Somehow all of this was connected with Aenarion and his cursed blade. It would have been better for the elves if it had never been drawn from its altar.

Another image sprang into his mind – a great metal mirror, forged in the ancient manner, had been set up within the pavilion. Potent spells were woven into its magical glass, a strange intelligence glittered in the crystal eyes of the metal dragons that held the frame in their claws. The glass itself was many-layered and magical. It could be used to communicate across distances by those who knew how.

Before it stood a powerful-looking dark elf in the elaborate armour of a high officer. His head was bowed as if in grief. That surprised Caledor. It was not what he would have expected at all. The dark elf was waiting for someone or something. He had already invoked a spell. There was a sense of a powerful cold mind being brought to bear through the mirror. Caledor knew that mind, or had done in the past, although back then it did not have the aura of ruthless evil it emitted now. It was Malekith, son of Aenarion, much changed from the quiet lad he had once been.

Caledor expended a morsel of his carefully husbanded power, disrupting the spell that the mirror contained, making it impossible for its master to look out of it or speak through it.

'Interesting,' said Death, 'although I don't see what good it does you. A messenger will work as well as that mirror albeit more slowly.'

Caledor smiled at him, knowing that in this game tempo was all-important. Time might work as well for him as it did for his enemy.

Death reached out to pick up a piece. 'I believe that was a mistake,' he said.

'We shall see,' said Caledor, wishing that he felt as confident as he tried to sound.

GENERAL DORIAN, MARSHAL of the North, by Grace of Malekith the Great Commander of the First Army of Conquest, stared into the mirror bleakly. Cassandra was dead. The thought hit him harder than he would have expected. In some ways it weighed on him more heavily than his failure to capture the Everqueen; and that was most likely going to cost him his life.

What did it matter? Life seemed bleak and empty now. He felt the woman's absence in a way he had never felt her presence in life. Or perhaps he had, and had just never noticed until today, the way one never notices the presence of a limb until it is amputated. He told himself it was only a foolish, sentimental attachment – as a druchii such things were meaningless to him. He could not convince himself of the truth of that.

He glared into the mirror, willing it to come to life so that he could get things over with, but all he could see was his own reflection: pale, angry and scared, glaring back at him. His armour was dented, his face was bruised, his lip was split. His side was bandaged and bloody.

He did not look like a successful druchii general. He looked like the broken survivors he had sometimes seen after a great defeat. He wore the expression of one of the slaves he used to capture when raiding the Bretonnian coast immediately after it had been put in chains.

He forced himself to smile coldly, to make his face a mask of confidence and command. The expression was not convincing.

What was taking the Witch King so long? Dorian had already made the offering of blood and invoked the spell that should have let him speak to his master over the long leagues of Ulthuan. Why had Malekith not made contact? He had never taken this long before.

Was his master toying with him, like a great predatory cat tormenting its prey?

He thought about the warrior who had done this to him. It should not have been possible. One elf could not simply stroll through a formation of druchii soldiers, walk into the presence of its general, slaughter half the command staff and their bodyguards and then walk out again, taking their prisoner and prize with them.

It beggared belief.

It was the sort of thing that happened in old tales, in the legends of Aenarion and Caledor. It did not happen in reality.

Still, this had been a gathering of champions, where a group of the mightiest warriors in Ulthuan had come together to compete for the favour of the Everqueen and to become her champion. If ever there was a place for a hero to emerge from, it was here. It was not something that the Witch King had calculated upon, apparently. He could imagine it becoming the start of a new epic, a myth of the asur, if the elf who had done it got away with it.

He shook his head and his reflection in the mirror did the same, mocking him. He felt like striking the magical thing with his sword, but he doubted it would do any good. This mirror had been forged beneath Naggarond by Malekith himself. The mage-steel frame was marked with dragons and looked as hard as the Witch King's armour. The glass only appeared fragile. It had been made to survive being taken on campaign with an army. It was, after all, how Malekith kept in touch with his generals when they were in the field and needed his personal supervision.

He thought about his lord and master. Malekith was not forgiving. He despised failures and he punished them; up until an hour ago Dorian would not but have agreed with that policy.

Why preserve the weak?

They needed to be winnowed out so that the strong might prosper. Of course, that had been before he had become a failure himself. Somehow he did not see the Witch King making an exception to his policy in this case. This was failure on a monumental scale. Dorian had imperilled a plan that had been a century in the making.

It was unfair. It had all gone perfectly. Right until the end. They had destroyed the great tournament camp and taken prisoner or slain thousands of the asur. They had captured the Everqueen. She had lain bound on the floor of this vast florid pavilion before him. The god-queen of the asur had been his prisoner.

For all of twenty minutes, he thought sourly. Before a solitary warrior had stolen her away.

As if that was not bad enough, his aides were bringing him news that some others had cut their way out of this trap. A group of elven knights under the banner of Arhalien of Yvresse had fought their way free.

Arhalien was a famous warrior. Was it he who had come back to undo Malekith's plans, slay Cassandra and lay waste to Dorian's life?

The Everqueen was a potent symbol to her people, their living goddess, an incarnation of their spirit. While she was free she would provide a rallying point for her people. They would not give in without a fight. It had been Malekith's master-stroke, capturing her. Or it would have been, if Dorian had succeeded.

At least it was peaceful here, he thought. He was alone with his grief and his sense of failure and shame. None of his officers dared enter this part of the tent. None of them wanted to catch the Witch King's eye when he was wrathful.

If Dorian had been reporting success, as had seemed so likely a few hours ago, they would have crowded around him, elbowing each other out of the way to come into the view of the mirror's great watchful eye. Now, there was no one except him there. Outside, all was silence. He knew the survivors of his staff were listening intently to see what transpired, to eavesdrop for any hints of their own fate.

He wondered if the sense of failure had started to ripple out through the army yet, if they realised exactly how bad things were or could be, if Malekith became really wrathful. They were hundreds of leagues behind enemy lines, in the heart of the oldest forest in the world. They were being supplied through a mystical portal created by an enslaved daemon who might turn on their master at any time. They were in a land they did not know and surrounded by an enemy who knew every inch of it. They had lost the element of surprise, which had been their greatest weapon.

He told himself not to be so defeatist. All across Ulthuan, the Witch King's armies were striking unexpectedly in the heart of Elvendom. A gigantic host of Chaos marauders was descending on the elven realm from the north. This was the greatest invasion of Ulthuan since the time of Aenarion. It was not going to fail.

And yet, Dorian thought, he had. One solitary elf had turned the greatest of victories into the most disastrous of defeats. He glared into the mirror, willing his master to appear so he could report his failure. Nothing happened.

What was going on, Dorian wondered?

He reached out and touched the mirror. It felt cold and dead. It was inert, without the faintest trace of magic in it.

He waited for an hour. Malekith still did not communicate. Slowly it came to Dorian that he was not going to die immediately. If the delay was sufficiently long, he might not have to die at all. If he could just recapture the Everqueen…

And why not? He still had a powerful army at his command. He still had the advantage of surprise. His foe was only a solitary elf, in the company of an Everqueen who had yet to come into possession of her legacy of power. If he acted quickly, he might still be able to save the situation, his career and his life.

Filled with a renewed sense of purpose, he squared his shoulders and strode out of the tent, bellowing orders to summon his captains, his scouts and his magicians to him. At the very least, he thought, he would get revenge for Cassandra's death.

# CHAPTER THREE

AS THE SUN rose higher, Tyrion's natural good spirits began to assert themselves. He was still alive and so was the Everqueen, and that meant that whatever the Witch King had planned could still be stopped. Ignoring the pain in his side, he vaulted over a fallen log.

He was not sure what that ancient evil being had in mind for the Everqueen, but he knew that it could not be anything good. At the very least, having her in captivity would allow him to exert a great deal of pressure on her people, who would naturally be very concerned for her safety.

Perhaps Malekith thought that if he had the Everqueen in his hands, he could use her as a figurehead for his occupation. Perhaps, by the use of magic or torture or some combination of both, he might even be able to make her act the part.

It would be a very bad thing for the people of Ulthuan if the Everqueen was to fall into the Witch King's hands. The best thing he could do for his people might be to ensure that it never happened.

Looking at the beautiful girl walking beside him, he was not sure he was capable of killing her. She was not his enemy, she was his queen. It was his duty to keep her alive if he could, and that was a duty he intended to perform for as long as there was breath within him. The Everqueen caught him looking at her from the corner of her eye and looked at him quizzically. 'What are you thinking about, Prince Tyrion?'

'I'm thinking about my duty, your serenity, and what I may need to do to perform it.'

'I'm sure that you will do whatever needs to be done, Prince Tyrion.'

'There are some things that I hope never become necessary.'

'We all have had such duties to perform. When the time comes, you must put aside your personal feelings and do what is needed.'

Tyrion wondered if she knew that she was signing her own death warrant. He half-suspected that she did.

SUNLIGHT DAPPLED THE path. Alarielle gave a shout and dropped downslope. She picked up something, studied it and nodded.

'What are you doing?' Tyrion asked. He was still taken aback by the suddenness of her action. He glared around, half-expecting some threat to emerge from the trees.

'I saw this,' said Alarielle, raising the long piece of wood in her left hand.

'Very good,' said Tyrion. 'You found a stick.'

'Not just a stick,' she said, already cross-legged and whittling away at the wood. 'I can make this into a bow.'

'I am not sure that will help us against the armies of Malekith,' he said.

She kept stripping the bark from the wood with her knife. 'No, but it will help us to eat.'

'Only if you can hit something with it,' he said.

She smiled. It was as dazzling as the sunbeams filtering down through the gaps in the leaves. 'I think I might be capable of that.'

'How long is this going to take?' He glanced around, as much to let her know that even now enemies might be creeping up on them as to give himself a chance to spot pursuit.

'A while,' she said. 'You may as well make yourself comfortable.'

'Let us hope our enemies are doing the same.'

'You were not brought up in Avelorn, were you, Prince Tyrion?'

'You know it.'

'It's easy enough to see. You do not move like an elf of Avelorn. You do not cover your tracks like an elf of Avelorn. You do not think like an elf of Avelorn.'

'I suspect all of this is leading towards the inevitable conclusion that I am not an elf of Avelorn, and that you are…'

'How long do you think this pursuit may go on?'

'I don't know. Weeks, perhaps months.'

'Indeed.' She inspected the bow which she had stripped of all bark now. 'Improvised, but it will do.'

'What has the time got to do with it?'

'How do you propose we eat?'

'We forage for edible roots, we bring down small game.'

She was making a string from the lacings of her dark elf tunic now and winding it around the bent piece of wood, drawing it taut. Tyrion could see a bow beginning to take shape.

'And how are you proposing to do that?'

'I was brought up in the mountains of Cothique. I can use a sling.'

Alarielle took some other pieces of wood and began to sharpen them. She was making very basic arrows.

'I don't see a sling,' she said.

'They are easier to make than a bow,' said Tyrion. 'You can use leather or cloth. Leather by preference.'

'And you are good with this improvised weapon?'

'I am good with any weapon.'

Alarielle took her hastily made bow and sighted at something in a nearby tree. She aimed, drew and fired. A bird fell, improvised arrow sticking from its breast.

'And I am good with a bow,' she said. 'All the children of Avelorn are.'

She walked over to where the bird's corpse lay, picked it up and began removing feathers. Tyrion already knew she intended to use them on her arrows.

'I could have brought that down,' he said, a little

defensively, 'with a thrown stone.'

'You may not always be here to ward and feed me. I think it best to be prepared for that eventuality.'

As she said this, she turned and fired again. Another bird fell.

Tyrion could think of nothing to say. She was correct.

DORIAN LOOKED AT the chief scout then at the dead witch elves.

'You see it?' Scout Commander Malak asked.

'The wounds have been cauterised.'

Malak nodded. 'Unless a passing torturer decided to mutilate the corpses with red-hot pokers, I would say they went this way.'

'Good. I want this elf found and I want him dead, and I want the Everqueen back in my hands before this week is out.'

'Perhaps you should simply leave the matter in my hands, general,' Malak said. 'I can do what needs to be done, and someone needs to be in command of the army.'

'You think to teach me my duties, or how to run my command?'

'Of course not, general.'

'Good. Let me explain something to you. There is nothing in the whole wide world more important than finding the elf with the burning sword and the woman who is with him. Is that clear?'

'Yes, general.'

'If he is not found, none of our lives will be spared. The

Witch King will make an example of us all.' Dorian paused and studied Malak's expression. If the scout thought that the general had gone mad, no sign of it showed on his face. If he was laughing inwardly at Dorian's failure, it was cleverly concealed. He had spoken loudly so that his words would reach all nearby ears. Soon it would be communicated to the whole army. He thought he had better emphasise the point.

'If we find the Everqueen, our rewards will be unimaginable. If we fail, the tale of our deaths will cause druchii everywhere to shudder for twice ten thousand years.'

'We will not fail, general,' said Malak.

'Good. Now let us get about our business.'

Bending over the tracks like a hound sniffing at a trail, Malak looked for clues. After a moment, he said, 'There were only two of them, a male and a female. They were garbed as druchii or at least wearing the boots of our soldiers.'

'I think it safe to assume they are in disguise then…'

'Indeed. They fought against a dozen witch elves and killed them all. The weapon used by one of them was a magical burning sword. It is definitely the elf you want, general.'

'How long till we find them?'

'They are travelling fast and light but my scouts can overhaul them. I recommend we fan out our force on either side of the trail in case they are hiding. I will assign a tracker to each company. We can send scouts on Cold Ones ahead down the trail and hope to overhaul them.'

'So be it,' said Dorian. 'Let us get to it.'

Already he was thinking that it might be best not to rely on the skills of his scouts. It might be best to invoke sorcery. He would need to talk with the witches.

TYRION ADDED SOME more twigs to the fire. The night was cool and there were beasts about. He had made camp in a hollow which would put their fire out of sight. In the darkness, he did not fear that woodsmoke rising skywards would give them away, although perhaps the scent of it would if their enemies got close. They needed warm food and comfort more than that slight risk at the moment, he decided.

The Everqueen looked at home here. Her face was smudged with soot. She had dressed the birds she had shot earlier and was cooking them on an improvised spit, baking tubers in the same fire. He was glad she had turned out to be competent at this. He was not sure he was going to be able to get her all the way out of the forest. His side was paining him already and he did not know how long they would have to flee.

They sat in silence as the pigeons cooked, then ate quietly, stripping the birds right down to the bones. Afterwards they sat down by the fire. Alarielle stared into it.

'I used to love doing this when I was a child,' she said. The sound of her voice was surprising in the night.

'Doing what?' Tyrion asked.

'Staring into the fire I could see all sorts of things in it: castles, clouds, gods, elementals, daemons. I used to tell myself all sorts of stories.'

'I would have thought there was always someone there to do that for you.'

'You don't like me, do you, Prince Tyrion?' There was truth in that, but now did not seem like a time to say it.

'I don't know you.'

'And yet you still don't like me – why is that?'

Tyrion sighed. 'Does it trouble you so much that one person does not like you? I would have thought the adoration of all the rest made up for it.'

'Is that what bothers you? The way the people worship me?'

'Perhaps worship is too strong a word.'

'No, it is not, and the truth is that it bothers me too.'

Tyrion looked at her sharply. 'Why?'

'Because it was not always so. I was once an elf maid like any other. Now people treat me as a living goddess. Even you, in your strange, sullen way.'

Tyrion felt that was unfair. Her words stung. He was not used to being talked to like this either. 'Perhaps because you *are* a goddess.'

'It was not my choice.'

'Poor child.'

She smiled, and something in her smile made Tyrion feel ashamed of himself. 'No. Really. It was not my choice. And I would much rather my mother was alive than I was possessed by this thing.'

'Possessed? That is an interesting choice of words.'

'It is an accurate one, Prince Tyrion. I share my body with something else. I am not even sure what that something is.'

'It is the spirit of the earth goddess. Even I know that.'

'You may know the words, Prince Tyrion, but I very much doubt you can have any inkling of what they mean.'

'I have met the Phoenix King.'

'I have not. Do I remind you of him?'

'No. Yes.'

'You are not normally so indecisive.'

'There is a spell around you. Even I can see that.'

'Why do you say *even*?'

'Because my magesight is not good. It has always been worse than most other elves.'

'I would not have thought you had any flaws. You don't behave as if you do…'

Tyrion laughed. 'You don't like me either, do you?'

'It's difficult to like someone so hostile.'

'I am not always so hostile,' Tyrion said. He decided it was best to be honest. 'You bring it out in me. You did before ever I saw you, if truth be told.'

'Why?'

'I did not want to become your champion. I was blackmailed into it.'

'By whom?'

'By my aunt, a very great and gracious elf lady, not unlike yourself.'

'You don't like her either?'

'On the contrary, I like her very much. I just don't like being made to do things.'

'We are all made to do things we don't like, Prince Tyrion.'

'Now you sound like her. She said very much the same thing.'

'Perhaps because life is like that.' She sounded sad again. Tyrion did not like that. He did not like seeing her as a person.

'What would you know of that?'

'I was born to be the Everqueen.'

'And you did not want to be the goddess of an entire people, of course?'

'Of course I did. When I was a little girl I dreamed of it. It was only later, when I saw what it really meant, that I had my doubts.'

'When you saw what it really meant?'

'What it did to my mother and to me and my sister.'

'What do you mean?'

'My mother loved me, Prince Tyrion.'

'Is that such a bad thing?'

'And I loved her.'

'So?'

'We almost never saw each other. We almost never saw my sister either.'

Tyrion thought he already knew the answer but he spoke anyway – she seemed to need to talk. This was the odd intimacy of strangers met around a campfire, telling things to strangers they would not tell to their best friends. He had experienced it before on his travels. 'Why?'

'Because she was the Everqueen and we were her heirs and we could not all be in one place at one time in case we were all slain or captured together. There must always be an Everqueen.'

Tyrion saw the logic of it. 'Don't put all your eggs in one basket.'

'A crude way of putting it, but essentially correct. I was taken away from her and put in the care of my aunt when I was small. I never saw my mother until my sister was born.'

'So you both could not be killed at one time.'

She nodded. 'My sister and I were not allowed to be in one place together. My mother could see one of us only on special occasions under conditions of highest security, and only for very short times.'

'After the events of the past few days, I think you can understand why.'

'I always understood why, Prince Tyrion. It did not make it any easier. I never saw my mother again after my sister died.'

'Died?'

'An accident. She fell from a tree into deep water. There were rocks, they say. I don't know, of course, for I was not there.'

There was something shocking and accusing about her grief. He did not want to hear it. He felt like he was standing in for the world that had forced this young woman to live apart from her family. In Lothern, he had seen many examples of the way elven society made the people in it cold and distant. He had not expected to encounter the same here.

'You have a brother,' she said. 'The famous magician.'

'Yes.'

'Are you close to him?'

'Yes.'

'And your mother?'

'She died when we were born. It was a difficult birth, so they say – twins.'

'I am sorry.'

'Why? You never knew her.'

'Nor did you. Perhaps you would have been different if you had.'

He did not want this conversation to go any further. 'I am going to take a look around,' he said. 'Make sure there are no dark elves sneaking up on us.'

He moved off into the quiet of the night and did not return until she was asleep or pretending to be. He stared into the fire for a long time, thinking of daemons and gods, castles and the lovely stranger lying so close by the fire.

The fire had burned down and the sun had already risen when he came awake suddenly. The woods around them were filled with the noise of an approaching army. Alarielle was already awake, staring at him with fear-filled eyes. Sometimes he thought he saw something else staring out at him, something ancient and alien and strange.

'We need to run,' he told her. 'Now!'

# CHAPTER FOUR

'WHAT'S THAT?' ALARIELLE asked. Tyrion could understand why she was disturbed. He recognised that eerie high-pitched screeching sound. He had heard it before in the cold northern lands of Naggaroth. It was a sound that meant terror to the warriors of Ulthuan.

'Cold Ones,' Tyrion said.

'The great lizards that the dark elves use as cavalry? What are they doing here?' Alarielle asked.

'Looking for us,' Tyrion said. 'That would be my guess.'

'I mean in Avelorn.'

Again he understood her shock but he chose to wilfully misunderstand it. 'Doubtless they got here the same way as their riders. One day, if we are lucky, we will know how that happened.'

'Cold Ones,' she said softly, as if not quite believing either

her own words or the distant bellowing of the great beasts.

'We need to move. They can smell warm blood. They are trained to be particularly receptive to the smell of high elf blood.'

Almost as if the creatures could hear him, the bellowing came closer.

'It sounds like there are a number of them,' Alarielle said.

'One would be too many,' Tyrion said. He was already starting to jog down the track, trusting to Alarielle to follow him. She kept up easily. His side hurt from where the witch elf's blade had bit home. It was going to be difficult for him to keep up any speed over long distances.

Tyrion could hear the sound of branches breaking as the Cold Ones' massive forms forced their way through the forest. Horns sounded, nearby and farther in the distance, as the dark elves exchanged signals. They were on the track of something and it seemed safe to assume that the trail which had been found was their own.

'They've caught our scent,' Alarielle said.

'Some of them can smell warm blood at a distance of a mile,' Tyrion said. 'I don't doubt that this is why these riders were sent ahead.'

'We can still lose them if we can find a way to water. That throws hounds off the tracks and wolves. It ought to do the same for them.'

'Do you know where we can find a stream?' Tyrion asked.

'I can do better than that,' Alarielle said. 'There is a river ahead. If we can reach it we can probably get them off our trail.'

'Lead on,' Tyrion said. Behind him he thought he already heard the sound of elves moving through the forest nearby. He doubted they would be friendly.

TYRION LOOKED OUT of their rocky hiding place and studied their enemies. Alarielle had chosen it because it would be impossible for their foes to track them over this ground. She had gone off and left a false trail beyond it and circled back to him. He had not liked letting her out of his sight, but he had no choice. She knew about these matters and he did not.

They had been running for most of the day and no matter how they tried, it seemed impossible to outdistance the pursuit. Always, the woods were full of the sounds of horns and druchii battle-calls, as the various components of the army kept in touch. Gradually, some of the noises had faded into the distance, but others had managed to keep up, no matter how quickly he and Alarielle ran.

Looking back now, he could see why. These were not standard infantry. They were lightly armed and armoured and moved with the easy authority of the highest echelons of combat troops.

Their very appearance here was shocking. The dark elves moved confidently along the trail. They gave every impression of being at home, of having utter confidence in their right to be there in the heart of the most sacred place in Elvendom. There was no fear in the way they walked. They were the hunters, not the hunted.

The cockiness in their manner almost compelled Tyrion

to leap out and slay them. An insane anger burned deep in him, filling him with the urge to rend and slay. He wanted to wipe the confident smile off the smug face of the dark elf sergeant giving orders to his troops. He wanted to see fear blossom in the eyes of the two druchii warriors sharing a joke, doubtless at asur expense. His hand tightened on the hilt of Sunfang.

A hand gripped his. He turned and glared angrily at Alarielle. She shook her head. I can kill them all, he wanted to say. There were only a score of them. With the advantage of surprise, and the power of Sunfang, it was possible he could do it too, even with the Everqueen clinging to his arm.

He let out a long breath, realising how mad the thoughts cascading through his brain had suddenly become. Attacking a score of armed veterans was not a sensible thing to do. The chances were that he could not kill them all, even if he could he might be wounded or slain in the process. It was a mad risk and there was nothing to be gained from it, save the satisfaction of a bloodlust that he had never even suspected he possessed.

Was this the Curse of Aenarion finally coming on him in full force? Or was it something else? Had the wound from the witch elf's blade infected him with something else, a taste of their reckless madness perhaps? He stayed frozen in place, waiting tensely to see if the dark elves discovered their trail.

One of them bent down and said something to the others. Had he spotted a track? Tyrion readied himself to spring into action if that was the case. It looked like his bloodlust might be slaked after all. Part of him would have welcomed it.

He could feel Alarielle tense beside him. If the dark elves overcame him, she might end up their prisoner once more. If that happened, she would eventually end up within Malekith's iron-gauntleted grasp.

After a long moment, he felt her exhale. The dark elves moved on, still scanning the woods around them, hunters seeking prey. It seemed like a very long time before they were out of sight.

Tyrion and Alarielle lay in the undergrowth, slumped out of sight, close as lovers. Eventually they smiled at each other. It seemed that danger had passed them by for a while. Some buried instinct urged him to stay here, but he knew it was foolish. The horns in the distance were coming closer. It was only a matter of time before the larger force of druchii overhauled them and they would have the numbers to search thoroughly. They needed to get moving by another path than the ones the pursuing scouts had taken.

Reluctantly, he rose from the hard ground. He felt a small sharp pain in his side, where the witch elf had wounded him. It seemed to be getting worse.

Alarielle stopped walking, raised her head and looked around. 'What was that?' she asked. Her jawline was set tight and every muscle was tense. Tyrion reached out to touch her shoulder and he could feel the tightness of the muscles beneath. She shrugged off his touch and glanced around, wary as a deer that has caught the scent of a hunter.

He understood why. There was a sudden tension in the air that had not been there before. Fewer birds sang. Fewer small creatures moved through the undergrowth. He realised how tightly wound the Everqueen must be to spot this before he did. Normally he was the person most aware of his surroundings. She gestured for him to take cover and threw herself under a nearby bush. Tyrion burrowed into the undergrowth, not a moment too soon.

A group of druchii emerged into the clearing, moving carefully and calmly. They carried small hand crossbows and had wicked-looking blades at their sides. Their movement was stealthy. There was something shadowy about them. They looked like creatures of the night, feral, predatory and deadly.

Their leader studied the ground where Tyrion and Alarielle had stood. He made a gesture using hand signals that could have meant anything but which Tyrion suspected meant they are close, be careful. He looked around the clearing and seemed to pick up their tracks. Tyrion knew the game was up and that he could only hope that there were not too many other druchii nearby. Alarielle clearly recognised what was happening. She stood up with her bow aimed directly at the scout leader. All of them turned to face her.

'It seems we have found our prey,' the leader said. His voice was as cold as the winds of the north. He sounded like a true son of his harsh land.

'I will put an arrow through the first one of you who moves,' Alarielle said.

'Perhaps,' said the druchii. 'And then you will be pin-cushioned by the rest of us.'

'It will be better than the fate that awaits me at your hands.'

'Our king wishes you delivered to him unharmed.' The dark elf's tone was reasonable.

'That was the fate to which I was referring,' Alarielle said.

'Shoot one of us and the rest will shoot to wound you,' the leader said. Tyrion knew his words were aimed at his followers. He did not want them making any mistakes in this tricky situation. He was obviously a careful elf. He glanced around the clearing again, puzzled, and Tyrion knew that he was thinking about the second person who might be there.

He had no recourse but to act. He leapt from the bushes, driving Sunfang into the back of one of the scouts. He heard a scream from nearby and, turning, saw that Alarielle had put an arrow through the eye of the leader. The remaining pair of druchii were distracted for a moment, unsure who to shoot at, the sight of a warrior in their own armour bearing a blazing sword confusing them for a crucial second.

Tyrion covered the distance between him and the closest in three strides. The immediate threat made the druchii swing his crossbow towards Tyrion. Sunfang swept down and cleaved it in two. Tyrion dropped the dark elf with his second cut and turned in time to see the last scout's crossbow pointed directly at him. There was no way he could close fast enough to avoid being shot. The dark elf's finger squeezed the trigger. An arrow flashed through the air and took him in the side of the neck, sending him falling to one side, spoiling his aim. The crossbow bolt flashed past Tyrion's ear, so close that he felt the wind of its passing.

Tyrion sprang forwards and beheaded the scout before turning to face Alarielle. 'Thank you,' he said. 'You saved my life.'

She was not looking at him and she did not respond. Her face was very pale, and Tyrion turned to see what she was looking at. In the shadows beneath the trees hundreds of druchii marched, an army on the move; he did not doubt for a moment that it was seeking them.

Already crossbow bolts were starting to flash towards them. Fortunately the bushes, the shadows and the low branches interfered with their flight, but it was only a matter of time before they got the range.

'Run!' shouted the Everqueen. She did not have to tell Tyrion twice. They sprinted away through the trees with what must have been the better part of a regiment of druchii in pursuit.

TYRION AND ALARIELLE sprinted through the woods. Now and then they could hear the sound of the druchii screaming. The enemy had caught sight of their prey and felt it within their grasp. The woods echoed with the shouts and war cries of the dark elves. Tyrion's heart pounded within his chest. Alarielle looked back at him over her shoulder. She could run like a gazelle when frightened, and she was frightened now.

Despair filled Tyrion's heart. He could not see how they were going to escape the jaws of the enormous trap that were snapping shut. From all around now he could hear druchii voices. It seemed like an entire army filled the wood, stretched out in a vast crescent, like beaters driving pheasants before them on a hunt. Tyrion began to understand what it must feel like to be hunted in that way.

He stretched his legs and began to overtake Alarielle. He was already breathing hard, much more so than he ought to be for this amount of exercise. It seemed that the wound in his side was already beginning to drain his strength – he did not like that in the slightest. Just when he needed it most he was losing his fitness. He cursed the witch elf once again, hoping that her wicked soul rotted deep in hell.

A few crossbow bolts fell around him. They had come a great distance and lost much of their power. A bolt clattered off a tree in front of him. He could hear the *whoosh* of arrows behind him. He had heard the sound before on the field of battle but he had never known so many missiles to be directed at only two people. It seemed only a matter of time before one of them hit home and either he or the Everqueen was impaled. That would be the end of the chase.

He began to zigzag, moving from side to side to confuse the archers, but he realised that this was not such a clever plan. The people chasing him would be able to run directly after him and thus gain ground. Alarielle was pushing on and with great woodcraft was simply weaving in and out of the trees, moving in as straight a line as possible while gaining as much cover as she could. Tyrion decided to do the same.

He heard another terrifying sound now. It was one that he

had heard before in the cold northern lands of Naggaroth. It was a high-pitched noise somewhere between a scream and a roar. He ran abreast of Alarielle.

He risked a glance backwards and saw some of the great lizards striding forwards through the massed ranks of the druchii troops. Cold Ones were bipedal wingless reptilian creatures who carried armoured knights upon their back. Their movements seemed oddly slow and bouncing but they covered the ground very swiftly with their enormous strides.

It was only a matter of minutes before the Cold Ones reached them, if that. He heard the running water up ahead. Just from the sound of it he could tell that it was a mighty river. It seemed as if they were trapped. Tyrion prepared to turn around and fight. Even a battle against hopeless odds seemed preferable to being captured.

'What are you doing, idiot?' Alarielle asked. 'That is the River Everflow. We have a chance to escape if we are swift.'

'They will shoot us while we try to swim across.'

'There is another way.'

'Lead on,' Tyrion said. 'I hope you know what you're doing.'

# CHAPTER FIVE

THE COLD ONES were closing the distance with appalling speed, outpacing the soldiers behind them. Tyrion could hear them thundering along the trail even now. The screeching echoed out through the forest, terrifying the birds and sending them racing skywards in fear.

'How much farther?' he gasped.

'A few hundred yards, if I remember correctly,' Alarielle said.

'I don't think we are going to make it,' he said.

'Run faster,' she replied.

It was already too late. Three riders closed the gap swiftly. The creatures gave off an awful stink that Tyrion well remembered. They had gigantic jaws capable of ripping off a limb in one bite and crunching through armour as easily as flesh.

Alarielle sprang upwards, grasping a branch and somersaulting onto the one above. Tyrion considered doing the same, but he needed to hold the attention of their pursuers, so he held his ground on the track as the dark elf riders thundered closer.

They howled in triumph even as their beasts roared at the prospect of devouring prey. Tyrion could see saliva glistening on massive dagger-like teeth. He braced himself to face onrushing death. His heart beat a little faster. His grip tightened on the hilt of Sunfang as he ripped it from its scabbard. He raced towards the oncoming Cold Ones. If nothing else he might be able to distract their pursuers and give the Everqueen time to escape.

The jaws of the leading Cold One snapped shut. Tyrion sprang to one side. He could smell the foul beast's breath. Its rider struck down at him with his sword. Tyrion rolled forwards, lashing out with Sunfang, aiming at the Cold One's ankle. His blade bit home, drawing blood and sawing through the tendon.

The Cold One shrieked and turned to snap at him, lowering its head to reach him. As it did so, its left leg gave way beneath it and it tumbled to one side, hitting the ground with a thud. It tried to rise, small arms waving desperately.

Its rider groaned and tried to wriggle free, his leg trapped beneath the beast's great bulk. Tyrion rolled to his feet, favouring his side. The poisoned wound ached. He struck out with Sunfang, catching the dark elf in his thigh as he was trying to get clear, severing the artery. Sunfang partially cauterised it, but blood still flowed from the wound and the dark elf desperately tried to stop it with his hands. Sensing the wetness flooding its back, the Cold One twisted to snap at him. It could not quite reach him but the two of them became progressively more entangled.

The other two riders charged towards Tyrion. Their beasts bellowed deafeningly. Tyrion watched the two massive monsters close with him, following the play of muscles beneath their scaly skin, readying himself to face them. A few hundred strides behind came a company of druchii soldiers.

An arrow whizzed out of the background and took the left-hand rider through the visor of his helmet. It was an awesome shot with an improvised bow.

The rider slumped in his saddle but his beast kept coming. Tyrion sprang, getting his foot into the stirrup of the dead rider's saddle. He was just outside the range of the Cold One's snapping jaws. He drew Sunfang across its throat, sawing with the blade so that even the cauterising effect of the magic could not seal the wound on its jugular.

As he did so, the last monster snapped at him and he just managed to pull his arm clear. Its teeth snagged on the sleeve of his jerkin and pulled him from the saddle. He twisted as the sleeve tore, dropping to the ground, facing the creature. Desperately he parried the rider's attack. Steel clashed against steel as the blades met. The beast bit at him again and he jumped backwards, away from its snapping jaws.

Its rider applied his spurs to its flank and brought the Cold One jogging forwards. Tyrion noticed how slow its stride seemed compared to the distance it covered. Another arrow flashed past overhead, but this one was not so accurate or so lucky. It buried itself in the rider's chest but was partially stopped by his armour. It put him off his stroke and enabled Tyrion to concentrate on avoiding his mount. He tried to hamstring the reptile but was too slow and merely scraped at its taloned heel. The Cold One buffeted him with its tail, sending him staggering backwards off balance. The strike hit him on his wounded side, and the pain was all but overwhelming. Sensing its advantage, the beast rushed closer, its jaws open wide, its foetid breath emerging in a poisoned cloud. Tyrion knew there was nothing he could do to stop it. He could barely move, so stunned was he.

Sunfang seemed to twist in his hand of its own accord until it was pointing directly at the onrushing Cold One.

Something sparked inside Tyrion's mind. A connection was made with the blade. The flames blazing along its length intensified for a heartbeat, turning bright red and racing towards the blade's tip, forming themselves into a sphere of fire. After a heartbeat, a fireball erupted from the sword, arced towards the Cold One and impacted in a huge explosion that sent the creature tumbling through the air to land in a fire-blackened heap.

Tyrion picked himself up groggily and stumbled over to Alarielle's perch. She dropped lithely to the ground and raced over to him. 'How did you do that? I thought you said you were no mage...'

'It was not me, it was the sword,' he said. 'Some sort of spell was woven into it.'

The flames along the blade had died down now. They did not blaze with quite their normal intensity. The blade did not feel so light in his hand. He remembered Teclis's warning that trying to summon the power within it too often would kill the spirits bound into it and make the sword useless.

'I still don't understand how you triggered it,' Alarielle said.

'Neither do I,' said Tyrion. In the distance he could hear more Cold Ones bellowing, and the shrieks of the druchii infantry as they came closer. 'We've got to go.'

They ran, with the hordes of Malekith howling at their heels.

DEATH LOOKED OVER the gameboard at Caledor. He smiled appreciatively. 'A good move,' he said, 'triggering the sword.'

'Tyrion could have done that anyway,' Caledor said. 'I merely nudged his hand.'

'Still, it's fortunate that you did, or you might have lost one of your most powerful pieces.'

Caledor studied the board and the image of Tyrion sprang into his mind. The poisoned wound was still there, aggravated by Death's magic. It could kill the elf prince at any time. A horde of pawns was closing in around Tyrion's position.

'I still might,' Caledor said. 'You have been playing very subtly yourself.'

'Such is my nature,' said Death.

He reached down and began moving more pawns. The

net of living steel around Tyrion and the Everqueen started to tighten.

AHEAD, THE WIDE rushing river swept past Tyrion in a great curve, disappearing under the shadow of titanic trees. The branches of the largest trees overhung the river. Vines dangled down almost to the waters.

Behind them, he could hear the sounds of pursuit drawing closer. Tyrion's side hurt from the running and the poisoned wound. He knew that he would not be able to go on for much further and still be able to fight – there was no chance of being able to overcome a force of the size that pursued them.

They did not have time to swim. The dark elves would be able to use their crossbows to shoot them before they reached the other bank. They might abstain from shooting Alarielle because she was the Everqueen, but they would certainly kill him.

He would have been willing to let that happen if he thought that it would enable her to get away, but he doubted that it would. They might shoot to wound her and that might have disastrous consequences. A wounded swimmer and a strong current were a recipe for disaster.

He looked over at Alarielle. She was as winded as he was from the long chase. Her breath came out in pants and sweat stained her clothes. Her hair was lank.

'This is the Everflow,' she said. 'We used to come here when I was a girl.'

He smiled sourly. 'That's nice. Perhaps you would care to

share the story with the dark elves when they get here. I'm sure they will be charmed.'

'I think I will save my girlish reminiscences for more congenial company,' she said. 'We need to get across the river.'

'A short swim would seem to be in order,' said Tyrion.

'You are in no condition to cross this river while wearing full armour. I have seen strong swimmers sucked under by the current here. I would not give a crumb of waybread for your chances.'

'It is not beyond my wit to take off the armour.'

'There is another way,' she said. She looked up at the vines overhanging the river.

'Are you serious?' Tyrion asked.

'We used to do it all the time when I was a child.'

'I'm surprised your guardians let you.'

'I never said anything about them letting me,' she said, smiling.

'You disobedient child,' he said. Alarielle was already beginning to scramble up the nearest tree. Behind them he could hear the pursuit coming ever closer, the dark elves whooping with triumph, knowing that their prey was within easy reach and sensing the river had cut off their escape.

Tyrion followed her up the trunk of the great tree. Every time he tried to use his left arm, the pain in his side almost crippled him.

Slowly, painfully, he pulled himself up hand over hand. Alarielle was already poised, graceful as a gazelle, on the main branch above him.

He smelled the moss that clung to the side of the great tree. The tips of his fingers were green from the moist substance on the bark. His breath came in gasps.

He was grateful when she reached down and offered him her hand. She pulled him up with surprising strength. They stood looking into each other's eyes for a long moment, then she turned and sprinted along the great branch, leaping into the air, reaching out and grasping the first vine. Her momentum carried her out over the great river and at the last second she let go, reaching out to grasp another vine. On and on she went, lithe as an acrobat, until she reached the far side and landed in the bole of one of the enormous trees.

Her passage had made his more difficult by setting the vines in motion. Now they were swinging backwards and forwards. He took a deep breath. He did not have much time. The dark elves would soon be upon them and he did not want them to notice how he and the Everqueen had disappeared.

He offered up a prayer to whatever gods might be listening and ran out along the branch. It was as wide as a footpath and solid as a rock at the point where he was upon it. He saw the first of the vines ahead of him and he sprang, reaching out to grasp it. Pain surged through his side as he put strain on his left arm. That accursed wound was going to be the death of him yet. He began to rotate; he knew that that would be bad because it would put him in the wrong position when he needed to let go.

He twisted to get his line back and the pain in his side

increased. He gritted his teeth and bit back a cry. Beneath him the waters of the great river surged. He noticed the rocks. If he let go now he would fall upon them and most likely be dashed to pieces.

He knew he was not doing this well. He was heavier than Alarielle and not in such good condition. He tried to judge when to let go through tears of pain. For a few seconds he was flying free over the waters far below, feeling out with his hands, desperate to grasp the next vine in the sequence.

There was a sickening feeling in the pit of his stomach when he caught nothing, then a heartbeat later his fingers closed on something slick and green. He felt as if his arm was about to be torn from its socket by the strain.

His fingers slid and his hands burned from the friction, but he refused to give up and let go until the time was right. There were a few seconds of relief while he swung forwards, and then it was time to let go again.

It seemed as if his fingers were not about to respond. He forced them open and once more was flying through space. He could see that the vine was still swinging from Alarielle's momentum. He prayed that it would move back into position in time for him to grasp it.

It began to swing back. He was still moving forwards. He was going to make it. He reached the furthest extent of his vine's swing and let go. The other vine kept coming back towards him. He stretched out as far as he could, trying to catch it.

Closer it came, its path converging with his own. He stretched out farther, extending his fingers as far as he could, as if somehow that would give him the extra reach. It came to him then that he was not going to make it. He had already begun to fall through space towards the water below.

The vines swished past overhead. He wondered whether he had time to twist into diving position and whether the water was deep enough for it to make any difference. He tumbled like an gymnast, trying to get his feet below him. He could see the moving water and the rocks and the far side of the river – it was much closer now. He thought he caught sight of Alarielle's horrified features. Everything seemed to slow down. He was abnormally aware of every motion and every muscle in his body.

The water rose to meet him. It smashed into his body with the force of a giant club. For a moment he thought he'd hit a rock, but then he was tumbling deeper and deeper into the water, his mouth filling with liquid, his eyes stinging.

All of the breath had been knocked out of him and he knew that he would not be able to survive long before drowning. He kicked out, hoping that his legs would still function, hoping that he was moving in the right direction, heading towards what he thought was the light.

His head broke the surface. He could feel the current pushing him downriver. He kicked out with his legs, trying to use his arms as little as possible to avoid irritating his wound. After what seemed like a very long time, he reached the far bank. Away on the other side, he could hear the dark elves shouting to each other.

It took what little strength he had remaining to pull

himself up onto the bank and lie there, staring at the branches above him. Slowly, the sickening knowledge of his failure percolated into his mind. He had become separated from the Everqueen. She was out there now alone and hunted by her enemies.

# CHAPTER SIX

CALEDOR STUDIED THE gameboard, his attention momentarily away from Avelorn by the complexity of the action. It was becoming intricate and ever more confusing to follow. Armies moved all across the continent of Ulthuan.

He saw the Phoenix King in Lothern, looking from the great sea wall of the city. Out in the waters of the bay beyond lay not one but three Black Arks, mountainous druchii ships with their attending fleets of smaller vessels and sea monsters. The hills around the city were full of druchii soldiers. Siege engines sent fiery death hurtling towards the walls of the city-state. Sorcerers aimed deadly spells. Legions of tightly disciplined druchii hurled themselves at the gates while the asur fought against traitors within their own walls.

In the mountains, hordes of Chaos-worshipping

barbarians chanted outside the walls of the mighty fortresses built by Caledor the Conqueror. Their armies had already overrun much of thinly populated Cothique and were ready to move south.

Along the coast of Tiranoc, druchii warships controlled the seas. The great fleets of the asur were rushing hither and yon in confusion, while the dark elves knew exactly what to do and where to strike.

Caledor sensed the disruption to the fabric of reality caused by N'Kari's magical gates. The Witch King was using them to move his forces all too easily around Ulthuan. It gave him a great advantage, being able to take his foes by surprise and concentrate his forces wherever he wanted. Such mobility magnified the potency of his army many times over. Something needed to be done to neutralise it, but that could be achieved by nothing less than the destruction of N'Kari, and that was not a feat that many of Caledor's pieces were capable of, and none of them were in the area of the city.

He knew he should not allow himself to be distracted. There were things that needed to be done. He reached down and picked up the piece called Teclis.

TECLIS WOKE. HIS mouth felt dry and his head felt fuzzy. His thoughts came with uncharacteristic slowness. On the table in front of him was a book of spells, and diverse other things including High Loremaster Morelian's translation of the Slann tablet Teclis had found in the ruins of Zultec. It all came back to him. He was in a chamber that was part of the Maze of Books below the White Tower of Hoeth.

Teclis shook his head. It was a mistake. The contents of his stomach roiled volcanically and for a moment the room tilted. It was more than just his physical frailty reasserting itself. It was something else, a reaction to his dream, if dream it had been, and he was enough of a sorcerer to very strongly doubt that. It had seemed so real, so concrete.

Had he really talked to the Archmage Caledor, an elf more than six thousand years dead? Had he spoken to the ghost of the creator of the Vortex, the huge spell that kept Ulthuan above the waves and the world safe from being overwhelmed by the dark cosmic magic of Chaos? Had the archmage really told him to protect his brother Tyrion, when all his life it had been Tyrion who had protected him?

It all seemed so unlikely, yet he did not doubt its reality for a moment. He had been given a warning and he had better deliver it at once to the head of his order. He had been sent to tell the High Loremaster to prepare for war.

He felt something else, a premonition of disaster even stronger than the one that had been hanging over him ever since he and his brother had returned to Ulthuan from the jungles of Lustria. He rose unsteadily to his feet, picked up the papers on the table and made for the exit of the small chamber, praying that this time he did not get lost in the spell-warped maze beneath the tower.

The corridors did not twist and turn around him in a way that would baffle his senses. Spells did not prevent him from finding the stairwell that led back up into the library.

Even as he emerged into the great book-filled chambers,

his sense of unease grew stronger. The rooms were deserted. He had never seen that before. It seemed somehow unnatural that there should be no scholar in the Great Library at Hoeth. He doubted that such a thing had happened in an age of the world. There was always someone in the library, no matter at what hour of the day or night.

It was as if some great disaster had struck Hoeth while he was in the Maze of Books. For a brief moment, Teclis entertained the fantasy that some dreadful magical catastrophe had swept through the White Tower and he was the only survivor.

Impossible, he told himself. No enemy could have found their way to the tower. It was warded by some of the most powerful protective enchantments ever created, surrounded by spells that could deflect even the most terrible curses and destructive spells.

Nothing could possibly have happened. Could it?

As he emerged from the library, Teclis was relieved to see a Sword Master, one of the warrior-guardians of the tower. The elf seemed surprised to see Teclis. It looked like he had not expected to encounter anyone coming from the library.

'What is going on?' Teclis asked.

'Haven't you heard the news?' The Sword Master asked.

'What news?' Teclis asked.

'Avelorn has been attacked! The Everqueen is dead! So is everyone with her!'

Teclis's eyes narrowed as he stared at the guardian. He shook his head. 'That cannot be true! My brother is there.'

'The word just came in an hour ago,' said the Sword Master. 'It was brought by one of the eagles of the forest. The Loremasters have verified it with their scrying crystals.'

Unbidden, the image of his brother's body lying sprawled in a pool of blood came into his mind. He shuddered. He told himself that was only his imagination. It was not a vision. He took a deep breath and tried to calm his racing senses. He was sweating. His heart raced.

It was impossible that Tyrion could be dead without him knowing. And yet, what if he was wrong? The powerful wards that surrounded the Tower of Hoeth might stop him from sensing such a thing. Perhaps this was the reason he felt so bad and had such a strong sense of foreboding.

He refused to believe it. The bond that existed between him and his twin ran deep. There was no barrier it could not penetrate. He was certain of that. Tyrion could not be dead. He would not believe that until he looked upon his brother's corpse with his own eyes.

Even thinking that felt like a betrayal. It was admitting the possibility that the guard might be right and that he might be wrong.

'What happened?' He felt like taking the guard by the collar of his jerkin and shaking him until he answered.

'The dark elves attacked.'

'The druchii attacked Avelorn? Nonsense!' Teclis almost shouted. He could hear the almost hysterical edge to his own voice. It was simply impossible that a dark elf army could have got so far into Ulthuan.

'It was the dark elves,' said the guard. 'And they did not

just attack Avelorn. Their fleets are at sea off our coasts and their armies have attacked in other places. The news keeps coming in and none of it is good.'

'Where?' Teclis demanded. He felt as if he were caught up in a nightmare. Last night he had gone to sleep in a land of peace and plenty. He had woken up in a land torn by war. His mind rebelled against the very thought of it. It was as if thunder and lightning had come out of an empty sky in which there had not been a single cloud. It was impossible, simply impossible.

The Witch King could not have prepared an invasion fleet without it being noticed. Naggaroth's ports were constantly watched. He could not have built up a fleet without it being noticed by the scout ships of the high elves. No army could have found its way into the very heart of Elvendom in so short a time without being spotted by a single person. A legion of Shadow Warriors could not have achieved this goal, let alone an army of heavily armoured dark elves. Even Teclis knew that and he was no soldier.

Yet, in spite of all this, there was a Sword Master standing in front of him telling him that Avelorn was invaded and that his brother and the Everqueen were dead. He forced himself to get a grip on his racing thoughts.

'I must have words with the High Loremaster,' Teclis said.

'Good luck with that,' said the guard. 'Everyone feels the same today.'

'Then I had best get going,' Teclis said. He strode off through the oddly deserted paths of Hoeth.

* * *

AS HE WALKED through the tower, Teclis understood where everyone had gone. All of the students, all of the masters, all of the guards and all of the elves who served them had gathered in the great open spaces. All of them were talking of the attacks and all of them looked frightened.

As well they might, Teclis thought. No such invasion of Ulthuan had happened in their lifetimes. Everyone has assumed the druchii were a spent force. No one had wanted to think otherwise.

Teclis overheard scraps of conversation. It seemed that rumour bred rumour and no one had any idea what might be true or false.

'An army of Chaos worshippers has landed in the north.'

'A thousand daemons lay siege to Lothern.'

'A million barbarians with Morathi at their head are riding to Hoeth and will not be turned aside by the warding spells.'

'The High Loremaster is working magic to scry the land.'

'The Vortex is failing. The ghost of Caledor himself has spoken to a dozen people in the tower.'

Crowds surged around the doorway of the High Loremaster's chambers. It seemed everyone wanted an interview. Everyone had questions. Everyone had something to say. Even in the most secure heart of the tower there was an aura of panic and fear.

Belthania emerged from the Loremaster's sanctum and caught sight of him. The tall sorceress gestured for him to come over. Teclis was not strong enough to elbow his way through the crowd and it would not part for him. Belthania gestured to someone within the office. Two Sword Masters emerged and began to force a way through the crowd for him.

A short minute later he was within Morelian's chambers. The High Loremaster looked up at him. He had looked old the last time Teclis had seen him, but appeared to have aged centuries within the past few hours. His already ancient frame seemed withered and bent almost double. The Sword Master slammed the door shut as soon as they entered and the hubbub from the corridors and chambers beyond subsided to nothing. A spell was at work there, Teclis realised.

'I can tell from your expression you have heard the news,' said Morelian.

Teclis said, 'My brother was in Avelorn.'

'Then he is most likely dead,' said Belthania.

'I would know if he was.'

'Where have you been? No one has seen you for hours. I have had people searching,' Morelian said.

'Why?'

'I had a peculiar dream concerning you.'

'What was its import?'

'The Archmage Caledor spoke to me. He told me you would be going on a journey, one very important to us all, and that I was to see you were prepared for it.'

'I too had the same dream,' said Belthania. 'As did every other Loremaster in the tower.'

'And all of those scattered across Ulthuan, for all we know,' said Morelian.

'I see,' said Teclis. 'If one Loremaster has a dream it may

be meaningless. If all of them have the same dream – it is significant.'

'It was more than a dream,' said Morelian. 'It felt extraordinarily real. I stood near the centre of the world and watched the ghosts of the Five enspell the Vortex. And they were failing.'

'I saw the same thing,' said Belthania.

'When did this happen?'

'In the small hours of the morning. After we last talked.'

Teclis nodded. 'That would be after I cast the spell.'

'What spell?'

'I was lost in the Maze of Books. I found a chamber and in that chamber was an ancient spell. I was compelled to cast it by some force. I could not have stopped myself even if I had wanted to. I thought the spell affected only me but it seems that it reached out to all of you as well.'

'Those of the Loremasters who were not asleep fell into a faint,' said Morelian. 'When they came out of it, they too had seen the same thing as the rest of us. That would explain it.'

'It might mean nothing,' said Teclis. 'It might be the work of the enemy.'

'No inimical power has ever reached into Hoeth.'

'There is a first time for everything,' said Teclis. His two fellow Loremasters looked disturbed by that prospect.

'I do not believe it possible,' said Morelian eventually. 'And if it was, why afflict us with such a vision? Why not something that would be of more material assistance to our enemies?'

'Indeed,' said Belthania. 'I am willing to believe this spell of yours contributed to the vision, but I doubt anything hostile was behind it. I am more likely to believe it was the spirit of the tower itself helping us in our time of need. I don't think it's a coincidence that this happened at the same time as Avelorn must have been attacked.'

'Not just Avelorn,' said the High Loremaster. 'Lothern, Tor Yvresse, Mancastra and a dozen other places. All of Ulthuan is besieged by the dark elves and their Chaos-worshipping allies. The Everqueen is missing, presumed dead. There are rumours of treachery everywhere. Members of the Cult of Luxury have risen up to aid the invaders. This is the gravest threat Ulthuan has faced since the Sundering.'

'And yet in the middle of this, Caledor, if Caledor it was, chooses to tell you that I will be going on a journey. You would have thought he would have more important things on his mind.'

'This is not a subject for jest, Teclis,' said Morelian. 'The first archmage must have known we would find out all the rest for ourselves soon enough. It is a mark of your importance in the great scheme of things that he chose to speak to us about you.'

'Why me?' Teclis asked.

'You are of the Blood of Aenarion,' said Belthania.

'And you and your brother are heroes,' said Morelian.

'I am no hero,' said Teclis.

'If you are not now, I fear you will be before all of this is over,' said Morelian.

'I am going to find my brother,' Teclis said. 'And to do that I will need a weapon.'

'We shall see what we can provide,' said Morelian.

'I shall make my own sword,' said Teclis.

'Then you had best get started,' said the High Loremaster.' I shall see that a forge is put at your disposal.'

QUICKLY TECLIS TOOK a fresh piece of parchment and sharpened a quill before dipping it in ink and sketching out the runes and magical equations that would be needed to make the sword. For long hours he sat hunched over the desk in his chamber, working swiftly and easily.

He had studied Sunfang and he felt certain that he could duplicate at least part of the magic that had gone into creating it. The basic spells that would go to making the blade sharp and deadly would need to be every bit as potent and as well constructed as the magic of Caledor.

As he worked he wondered why he was really doing this. He did not have any great use for a blade – he was no warrior. He had no plans to run around like his brother, cutting things up with a sword. The only thing he was likely to be able to hurt was himself.

Anything that had got close enough to him that he would need to use a sword upon was already too close. He did not need to do anything as spectacular as the fire magic that had been woven into the sword. That would be difficult to do without access to the volcanic fires of Vaul's Anvil. He was no warrior and he did not really need the blade to do anything so spectacular anyway.

It was the creation of the sword itself that was important. It was a test that he had set himself. If he could recreate this part of Caledor's work, he could recreate other parts, at least that was what he told himself. He was setting himself on the same path as that great master-wizard. He was making a statement to himself and to the world about what he could do and what his intentions were.

In the end, it did not really matter what his motivation was. What mattered was that he completed the work he had set himself. The mystical diagrams and the potent incantations flowed freely onto the parchment, seeming almost to write themselves. He kept at work long into the night, using more and more parchment, constantly having to sharpen the nib of his quill, burning the candles in his chamber low.

Dawn was breaking by the time he had completed his work, but he did not feel tired. It was not merely the drugs that he used to give himself energy that made him feel so lightheaded. He had a sense he was becoming the person that he was intended to be; finally he was on the right path to fulfilling his destiny. Making this blade just felt right.

This was a sword that would never lose its sharpness no matter what it was used to cut and which would be able to cut through almost anything. It did not really matter to him that he had no real use for it – it was something that he could build upon, a structure into which you could eventually fit other spells in exactly the same way that Caledor had.

Yet even as he completed the design, a vague sense of dissatisfaction filled him. He was merely recreating the work of another. What he had done was a work of genius, but it was a work of someone else's genius. It pleased him to be able to do this, but he knew that he would never be truly happy until he had managed to create a work of equal magnitude of his own. He wanted to make his own masterpiece.

As that thought occurred to him, a sardonic smile twisted his lips. He could see where that path was eventually going to lead him. He was putting himself in competition with the greatest mage who had ever lived. Caledor's masterpiece was the Vortex, a spell that had saved the entire world and which even to this very day protected his homeland.

How could you compete with that?

He already felt certain that he was going to try and find a way. He strode down to the forges.

It took long hard hours wielding the heavy hammer, sweating at the forge, using all his strength while weaving potent enchantments into the metal. It required him to perform two very difficult tasks at once, and it taxed his mental and physical strengths to the limit. By the time the finished blade gleamed in his hand he was exhausted – it was all he could do to drag himself to his chambers and throw himself upon his bed. Sleep took him almost instantly. Visions of Tyrion and the Everqueen being pursued through dense forests by armies of druchii dogged him. Over everything loomed two gigantic figures: one was robed and cowled and radiated a chill aura of deadly power, the other was the Archmage Caledor. They seemed to be involved in some titanic battle of wills, and he knew he was part of that struggle.

He awoke with a growing sense that time was running out.

# CHAPTER SEVEN

'I CANNOT SAY I am pleased to lose you,' said Morelian as Teclis entered his chamber. He glanced significantly at the new blade that hung scabbarded at Teclis's side. 'Your power and your skill could be of great use here in Hoeth.'

'The tower does not need another defender,' said Teclis, wondering why the High Loremaster had summoned him.

'That remains to be seen,' said Morelian, although he did not say it loudly lest they be overheard. 'In any case, I have some gifts for you to use on your quest.'

'Any help will be gratefully received,' said Teclis.

'I suspect you will need all of it by the end of your journey. I fear you go along a very dark road.'

'Your words are not calculated to improve my morale.'

'You are not riding into such circumstances that overconfidence would be justified.'

'I trust that your gift does not consist merely of advice, no matter how well meant. If you continue in this vein it may discourage me from departing entirely.'

'Hopefully you will find this a somewhat greater mark of my faith in you,' said the High Loremaster. From behind his desk, he produced a helmet that Teclis recognised. It was a winged crown that had once sat in the vaults beneath the tower.

'The War Crown of Saphery,' he said. It was difficult to keep the awe from his voice. 'You're placing a mighty trust in me.'

'Let us hope that it is justified,' said Morelian. He raised the crown reverently with both hands and placed it upon Teclis's head. Almost at once, Teclis felt a difference. His eyesight and his hearing both became much keener. He could see the High Loremaster's face in much more detail than he had ever been able to do before, with his weak eyesight. Concern was written in the old elf's face, and something else too, something like respect.

'I will do my best to see that it is,' Teclis said. His own voice sounded different now. It was louder and more decisive. He was much more aware of the flow of magical energy about him. He was not entirely sure of all that the crown was doing for him, but he was certain that it was enhancing his power in many ways.

'It is a princely gift,' Teclis said.

'Think of it more as a loan,' the High Loremaster said. 'For as long as you live, you will hold it in trust for the tower. On your death, it will be returned to us.'

'It shall be as you say,' Teclis said. 'And once again I must express my gratitude. Never did I expect to be granted such a boon.'

'It may well be that you carry the destiny of us all with you,' said the High Loremaster. 'It is the least that I can do. And it is not the only thing. Come with me.'

He led Teclis from his chambers and by devious and secret ways took him out of the tower, avoiding the throngs that sought audience with the High Loremaster. Two Sword Masters dogged their steps. It was a measure of the High Loremaster's worries that even here in the tower, bodyguards followed him everywhere.

Had things really come to this, Teclis wondered?

They emerged into the sunlight. The day was bright and beautiful and one would never have suspected that somewhere far-off wars were being fought and elves were dying. The High Loremaster trudged on, leaning on his staff, and Teclis was all too aware of how old Morelian was and what a great weight of responsibility pressed down upon his shoulders.

They came eventually to the open fields where many beasts grazed. They passed the corrals in which the steeds of the Sword Masters were penned. They came at last to an oddly constructed stable on the very outskirts of the tower's domain. From inside came the whinny of a great horse. It seemed to greet the High Loremaster as if the beast was welcoming an old friend.

'Peace be upon you, Silver Wing,' the High Loremaster said. The horse snorted in response, or at least Teclis thought it was a horse until he entered the stable. Then he saw it was something quite different.

In some ways it looked like a great white stallion, as noble a beast as he had ever seen. It looked old but still very strong. In one important way it differed from a normal horse. Two great wings were folded against its flanks and when it reared to welcome its master, the wings extended and their flapping sent great gusts of air billowing around the room, making the wizard's robes flutter.

Morelian said, 'Silver Wing and I are old friends. He carried me on many a quest when we were both younger. He will bear you on this one at least as far as Avelorn.'

Teclis knew that he should feel grateful, and he did, but he could not express his gratitude. He found the prospect of riding upon this great beast terrifying. It could bear him to Avelorn faster than any horse could. It would take him through the air with the speed of a bird.

That was the problem. Just the thought of getting into the saddle and riding through the sky almost paralysed him with fear.

'You do not seem entirely enthusiastic,' the High Loremaster said. 'I confess I had expected a somewhat greater display of gratitude. It is not every day that Silver Wing extends this privilege.'

Teclis considered his words with care. 'I am grateful to you both. I was merely overwhelmed by the immensity of the favour that you're doing me.'

'That and something else,' the High Loremaster said. He looked as if he was struggling to keep from smiling. 'I can tell.'

Teclis decided that it would be simplest not to conceal his reservations. 'I find the prospect of flying more than a little daunting. I might even go as far as to say I find it terrifying.'

'I felt exactly the same way the first time I ever had to bestride a pegasus.'

'Without wishing to insult Silver Wing or demean the generosity of your offer, perhaps it would be better if I took a normal horse to Avelorn.'

'I was under the impression that every minute, every second, counted.' Teclis got the impression that this evil old elf was rather enjoying his discomfiture. 'I thought there was not a moment to be wasted.'

'And indeed, this is the case,' Teclis said. 'On the other hand, it would probably be for the best if I actually arrived in Avelorn and did not fall out of the saddle as I streaked through the sky.'

'Fortunately, we have provided for that contingency,' the High Loremaster said.

'I suspected that you might have,' said Teclis. He did not entirely succeed in keeping the sour note from his voice.

'The saddle of a pegasus rider is not like a normal saddle. It contains an arrangement of straps designed to restrain the rider in place as much to keep it attached to the pegasus.'

'That goes some way towards reducing my reservations,' Teclis said. 'But I am forced to confess that I have some more.'

'Doubtless you're wondering how you will guide Silver Wing.'

'You show an understanding that verges on the telepathic.'

'Silver Wing is very old and very wise and will respond to

voice commands. If I may say so, he is considerably more intelligent than many elves although he cannot speak.'

'I suppose you will have ready answers to any other objections I might raise.'

'I would deem such an eventuality very likely. Pegasus is undoubtedly the fastest way for you to get Avelorn unless you propose inventing a spell of long-distance teleportation within the next few hours.'

'Would that I were capable of such a prodigy of research.'

'I have taken the liberty of not only providing you with the special saddle, but also with saddle bags containing rations and enough space for any medicines that you might need to carry.'

'It seems that you have thought of everything. I wish I could find suitable words to express my gratitude.'

'You have done quite well enough so far,' the High Loremaster said.

'When do you propose that I depart?'

'Once again, I was under the impression that there was not a second to be lost. You seemed most insistent upon this the last time we talked about this matter.'

'Forgive me for saying so, but you seem to be taking some pleasure in using my own words to discomfit me.'

'When you reach my age,' the High Loremaster said, 'you will understand that one must take one's pleasures from what one can, no matter how petty those enjoyments may seem to those younger than you.'

'I hope that when I reach your age I should be somewhat more generous of spirit.'

'A noble wish, but I fear it will not be the case.' The old elf was smiling. 'I would like to be here to wish you a safe journey, but I do not have an infinite supply of time to take off from my duties.'

'It seems that you have prepared all that I need. All that remains for me to do is to wish you farewell.'

'And to mount your new steed,' the High Loremaster suggested.

'Indeed,' said Teclis. 'I would not wish to deprive you of the pleasure of witnessing that.'

Cautiously Teclis approached the pegasus. As he got closer, he realised exactly how massive it was. Its head was taller than his own. Huge muscles bunched as it moved. He reached out to gently stroke its muzzle, and it lowered his head as if accepting him and his touch. His hands trembled as he stroked the creature's cheek and looked into the huge, deep black eyes. There was an intelligence in them greater than in that of any horse he had ever encountered. The pegasus whinnied softly and stopped prancing.

The High Loremaster himself came forwards and fixed the saddle onto the beast. It was larger than a normal saddle, with far more straps holding it in position. At front and back, it was higher and the saddle posts were larger. As it was fixed in place, Teclis could see that there were a number of straps left unbuckled. Doubtless these were intended to hold the rider in place. Carefully, he put one foot in the stirrup, threw a leg over the saddle and got himself into position. The High Loremaster showed him how to fasten the restraining straps that would hold him in.

The beast shifted below him as it adjusted to his weight on its back. Its wings flapped. Teclis was all too aware of their motion very close to him, of the great muscles moving in the beast's flanks. Mighty as the creature was, he could not see how those wings alone could get it airborne. There had to be magic involved. He sensed a reservoir of energy within the pegasus and he suspected that it was as much needed to get the winged steed aloft as its pinions.

'Very good,' the High Loremaster said. 'You look as if you were born to do this.'

'I don't feel like it,' Teclis said.

'Desist from complaining and learn to simply enjoy the circumstances you find yourself in. That would be my advice to you.'

'It is easy enough for you to say that,' Teclis said. 'You're the one standing with his feet on the ground while I am trussed up like a prisoner awaiting torture.'

'Believe me, I wish I could take your place. There is nothing quite in comparison with the sensation of racing through the sky with the wind tugging at your robe and the ground a thousand feet below.'

'I find that I am inclined to let you take my place if you desire the experience so much.'

'My heart has already thrilled to that particular delight. I shall leave the joys of flight to you. And there's no time like the present – Silver Wing, take to the skies!'

On the High Loremaster's command, the pegasus raced from the stable. Its wings beat steadily and Teclis felt the build up of magical energy within the creature's breast. It took a dozen strides and then sprang. At first, Teclis thought that it was actually going to be in the air. The leap went on for longer than any normal jump by a normal horse, but the pegasus returned to the ground, took three more strides and then sprang again. This time it stayed airborne for a dozen heartbeats before returning to the ground. It made a third attempt to get aloft, wings thrashing, and this time it stayed aloft.

Teclis watched the trees of the surrounding forest race ever closer. He feared that his career as a flier was going to be cut short by the brutal impact of their branches. At the very last second, Silver Wing gained height and skimmed just over the treetops. Teclis clung on desperately, his knuckles white against the saddle post.

Silver Wing circled, gaining altitude as it flew round and round the tower. At first, it was all Teclis could do to hold on. He kept his eyes resolutely closed and fought against dizziness and nausea. When he looked down, the ground seemed a long way below and the faces of those who stared up at him appeared tiny.

His weight strained against the harness that held him in the saddle. The fear that he was going to fall or that the leather straps would break and send him tumbling to the earth far below dominated his mind.

Every little creak that the harness made seemed an ominous warning that it was about to snap and send him to his doom. It felt impossible that an animal as large as Silver Wing could be kept aloft merely by the thrashing of its wings. At any moment the power of the spell could run out and the two of them would be sent tumbling earthwards...

After a few minutes, he managed to keep his eyes open despite the tears from the roaring wind that threatened to blind him. He had enough presence of mind to speak a shielding spell. It was the same cantrip he used to protect himself against the heat of the jungles of Lustria, but it served just as well to protect them from the passing breeze.

He saw that they had climbed far above the trees but still had not managed to equal the height of the great Tower of Hoeth. It loomed enormously before them. Seen from this angle he was able to appreciate both its massive size and its astonishing grace. It was indeed true – there never had been a structure built upon the face of the world to match this tower in beauty or scale.

The High Loremaster waved to him. Teclis did not dare let go of the saddle posts to wave back.

Silver Wing soared northwards towards the distant forest of Avelorn.

IT WAS MERE minutes before the area surrounding the tower faded from view and Teclis found himself flying over the dense woods of Saphery. It was strange to see the world from this angle, to look down upon the tops of trees and watch the clusters of leaves swaying in the wind, to see the birds rising up from beneath him as they were startled by the passage of the pegasus's shadow. It was odd to find himself flying alongside flocks of starlings.

Teclis was not sure how long he was airborne before he started to get used to the sensation of flight. He doubted that he would ever become totally accustomed to it, but eventually his stomach settled and he lost some of the fear of falling to his doom. Silver Wing had managed to stay aloft for a sufficient length of time to reassure him that it was not an accident and that the pegasus was actually capable of flying for long distances.

He had grown accustomed to being able to work the most powerful spells of the magical art, but he was upset by simply being mounted upon a flying horse.

He had a suspicion as to the reason why that was. When working magic, control of the ritual was his. Flying this way, he was utterly reliant on the ability of his steed. He knew that there were spells that would slow the fall of anyone dropping from a great height, but he had never taken the trouble to learn any of them. He made up his mind to rectify this omission as soon as he was given the opportunity, if he ever was. It had been a lamentable oversight in his magical education. In fact, he thought, as he flew he would do his best to derive some from first principles.

The saddle creaked. He tried to push thoughts of the straps coming undone from his mind.

AFTER MANY HOURS of flight, Teclis saw the curve of a vast silver river below him. From his memory of the maps he had once studied in the tower he reckoned this was the Everflow, which at this point marked the ancient boundary between Avelorn and Saphery. Here the rule of the wizard-princes gave way to that of the Everqueen. He knew the river ran a long way northwards to its sources in the mountains of

Chrace, but it was at least a landmark to navigate by.

The forests beneath him were changing. The woods seemed deeper, older, the trees taller and darker. These woods were quieter than those of Saphery. There was a magic here just as deep but more still and subtle. In Saphery the magic felt like the product of intelligent intervention, of spells, old and well woven. Here the land itself was magical. Power flowed through it and sometimes formed deep pools. Not all of those pools were pure. In some places, Teclis sensed the taint of an evil as ancient as the world. It seemed somehow appropriate. No place was entirely free of the taint of darkness, not even ancient, noble Avelorn. He wondered if Tyrion had found this out yet.

The thought struck him that Tyrion might have found this out and died. He pushed that thought to one side. Such a contingency was simply not possible. He would know if it had happened. Another thought, just as discouraging, replaced it. This was a quest that was more difficult than looking for a needle in the proverbial haystack or a single grain of sand on a beach. Avelorn was a vast land, mostly wilderness, and he was no woodsman. How was he going to find his twin? Looking down from above, he could see almost nothing through the canopy of leaves and branches. Even being mounted on a pegasus was not going to be much of an advantage.

He could try a spell of location. Normally he would have been dubious of its efficacy over so wide an area, but he had some hope that given the strength of the bond between him and Tyrion he could make it work. Of course, that would mean returning to the earth and sacrificing the advantage of speed and mobility that flight gave him. The best bet seemed to be to head towards the tournament grounds and try and pick up the trail there.

He found that in an odd and half-scared way, he was coming to enjoy the sensation of speed, of skimming over the surface of the world and being able to see to the distant green horizon. He doubted that he would ever get used to it, but he was starting to find the wonder within the terror. As if in response, Silver Wing snorted, almost derisively.

'You stick to flying, and leave the sarcasm to me,' Teclis said softly. Onwards they flew over a land that was now in the hands of the enemy.

# CHAPTER EIGHT

TYRION LAY GASPING on the bank of the Everflow. His mail shirt felt as if it was made from a ton of rusting metal. His clothes were sopping wet. Water had almost doubled the weight of the tabard. It dripped into his eyes through the eye pieces of the helmet. His side burned, and with more than the effort of swimming.

He pushed himself upright with both hands and looked around. On the far side of the river, somewhat upstream, a company of Cold One riders had come into view. Their beasts were screeching with frustration. One of them, obviously the leader, started bellowing orders and they split up into multiple parties, some of them heading north along the riverbank, some of them heading south, some of them starting to swim across the river. They had obviously underestimated the strength of the current, for it started to sweep even the great beasts away, bringing them in Tyrion's direction. More and more dark elves came into view on the far bank of the Everflow. They halted, reluctant to press on across the water in the fading light.

The cold water seemed to have leeched all strength from Tyrion. He struggled to pull himself into the undergrowth before he could be spotted. He had to dig his fingers into the soil to gain purchase. Pain stabbed his side. His knuckles were scratched and the palms of his hands had friction burns.

He was not in any state to fight. Somehow, with as much effort as it would once have taken him to run several leagues, he managed to fight his way in among the roots of a bush. Twigs scratched against the outside of his helmet, monstrous fingers scraping against metal. He let himself lie there, more exhausted than he had felt in a very long time.

The Cold Ones emerged from the water upstream but still closer to him than he would have liked. He wondered if they were already on his trail, catching his scent with sensitive, bestial nostrils.

He just lay there, thinking that he ought to do something, but not sure what. The most logical thing to do was to lower himself back into the water so that they could not catch his scent, but he was not sure he had the strength to hold on if he did that.

He feared for Alarielle. She was alone.

What was she doing right now?

Hopefully she had sense enough to take cover or flee. He told himself not to worry. She had grown up in these woods. She was better at this sort of thing than he was, as she had already proved. He was the one he needed to worry about right now. He doubted that the magic sword was capable of saving him twice in one day. It seemed mostly luck that he had been able to trigger it in the first place. He had no confidence that he would be able to do so again.

He could hear massively heavy forms crashing through the undergrowth nearby. Something enormous bellowed its hunger and its hate. He had no choice. He had to get away before it caught his scent. Steeling himself against the cold, he pushed off, sliding down the bank back into the water with a splash that was louder than he would have liked. The cold water closed over his head again. Bubbles of trapped air emerged from his helmet and clothing. Instinctively, he pushed himself to the surface, making even more splashing noises that sounded as loud as the trumpets of an army in his ears.

Very good, Tyrion, he thought. Very stealthy.

He reached out and grabbed the root of a nearby tree to hold himself against the current. The cold of the water already seemed to be seeping into his fingers, paralysing them, numbing them, making it more and more difficult for him to hold his grip. He could see the vague outlines of massive forms moving through the undergrowth, displacing it. He could hear the jingle of harnesses and the bellows-like breathing of the monstrous animals.

Once, he saw the cold glitter of one of their eyes turned on him. He did not move, fearing that any motion would simply draw their attention.

Yes, he could see the outline of one of those great reptilian heads. It was turning backwards and forwards, nostrils flaring, as if attempting to catch his scent on the wind. Tyrion considered letting himself drop back under the water, but he resisted the impulse although his heart was pounding and his breath was coming in short, shallow gasps.

The beast stood there for a very long time, and he felt certain that it knew he was there. It made a small mewling noise as if it was confused, then its rider hit it with the butt of his sword and it moved on, followed by a long line of its scaly brethren. It seemed to take hours for them to pass although it could not have been more than a few minutes.

When they were finally gone, Tyrion pulled himself back out of the water and lay there, too exhausted even to think about what might have happened to the Everqueen. He knew that he had to do something. He had to take off his soaking clothing before he caught a chill. He needed to look after his armour or it would rust. He prayed the dark elves would not cross the river and find him.

TYRION PULLED OFF his metal jerkin and place it on the ground beside the tabard. He stripped off his shirt and britches and began to wring them out. Water sopped over his scraped knuckles and abraded palms. He was shivering from the cold and wet. He could hear the dark elves receding into the distance but that did not mean he was safe. It was possible that there were other silent hunters nearby. It would be foolish to assume that the Cold Ones were the only things looking for him.

He drew Sunfang from its scabbard and placed it on the ground. Its flames blazed up, not as bright as usual but still enough to give some heat. He drove the tip of the blade into the ground and sat down beside it, letting its warmth heat his body and dry his clothes.

He draped his shirt and britches over a piece of wood so that they would catch the heat and form a small windbreak which he hoped would also shield the sword from view. He inspected the chainmail shirt he had taken from the dead dark elf what seemed like a lifetime ago. It had been well oiled, but the water had removed that protective coating and he could see that some of the links were already beginning to rust. There was nothing he could do about it since he did not have the tools needed for maintenance. Instead he put the mail shirt to one side and thought about what he was going to do next.

He had become separated from the Everqueen because of his own weakness – even now she might be in the hands of the druchii and he would not even know it. He had to fight down the impulse to rise and run off into the woods and begin searching for her immediately. He was even tempted to shout her name, although that would be madness since it would alert the children of Naggaroth to his presence and possibly to hers as well.

He hated this feeling of weakness, of not being able to do anything. He clenched his teeth and fought down the urge to punch the ground with his fist. That really would not do him any good at all, given the condition of his hands. He was suddenly aware of what a fragile thing his body was.

He had never felt this way before. It had not taken much to transform him from an efficient fighting machine into something barely capable of movement. All it had taken was a little hardship, a little cold and the strangling strength of the river.

He looked at where the witch elf's blade had bitten into his side. The wound had gone a strange colour around the edges, a sort of blackish-purple, and the area was strangely tender. Worse than that, it felt as if something in it was draining the strength from his body. It seemed all too likely that he had been poisoned, and there really wasn't anything he could do about it.

Perhaps his aunt or Teclis would know what to do – they were alchemists after all. He had no such knowledge. He knew only the basics of field medicine that any elven soldier picked up on campaign.

Sitting here feeling sorry for himself was not going to achieve anything. He needed to do something. The heat from his sword had given him back a portion of his strength. He would wait until his clothing was dry and then he would set out in search of Alarielle, although he had no idea where he could find her.

Having made that resolution, he felt a little bit better. He wished he had something to eat but there was nothing. At least there was no shortage of water, he told himself. He supposed that given some time he might be able to catch fish in the river, although he was not sure, given the speed of the current.

It was dark by the time his clothes had dried. His blade

crackled with its flames, sending shadows dancing away from him. He knew he really should put it back in its scabbard, for its light would probably attract pursuers. The small windbreak that he had created from his clothing would shield it from certain angles, but all it would take would be the Cold One riders to turn up the path they had been following and they would see it. He did not fancy fleeing from one of those hunting reptiles through the dark. It would be able to track him by scent. There was something unnerving about the prospect of being pursued through the night-shrouded woods by one of those great cold-blooded monsters.

He rose and donned his shirt and leather underjerkin and then put on the mail shirt. It jingled slightly when he moved and the noise was all the more noticeable at night. He wondered why that was – why did sound always seem so much louder at night? No doubt Teclis would have some explanation – he always did. All Tyrion ever really had were questions.

He picked up the blade and put it back in its scabbard. Suddenly the night seemed very cold, colder than it ought to have. He was almost tempted to draw the blade again so that he would have more light, but that was madness. He stood there waiting for his eyes to adjust, letting himself become more accustomed to the shadowy mass of the woods around him. Nearby the river continued to race by. The sound of water on rocks was like quiet thunder.

Tyrion figured that he would need to head back the way he had come to pick up the Everqueen's trail. She had been north of him when they had tried to cross the river and it seemed only logical that she still would be. Of course, it was always possible that she had somehow passed him by in the darkness. He dismissed such thoughts from his mind. If he allowed them to influence his decision, he would never do anything.

TYRION CONSIDERED HIS options. It seemed foolish to be blundering around in the dark, wearing the armour of a dark elf. If Alarielle saw him she may put an arrow through him. If a druchii saw him, he might be mistaken for a deserter. His disguise certainly had not fooled the Cold Ones, so it was not a great deal of use to him under the present circumstances.

On one hand, the mail shirt was certainly useful as armour, but then again it was noisy and might give away his position when he was trying to move stealthily. Reluctantly, he decided that he would need to get rid of it. Stealth was more important than protection at this point, and the truth of the matter was that the armour was hurting his wounded side and its extra weight was slowing him down.

He decided he would keep the leather underjerkin because it offered a measure of protection and did not make any noise when he moved. The dark elf helmet was of a very distinctive shape and if Alarielle saw him it might cause her to mistake him for one of the enemy. He decided that he could not afford that either. She knew his face and it would be best if she could see it.

He took the armour he was going to discard, wrapped the

helmet in the mail shirt and tossed it out into the river. He did not want to leave it here because it might give away his position to the Cold Ones when they returned. It was best to leave as few clues as possible behind him.

He felt better for not carrying the extra weight, and made his way down onto the trail. He discovered some evidence of the Cold Ones' passage almost immediately. Large lumps of excrement, foul-smelling in the extreme, dotted the path.

He kept moving, keeping to one side of the trail, so that he could dive into the undergrowth as quickly as possible. His night vision was good, even for an elf, so he did not have much trouble picking his way along in the darkness now that his eyes had adapted to the lack of light.

He paused now and again to listen, filled with foreboding that some enemies might be creeping up on him in the dark. At night, small sounds filled the forest. A white owl passed by overhead, gliding on silent wings, seeking its prey among the shadows. Tyrion felt a certain sympathy for the creatures it hunted. Occasionally, he caught the glitter of bestial eyes in the undergrowth. A fox, perhaps or maybe a wild dog. Whatever it was, it was silent and it retreated as he approached.

As he marched along, a sense of futility overcame him. What was he doing? He was never going to be able to find Alarielle in this gloom. She must be leagues away, or perhaps she was in the clutches of Malekith's minions. He could pass her in the darkness if she lay sleeping, and the chances were that he would never spot her. Nonetheless, some instinct told him to keep moving. It was his nature to do so anyway. He preferred action to inaction. At least this way he felt as if he was doing something and he was, in some small way, master of his fate.

He wondered if he should call out to her in the darkness, perhaps just whisper her name quietly, but this too struck him as a species of madness. It was the counsel of desperation. He was infinitely more likely to give away his position to any hunters that might be looking for him in the night.

He told himself that he was over-thinking things. Why should the dark elves be abroad now? They would most likely be making camp and laying themselves down to sleep, which is what he would be doing if he had any sense. Nonetheless, by the light of the fading moon, he kept walking, and occasionally when instinct told him that he was safe, he whispered the name of the Everqueen as if it was a talisman or a desperate prayer.

In his hand he clutched a dagger, and held himself ready to lash out at anything that might spring upon him from the darkness. He almost hoped that something would attack. At least it would break the tension, and it would give him a sense that he was not alone in the night.

He wondered how many other people were abroad in the darkness. Not too many, he suspected. If they were, they were likely to be enemies. He told himself that he was being too pessimistic. It was possible that there were other elves friendly to the Everqueen in this forest. Not all of them could have been massacred or captured by the dark elves back when they attacked the great tournament grounds. Perhaps there were even natives of Avelorn in this area who had not been at the tournament.

Of course, if that was the case, it was more than likely that the Cold Ones had scented them and they were now dead. It galled him to be wandering on his own through the night when his homeland was under attack by their ancient enemies. He wished that he was with an army right now, getting ready to fight against the invaders.

Perhaps there was no army anywhere in Ulthuan capable of fighting any more. The enemy had reached the heart of Avelorn and had almost succeeded in capturing its queen without anyone opposing it. Perhaps the same thing had happened elsewhere. Perhaps the armies of the Phoenix King had been taken completely off guard and overwhelmed by the same sorcery that had allowed the dark elves to penetrate so far into the forest kingdom.

He dismissed such speculation as futile. It could not be so. There were not enough druchii in Naggaroth to overwhelm all of the elven lands. Somebody, somewhere must be fighting against them, and while they did so, there was hope. Tyrion smiled sourly. It was one thing to tell himself that logically this must be the case. It was another thing entirely to make himself believe it, in the night, while hunger gnawed at his belly, and the witch blade's poisoned wound sapped his strength.

From up ahead came the sound of voices.

Tyrion could see a fire and hear the muffled, rasping breath of the Cold Ones. He paused, fearing that it was already too late to avoid detection and that at any moment the creature's bellowing would give the alarm and warn their riders of his presence.

He froze, becoming just another shadow amid shadows. No alarm was given. No monster sprang to life. The rhythm of their breathing was undisturbed. They were either asleep or made sluggish by the darkness. He let out his breath in a long, soft sigh, and crept forwards. He could see a group of druchii knights gathered around a fire. Their great mounts were tethered to metal stakes driven into the ground close at hand.

Slowly, carefully, Tyrion moved closer, writhing along on his belly, balancing himself on his palms. He got so close he could make out the features of the dark elves around the fire. They had removed their helmets so they could eat, and that action made them seem strangely vulnerable. They could have been elf soldiers anywhere on the seven continents, fighting a war far from home. Just watching their familiar actions gave Tyrion an odd pang of homesickness for the camps he had known.

One of them was leaning forwards, turning the corpse of some small animal on a stick-spit. Another was passing around his flask. From where he crouched, Tyrion could smell the alcohol. Two more were lying on the ground, looking at the stars. Another, the loner of the group, sat on a log and whittled something from a twig with his knife. It did not seem possible, looking at this homely scene, that these were the same fierce invaders who had killed so many at the tournament grounds.

And yet, they were.

If he wanted, he could take them by surprise. He could kill them all before they realised what was happening. It would be easy. He would circle the fire and take the first two from behind, then kick the embers of the fire on the ones facing them. A few strides and he would skewer them, leaving only the whittler and the ones on the ground. He had no doubt he could handle them, even in his weakened state, provided their beasts did not wake and join the fight.

There was nothing to be gained from doing so though, other than the slaking of the thirst for revenge that burned in his gut. He might even get himself killed, which would do no one, not the Everqueen and certainly not himself, any good. He had established that Alarielle was not their prisoner at least, which was one thing. He could be on his way.

Yet something held him in place. Perhaps it was loneliness. He found himself drawn to the fire and to vicariously participating in the soldiers' comradeship, and he was reluctant to leave just yet and wander off into the darkness.

'Do you think we'll find them?' one of the dark elves asked.

'They are leagues away if they have any sense,' the whittler replied. Tyrion knew his type. There was always one in every group, the loner, the one who had to be negative, who needed to bring his comrades down.

'What would you do with the reward?' the drinker asked.

'Forget the reward. I would just like to get my hands on the Everqueen for a few hours,' said another soldier.

'A few minutes,' one of his companions said.

'A few seconds more likely,' said Whittler.

'You had better hope those seconds are worth it,' said one with the voice of authority and the badges of a leader. 'She is to be returned to Malekith untouched and unharmed. I think the Witch King wants to bed her himself.'

This led to a burst of ribald speculation. 'Soon we might have two queens in Naggaroth,' Whittler said.

'The gods preserve us, one is enough,' said Drinker. 'Not that I would kick Morathi out of bed, you understand.'

'That's very generous of you,' said Whittler.

'I am free with my favours,' said Drinker, 'although not as free as she is.'

'You have not had seven thousand years of practice.'

'Well, tomorrow we have another chance at the reward, if the trackers have not already found our high, bitch-goddess majesty,' said the leader.

'I thought Morathi was in the north, selecting some new barbarian lovers for her harem,' said Drinker.

'I was talking about the Everqueen, as I am sure you would realise if you were sober.'

'Which way did the scouts go?' asked one of the sleepers lying on the ground.

'You know what they are like. They are always creeping about, going their own way without anyone seeing them.'

'I thought we had them today,' said Drinker. 'When old Sharptooth caught the scent. I didn't think anything on two legs could get away.'

'And yet somehow they did,' said Whittler. 'And they killed three good riders while they were doing it.'

'They say Harek and his boys were burned by magic,' said one of those on the ground. 'You think this famous warrior is also a sorcerer?'

'I don't know. I heard he walked into the pavilion and slaughtered the general's bodyguard all on his own. He was carrying a burning blade, just like the one Aenarion used to carry before he picked up the Sword of Khaine.'

'Maybe it was Aenarion,' said Whittler, with heavy sarcasm. 'Maybe he returned from wherever he flew off to just to save the Everqueen.'

The silence that fell told Tyrion that Whittler had said the wrong thing. Not even those sacrilegious druchii wanted to hear jokes about Malekith's father. Or contemplate the prospect of his return.

'We'd better set some watches,' said Leader. 'I would not want to be taken off guard, just in case this famous warrior comes for us.'

Tyrion knew a cue when he heard one. He left their corpses for the Cold Ones to feast on.

# CHAPTER NINE

'YOU SEEM UNABLE to resist slaughtering things, Prince Tyrion,' said a voice from behind him.

Tyrion turned to see the Everqueen standing there. She held her makeshift bow in her hand and she looked ready to use it. He was not sure whether she intended to use it on him.

'In case you had not noticed, your serenity, these are our enemies,' Tyrion said. 'Or they were.'

'You're leaving a trail of dead bodies around Avelorn that a blind elf could follow,' she said. 'Perhaps you ought to learn some self-restraint.'

'At least I had made it easy for you to find me,' he said. 'I presume you sought out the sounds of carnage.'

'I was looking for you,' she said. She moved over to the pile of corpses that Tyrion had left and inspected them distastefully. It was not a pretty sight.

'Well, you found me, though it took you long enough.'

'I was pursued by an army of dark elves,' she said. 'I had to flee before them and then double back.'

'How did you escape them? I thought those Cold Ones would never give up, once they got your scent.'

'I took to the trees. Some of them grow very high here, and I think that kept me out of range of the hunters' nostrils. I came back here by climbing through the branches over their heads.'

'Very clever,' he said. 'I see I was wasting my time worrying about you.'

'Here's an idea you might like to drive into your head, Prince Tyrion. I was born here. I grew up in these woods. I know how to take care of myself. More than you do, it seems.'

Tyrion thought back over the events of the day. 'You're right. I am more at home on a battlefield than being pursued through a forest. My instinct is to turn and fight. It galls me to have to watch these scum overrun our homeland.'

'As it does me, Prince Tyrion. But there is a time to fight and a time to flee, and I think we both know which time this is.'

'How did you find me?'

'I doubled back along the trail. I looked down the river to the place where it seemed most likely you had come out of the water.'

'Did you find my trail?'

'No. I am no great tracker. I could not follow in this light.'

'And yet you found me.'

'It was simple enough. I merely asked myself what I would do if I were you. And naturally I found you slaughtering dark elves, so my method was proved correct.'

'You're being too glib.'

'I thought you would head north, looking for me. You seem determined to be my protector.'

'And you obviously don't need one.'

'I think we both need one. I lack your talent for killing things. You leave a trail through the woods that a child could follow, at least a child of my people. We have to assume that the dark elves have trackers just as competent.'

'I stand chastened,' he said. 'What do you suggest we do?'

'I suggest we search these bodies for supplies. They most likely have some things that we need. After that, I suggest we leave this place as quickly as possible.'

'I could probably have managed to think of that all by myself,' he said.

'Once we're far enough away, we can build a sleeping platform in the trees.'

'I will leave that to you,' he said. 'It's not something I have a great deal of experience of.'

'Don't worry, I shall show you how it is done.'

'WELL, THIS IS novel,' said Tyrion, looking down from the bole of the great tree. The ground was a very long way below, but he had always possessed a good head for heights.

'Great oaks are good places for this,' Alarielle said. 'Their branches are broad and there are boughs where they join the trunk. Even better, there are often hollows such as this one.'

She threw herself flat inside the small cave-like opening in the tree's side. 'Out of the wind, see?'

She was showing off and revelling in her superior knowledge, but he did not mind. She had charm when she chose to use it, and anything that made her feel more confident was a good thing as far as he was concerned.

'What about beasts?' Tyrion asked. 'I would imagine some things use them as dens.'

'Tree panthers, oak hawks, leaf pythons,' she said. 'But there are none of them here. I checked. Nothing has used this place for a long time.'

'Perhaps there is a reason for that,' he said.

'The main thing is that we are off the ground, and away from the trail.' Tyrion wondered about that. They had clambered up a lesser tree and then made their way here following the broad branches. It had not been the easiest of feats in the moonlight but they had managed it.

'Won't anybody tracking us wonder that the trail suddenly vanished?' he said.

'That's why I picked a tree surrounded by rocks in a rocky area,' she said, 'and that's why we climbed up them first. If anyone can track us over that, they are using magic, and we have other things to worry about.'

'I am glad you reminded me of that. I think it's safe to assume that there will be sorcerers amid the dark elves.'

Her smile vanished like the sun behind a cloud. 'True. But we've done what we can.'

'Can't you work magic to hide us? I have always heard that the Everqueen was a great sorceress.'

'It is not so simple, Prince Tyrion. I have the power but I don't know how to use it… yet.'

'I would respectfully suggest that you learn.'

'If I could, I would. Anyway, that is a problem for tomorrow. Tonight we shall sleep.'

'You sleep first,' he said. 'I will keep watch.'

She looked as if she wanted to argue, but then said, 'Wake me in a few hours.'

'That I will,' said Tyrion.

GENERAL DORIAN STRODE through the woods. He was coming to hate this place. He disliked being surrounded by the gigantic trees. He wished that he was home in the cold wastes of northern Naggaroth, fighting against a foe that he at least understood. He disliked being surrounded by gigantic plants that obscured his field of vision, and low bushes in which predators could lurk. He preferred the rocky wastelands.

This was like hunting for a shadow in a darkened room. Even his army, which had seemed so large when he set out, seemed inadequate to the task. He had hundreds of trackers looking for the Everqueen and her mysterious protector, all of them following different trails with different forces. He was starting to wonder whether that was wise. Already the queen and her protector had more than once turned at bay and slaughtered those who should have been hunting them.

He wondered if he was only doing this in order to lengthen his life. All he was really doing was putting off the evil moment when he would need to go back and confess his failure to Malekith.

No! He would not give up. He would find the Everqueen and where she hid, no matter how long it took. It was only a matter of time before the trackers found the right trail and he would be able to bring his overwhelming force to bear. Once that happened, he would be able to report to his master the good news and claim the reward that would be his due.

He suspected that he was not even fooling himself. He very much doubted that there would be any reward for him except a painful death. Malekith did not like to be kept waiting.

Even though it was not his fault that the mirror had not worked, Dorian knew that he would take the blame for it. He should have stayed at his post and waited instructions. He had not. He had taken it upon himself to go and seek the Everqueen. It was the only sensible decision. There was nothing else he could have done under the circumstances. That would make no difference.

Dorian decided that it was time to employ new methods to find the Everqueen and her guardian. Conventional scouting and tracking had failed, so it seemed that the time had arrived to use magic. He had been putting this off because normally he relied on Cassandra to perform the sorcery that he required or to pass on his commands to her fellow witches. Doing this reminded him of her absence and of his own weakness. Nonetheless, the time had arrived.

Alexandra, the chief sorceress, arrived flanked by her sister-witches. They stared at Dorian with cold, malevolent eyes. He matched them glare for glare. He knew they were used to intimidating most druchii, but he had not reached the rank of general by allowing himself to be intimidated.

'Yes,' Alexandra said. Her gaze was particularly cold. She had once been his rival for Cass's affections, and it meant that no love was lost between them.

'We need to find the Everqueen. She continues to elude our scouts.'

'And you wish us to use our magic.'

'No, I expect you to strip naked and race through the woods shouting her name until she answers.' That drew a laugh from the surrounding soldiery which was quickly quelled by the glares of the witches.

'You are not requesting our aid very politely.'

'I am not requesting your aid at all. I am ordering you to do it as your commanding officer.'

'I answer to Morathi.'

'You will answer to Malekith soon if the Everqueen is not found. I doubt even your mistress will protect you from his wrath.'

'Your failure is not our failure, general,' said Alexandra. She had clearly decided that this was the line to take.

'And I am sure the Witch King will take your assessment of that at its true value,' Dorian said. 'I will be sure to mention you specifically when he questions me about this matter.'

Dorian wanted to make it very clear that he was not going to go down for this alone. The witches were no more going to be able to wriggle out from under Malekith's vengeance than he was. He smiled coldly at her to emphasise his point.

'Accidents happen, general. You may not live to be questioned.'

'Some would say that would be a fortunate event for me, given the current situation. I am sure Malekith would conduct his own investigation should that eventuality arise, and he will be generous in apportioning blame.'

Alexandra clearly got the point.

'There is no need for this senseless bickering, general. My sisters and I will get you out of the mess you and your scouts have got yourself into.'

'I welcome your acquiescence.' Her glare told him he might be pushing things a little too far.

Alexandra led her coven out of the tent and Dorian followed. He was curious, and knew that watching her perform their rituals would provide him with distraction from his grief.

The witches scratched a hexagon six paces wide on the ground and then a circle that connected to its corners. Each of them then inscribed a smaller version of the same figure at a corner.

'Are you sure you want to stay, general?' Alexandra asked. 'If something goes wrong you may suffer from the backlash.'

'I am sure my amulets will protect me,' said Dorian, although he was not sure at all. He was simply beyond all caring. He took a few steps back though, to put some distance between himself and the ritual.

Alexandra started to chant. One by one the witches took up the chant. It was in the ancient elvish tongue interspersed with some words in another language which made the hairs stand on the back of Dorian's neck. He recognised some of them from Cass's grimoires. They were in one of the daemon tongues. Curious birds fluttered overhead, cawing raucously, obviously disturbed by what they saw.

As the witches repeated the words a cold breeze sprang up which carried on it strange odours. Small firefly-like points of light shimmered in the air around the hexagon until the witches were obscured by their swarming. The tones of the chant changed and the motes drifted outward. One of them touched a hovering raven. The bird let out an unearthly shriek. Its eyes glowed with the strange corpse-light of the mote. It began to move and circle with a new intelligence, buffeting some of its companions down into the cloud with its wings. They too were limned in light and shrieked loudly and were merged with the possessed flock.

The motes continued to drift outwards, touching animals and birds as they went. Every one that was touched joined the great swarm, and circled around the witches, a mass of birds, foxes, weasels and other animals, all moving in eerie unison, like a great shoal of fish changing directions in a current.

One of the motes drifted close to where Dorian stood. He was almost curious enough to reach out and touch it. It moved closer and circled him, coming close to the amulets he wore before veering away. He had a sense of malign intelligence in the thing. It buzzed into a nearby bush, and something shrieked and scuttled out of the undergrowth and headed back towards the ever-growing swarm.

Alexandra was talking to it, and it was responding in the same odd language, all of the creatures' voices blending together into one cacophonous roar that made the air vibrate with its words. He knew without being told that the witch was giving this composite creature its orders, telling it what to seek and what to do when it found its prey.

The roar sounded angry and defiant. Alexandra's tone was by turns threatening and cajoling. Eventually some accommodation seemed to be reached. The birds fell upon the ground-based animals, pecking out their eyes, devouring their flesh and drinking their blood. As they did so, imprisoned sparks were liberated and drifted free to seek out another avian host. Eventually the air was filled with birds, swarming in a vast flock, which suddenly erupted skywards and hurtled east as if seeking a trail.

'SOMETHING IS WRONG,' Alarielle said. 'I can feel it in the air.'

She had been nervous all day, full of dire premonitions.

Tyrion just looked at her. Studying their surroundings, he could not see any threats at all. It was not that the woods were quiet. They were never really that. There are always some small animals or birds moving through them somewhere but he could not discern any threat, particularly compared to previous days when it had seemed that the surrounding forest teemed with dark elf soldiers. She tilted her head to one side and said, 'There is something wrong – it has something to do with magic. That is all I can say.'

Tyrion understood this – he had never been good at sensing the winds of magic. In fact, he was much worse at it than most elves. It was a species of blindness that he suffered from compared to most of his people, and he felt its lack now.

Even as Alarielle spoke, a dark cloud appeared overhead. It was a mass of birds, all flying together with a strange rigidity and precision in their formation. His magesight was not the best but there was nothing wrong with his eyes, and he immediately saw the sinister nature of the flock.

It consisted of birds that should not have been flying together, such as rooks, sparrows and swallows. Its composition was random and there was something strange and malevolent about the eyes of the birds. Looking closely he could see that they glowed with tiny pinpricks of red light. Even as he noticed this, they swooped down towards him and swirled around in a storm of wings. He could feel the wings beating against him, the feathery mass obscuring his vision temporarily. He regretted that he was not wearing a helmet for he feared that the birds would start pecking at his eyes. They did not attack, and shortly thereafter they withdrew. One of them was soaring off into the distance and he could hear it cawing with a strange intelligence. The birds returned to swooping above them in a holding pattern, circling overhead. If they had been on open ground he would have worried that such a strange formation of flying creatures would have given away their position at a distance, but he strongly doubted that anyone would notice that unless they were close enough to hear the birds shrieking.

'It is a spell,' Alarielle said. 'Those creatures are possessed, I can feel it.'

It came to Tyrion exactly what was happening. 'One of them has returned to whoever sent it.'

Alarielle nodded. 'And I do not doubt that there is a link between it and the rest of the flock so that it will be able to find where we are again.'

'We should kill them,' Tyrion said.

'And how do you propose to do that, Prince Tyrion?' Alarielle said. 'I have a limited number of arrows and they are flying among the branches and I doubt that we can even see all of them.'

'We have to do something,' Tyrion said.

'The best thing that we can do is to try and run ahead of them and hope that we can outpace our pursuers.'

Tyrion could not think of anything else to do, so he started to jog along among the trees while Alarielle easily kept pace beside him. Overhead the birds followed, mostly in ominous silence but sometimes cawing loudly as if to summon pursuers who might be lurking in the woods.

'There has to be some way to get out of their sight,' Tyrion said.

'I can only think of one,' Alarielle said. 'We could head for Winterwood Palace.'

'Where is that and how will it help?'

'Save your breath for running, Prince Tyrion. You'll see when we get there.'

The shadow of the daemonic birds fell upon them as they ran.

# CHAPTER TEN

IMPATIENCE GREW WITHIN Malekith. What was going on, he wondered? Why had he not heard from Dorian? He glared at the mirror once more and willed it to work. It stubbornly refused to respond, just as it had done for the past several days. He clenched his fist and fought down the urge to smash it. He knew that it would do no good – after all, he had designed the thing and caused it to be created. It was intended to be able to withstand much greater force than even his massive strength could bring to bear.

He turned his burning gaze on the rest of the druchii in the command tent. They quailed, sensing his mood. Only N'Kari, the greater daemon that he had bound to his service, refused to care. The daemon still wore the form of a beautiful, naked elven woman. Today, she was tattooed with the runes of Slaanesh.

Malekith rose from his throne, looming over every single person in the room. He strode down from the dais on which his seat had rested and marched across the chamber, wrestling with his own anger.

Be calm, he told himself. Restrain yourself. Before you can rule others, you must first rule yourself. There was no need to be impatient. Everything was still going according to plan. All of the reports coming in told him this.

In the north, the vast force of human Chaos worshippers led by his mother surged across the lands of Yvresse with fire and the sword. In Lothern, the rebellion his supporters had fomented was tying down the great city-state's military strength even as his fleet laid siege. In a dozen different places, armies led by his generals had seized crucial objectives, fortresses, mountain passes that dominated supply lines and ports. From everywhere came reports of uninterrupted success. The plan was working. As he had known it would.

Except in one aspect.

He had heard nothing from Dorian. It had been days now and still there was no contact. He did not know whether the Everqueen was his prisoner or not. He did not know whether the spiritual leader of the elves was alive or dead. He did not know whether his army was victorious or had been destroyed.

For the first time in centuries, the magical mirror he used to keep in touch with his agents and lackeys all over the globe had failed to make contact with its counterpart. It seemed ominous that for the first time, that potent magical instrument had failed. What did it signify?

Had his army been defeated? Was the mirror even now in the hands of his enemies? Had it been destroyed? He doubted it was the latter. He would have sensed that.

Perhaps there was some more reasonable explanation. Perhaps there was some form of magical interference. He knew that protective spells might be at work in the area of Avelorn where the Everqueen dwelled.

Partially, it was his own fault. He had let things slip. He had been too busy issuing orders to the force he himself commanded. He had been too busy overseeing the destruction of the ancient elven city of Mancastra. He had neglected his duties. It was his first field command in many decades. He had allowed himself to succumb to the pleasure of watching his troops smash through the walls of the ancient city and search through the streets, killing and enslaving the inhabitants. He had allowed himself to be overcome by the pleasure of destroying his enemies with his own hands. For the first time in many years he had killed using his own sword.

It had been a foolish mistake, he now thought. He pushed his doubts to one side. He did not know that any mistake had been made. He needed to find out what was going on. The capture of the Everqueen was a major part of his strategy. It had been stupid to delegate responsibility to any underling, no matter how competent.

He had let his own secret, nagging fears dominate him. It was something that he had trouble admitting even to himself. The prospect of facing the god-queen of the elves had worried him. There was always the possibility that he had miscalculated, that his spies had missed something, that there were ancient, potent spells in place in Avelorn that might be able to slay even him.

Perhaps that was in fact the case. Perhaps that was why General Dorian was not in contact with him. Perhaps some hidden magic had risen up and destroyed his follower and the force he led. Perhaps it had been wisdom, not fear, to avoid going to Avelorn himself.

In any case, it was no longer permissible for him to stand by and do nothing. He needed to know what was going on there. He needed to know what had happened to his army there. He needed the information so that he could deal with any problem that might have arisen.

He could not send another army just yet. In fact, it may not be wise to do so. If one army had already been destroyed, he would only be weakening his forces unnecessarily by sending them into the same trap. He needed to do something else. He looked at the daemon, wondering suspiciously if N'Kari had anything to do with what was going on here.

The daemon smiled blandly. Malekith knew he would need to use its services to get what he wanted done. A chamberlain announced the presence of those he had summoned. He turned his burning gaze to greet them.

Malekith inspected the four elves. They did not look immediately prepossessing. No one would suspect them of being among the most deadly elves who have ever lived. Which, of course, was the whole point.

These four were almost as dangerous as the great Urian himself. Each of them was only a hair's breadth less dangerous in his or her field. All of them now looked at their ruler expectantly. Malekith stared back, daring them to show the slightest quantum of defiance. They were all too clever for that.

Malekith walked around them, surveying them. Amara looked as beautiful and innocent as a maiden from the foothills of the mountains of Cothique. She might have been a dairy maid from some small elven village in the wilderness. Her hair was long and blonde. Her eyes were wide and innocently blue. Her nose was small for an elven aristocrat. Her lips were wide and pouting. She looked innocent, trusting and ever so slightly stupid.

She was none of these things.

To Malekith's certain knowledge, she had slain over a thousand elves. She had done it with daggers, poison, garrottes and even a long slender blade which she wielded very expertly when she needed to. She was one of his deadliest spies, a consummate actress who had travelled undetected across Ulthuan on hundreds of occasions. She could appear to be a merchant princess from Lothern or a barmaid from a tavern in some remote village in Yvresse just as easily.

She was an expert of winning the trust of other elves and seducing them to her cause. Now she was dressed in the raiment of an officer of his guard, which was the position she occupied at his court when she was not dispatched on some mission. She kept her eyes modestly downcast but he knew she was listening attentively and without flinching as his metal footfalls passed behind her.

Balial was big and brutal. He was almost as large as Malekith himself. He was enormously broad and enormously strong and he delighted in using his strength. He could break the neck of a human blacksmith with a twist of his hands. He could wrestle monstrous bulls to the ground. He could chop through an outstretched neck and a heavy wooden log on which it rested with one sweep of the giant double-bladed axe that he carried across his back, unusual in that it had an axe-head at each end. There was nothing subtle about Balial. He killed face-to-face in combat. He liked to feel blood splatter his face as he did so.

He had started off as a pit fighter who had attracted Malekith's attention through his sheer ferocity and brutality. For a time, Malekith had thought to make him his executioner until he had discovered that a sly intelligence lurked beneath his brutal mask. Balial was perhaps the deadliest warrior in Malekith's entire retinue. Strangely enough, he possessed a certain charm that was able to win the trust of other elves. Malekith had often infiltrated him into groups of captured slave gladiators to find out what they were thinking, to pick their brains for intelligence about their homelands and to motivate them to fight and win and thus put on a better show. Balial had an excellent memory and a sound grasp of strategy; he was utterly trustworthy, which was not something that could be said of most dark elves.

Khalion looked like he liked his food, his wine and his drugs too much to be a fighter. That was deceptive too. He was a master sorcerer. He was particularly good at spells of illusion and deception, and being good at such things, he did not often fall for them himself. Malekith often used him to bring rebellious wizards to heel or to death's door if they could not be disciplined. Khalion looked amiable but he was cruel almost beyond belief, even by the standards of dark elves. He liked to torture his victims and devour their souls or offer them up to daemons in a most unpleasant manner.

Vidor looked like an inhabitant of Avelorn. He could almost be one of the primitive asrai of the far eastern continent. He dressed all in leather, in a hooded jerkin. In his right hand he carried a great longbow which he could use with a proficiency that would do credit to even one of the elves of the forests across the ocean. He was a deadly shot and just as deadly with a sword or knife. He liked to hunt, and most of all he liked to hunt intelligent creatures such as humans and elves. He was a famous tracker who often returned escaped slaves to their masters. He delighted in doing such things.

Malekith knew his secret. Not only was he a great tracker, but Malekith had ordered his sorcerers to alter the olfactory centres of Vidor's brain. It had been an interesting experiment, a precursor to the much more elaborate ones that he had worked upon Urian and others. Vidor was capable of tracking like a hound. He had a sense of smell as keen as a wolf. Something about the sorcery had altered his brain and let him derive an almost sexual pleasure from the hunt and kill.

Malekith said, 'You are being dispatched on a mission of

utmost importance. You will travel to Avelorn and ascertain what has happened to our army there.'

They knew better than to ask any questions at this point. If he wanted to explain, he would. If he did not, they would need to interpret his wishes according to their own understanding.

Tersely Malekith explained the situation and gave them their instructions. 'You are to seek out General Dorian's force and seek an explanation as to why he has not been in contact. If this explanation is not satisfactory, you are to see that General Dorian is replaced by his immediate subordinates. If the Everqueen is present, return with her to me. If she is not present, find her and bring her to me if that is possible. If it is not possible, kill her and bring back her head so I may use it as a standard for my army.'

He gestured to the small gemstone amulets in the shape of a bird that lay on a nearby table.

'You are each being given a stone raven. Use it to communicate with me if the need arises. I do not need to explain to you that it is of the utmost importance that you succeed in this mission. So far, the conquest of Ulthuan has occurred precisely as expected and according to plan, with the single exception of General Dorian's command. To you falls the great responsibility of bringing that part of the plan back on track. Any questions?'

'Am I to take it that we have your authority to do anything we require, sire?' Balial asked.

'You will be given black signets. You speak with my voice for the course of this mission.'

Balial looked satisfied. There could be no greater mark of Malekith's trust.

'We may remove any who get in our way, no matter how highly placed or no matter whose favour they enjoy, sire?' Khalion asked in his annoying, high-pitched voice. He was well known to have feuded with several of Morathi's most devoted sorceress followers. He hated them with a passion, possibly because all of them had rejected his overtures.

'You do. No matter who they claim protects them. Your actions will be assessed afterwards. If they are found to be unnecessary, you will answer for them.'

Khalion smiled. He knew that success would absolve him of many sins. Malekith knew this too. He did not wish to state it overtly, however. There was no need to provoke his mother's enmity unnecessarily.

'How will we get there, sire?'

'N'Kari will take you. I have assigned her to this immediately. It is a sign of the importance of your mission.'

'I am ready to depart, sire,' said Vidor.

All of them nodded. 'Go!' said Malekith. 'Bring me the Everqueen dead or alive, and you may name your own rewards.'

That startled them. It was an offer of fantastic generosity. They hurried from the pavilion.

THE FOUR ASSASSINS stepped into Avelorn, leading their four large black steeds. They glanced around at what looked like a partially abandoned camp.

'Not a lot of people here,' said Balial.

'Very observant,' said N'Kari.

'I did not ask for your opinion,' said Balial.

'I did not ask to endure your stench and yet I must,' said the daemon. 'And now I must go. I apologise for not waiting until your slow wits could formulate a reply, but I do not have a month to waste.' With that the daemon was gone. The magical portal closed behind it.

'You!' Balial bellowed at one of the dark elf soldiers who stood nearby watching. The soldier marched over.

'Sir,' he said cautiously, for he was unsure who the newcomers were although he suspected they were important.

'Where is your commander?'

'Captain Marin is in the field, sir. We have heard nothing from him for several days. Our last order was to hold this spot and wait for the portal to open.'

'Where are your captain and the general?'

'They both went to the tournament fields, sir, to capture the Everqueen.'

'They are there now?'

'We have heard nothing from them, sir, since we received our orders.'

'They have captured the Everqueen?'

'I believe so, sir.' The soldier did not seem at all certain.

'Then why has the matter not been reported to the Witch King?'

'General Dorian does not explain his decisions to me, sir. Perhaps you should ask him yourself.'

'I will do that, soldier,' said Balial. Vidor had already picked up the track and was riding down it. Clearly he intended to be the first to report success if he could.

Balial mounted up and followed the rest of them. It was clear the army had not been wiped out, or at least this contingent of it – the base camp had not been either. He wondered what they would find at the tournament grounds.

'A REMARKABLE NUMBER of slaves,' said Vidor, inspecting the captives. They had that beaten look he knew from the faces of new captives everywhere. There were hundreds of them. He had never seen so many enslaved elves in one place before. The smell was quite distasteful. These elves clearly had taken defeat badly. They were unwashed and stank like humans.

'A less than remarkable number of guards,' said Amara, in her soft, husky voice.

'There are enough,' said Balial. 'Dorian knows his business in this at least.'

'He seems to have let the Everqueen slip through his fingers,' said Khalion. He sounded almost disappointed. Vidor wondered what the sorcerer's plans were if he got his hands on Alarielle. Nothing pleasant, that was for sure.

'Taking most of his army in pursuit of her seems almost a dereliction of duty,' said Khalion.

Balial shook his head. 'It is entirely according to his orders. Taking the Everqueen dead or alive is of the highest priority both to him and us.'

'It seems he had her and she escaped.'

'Accompanied by a warrior with a burning sword, if the reports are to be believed,' said Vidor.

'I would like to meet this fighter,' said Balial.

'So would I,' said Amara, although she sounded as if she had a different purpose in mind to the burly warrior.

'Let us see what we can do about finding him,' said Khalion.

'IT'S NOT THE easiest thing to see what was going on here,' said Vidor. 'Too many others have been around and spoiled the traces.'

'Surely the master tracker can tell us something,' said Khalion. The sneer was evident in his voice. Vidor looked at him as if he wanted to put an arrow through the sorcerer's throat.

'There are still some traces,' he said as if lecturing an idiot. 'Over here we can see where the Cold Ones were. Their breath poisoned the leaves above them. Their riders were sitting by the fire over here. They were talking or drinking or both.'

'Such a brilliant tracker,' said Khalion. 'He can even detect the fact that people were talking.'

'It's not a difficult thing to do,' said Vidor. 'From your tracks I could easily deduce that an idiot would be talking. Anyway, I can tell from the scent that the stranger came from over here. He was hiding in the bushes watching the knights. He came out of them and then he killed them.'

'He killed half a dozen knights on his own,' Amara said. 'Impressive.'

'Not quite so impressive if he took them by surprise,' said Balial. 'And I don't doubt that he did.'

'There was another one here. She was watching him. I can catch her scent too. She is the one we are looking for. The trace is very distinctive.'

'I will take your word for it,' said Balial. 'You think you can find their trail from here?'

'I can do that easily enough if I am not distracted by Khalion's inane ramblings.'

Khalion poured some black liquid into a small goblet and took a sip of it. He shuddered with pleasure after he swallowed the first mouthful. 'What reward will you ask of our glorious king?' he asked.

'I am tempted to ask for your head,' said Vidor, 'with the empty space inside it filled with gold. That would make me a very wealthy elf.'

'I think I will ask for copies of all Morathi's grimoires. I will be capable of astonishing things once I have mastered the knowledge in them.' He turned the words into a very ominous threat.

'I will settle for a mansion and a royal title,' said Balial. 'And the right to raise my own personal army.'

'How about you, Amara?' Khalion asked. He leered as he spoke. 'What does your heart desire?'

'Nothing that you could provide,' she said.

'I would not be so sure of that,' he said. 'The sorcerer's arts are not the only arts I have mastered.'

'I am sure many a maid has fainted under your caresses,' said Amara. Her tone made the words very ambiguous.

'We do not have all day to stand here,' said Vidor. 'We need to get on the trail as soon as possible, or the only reward any of us will get will be a painful death.'

All of them nodded in agreement and mounted their horses, following him off along the trail. Excitement filled them. It was only a matter of time before they overhauled their prey.

# CHAPTER ELEVEN

MALEKITH STARED INTO the mirror. His mother looked as clear and steady as if he was looking at her through a crystal window rather than by means of a spell that crossed the leagues between them. She smiled sweetly so he knew she was about to place one of her daggers ever so delicately through some chink she believed she had found in his armour.

'It goes very well,' she said. 'The asur were taken completely by surprise. We have taken a dozen of their towns and villages. They are learning humility under the gentle caresses of our barbarian allies.'

'Good. It will make them all the more grateful when I restore the natural order of the world,' Malekith said.

'The barbarians may not take to discipline quite as easily as you imagine.' Morathi's smiled widened. She was about to deliver the bad news. At least, he felt certain it would be bad news from his point of view.

'What makes you say that?' He allowed the merest fraction of his annoyance to glitter in his voice. Anyone else would have blanched with dread. His mother was amused.

'They have their own priests, their own cults, their own ideas of destiny.'

'I would have thought it would not be too difficult for you to subvert all of those to our needs. You have a gift for such things, mother.'

'Under normal circumstances, I would have to agree with you, but these are not normal circumstances. The winds of magic blow strong and they are tainted by Chaos. That should tell you something.'

'It tells me I am about to hear you make excuses about why you cannot do what is required of you.'

'Do not sound so petulant, Malekith. It ill befits the greatest ruler of elves the world has ever known.' How typical of her to mingle a compliment with a reprimand. Or perhaps it was a secret sneer at what she felt was his vanity. Even after all this time, with his mother, it was difficult to tell.

'Make your excuses, mother.'

'The winds blow so strongly because the northern gates awake from dormancy.'

'We both knew this before we started. In fact we counted on it.'

'What we did not count on, my son, is that those who lurk beyond those gates might also become more active. The old dark gods are reaching out and making their worshippers restless.'

'You are saying the daemon gods of Chaos are preparing to intervene.'

'They have intervened. They have spoken in the dreams of their priests. They are giving their followers ideas above their stations.'

'Why have you not discouraged this?'

'Our situation here is delicate, Malekith. I stand at the head of an army of ten thousand druchii. The barbarians have twenty times that number and that is but a fraction of their force. If we are to ride this whirlwind, we must be subtle. We cannot stand in its way. Not yet. We have unleashed a daemon that will be difficult to banish again.'

'We shall see about that in time.'

'The barbarians have started to act on their own account. The great army is splitting up into marauding hordes, bands of savages are following their own prophets, covens of magicians are going their own way. Many have headed south.'

'So much the better. They will still cause havoc and they will be much easier to deal with piecemeal than as one unified force.'

'Let us hope so. Many of their mages have already departed southwards. More and more of the barbarians are preparing to follow.'

Malekith understood. His mother was taunting him. She was showing him the mistake he had made in his calculations. She had planned this all along. She wanted him to know how clever she had been, organising it, working it into his plans. She was planning something herself, and doubtless would dispatch agents to work her will. The question was, what was she up to?

'It seems one of us has made a miscalculation,' he said, and broke the contact. Let her think about that for a while.

SIGNS OF LIFE became evident below Teclis as the sun lowered itself on the horizon. He did not welcome them. Large creatures prowled below, even as he looked for a place to put down for the night. Silver Wing was weary – flying on by moonlight did not seem like the smartest of things to do.

Teclis found a clearing and patted the pegasus's shoulder and pointed down. Silver Wing had no difficulty understanding. The steed circled cautiously, as if looking for threats, and then descended.

There was a brief, half-terrifying, half-exhilarating sense of moving far too fast over the ground as the winged horse touched down. The pegasus beat the air furiously with its wings and they slowed. Teclis had a few moments to worry about Silver Wing stumbling on a hidden pothole and sending him tumbling to a broken neck before they came to a halt.

Nervously, Teclis unstrapped himself, dismounted and looked around. He felt alone and vulnerable, as he never had before in the woods of Ulthuan. It was more than simply the fact that he knew there was a hostile army out there that would gladly torture him to death if it found him. It was something to do with being on the ground again, away from the sky and the wind and the lonely heights where nothing could threaten him but the birds. He found that now the motion had stopped, he missed it.

He could see much better in the gathering gloom than he ever had been able to do before. That was obviously the War Crown's work. He took it off, and found the circle encompassed by his sight and hearing shrank. The world blurred and became far more difficult to see. Despite its weight, he put the helmet on again. Everything became sharp and clear once more. It saddened Teclis to know that he needed magic and artificial aids to make him the equal of a normal elf. It came to him that in some ways this quest was madness. He was not fit for this, but then if he was not, who was?

He began to rub down Silver Wing with a saddle blanket. The pegasus began to graze, occasionally pausing to sniff the air and whinny. The sound was not exactly fearful – Silver Wing was not the sort of animal that gave a sense of that – but it was uneasy, as if the pegasus was catching the scent of something it disliked.

Teclis moved to the edge of the forest and gathered wood. He returned to the centre of the clearing and piled it up. He put his body between the pegasus and the wood before he spoke the word of power that turned the kindling into a blazing fire. It was likely the flying horse was used to such magic, but there was no sense in taking the chance of spooking it.

The pegasus returned to where he sat and nuzzled him gently. Teclis patted its head, grateful for the company. The scent and warmth of the huge beast was reassuring. At night, Avelorn did not sound like the more domesticated woods of Saphery. Out there, huge beasts roared, and other animals shrieked as they died. A massive white owl glided across the clearing, and stooped on some small prey.

This was nature, Teclis thought, a place where living things ate each other raw. He did not much care for it.

He was contemplating setting his wards for the night when he looked up, startled. He was surrounded by elves. They did not look exactly menacing, but they did not look friendly either. Several of them had bows trained on him. It seemed the Crown had not amplified his senses quite enough. It came to him that perhaps he had a problem.

'I had heard the elves of Avelorn were stealthy. Let me congratulate you on living up to your reputation.' He was proud of himself. His voice was steady. He had managed a deadpan politeness worthy of Prince Iltharis.

'It does not look like a druchii,' said a voice.

'I am not a creature of indeterminate sex,' said Teclis. 'I would be obliged if you referred to me as he.'

'It does not sound like a druchii,' said another. 'More like an effeminate scholar.'

'This effeminate scholar will be forced to teach you manners soon,' said Teclis. He really was starting to sound like Prince Iltharis.

'And how will you do that? With that pretty slender blade at your side? It looks good but you must be able to use it.'

'So this is the legendary hospitality of Avelorn. It seems somewhat over-rated.'

'You do not sound as troubled as I would expect someone

a heartbeat from death to sound.'

'If you use your eyes, you will notice I am a wizard. I am protected by several powerful charms against arrows. I am quite capable of killing you all with a word, which I would rather not have to do, since I have a natural aversion to killing simpletons. It does not seem quite fair somehow.'

Teclis was surprised by how calm he sounded, how easily the words came. He had a mission. He was not going to let anything stand in the way of his completing it. He was even prepared to put his fellow asur to death if they tried to obstruct him.

'I don't think a druchii spy would talk like that,' said one of the voices.

'You've met a lot of Naggarothi spies, have you?' asked the first voice, obviously the leader.

'I am Teclis, Loremaster of Hoeth. I am seeking my brother, Prince Tyrion, who will be, if he follows his usual lecherous habits, in the company of your Everqueen.'

A stunned silence followed that announcement. Teclis wondered if perhaps he had overdone the insouciance.

'The Everqueen is dead,' said the one who sounded like the leader. 'If he is with her, your brother is too.'

A shock ran through Teclis. 'You have seen this with your own eyes?'

'We have met those who were at the tournament grounds when the druchii attacked. They saw it.'

'I would talk with them,' said Teclis.

'We still have not decided whether you are a spy or not.'

'I come here riding on a pegasus and wearing the War

Crown of Saphery, and you ask me if I am a dark elf spy?'

'Anybody can make outrageous claims,' said the asur. 'Talk is easy.'

'Obviously thinking is harder.'

'If he was a dark elf spy he probably would not be so rude,' said a voice from the gloom. Teclis could sense a shift away from outright hostility to something else. They did not see him as an immediate threat. Most of them seemed to be prepared to take him at face value.

'I am seeking my brother and the Everqueen. If they are alive, I can find them and help them. If they are dead, you will be doing no harm.'

'You might be trying to find out where our camp is.'

'Bring your friends here to me then and I will talk to them.'

The leader nodded. 'Jaq, go and fetch the survivors. We'll stay here and keep an eye on this fop.'

'If you have no objections, I will prepare my medicines.'

'Your medicines?'

'I require them for my health.'

'You carry some sort of plague?' the elf leader asked him.

'I have been troubled by ill-health since birth.'

'You are a strange one. I think I am starting to believe you.'

'I am touched,' said Teclis. He took out some waybread and offered it around. The elves refused although they looked hungry. He shrugged and ate, and began to mix his potions in their alembics. He removed the War Crown so he could drink. He had finished with them when the scouts returned with some stunned, haggard-looking elves. Their gaudy celebrants' clothes contrasted oddly with their staring, haunted eyes. A few of them were heavily armoured warriors leading huge warhorses. Their leader was a tall, noble-looking elf.

'Our friends here say you claim to be Prince Tyrion's brother,' he said.

'I am his twin, Teclis.'

'I am Arhalien of Yvresse.' He came closer and inspected Teclis closely. 'It is odd. You are much gaunter and darker than your brother, but there is a certain resemblance.' The other elves present relaxed when Arhalien said this, becoming a fraction less wary and on edge.

'You have seen my brother?'

'I bested him in a tournament a few days ago.'

'Then you are one of the few elves living who can say that.'

'That I can well believe. I have never seen a better elf with a blade. He used weapons as if born to them.'

'I would be grateful if you would not refer to him in the past tense.'

'It would be a miracle if he were still alive. The tournament grounds were overrun by a vast dark elf army...'

'And yet, you are still here...'

Arhalien smiled ruefully.

'It was good fortune. I was camped by the edge of the tournament grounds with my retainers. I could not sleep after the excitement of the day and I was checking our sentries when I noticed one of them seemed to be asleep. When I checked I found his throat had been cut. A moment later I was beset by assassins. I cut them down and shouted the alarm. Within moments the whole camp was a battleground.

'I rallied my warriors and we made a stand. After that I tried to cut my way to the centre of the camp but it was hopeless, there was an army between us and them. We were sore beset and only just managed to cut our way free.'

'So you never actually saw my brother fall.'

'I passed his encampment. I thought to join forces with him, but by the time I got there all were dead.'

'You saw his body?'

Arhalien shook his head. 'I saw a dozen of his friends, Atharis and others. Corpses were piled in heaps all around. It was howling chaos. But honesty compels me to say I saw no body, of Tyrion at least.' Honesty seemed to be something of importance to this elf.

'So you cannot be utterly certain that my twin is dead.'

'No.'

'Or the Everqueen? Did you see her body?'

'No. You are making me feel very foolish and guilty, Prince Teclis.'

'An elf is the best judge of his own conduct.' Teclis knew he was being rude and unsympathetic. Arhalien seemed decent and brave – he must be a very great warrior indeed to have beaten Tyrion and fought his way clear of the massacre.

'I will accompany you on your quest. If your brother and the Everqueen are still alive, they may need aid from both of us.'

Tyrion gestured towards Silver Wing. 'Unless your horse

grows wings you will only slow me down.'

'You think it likely your brother and the Everqueen are still alive?'

Teclis shrugged and spread his hands wide. 'Since we were very young my brother and I have shared a bond. We have always known when the other was hurt or in danger. I have a terrible nagging fear concerning Tyrion, but I do not think he is dead. And if he is alive, the Everqueen may be too. I have no reason to say so but hope, however.'

Arhalien sighed. 'I had hoped your magic had given you a vision of something better. You are said to be a very great mage. And you are not without courage. These woods teem with druchii.'

'Have you any idea how they got here?'

'You are the wizard. I was hoping you could tell me.'

'Once again I must dash your hopes.'

'Perhaps you will uncover the secret on your travels.'

'It is a great one, if it has let the dark elves penetrate into the very heart of Avelorn and beyond.'

That got the attention of the elves around him. It came to him that they had all been trapped in these vast woods and could not possibly have had news of the rest of the kingdom.

'Beyond?' Arhalien asked.

'Ulthuan is invaded. A horde of human barbarians led by Morathi is in the north. Malekith himself leads an army to the west of here. Lothern is beset by traitors from within and fleets from without. That was the word at the White Tower when I left.'

A shocked murmur rippled away into the darkness. 'These are terrible tidings,' said Arhalien. 'The Witch King himself… He has not set foot on Ulthuan since the time of Morvael.'

'I suspect he has returned to claim his father's kingdom.'

'We respect Aenarion, but Ulthuan was never his fiefdom. He did not own it.'

'I doubt Malekith would agree with you.'

'What can we do?'

'You must fight,' said Teclis. 'And you must win.'

'How?'

'Ah… that is the hard part.' They laughed at that. They sounded like elves who had not laughed in a long time.

'Sleep, wizard, we will guard you,' said Arhalien.

'I will set my wards,' said Teclis. 'I was going to do so when you interrupted me.'

No one objected.

TECLIS LAY IN the forest. His side hurt like fire. He sat up and looked at the beautiful woman sleeping nearby. He stood easily, much more easily than Teclis had ever found natural, and looked around with an eyesight that was keener than even that the War Crown gave to him. He was tired but he could not sleep. Somewhere out there in the distance the druchii were moving, coming ever closer.

Part of Teclis knew this was ludicrous. He was asleep and he was dreaming that he was Tyrion. It was one of those special dreams that had been very common when they were children but much less so as they got older. He was glad.

His brother was still alive and so was the Everqueen. This was the first conclusive proof he had of it. He was not on a fool's errand then. There was still a chance of finding his brother before it was too late.

He tried to memorise any of the things that Tyrion could see, hoping for some clue as to where he was. It was hopeless. He was surrounded by trees, and all the different parts of the forest looked alike to Teclis. He could hear the sound of running water nearby. His brother was near a powerful river, that much was certain. The only large river that Teclis knew of that was near here was the Everflow although it was a river of great length. At least he had a direction to head in.

Things twisted, as was their wont in dreams, and he was no longer in Tyrion's body. He was standing on a high ledge, overlooking a vast intricate pattern. The pattern was starting to fade in places despite the efforts of the ancient ghosts who maintained it.

Things twisted again and he was standing in a chamber that seemed familiar, where Caledor leaned forwards over a gameboard and moved a piece. Opposing him over the table was a shadowy figure that Teclis knew it would not be good to look too closely at. As if sensing his presence, the figure turned its head and looked up at him with cold empty eyes. Teclis felt himself falling forwards into those eyes and into oblivion.

He woke in a cold sweat, feeling as if he had just had a very narrow escape indeed.

* * *

Teclis rose with the dawn. He felt like blasting the birds singing so cheerfully in the trees. His shoulders felt as if someone had been punching them all night. His back hurt and so did his hip. Sleeping on the ground did not agree with him.

Arhalien was already awake and inspecting Silver Wing with his knightly companions. The elves of Avelorn were not visible. Teclis put on the War Crown, although it felt like the weight of it might break his neck this morning. Immediately his eyesight improved and he saw a few elves asleep in lean-tos under the eaves of the forest. He suspected there were others out there guarding them.

Arhalien walked over. In the early morning sunlight, Teclis could see his surcoat was grubby and blood-spattered. His armour was dented. The links had been broken and hastily repaired in some places. The ornate working on the hilt of his blade was dented and damaged. His companions looked to be in similar straits. He really did look as if he had fought his way clear of a brutal battle and spent the last few days racing ahead of terrible enemies through muddy woods. Teclis invoked the spell that kept his robes clean and his gear sparkling bright.

'You woke bright and early with the woodlarks,' said Arhalien, smiling.

'If it was not for those damnable winged vermin I might still be asleep.'

'You intend to go ahead with your plan?'

'I dreamt last night of my brother and the Everqueen. I believe they are alive and in danger. Dark elves pursue them through the forest.'

'Do you know where?'

'Would that I did! I must go to the tournament grounds and try and pick up their trail there.'

'How will you do that?'

'Magic.'

'I wish that I could come with you.'

'I would welcome that, but it is not to be. Silver Wing can carry only one of us.'

'I believe I will take my warriors north and see if I can be of some help.'

'It might be better if you escorted the refugees southwards to the White Tower. It is the only place where they will be safe.'

'I am not sure any place is safe any more,' Arhalien said.

'You may well be right.'

'May Isha watch over you,' Arhalien said.

'May you live a thousand years,' Teclis responded, but with foreboding.

# CHAPTER TWELVE

TECLIS FELT STRANGELY lonely as the ground fell away below him. His companions of the night waved farewell. Silver Wing circled, giving him a chance to respond. After that, they continued to fly northwards, following the line of the Everflow.

Teclis was as nervous as ever, strapped into the saddle, but he found he was able to concentrate on some of the things happening below him. It was fascinating, seeing the great forest from the air and noticing the way the river carved through it. There were a number of waterfalls and in places the current looked very swift.

After a time, he noticed that he was not alone. Below him he could see large bodies of elves moving. Logic told him that they had to be interlopers, druchii, the invaders of whom he had heard so much and seen so little of previously.

He nudged Silver Wing to descend. The pegasus responded reluctantly, as if it sensed danger. Crossbow bolts begun to whizz by, some of them only deflected by Teclis's magic. He caught sight of heavily armoured dark elf warriors firing up at him.

With the power of the War Crown of Saphery enhancing his eyesight, he could make out the decorative metalwork on their helmets and the insignia on their shields. He could tell that there was a magician down there because he felt the shift in the currents of the winds of magic. He readied himself for the attack that was not long coming. A bolt of pure magical energy lanced upwards towards him.

He invoked a swift counterspell and neutralised it.

Silver Wing whinnied and pulled upwards into a steep climb, instinctively avoiding the terrible magic that had been unleashed beneath it. A few half-hearted crossbow bolts succumbed to gravity behind him and there was no further spell from the wizard who had previously attacked them.

The pegasus flew on, northwards, leaving the line of the river, heading towards the tournament grounds. Teclis dreaded what he would find there.

EVEN BEFORE HE saw the tournament grounds, Teclis was filled with a sense of wrongness. The winds of magic in the area were curdled, tainted by some dark power whose aura was ominously familiar.

He sensed the psychic stench of a powerful daemonic force. It had faded and he doubted that it was present now, but something of it lingered in the air, the way the smell of a rotten corpse hung in the air near a charnel house.

He saw that there were the remnants of a vast military camp below him. A powerful force of dark elves was still down there. At the moment, Silver Wing was flying too high to be shot at and it would have taken a very powerful wizard indeed to be able to propel a spell to this height.

He could see that his arrival had created quite a stir. Dark elves had emerged from tents to stare at the sky. He was tempted to send a wave of destructive magic raining down on them. He resisted the temptation. He needed to preserve his strength in case of an emergency. He was alone here, without bodyguards or friends, and it would not do to waste his resources in pointless shows of strength.

He could see that the dark elves were camped within the boundaries of what had been an even larger campground. This was certainly where the great tournament for the favour of the Everqueen had taken place. It looked as if the vast tent-city had been overwhelmed very swiftly indeed. There was a nasty smell of death in the air as well as tainted magic. He suspected that huge piles of bodies must have been burned. It certainly was not a pleasant aroma.

He kept Silver Wing circling. Guards watched over huge pens full of enslaved high elves. It was what he would have expected. It was what he had been half-dreading all day. The dark elves were not wasteful except when it came to making sacrifices to their daemon gods. Living, sentient creatures represented wealth to them. They were slavers. Those were his people down there, but he could not take the risk of trying to free them. He might just be throwing away his life.

From this height, he could see that the earth had been churned as if by the passage of thousands of feet. There were many tracks. They ran everywhere. From above, they looked like the outline of some mad maze created by an insane god. Teclis knew that he was looking at the paths over which units had marched and crowds had fled, but he was not skilled enough in tracking to understand what they meant. One thing was clear though: the largest path led away from the camp in the direction from which he sensed the strongest stench of dark magic. Instinct told him he might find some answers there.

He turned Silver Wing in that direction, following it outwards as it ran through the forest. Sometimes, he lost sight of the tracks where the trees overhung the path, but always it emerged again. Even if it had not, he knew instinctively that all he needed to do was follow the strange psychic spoor of the dark magic. After what was not a very long flight, he came upon another, smaller dark elf camp.

Nearby was a tall standing stone carved with intricate runes and patterns. It was a waystone – part of Caledor's vast, ancient spell. A company of dark elf soldiers stood near the point where the tracks vanished. They simply ended as if the whole crowd of people that had made them vanished. What was going on here, Teclis wondered? He knew it was imperative that he find out.

He directed Silver Wing downwards. The dark elf soldiers ran to meet him. They were clearly uncertain as to who he was, but they were wary and they were levelling their crossbows. Teclis spoke a spell and when they unleashed their bolts, the projectiles caught fire in the air long before they reached him. Teclis invoked another spell – chain lightning danced around him, leaping from dark elf to dark elf, sparking from blade to blade, killing everything it touched. The smell of scorched flesh filled the air, mingling with the ozone stink of the electrical bolt. The remainder of the druchii turned and fled. Teclis proceeded with his investigation.

The aura of dark magic was strongest near the waystone. It was also very familiar. His senses had grown much more discerning since the last time he had encountered this particular spiritual stink, but it was not something he would ever forget and it brought a chill of terror to his heart.

The Keeper of Secrets N'Kari had been here. The daemonic enemy that had sworn to destroy all of the descendants of Aenarion had walked on this very ground. Teclis glanced around warily, fearful that the daemon might suddenly manifest. Potent wizard as he was, he knew he was nothing compared to a greater daemon of Chaos. All of the confidence in his own power that had been building over the past few days flowed from him like wine from an overturned decanter.

If Malekith was in league with such a creature, it explained a very great deal. When he was very young, an army had been moved around Ulthuan with similarly astonishing speed by N'Kari. He had managed to lay siege to a number of elven towns and even the shrine of Asuryan itself within the space of one month. No one had ever worked out how the daemon had done this, but just the fact that it had done so showed that it was theoretically possible, at least if you were a greater daemon of Slaanesh.

Or had access to the services of one.

That thought chilled Teclis's heart. It was virtually impossible to imagine someone compelling a Keeper of Secrets, but if anyone had such a power, if any sorcerer possessed enough skill and knowledge, it was Malekith or his mother Morathi.

Teclis did not want to believe that it was possible, that this could have happened. His mind reeled at the possibilities. N'Kari was a daemon with a great thirst for vengeance, at least part of that thirst would be slaked by drinking the blood of Teclis and his brother. The daemon had sworn vengeance against them personally.

Was it possible that Malekith had known this and used it as a bargaining chip to win the services of the daemon?

But Malekith himself was of the blood of Aenarion, and N'Kari had sworn vengeance against all of the descendants of the first Phoenix King. Surely he would want to destroy Malekith as well as Tyrion and Teclis.

Those things were not mutually exclusive, Teclis thought. The daemon was a being of great cunning. It was perfectly capable of cutting a deal with the Witch King and then turning on him once it had achieved its vengeance on the twins.

The more he thought about it, the more Teclis thought that he had hit upon a potential explanation for what had happened, or at least part of one. The question was: what could he do with this knowledge?

He needed to tell someone – the High Loremaster was the best candidate for this, but how could he send the message? And after he had done that, what should he do – turn back to Hoeth with news of the discovery and attempt to find a way to thwart the Witch King's magic, or press on with his quest?

Teclis heard booted feet racing closer through the trees. He saw a group of druchii emerging from the forest. They raised their crossbows and sent a hail of bolts flashing towards him. His charms repelled most of them. One or two found their way through, most of their energies spent. The impact was still painful though, and the sharp edge of one sliced his hands. Nearby Silver Wing whinnied and reared. Teclis turned to see that a bolt had bounced off his protective charms and hit the pegasus.

Realising they could not harm him with their weapons, they were, with the merciless vindictiveness of their kind, concentrating their fire on Silver Wing.

Teclis raced towards the pegasus, hoping to envelop it in the protective globe of his charms. Before he was within range, the winged horse screamed again. A dozen bolts had penetrated his hide.

Silver Wing fell, gasping. Bloody froth emerged from its nostrils. Its breathing was like the wheezing of a drunk man. It was drowning in its own blood. The pegasus looked up with sorrowful eyes. Teclis could see the intelligence fading from them. It was like watching the death of another elf.

He could try speaking a healing spell, but he did not have the time to do so and to protect himself. He was not familiar with the anatomy of pegasi and he doubted that any of the spells that he knew would be of much use. Even as these thoughts crossed his mind Silver Wing gave one last gasp, its wings twitched as if its spirit was making one last leap for the sky, and then the winged horse was still.

Fear dried out Teclis's mouth. The fate of the pegasus would be his if the dark elves had their way. More than that though, he was enraged that he had failed to protect the creature. What was worse, he had lost the thing that would allow him to find his brother quickly. He was going to have to proceed on foot through the wilds of Avelorn, and this was at a time when speed was of the essence.

The war cries of the druchii were triumphant now. That they had killed something beautiful only pleased them more. A cold, cruel rage took hold of Teclis, burning away his fear, leaving him thinking with a terrible clarity that he had never enjoyed before.

He spread his arms wide and invoked his power, drawing the winds of magic to him with a force that could not be denied. It was as if he stood at the centre of a vast whirlpool of power, sucking all of the magical energy into himself. Once, such a thing would have killed him. Drawing on so much power so quickly might have burned out his gift for wielding it, overloaded his brain, driven him mad.

Perhaps that was happening anyway, perhaps he was deluding himself that he could handle so much of it. Blazing light surrounded him now. The patterns of the winds of magic themselves were visible in the air. Shimmering lines of light were drawn to him in all the colours of the rainbow and some colours that were not natural for the eye to see at all.

His body was on fire. He burned but he did not feel any pain. His skin tingled. When he breathed, the air he took into his lungs felt incandescent. He kept chanting, drawing more energy to him.

The shouts of the druchii faded. At first he thought it was because of the effects of the magic upon his hearing, but then he realised that they were silent out of dread and they were right to be so.

He was going to give them a lesson in the use of power that they would not live to forget.

There were wizards present among his enemies. They sensed what he was doing and tried to interfere. One of them sent a bolt of lightning arcing towards Teclis. It was like trying to put out a fire by throwing pitch upon it. Teclis merely drew on its energy and it dissipated harmlessly before it reached him.

He added it to his own and began to shape it. The other dark elf mage attempted to dispel the magic he was casting. Teclis squelched his spell as he would an insect underfoot.

He was drunk with power now. He was like a giant who could reach out and knock down the trees with his hands. He felt free for the first time in his life; free of all restraint, free of the restrictions he had placed upon himself out of fear of his own strength.

Hatred burned in his heart. It was not a new hatred. It

had been there for a very long time. The druchii merely provided it with a focus. They were, after all, elves. They looked like the people who had sneered at him and tormented him all his life. They looked like every enemy he had ever had. Every female elf who had ever rejected him. Every male elf who had ever laughed at him or bullied him or sneered at his ill-health.

Living in Ulthuan, among the asur, he had needed to restrain himself. Even though he was an outsider, he was still a member of a society. The druchii were not his people. No law protected them. No one would punish him if he destroyed them. There was no need for him to restrain himself.

He laughed out loud, there was a wild, cackling evil in his voice. Some of those who heard it turned and fled.

He wove a spell of awesome, ominous power. Words emerged from his throat and seemed to take shape in the air, becoming glowing runes of light formed by the very vibrations of his voice. They swirled around him, forming ever more complex patterns, daemonic in their complexity, moving ever faster around him until they seemed to leave lines of fire behind.

Finally, when maintaining the spell was all but unendurable, he unleashed it. It flooded outwards, surging in lines of light towards the trees, lines dividing and re-dividing until there were hundreds of them. Each line sought out one living thing, one dark elf, and pursued it through the forest. Where those lines touched flesh, the targets screamed and died, becoming incandescent and then turning to dust which was blown away on the wind caused by the vortex of Teclis's might.

A few wizards tried to shield themselves, but Teclis's spell smashed through their defences like an axe through rotten timber. Within heartbeats all of the druchii were dead, and Teclis stood in the centre of the clearing, over the dead body of the pegasus, howling with mad exultation.

A small wary part of Teclis's mind realised something.

Part of the rage and part of the anger was most definitely his, but part of it came from somewhere else. It was fuelled by the dark taint on the winds of magic, the even darker taint of the place where he stood, on ground upon which a greater daemon of Chaos had once trod and woven potent magic.

He sensed a darkness creeping into him, blighting his spirit and making him into something he had not intended to become. He knew, for he had been taught by true masters of magic, that there was always a chance of daemonic possession when working high and powerful magic, that things reached out from the Realm of Chaos when a wizard drew upon them for power. Something was doing that to him now. He closed his mouth and stopped his mad laughter with an effort of will, and began to utter ritual words of cleansing and to calm his mind with meditation.

It was a long time before he felt like himself again, even then he was both thrilled and appalled by what he had done, by the murder he had committed on such an epic scale. He felt for the first time in a long time the very dark depths within his soul, the awful potential for abomination that was his. He feared it and he loathed it, but he was entranced by its possibilities nonetheless.

He was shocked to find that he had enjoyed smiting his fellow elves far more than he had ever done any other foes. It came to him then that there was within him a terrible potential for evil. He started to understand why the dark elves took such pleasure in tormenting their foes. It was a way of asserting their personal power in a universe that did not care for them. In that moment, he was surprised indeed to find in his heart the truth that he was more like the spawn of Naggaroth than he would ever have previously cared to admit.

He looked at his hands and found that they were shaking. His mouth felt dry. His heart beat faster. He felt certain that he had crossed some personal bridge, had stepped onto a path that was going to take him somewhere that he might not like but that he felt was his destiny. He was starting to see that in this war he might find a crucible in which he would be transformed into someone very different from the person that he had previously thought that he was.

He began to understand his brother better than he ever previously had. Perhaps this was how Tyrion felt when he stood alone on a battlefield with all his foes vanquished.

Teclis had killed all the other wizards. He felt good about it. He had proved his superiority. He had not started that particular fight but he had finished it. He wondered at the moisture running down his cheeks. He had expected his spells to protect his eyes from the effects of the wind.

# CHAPTER THIRTEEN

TECLIS LIMPED THROUGH the woods, heading east towards the Everflow as he had done for the past few days. Birds sang cheerfully. He felt like blasting them with magic because he was anything but cheerful.

Only now that it was gone did he really realise what the pegasus had given him. It had allowed him to travel with amazing speed across this vast wooded landscape. It had enabled him to cover in a few days what would have taken him months on foot and weeks on horseback, to navigate through a realm that had no major, well-marked roads. Now he was reduced to walking, and he was even slower at that than most people would be because of his limp and physical weakness. Only now did he have a real sense of the size of the forest he tramped through. It was as vast as many countries.

Even wearing the War Crown of Saphery, he felt trapped in a dense world where he could not see peril as it came towards him. The forest limited his vision, huge trees and dense undergrowth making it impossible for him to see very far.

Anything could be out there, creeping up on him, taking aim at him with a bow or spear, and he would not know it until it was too late. His magic protected him somewhat – he had charms against arrows and other missile weapons that would deflect things fired at him. That did not make him any less nervous though. He was not used to travelling on his own through such wild lands.

He had thought that Avelorn would be like the forests of Saphery, but that was not the case. Saphery had been domesticated by the presence of wizards. The roads there were protected by warding spells, and dark and wild creatures shunned the paths that were likely to be protected by magic. That was not the case here. Huge predatory cats stalked through the undergrowth. He heard them prowling at night. Sometimes, he could see their eyes reflecting his firelight as they watched him.

It was not just that. He sensed the presence of patches of old, dark magic in the trees around him. There were places that were blighted and had been since the time of Aenarion. Sometimes, he could sense powerful malign intelligences waiting for unwary passers-by to draw into their web of magic.

Sometimes he came across the signs of war. He passed bodies left on the ground where they had been slain.

Sometimes, the corpses bore the marks of torture and they belonged to elves of Avelorn. It was obvious that the druchii were taking great pleasure in killing anyone they encountered.

That did not make any sense. The druchii were slavers. To them prisoners were wealth. They were looking for something and torturing the people they found for information. Part of him hoped that they were simply looking for the elves who opposed them.

Not all of the corpses he found belonged to high elves. Sometimes he came across the sites of ambushes where forces of dark elves had obviously been surprised by the natives of Avelorn. There, the bodies had been riddled with arrows and sometimes left nailed to trees as a warning. There was nothing honourable or chivalrous about the war being fought around him. It was savage, brutal, ancient hatred on both sides unleashed in the struggle.

He half-suspected that the dark elves were seeking news of Tyrion and the Everqueen just as he was. It was the only reason he could think of for them splitting their forces and searching through this vast, trackless wilderness with such fury.

No other military objective could be achieved by this invasion of the forests. Tyrion might have been able to tell him otherwise; his brother had always been a great expert on military matters. Teclis doubted it though. There were no fortresses here, no wealthy cities to be plundered, no towers full of magical knowledge.

This was the spiritual heartland of Elvendom but it was

mostly empty and far from civilised. The only place that would be counted as such had been very civilised indeed. That was the court of the Everqueen, but the dark elves had already destroyed that and killed most of the people who had attended it.

In some ways this gave him hope. It meant that it was likely that his brother and the Everqueen were still alive. Why would the dark elves be pursuing them otherwise? That only made the slowness of his progress more frustrating. He felt as if time was running out and that every second counted – being afoot was putting him at an enormous disadvantage in a race that he did not have much chance of winning anyway.

He wished that he could encounter some of those marauding high elves himself. He could have asked them for news concerning the druchii or the passage of those that were hunted by them. He half-hoped that his brother had found refuge among the nomadic warriors who harassed the dark elf army. At least he would have found shelter among locals. In theory, they would know where to hide and have the best chance of avoiding the marauding druchii.

Of course, there were other threats now. He had come across a few bands of humans. He had no idea how they had got here so quickly, but he felt that magic must be involved somehow. Maybe not. Maybe they had infiltrated the woods a long time ago and waited for their opportunity to come forth. He resigned himself to the fact that he might never know and trudged wearily onwards, not even certain he was on the right path.

All he could do was follow the feeling in his heart that this was the right way.

TECLIS LOOKED UP. Overhead he could see a group of wizards. They zoomed along on floating discs of light, leaving comet trails behind them. They were not elves, that was plain to see even at this distance. They were shorter and squatter – their robes could not conceal that. There was something about them that was deeply disturbing, a suggestion of dark magic worse than any Teclis had ever encountered among humans before. These were followers of Chaos at its most corrupt and wicked.

The thought that such creatures had found their way to the very heart of Avelorn was shocking. Such a thing had not happened since the time of Aenarion. They should not have been here. There should have been no way that they could have progressed so far.

Had they been carried here by daemons, or had they somehow found their way through with their own power? It was possible it was the latter since they could fly, but someone should have stopped them if things had been at all normal. They should not have been able to get here and they should not be travelling around unhindered. It was an insult to the high elves and the people of Ulthuan. Teclis supposed that they had probably come with Morathi and the huge horde that had appeared in the north.

It was clear that they were looking for something. He was not certain whether it was him or not. So far, it seemed like his spells of misdirection had protected him. Even as he watched, the formation split up and the wizards went their own way. They were definitely looking for something. This was the easiest way for them to cover more ground. Of course, it made them more vulnerable to being attacked. Teclis supposed that it was a mark of their confidence that they had done so. They did not feel threatened. He was going to have to see what he could do to change that if he encountered them.

He pushed that thought to one side. He was not here to brawl with wizards. He was here to find Tyrion and the Everqueen and save them if he could. He only wished he had a clearer notion of how.

DORIAN WATCHED AS the wizards came closer. He could see that they were not dark elves. They were humans, albeit humans of a very strange sort. They were flying through the air above the dark elf army, mounted on some kind of flying disc that seemed to be made of light. As soon as he saw them, he felt the old urge to enslave and dominate come over him.

They descended, circling warily, a glowing order of magic surrounding them which spoke of protective spells. One of his captains looked at him as if waiting for the order to fire.

Dorian shook his head. There would be time enough for that if things turned nasty. He gestured for his own wizards to stand ready in case this was some kind of trick or trap.

A few seconds later, an eerie figure hovered in the air before him, standing on a disc of floating light. The wizard was tall for a human, almost as tall as Dorian himself, and almost as slender. He was wearing a long robe of red and purple and a mask of purple cloth covered most of his face, leaving only the eyes visible below the hood of his robe. His fingers were covered in leather gloves and were unnaturally long for a human's, tipped with nails that were almost as sharp as talons.

'Greetings, druchii, from the great sorceress Morathi.' As soon as he heard Morathi's name, Dorian was instantly wary. He sensed intrigue and something else. Whatever it was, he knew it could not be good. 'Who are you, human?'

'I am Ferik Kasterman and I am the leader of the Coven of Ten.'

'You are a wizard then,' said Dorian, stifling a yawn. The officers nearby laughed.

'Yes, my lord, I am a wizard and dedicated to the great powers of Chaos which we all serve.'

'I serve Malekith, Witch King of Naggaroth and rightful ruler of this island continent of Ulthuan. I do not serve the ruinous powers.'

The wizard tittered. The sound even disturbed Dorian, and he was used to such mad mirth. 'Perhaps not knowingly,' the wizard said. 'But be assured we all serve Chaos, even your king.'

'I could have you put to death quite painfully for suggesting such a thing,' Dorian said. 'Our king serves only himself.'

'Believe as you wish. Some do not know the truth even when it is slapping them in the face.'

'Unless you moderate your tone, *I* will be slapping you in the face.'

'That would be most unwise. You do not wish to provoke the enmity of my mistress.'

'So Morathi has taken humans as lovers now. I suppose it was only to be expected. She has tried everything else.' That got another laugh from the nearby druchii.

'I shall make sure that your words are reported back to her exactly as you said them. I am sure she will be very interested to hear your thoughts on this matter.'

'She will most likely be flattered. She prides herself on her degenerate behaviour. It seems you do not know your mistress as well as you would have us believe.'

Dorian's attitude seemed to have taken the wizard off guard. He did not seem to know quite how to take things. He was obviously used to having people cringe in terror before him. Dorian supposed his attitude must work quite well among the worshippers of Chaos. It was not something that cut any ice with a noble of Naggaroth.

'I have been sent to aid you in your search.' It was Dorian's turn to be taken aback. He had not realised that any beyond his own army knew the truth about what was going on. Of course, it came to him at once, Morathi had her visions. She was able to see the future and things that would happen at a distance. It seemed that she had divined something about what was going on in Avelorn.

'What search would that be?' Dorian asked to give himself time to think.

'You seek the ruler of this land. She is lost in the woods. Once you had her in your grip but she slipped away. An elf with a burning sword took her and now you're desperate to get her back before your master learns of your failure.'

Dorian considered ordering the human killed. He did not like the wizard's tone and he did not like being spoken to in this way. On the other hand, the wizard had just proved that he had been sent by the Hag Queen of Naggaroth in a way that made his credentials indisputable. Dorian suspected that if he put this human to death, Morathi would know, and she would find her own way to take revenge. The wizard was right in one way. She was a very dangerous person to get on the wrong side of. Dorian was also curious not only about what Morathi knew but about how these wizards might help him find the Everqueen. Also, he reasoned, it would be easy enough to have them put to death once they had helped him find Alarielle.

'You say you can help us find her – how?'

'We are wizards. I should have thought the answer was obvious. Magic.'

'I would be interested to see what you can do that my own wizards cannot. I do not lack sorcerers in my service. Even now they close in on those we seek.'

That seemed to take the wizard aback. He had not been expecting such a response. Then the human laughed, as if regaining some fraction of his mad confidence. 'I doubt any of them possess the same gifts from Chaos that I and my coven do. There is a reason our mistress has sent us.'

'Then I will gratefully accept your aid,' said Dorian. 'Be warned though, if you fail us, we will treat you as we would any other human.'

'You are not in any position to make threats, general. We

both know that. Now I must go... We will need some prisoners for the sacrifices... Unless, of course, some of your own troops would care to volunteer.'

'Be careful what you say, wizard.'

'Both of us should be that, general.'

# CHAPTER FOURTEEN

FROM UP AHEAD Teclis could hear the sounds of battle. The full-throated roar of human warriors mingled with the shouts of elves. He had no idea who was fighting who here, but his trail led towards the fight. He could hear another sound – it was the rushing of water. Cautiously, he moved forwards. He left a trail and took to the trees, moving between them as quietly as he could. It did not really matter that he was not particularly stealthy. He doubted that anyone could hear him over the sounds of battle.

The air was getting moister. It swiftly became clear why. The rushing sounds came from the fast-flowing waters of a great river. He got down on his hands and knees and moved ever closer to the edge, poking his head out from the undergrowth.

By chance, it looked like he had picked a good spot. He

could see that a large force of humans were trying to ford the river at this point. There were hundreds of them, mostly tattooed barbarians, with a sprinkling of dark, armoured figures who appeared to be the leaders. They were being ambushed by a force of elves. At least, Teclis thought they were elves. He had some difficulty making them out at first sight. They were extremely well concealed in the undergrowth. What gave them away were the great clouds of arrows emerging from the forest on the far banks of the river.

For once, it looked as if he was about to witness an elven victory. The humans were caught in midstream, slowed down by the fast-flowing currents of the river. They were struggling to get across and get to grips with their hidden attackers.

Already the river was red with blood and corpses floated swiftly downstream. Teclis felt like cheering. It was amazing how swiftly he had been reduced to a barbarism similar to that of the humans. A few months ago it would have been impossible for him to imagine himself doing such a thing. Now it came all too easily.

There was no doubt that the humans were brave. Some of their leaders, mounted on massive armoured steeds, were thrusting their way through the water, bow waves forced ahead of their mounts by the speed of their passage. It looked as if some of them might actually make the far bank.

It seemed that the elves who were fighting with them had realised the same thing as Teclis had. They began to concentrate their fire on the riders. Even the powerfully driven elven shafts bounced off that evil, rune-encrusted armour. Obviously, the mounted Chaos knights were protected by more than mere metal. Some form of magic, similar to the charms that Teclis himself wore, deflected the incoming arrows.

Teclis could hear the inhabitants of Avelorn shouting to each other in Elvish. They were preparing to retreat back into the woods, not wanting to have to face off against such heavily armoured foes. It seemed entirely sensible. They could withdraw in good order, outrun their foes and return to attack them stealthily at night.

Even as the thought crossed his mind, Teclis heard a strange whizzing sound from above. He looked up and saw a sorcerer mounted on a flying disc pass overhead. It was one of the same wizards that he had seen previously. The mage was already starting to cast a spell, bringing down death on the elves in the woods. More of the sorcerers flashed into the air above the ford. Teclis counted ten of them, and all were potent wizards. The air shimmered around them as they summoned the winds of magic.

Clouds of poisonous gas erupted in the forest. Rains of ice and fire descended upon the elven archers. Their screams filled the air. The brutal bellowing of the humans rose in triumph. What had seemed like an imminent defeat had suddenly become a potential victory.

As the hail of arrows ceased, the Chaos worshippers surged forwards across the river, brandishing their weapons, shouting challenges and curses at their enemies.

Teclis wondered whether he should do something. Hundreds of elves were being killed out there. It was not his task, he told himself. He had work of his own to do and he should not take any risks. His brother needed him and the Everqueen needed him. On the other hand, it was possible that those elves over there might be able to help him. Perhaps they even had some news as to the whereabouts of those he sought. More than that, he disliked the sight of those human magicians slaying the inhabitants of Avelorn.

Before he had really thought things through, he was in motion. He spoke a simple charm of dispelling. It sucked all the magic out of the air near three of those wizards who were flying overhead. The discs supporting them in the air suddenly vanished. They fell, suddenly and spectacularly, into the river below. He was not sure whether the fall had killed them or whether they were simply stunned by the descent from such a great height into the chill waters, but he was sure that they were out of the fight at least temporarily.

He spoke another word of power and a bolt of chain lightning knocked another two wizards from the sky. It was all so sudden that those he attacked had no chance to realise what was happening. They continued to invoke their deadly spells upon the elves below them. Perhaps some of the humans had some inkling that something had gone wrong, for they had paused and started to look around.

One or two of the tattooed warriors pointed in his direction. He cursed the visibility magic gave him. Wielding such power made his aura incandescent. Surely there must be some way to do something about that. Not today though. He had too much else to do.

A group of the humans broke off from charging the far bank and came towards him. It was foolish and brave. They had to fight against the current as they tried to swim upstream. More by luck than judgement he had chosen a good place to make his stand. It was something he was going to have to remember in the future. Position was important. Such stuff had always come naturally to Tyrion but it was not something Teclis had ever given much thought to.

The humans were not being stupid, he realised after a moment. The water provided them with some protection against any fire spells he might invoke; they dived beneath its surface, hiding themselves from view for a time before they surfaced. He could see only their savagely twisted faces and their broad, muscular tattooed shoulders – and then only sometimes.

Right now, they were not his main problem. One of the mages had also noticed something was happening and was skimming towards him, low over the surface of the water, his disc undulating over the wavelets like a woodlouse moving over a log.

Simply dispelling the disc would send him into the water, but it would not take him out of the fight as it had done the others. The human mage was chanting a spell, summoning a pulse of destructive Chaotic power to him.

Teclis invoked a spell of shielding just as the Chaos bolt powered towards him. It impacted the shield spell with awesome destructive force. Teclis had to concentrate to maintain his defences. There was nothing subtle about the magic the human was using, but it was effective.

The human smiled as if he sensed he was putting his opponent under pressure. Teclis laughed aloud at his naivety. With a short chopping gesture he sent bolts of his own rocketing towards the human. The mage attempted to dispel them but failed to catch them all. One of the tiny circular spheres of energy hit the disc and exploded, shattering the flight spell and taking the human's legs off at the knees; he fell flopping into the water and vanished beneath the fast-flowing waters. He did not become visible again.

Enough, Teclis thought, it was time to finish this thing. He spread his arms wide and pulled a massive amount of magic to him. He spoke words of elemental fury. The sky darkened, the wind howled, the branches of the surrounding trees whipped backwards and forwards under its force.

It was as if an army of trees was giving a rustling war cry. The surface of the river turned white as the wind drove it on. A cloudburst of rain descended, putting out the fires on the far side of the river, wider and wider ripples appeared on the water's surface as heavier and heavier raindrops hit. The force of the wind increased till a hurricane ripped through the forest. Thunder cracked. Lightning flashed. A great tree toppled under the force of the wind. The humans swimming towards him screamed in panic. The sorcerers on their flying discs turned towards Teclis. They struggled to make progress in the teeth of the daemonic winds, as had been his intention.

Chain lightning flared again, dancing from disc to disc, overloading the mages' protective spells, causing the flying discs to disappear in a hail of sparks. It flashed down where armoured Chaos warriors stood, and danced from massive metallic armoured form to massive metallic armoured form. It impacted in the river and flash-fried those human warriors who were still trying to cross. They screamed and died, their bodies floating lifelessly downriver like so many logs.

Within minutes it was over, the mage storm had cleared the Chaos force from the river. Those humans who had made it to the far side were killed by the remaining elves. Teclis allowed the sky to clear and waited by the riverbank. It did not take long for the elves on the far side to emerge. He waved to them and they waved back. Teclis invoked a spell that let him walk across the water. He swayed as if walking on a fluffy mattress but managed to keep his balance. The elves cheered him as he came towards them.

'Greetings, wizard,' their leader shouted. 'We thank you for giving us victory. Hathar Ford is a name the forces of Chaos will long have cause to remember.'

'My name is Teclis. I am a wizard from Hoeth. I come seeking my brother, Tyrion, and the Everqueen. Perhaps you have heard news of them.'

The elf looked wary for a moment. 'Join us in our camp and I will tell you what I have heard. It is not much, but it may be of some help.'

'I thank you for the offer. I have spent a long time wandering these forests on my own. Some company for the night would be welcome.'

* * *

TECLIS WARMED HIMSELF by the fire and drank wine, an honoured guest of the elves of Avelorn. For the first time in his life, he felt like a hero. Many elves came over to thank him for his intervention, and many more offered him drinks from their flask or some of their pitifully small supplies of food.

He wandered among them, healing those he could, brewing medicines for the sick, drawing poisonous humours from the wounded. He was touched by their gratitude but he found himself becoming colder and more distant with every word of thanks.

He did not know how to behave in situations like this. He was not used to being popular. No one had commented on his pallor, his thinness or his limp. Everyone present had endured a great deal of hardship – perhaps they merely assumed he had done the same. Or perhaps it was something about all being in this fight together. They seemed prepared to overlook his shortcomings. The only one present dwelling on them was himself, he thought sourly.

Alanor, the leader of these elves, sat down at the fire across from him. 'You saved us all today. We miscalculated. We thought we could hit the Chaos warriors when they crossed Hathar Ford and melt away into the woods before they could catch us. We never counted on Ferik Kasterman and his Coven of Ten showing up.'

'Ferik Kasterman?'

'He was the leader of those sorcerers, a twisted and evil human if ever there was one.'

'It seems like every twisted and evil human in the world

has descended on the shores of Ulthuan.'

'You are right,' said Alanor. 'What are they doing here?'

'Helping the druchii, it would seem.'

'Why?'

'Because it suits their daemonic masters to do so.'

'What could they possibly want here?'

Teclis looked at the Avelornian. It seemed impossible that he did not understand what was happening here, but it was quite obviously the case. He sometimes forgot that not every elf was a magician or had access to the libraries at Hoeth. They did not encounter the maker of the Vortex in their dreams either. 'Nothing good,' Teclis said. The truth could not do any good here and would only help spread fear. 'You said you had something to tell me of my brother and the Everqueen…'

'Not very much, I am afraid.'

'Every little helps.'

'I know the druchii are still looking for them. Some of our scouts sneak in so close to their positions that they overhear them talking sometimes. We have our own people looking for them, but it is difficult for them to break through and seek among the dark elf soldiery. The last I heard, some dark wizardry was being used to hunt our queen. I do not know what.'

'They are sure of this?'

'Believe me, if General Dorian or his army had found the Everqueen, we would hear them celebrating all along the Everflow.'

'I guess you are right.'

'The druchii have split their forces in the hunt. It's the only thing that lets us strike at them, but they are getting more cautious. More and more of the humans are finding their way here as well. How are they doing so?'

'Some of them by magic, like Kasterman and his coven. The rest must be coming on foot.'

'How? How can they get through the mountains?'

'I think this is an invasion long planned. They have scouted well. The fortresses are besieged. It would be easy enough for warbands to slip by them under the circumstances.'

'Are things really so bad?'

'Worse.'

'You are not giving me much hope.'

'My brother is the great inspirational leader. I am merely a wizard.'

'There is nothing *merely* about that. You saved all of us today, and we are grateful. And we are grateful to you for helping the wounded as well.'

'Do you know where this General Dorian and his men are centring their hunt?'

'To the east of here. The trail always seems to lead in that direction.'

'Do you have any idea why that would be? What is in that direction?'

'The Winterwood Palace.'

'Could you spare me a guide to take me there?'

'I will ask for volunteers. If no one can do it, I will take you myself, although I think these people need me.'

'If I can find my brother and the Everqueen, I can save them.'

'If you can do that, you will be more than a wizard, you will be a miracle worker.'

'Will you help me?'

'I will do anything within my power.'

'Then let us set out in the morning. Now I need my rest.'

'Sleep well. You have earned it.' Teclis felt a sudden sharp stabbing pain in his side. He knew that his twin was feeling it too.

'What is it?' Alanor asked.

'Nothing good.'

URIAN ENTERED THE presence of his ruler for the first time in many decades. It had been a long hard ride to the waystone. He had not trusted the daemon sent to collect him or the strange portal through which they had passed, but now it seemed at last he was here in the great hall the Witch King had commandeered for his headquarters.

He stepped forwards with what he hoped was the correct air of humility. It would have been when he left Naggaroth, but Malekith was given to shifts of mood and formality. Sometimes he wished to be treated as if he were a barbarian potentate, at others with the formal courtesy of an elven lord. There were times when he played the simple warlord that he thought his father had been. There were times when he oversaw revels that would have put Morathi to shame, indulging vices by proxy that he could not any other way.

Today it looked like he was the warlord. He was surrounded by soldiers, generals and mages. Messengers bearing dispatches came and went, and the great mirror through which he communicated with distant corners of his empire stood uncovered in the middle of the chamber.

They had gathered in a palace on the outskirts of Mancastra, the first city of Ulthuan to fall to Malekith personally in centuries. The full panoply of the conqueror had been unfurled. The banners of hundreds of druchii lords hung outside, and pens full of weeping, captured slaves filled streets, plazas and courtyards.

Urian enjoyed the shock that rippled across the vast audience hall as his name was announced. Everyone here thought him dead for centuries. The only ones who knew differently were Malekith and the mages who had transformed him. Malekith rose from his throne and gestured in welcome. It was an almost unheard-of sign of favour. The murmur of conversation died immediately. Everyone smiled at him, knowing that he was, at least for the moment, the favourite of their king and thus a personage to be cultivated while he enjoyed access to Malekith's favour.

'Welcome, Urian,' Malekith boomed. 'Step forwards that we may embrace you.'

Urian did as he was commanded and was raised from the ground by Malekith's vast metal arms. It was the greeting of a comrade for a comrade, a mark of Malekith's approval unheard of in the lifetimes of any of those present.

'Let everyone hear the words of Malekith the Great,' the Witch King boomed. 'Urian Poisonblade has returned from long and secret service among our rebellious subjects of Ulthuan. All marks of our disfavour are erased. He is our chosen champion, our herald, and when he speaks, he speaks with our voice and is to be obeyed. He has been our instrument in matters of policy deep and subtle – he has slain many enemies of our cause. All hail him and salute him as we do.'

The Witch King placed Urian back on the ground and banged his armoured fist against his breastplate in warrior's applause. All of the other druchii present did the same. The women looked at him with smiles, the men with calculation. All of them applauded, for it was their lord's desire. Urian smiled ironically as he accepted it for what it was worth – the mark of a momentary approbation.

Tomorrow, he would find out what Malekith's favour was really worth. Today, he might as well enjoy it.

URIAN LOOKED DOWN at the armour Malekith had presented him with. It was, in some ways, a smaller replica of the Witch King's own. It was just as invulnerable. It amplified his strength in a similar way.

'You are my champion now, Urian,' Malekith said. His voice was confiding. They were alone in his huge pavilion aside from the Witch King's servants and slaves. No other druchii nobles were present. 'You must be armed and equipped as such.'

Urian bowed to indicate his gratitude. Malekith gestured for slaves to bring forward his gifts. Two hulking humans, blinded with their eyes sewn shut, brought forth a massive lead-bound, heavy wooden chest. They opened it and Urian saw two long black blades etched with runes that glowed greenly from within.

Malekith indicated that he should pick them up. 'Be

most careful with these. Do not touch the blades with your unprotected hands.'

Urian would not have done so, even without the warning. There was something about the way the rune-embossed metal shone that reminded him of warpstone, the terrible substance that some said was the crystallised form of pure Chaos magic.

He took the blades by their hilts and lifted them. They were feather-light and razor-edged; he knew without having to be told that they would cut through the heaviest steel armour. Malekith pointed to the massive armoured slave and made a chopping gesture. Urian tested the edge of the blade on the slave's huge, metal-encased form. As he had suspected it went right through the armour, the flesh and the bone, shearing cleanly through. It had another unexpected side-effect. The victim writhed, his skin blackening where the blade had touched, liquefying and becoming corrupt.

'Now you are Poisonblade indeed,' Malekith said. It seemed like he had actually put some thought into this gift. It was flattering as well as frightening.

'I thank you for the honour you do me, sire,' he said.

'You have earned it. These weapons will overcome the strongest healing magic. Once you inflict a wound, it will not be healed and the victim will die in extreme and very educative agony.'

There was no need to ask who would need to be taught such lessons. Anyone who earned the Witch King's displeasure must be subject to the harshest punishment.

* * *

General Dorian awoke knowing that there were others in his tent. He sat bolt upright, reaching for his scabbarded blade. A strong hand grasped his wrist, immobilising it. Another hand covered his mouth. A very sharp blade nicked his throat. Was he the prisoner of some sort of mutant? Did the intruder in his tent have three hands?

'Hush, general,' said a quiet voice near his ear. It belonged to a woman. It was husky and sensual. Despite his position, or perhaps because of it, Dorian found himself becoming aroused.

'The Witch King sends his regards,' said another voice. This one was male, deep and resonant. It sounded somewhat familiar.

'Lord Vidor?' Dorian said. He knew he was in trouble. At least two of Malekith's pet assassins were in his tent – not a good sign.

'None other,' said the male voice. 'Our master has dispatched us to make enquiries.'

'It seems that you have not contacted him,' said the female voice. 'He's curious as to what you have been doing.'

'I have been seeking the Everqueen,' said Dorian.

'There have been rumours,' said Lord Vidor. 'People have been saying that you found the Everqueen and then lost her again.'

Dorian felt his mind racing. He was not sure what to say. He was not sure of what these deadly assassins knew. He was sure this was the way they had intended it. He decided it would probably be safest to tell the truth. 'I captured her as I was ordered to do. I had her bound at my feet.'

'Very erotic,' said a female voice. She sounded as if she meant it.

'We were surrounded by my warriors. There was at least a score of us.'

'And yet she managed to escape?'

'She was rescued. A warrior came in–'

'One warrior?'

'One warrior. He was armed with a magical blade. It burned, like Sunfang, the legendary blade of the first Phoenix King.'

'So one hero entered the pavilion and snatched her from your grasp.'

Dorian could not miss the fact that Lord Vidor knew that the rescue had taken place in the pavilion. Someone had obviously been talking. 'Quite so.'

'And you were the only survivor of this rescue attempt?'

'The guards saw him enter. He was dressed like one of us. He was wearing our armour.'

'Is it possible he was one of us? Is it possible that he was a dark elf? A spy?'

'Of course it is possible, but I don't think it likely. I suspect he was one of the asur. I think he was wearing stolen armour – I think he took it from a warrior he killed.'

'That is certainly a possibility,' said the female voice. Dorian recognised the pattern now. The male voice was mocking and had no sympathy for anything he said. The female voice sounded as if she believed him, as if she wanted to be convinced by his words. It was one of the oldest interrogation techniques in the book. That did not make it any the less effective.

'So, this one warrior, with his legendary magical blade, slaughtered your entire high command and their bodyguards, unbound the Everqueen from where she lay at your feet, and then casually departed from the tent while none of your guards did anything to stop him. Have I stated matters correctly?'

'I would not have placed the emphasis where you have, but yes. He slaughtered everybody present and damn near killed me. I'm sure you've noticed the wounds in my side. Inspect them closely and you will note that they were partially cauterised. His blade did that. He shouted instructions to the guards to confuse them, slit the side of the tent and departed.'

'And what were you doing all this time?' Lord Vidor asked.

'I was bleeding on the carpet of the Everqueen's tent. I suppose I could have attempted to make him slip in a pool of my blood, but I was drifting in and out of consciousness at the time and the thought did not occur to me.'

'When did you come to consciousness?' the female voice asked.

'It was only minutes later. My guards found me and helped revive me. Once I was up and about I gave orders for pursuit, but the Everqueen and the one who rescued her were long gone.'

'I am given to understand that they slaughtered some witch elves on the way out,' Lord Vidor said.

'That is correct,' Dorian said. 'We think the witch elves tried to stop them.'

'And got chopped down for their pains.'

'Quite.'

'So this warrior also killed a dozen witch elves on his way out.'

'So it would seem.'

'It's almost like one of the ancient heroes of legend has come to life and fights against us,' said Lord Vidor, the sarcasm obvious in his voice.

'Almost,' Dorian agreed.

'There are, of course, alternative explanations.'

'I would be glad to hear them.'

'There may well be traitors in your force who have betrayed us to the enemy. They might even be very high in the command chain.' Vidor's tone left no doubt that the suspicion rested on Dorian himself.

'An interesting theory,' said Dorian. 'If a little fanciful.'

'Perhaps then it was simply incompetence on your part or the part of your officers that let the Everqueen escape.'

'Then my officers paid for their incompetence with their lives.'

'You have not.'

'I suspect you are about to change that.'

'No. I am not, general. I believe your story. I have seen the tracks of this warrior. I have noted the fact he was capable of killing a group of our strongest knights all but single-handed.'

There was no need to ask why Lord Vidor had performed the interrogation. No druchii would have passed up such an opportunity to humiliate another. Dorian suppressed his anger. He still had no idea where he stood with these assassins. They might kill him yet. They could do it before his guards could respond to a cry for help, and disappear into the night to escape vengeance.

'You have authorisation from our king?' Dorian asked. He was already trying to work out how to have the pair of them killed if he could. They were not the only ones who were capable of cruelty here.

A black ring, the seal on which Dorian recognised only too well, was shoved under his nose. There was no question of having them assassinated then. Malekith would make him pay very dearly indeed for that.

'We are here to help you recover the Everqueen,' said Lord Vidor.

'That will not be necessary. Our sorcerers have already located them. Even now the net closes around them.'

'Perhaps they will perform another miraculous escape,' said Vidor.

'Their luck cannot last forever.'

'I should certainly hope not. Oh, and in case you have any odd ideas, we are not the only ones our master has sent. If anything happens to us…'

There was no need for him to complete the sentence. 'What can I do for you?' Dorian asked.

They told him.

# CHAPTER FIFTEEN

'HERE,' ALARIELLE SAID.

'Where?' Tyrion responded. He could see nothing. This place looked like any other part of the great forest. Overhead huge ancient trees loomed. All around them was the tangle of massive, ancient roots. They were like the hands of wooden giants buried deep and trying to dig themselves out of the earth. The dismal birds circled overhead, cawing and giving away their location. They kept out of direct line of sight though, since Alarielle had taken to shooting them. The birds had pursued them for days, and once again Tyrion could hear the sound of Cold Ones closing in.

Alarielle stood like a statue for a moment and then danced over one of the roots, arms held wide, whirling like a child playing a game trying to make itself dizzy. She seemed unusually elated.

'I am glad you are so happy,' he said, 'but I don't see anything to be happy about. We are still lost in the woods. We are still pursued by enemies. We still have no aid.'

He did not mean to sound so angry. He felt very ill and his side was paining him. He was not sure how much further he could go without rest, and she did not seem tired at all. He was used to being able to go for days without rest if he had to. Now it felt like he could barely go for hours.

'I know where we are,' she said, her exuberance fading with her smile.

'Please, share the information with me!'

'We are at the Winterwood Palace.'

'I don't see any palace.'

'Perhaps that is because you do not know where to look.'

'If you would be so kind as to point it out to me...'

'I am standing on it.'

'I have always heard that the people of Avelorn were backward, but I never thought that even they could mistake a tree for a palace.'

'And I have always heard that the people of Lothern know nothing but stone houses.'

'I don't see any stone houses.'

She jumped down from the great root upon which she was perched and moved amid the tangle of them which formed something like a cave. She vanished from sight into the gloom and did not reappear.

'Alarielle!' Tyrion said. 'Alarielle!'

There was no answer. Tyrion walked forwards into the gloom, hands extended, expecting at any moment to encounter a rocky surface. Nothing happened. He kept walking, and ahead of him he heard mocking laughter.

'Wonderful,' he said. 'A tunnel for a palace. I suppose it's an improvement on a tree root, but not much.'

'Keep walking,' she said. Her voice echoed strangely in the darkness. He walked into something – a dead end. He moved his fingers along it and turned slightly, realising that the tunnel had reached a bend.

He repeated the process a number of times, all the while speaking her name and following the echo of her laughter through the darkness. It receded before him and then it got closer again until, reaching out, he touched her warm flesh in the darkness.

She laughed again and moved away from his grip and then spoke a word in the ancient tongue of the elves. A greenish glow emerged from the air itself and he saw something that took his breath away.

He stood in a vast cave, the roots of the trees thrusting out of the earth like beams in the dome of a great hall, forming a large arch overhead.

In the centre of the chamber was a huge dark pool, the surface rippling as if something in the depths was disturbing it. Clouds of steam emerged from it. The air was warm and slightly humid and it smelled of earth. Tyrion suddenly had a sense that they were deep underground. It was like being in the burrow of some great beast.

After a few further moments of inspection, he decided that was wrong. This place was the product of an elven sensibility. The earth had been shaped and sculpted to make this place exactly what Alarielle claimed it was – a palace.

They had not come through tunnels, they had come through corridors that resembled tunnels. This place looked as if it was the creation of natural formation at first glance, but you could see that the roots of the trees and the nature of the ceiling had actually been arranged to artfully suggest that. In fact, the whole chamber had a symmetry that could only be the product of intelligence at work.

Alarielle smiled. 'I used to love this place,' she said.

'I can understand why,' Tyrion said, surprised to find that he could. The chamber had an odd charm and the more he looked at it, the more he liked it. 'It is like nothing else I have ever seen.'

'We used to come here in the winter, when the snow lay deep on the ground, and be snug as badgers in their burrows. The hot springs keep the place warm. A certain amount of magic has been woven into the place as well.'

'Do you think that those who follow us will be able to detect that magic?'

'I don't know,' she said, looking thoughtful. 'This place was never intended to be a fortress or to be particularly secret. It was a refuge when the winters were hard, a place to come and sing and dance.'

'Let us hope that our pursuers can't spot us with their spells,' Tyrion said.

'This place is also a storehouse,' Alarielle said.

'Good. So we can find food here,' Tyrion said.

'And more than food.'

'What do you mean?'

'Wait and see,' she said.

'With bated breath.'

'We should be able to use the tunnels here to give our feathered pursuers the slip. There is more than one exit from here, and if we are careful and come out under cover of night, we can lose them.' She sounded more confident than she had in a long time. Tyrion wished he shared her confidence. His side hurt more with every step.

They moved deeper into the palace and each chamber was as large as the first, sometimes larger. Tyrion began to feel like a hunted animal that had found its way back to its burrow, a safe haven. He knew that feeling was deceptive though. It was perfectly possible that those who followed them could find this place just as easily as they had.

If that was the case, what Alarielle thought was a safe haven could easily turn out to be a very large trap. He told himself to stop looking on the dark side so much, but he could not help it. His side hurt. He felt weaker than he had at any time in his life; a sense of doom was creeping over him.

He felt as if great danger was approaching and there was nothing he could do to avert it. It had a nightmarish quality that was profoundly depressing. He started to understand his twin's temperament. For a great deal of his life, Teclis had laboured under ill-health of the worst sort. It was no wonder he was so sour.

'You look very thoughtful,' Alarielle said.

'I know that must be disturbing,' Tyrion said. 'But I am capable of it.'

'I never said you were not,' she said.

'I'm sorry, I was thinking about my twin.'

'You are very close to him?'

'Yes.'

'What were you thinking?'

'Nothing,' he said.

'You're not very forthcoming,' she said.

'You said there was more than just food here,' he said. She nodded. She gestured through some archways. Tyrion could see light springing into being within them. It was a greenish glow emitted by what looked like gems. Inside each chamber was a sleeping platform. Near each platform was a chest. Alarielle opened the chest. It contained bedding – furs and sheets.

'You said there are other ways in or out from this place…' Tyrion was curious as to how many escape routes they might have.

'There are many. You're thinking that we may be trapped down here, aren't you?'

'The thought had occurred to me.'

'You need rest,' she said. 'We both do. And this is the safest place we're likely to find in many leagues. We cannot be spotted from the air. It is difficult to find the way in if you don't know how. We will be safe here for a little while.'

'I hope you're right.'

'In any case, there are things here that we can use.'

'Like what?'

'You will see.' Her smile was enigmatic. She seemed to delight in having secret knowledge. He supposed he could not blame her for that. 'Wait here! Rest! I will find it.'

Tyrion wanted to protest. It would be dangerous for them to be split up again. It would be dangerous for her to wander off alone. She simply shook her head.

'I know this place. I grew up here. I can find you and I can get away from anyone who pursues me.'

'What if you're not the only one who knows how to find their way around here?'

'What do you mean?'

'This attack has been supremely well planned. I do not doubt that Malekith has had spies investigating your kingdom for centuries. It is possible that one of them has been here.'

'You're right, but what of it? Unless that person is here right now, the advantage will still be mine.'

'Who's to say that they are not?'

'Then I think I will recognise them and we will know who the traitor is, won't we? Now, stop fretting, lie down. I will be back soon.'

Tyrion lay down on the bed. He felt very dizzy. The room spun but only for a moment. He fell into a pit of sleep. There was nothing he could do to prevent it. If a legion of dark elves charged into the room at that very moment, he would not have had the strength to rise and fight them.

He knew that Alarielle was right. The best thing he could do was sleep and regain his strength, if that was even possible. He was useless to both himself and her in his present condition.

* * *

TYRION WOKE FEELING much better. Alarielle stood in front of him. She was garbed in fresh clothes and carried a tall winged staff which exuded an aura of power that even he could feel. She smiled and looked genuinely happy.

'What is that?' Tyrion asked.

'It is the Moonstaff of Lileath,' she said. 'It is an ancient artefact useful when you're casting spells. I hope that I will be able to find a use for it.'

'I hope you never have to,' said Tyrion.

'There are a number of other things that have proven useful. I found some of my mother's elixirs. I have been feeding them to you while you slept and sometimes when you were awake, although you do not seem to remember that.'

He ran his fingers through his hair and noticed that it was significantly longer. He had acquired the beginning of a beard, which was unusual because normally his chin hair grew very slowly. 'How long have I been asleep?'

'Three days.' She looked worried and he understood why. It was possible that their enemies were creeping up on them even now.

He sat upright very quickly. The motion made him feel very dizzy. He did not let that stop him though. He forced himself to stand although his legs felt weak and he could barely stay upright. He felt very hungry. The pain in his side had diminished somewhat, which was a blessing.

'Lie down!' Alarielle said. 'You need to eat and you need to get back your strength.'

'I have been unconscious for days?'

'Not all of the time. Sometimes you were conscious but raving. I needed to restrain you sometimes. I still have the bruises.'

She showed him her arms. They were patterned with small bruises that looked as if he had gripped them there very hard. 'I am sorry,' he said. 'I did not mean to hurt you.'

'You were not yourself. Think nothing of it.'

He sat down on the bed again and the room seemed to revolve. He lay flat on his stomach and waited for things to settle down. She touched him gently on the shoulder. 'Don't worry, you'll feel better soon.'

'I certainly hope so. I'm not used to this.'

'I found some new clothes. And some new armour. And a proper bow with real arrows. There is one for each of us.'

'You have been busy.'

'There is no need to sound so bitter. I have managed to collect some supplies as well. We won't be any worse off for the time we spent here. We might even be better off.'

'What do you mean?'

'I think the ones pursuing us may have passed us by. I saw no sign of them when I went up to take a look.'

'You saw no sign of them? When you went up to take a look? What were you thinking?'

'I was thinking that we need to know what was going on. I was thinking that *I* need to know what is going on. And I am thinking that I am your queen and it is not your place to use that tone of voice with me.'

'You could have got yourself killed or captured.'

'Why? Because you were not there? You were unconscious.

I doubt that you could have protected me.'

'It seems like you have been protecting me rather than vice versa.'

'I would not be here now if it had not been for you. I am grateful. And I'm going to need your help again, if we are to get out of here alive.' She sounded a little embarrassed and a little defensive.

'I need something to eat,' he said, 'if it is not beneath your royal dignity to serve me.'

'I think I might stoop to that,' she said. 'Just don't expect it to become a habit.'

He could see that she had already prepared waybread and cold meat. He began to eat slowly. The magic in the food lent him some strength and settled his stomach. A few moments later he felt himself sinking back into sleep. The Everqueen seemed to be singing a song. It sounded like a lullaby, but there was magic in it. He wondered what it was for.

TYRION WOKE, SENSING the presence of someone near. He looked around and saw Alarielle stretched beside him, fast asleep. With her eyes closed she looked much younger and much more vulnerable. He rose as softly as he could and padded across the chamber, head cocked to one side, listening for the presence of intruders.

He found clean new clothes in a neat pile lying near the bed. He donned the underwear, the linen shirts and then the leather jerkin and trousers of an Avelorn woods ranger. It felt more natural and more comfortable than the dark elf equipment that he had been wearing for so long before they came to this place.

He had to lace up the shirt and jerkin very gently because his wound still pained him – less than it had for some time, but still he sensed that it had the potential to become agonising. It was only a matter of time before the poison in it claimed his life.

So far, nothing that Alarielle had attempted had managed to clear his system of the witch elf's deadly venom. He strapped Sunfang onto his belt and did some gentle stretching exercises. The waybread and the elixirs had done their work. He no longer felt weak.

He padded through the tunnel-corridors of the Winterwood Palace. The place was vast and empty. The air was damp but warm. He felt himself starting to sweat, but it was a natural sweat, not the sweat of fever. He understood Alarielle's need to get out of this place. He felt a craving for fresh air himself. He thought that he could find his way back to the chamber in which the Everqueen slept. He pushed on, back along the route that had taken them to the chamber in the first place. He was heading for the exit.

As he did so, from up ahead he heard the sound of voices, speaking in the accents of Naggaroth. Swiftly, he backed away along the corridor and made his way back to the sleeping chamber. He shook Alarielle. She murmured something and turned over in her sleep. He shook again, more violently this time, and put his hand over her mouth so that she would not make any loud noises. She started to struggle against him, as if she feared what he was doing.

'Hush,' he whispered. 'They have found us.'

She nodded understanding and he took his hand off her mouth, still aware of the warmth of her breath against his palm. 'Where are they?'

'Down the corridor.'

'How many?'

'I did not wait to see. More than one.'

'I'm surprised you did not just slaughter them.'

'I prefer having you as an audience while I perform my heroics.'

'I am gratified to find that I have some part in your life.'

She spoke softly and in a joking tone, but he could see the fear in her eyes. She had the hunted, wild beast look to her again. It could not be pleasant, knowing that Malekith wanted you as his prisoner.

'We need to get going. You'll have to show me the other way out. We can't go back the way we got in.'

'What if they are watching the other exits?'

'That's a chance we will just have to take.'

ALARIELLE STRAPPED THE Moonstaff to her back, and snatched up her bow and her quiver of arrows. 'This way,' she said.

Tyrion followed her out into the corridor. He glanced right to make sure that none of the intruders had found them and then raced off after her.

'There is another way out,' Alarielle said. 'We just need to–'

Tyrion pushed her back into the sleeping chamber. A crossbow bolt flashed past her head. He heard one dark elf shout at the other, 'Don't shoot, idiot! The reward is greater for taking her alive.'

Tyrion stepped back into the chamber. They were trapped. There was no other way out. The dark elves could simply shoot them if they stepped out into the corridor. All they had to do was wait and bring up more soldiers.

'We waited too long. I'm sorry,' said the Everqueen.

'It's not your fault,' Tyrion said. 'If I had not become sick…'

'I could give myself up and they would not hurt you,' Alarielle said. Tyrion shook his head. He heard footsteps coming closer down the corridor. It would not be long now.

He drew Sunfang. Caledor's magic sword blazed brightly in his hand. He had left the doorway open. A dark elf, armoured and carrying a crossbow, appeared in it. Behind him there was another, with even more out of sight. Tyrion sprang forwards, even as the druchii aimed. Sunfang described a blazing arc downwards and smashed through the crossbow, setting it alight, before burying itself in the dark elf's chest.

Slowed by his wound, Tyrion could not attack the second dark elf before he had struck a blow. Tyrion raised his blade to parry and the dark elf stepped back instinctively, flinching before the flame. The two blades clashed together.

Tyrion struck. The dark elf fell. He tumbled backwards into his friends, getting tangled in them. Tyrion pressed his advantage and stepped forwards, claiming another victim.

'Get out! Run!' he shouted. Alarielle stepped into the corridor behind him. He sensed her presence and roared, 'Get going! I'll be right behind you.'

He could see that there were only a few more dark elves left, and in the confusion they were panicking. Disciplined as they were, they were not used to fighting in these narrow tunnels deep beneath the earth against a foe with a magical blade.

Several of them had already turned and run. The last one faced Tyrion, only to be chopped down with one brutal stroke. Tyrion considered pursuing the fleeing dark elves, but that would mean losing contact with Alarielle; he was not going to let that happen again. He turned and was surprised to see that she was still there, aiming her bow. Tyrion stepped to one side. She let loose her arrow and was rewarded with a scream from the far end of the corridor.

'Now they'll know that they're not the only ones who can shoot,' she said.

'Don't you do anything that you're told?' Tyrion asked. She shrugged.

'You looked like you could use the help.'

He grabbed her by the wrist and tugged her off down the corridor, regretting it immediately when the wound in his side began to ache.

'Don't you want to know where we are going?' she asked.

'Why don't you tell me as we run?'

ALARIELLE RAN LIKE a frightened deer, speeding along, turning left and then right decisively as if she knew exactly where she was going.

It occurred to Tyrion that if the dark elves had found

other entrances, there might well be a problem. They might run headlong into their pursuers.

The ceilings became lower. Tyrion had to crouch in order to keep going. Ahead of them, he could see a wooden doorway. It looked old and was covered in moss. The air here was colder and damper than it had been, and he felt as if the outside world was closer.

She reached out and touched the door, muttering a word of command. It swung open even before Tyrion reached it. A draught of cold air hit him in the face and he caught sight of shadows and gloom outside. It came as a shock – he had somehow been expecting to see daylight when the door opened, and he realised now that it was night.

Alarielle paused for a moment and listened. Tyrion realised that she was learning caution. She had not bolted straight out into the night as perhaps she might have been inclined to do only a few days before.

He felt winded as he had never done in the past, and he realised that his wound and the poison in it were still affecting him greatly. He felt his face flush. He was not used to being the weakest person present and he found it both irritating and embarrassing.

He tried to listen over the sound of his own rough breathing, but he could hear nothing. Alarielle waited for a few heartbeats, looked at him, nodded and gestured to him to go ahead. He drew his dagger, not wanting to draw Sunfang in case the flame of the blade gave away their position to any watchers. He advanced, balanced on the balls of his feet, ready to strike at anybody waiting in ambush, but there was no one.

He surveyed the bushes close at hand and saw no waiting enemy. They had emerged onto a wooded slope. Beneath them was a river. It was not as wide as the Everflow and there was a path of stepping stones just below them, doubtless put there deliberately to service this doorway into the palace. He gestured for her to follow him, and they both ran down the hill until they reached the stepping stones and crossed the river.

He kept glancing to left and right, suspecting that every shadow might conceal a watching archer, expecting at any moment to feel a crossbow bolt plunge into his chest. He kept low, squatting down to provide the smallest possible silhouette, to make himself the most difficult target he could. Copying his action, Alarielle did the same.

Where were the dark elves? Surely they must be out there somewhere. He felt as if he was walking into a vast trap of which he did not know the full extent.

There must be enemies out there, for not all of the dark elves could have entered the palace. That would be foolish. There must be scouts here somewhere, watching things, hoping to prevent their escape. It was what he would have done if he was leading the dark elves, and it would be foolish to assume that their leader was any less competent than he was.

Alarielle held her bow, ready to shoot any dark elf she saw. He realised she had come a very long way in a very short time. She was no longer the scared girl he had rescued. Perhaps she never had been. Perhaps that had only been the way he perceived her.

They had to come to a decision, he realised. They could not just stand here waiting like frightened rabbits for the dark elves to pick them up. They needed to move.

Something quivered in the ground at his feet. A crossbow bolt. He looked around to see who had fired it. An arrow whizzed past his ear and into a bush. A scream rang out through the night. Alarielle's shot had found its target.

Answering cries echoed through the night. They were surrounded.

# CHAPTER SIXTEEN

SHE WALKED ALONG a beach of black sand. Black gulls shrieked overhead, sometimes coming to rest on oddly shaped dunes. It took her a few moments to realise that the dunes were made of skulls, bones and ancient rotting armour. She was looking for something or someone she had lost a long time ago. She had been looking for ages and she had not found it. She feared she never would, no matter how hard she tried.

'Morathi…' The voice might have been the cold wind that blew in from the sea; it was just as monotonous, just as cold and just as cutting. Her cloak fluttered in the wind. A strand of her curly black hair escaped from beneath her hood. She turned around and could not see who spoke.

'Morathi…' She glanced back over her shoulder and still no one was there. Perhaps it was a ghost who taunted her. This was a haunted land. She felt the nearness of the Black Sword. It was a hideous presence, terrifying in its fatal potential and yet oddly reassuring. It reminded her of Aenarion. Its aura had always marked his presence. He had not been separated from the weapon in all the time she had known him.

Perhaps that was what brought her here so often. Perhaps something of him still lingered, unable to part from the blade even in death. She felt a certain bitterness. She had always thought the blade was more his mistress than she was. It was a more terrible rival than any mere elf woman could have been.

'Morathi...' She thought she had identified the source of the voice now, and began to follow it through the dunes of bones and wreckage, determined to confront whoever was its source and make it pay for mocking her.

She found him standing amid the rubble of some ancient broken shrine. The stone face of Khaela Mensha Khaine looked down upon him as he studied his reflection in the stagnant, scummy waters of the font. His back was to her but even before he turned to face her, she knew him.

His skin was near translucent. The muscles writhed below it like worms in a corpse. His eyes were mere pools of black light. His fingers were claws. He looked like an animated skeleton smeared with a thin layer of flesh. The expression on his face was a calm madness personified.

'Death does not agree with you, Caledor,' Morathi said. His lips quirked in a quiet, mad smile.

'I did not need you to tell me that, Morathi. He tells me

that himself.' She studied him closely. His limbs twitched. He licked his lips. He looked shrunken and twisted and lonely.

'You have gone mad, old ghost. Avaunt, begone and trouble my dreams no more.'

'This is more than a dream, Morathi. You know that. You sleep surrounded by wards to shield your thoughts. And yet I am here. Why do you think that is?'

'You grow lonely in your dotage, perhaps.'

'You are in my land now, Morathi. In the place I made. You should be careful what you say, careful what you think...'

She started. What the wizard said was true. He should not be in her dreams and yet he was. Who knew what else he was capable of? In life, there never had been another mage as subtle and powerful as Caledor. Who knew what he was capable of in death. Best be wary.

'You have something to say to me, Caledor, so say it and begone!'

'I know why you have come to Ulthuan. I know why you lead your army of barbarian Chaos worshippers. I will not allow it, Morathi.'

'What can you do to stop me? You are trapped with all your former students at the heart of the Vortex. You cannot leave it or it will collapse, and that will serve my purposes just as well.'

'Are you sure?' In truth she was not, but it would never do to let him know that, so she kept quiet.

'Listen to me, Morathi, and listen well... I created the Vortex, and before I let you use it for your twisted purposes I will destroy it myself.'

'Then you are as mad as I always suspected...'

'No. The destruction will liberate an enormous amount of magical energy and I will use it for one purpose...'

'And what would that be?'

'Though it be the last thing I do, I will slay you. On this you have my word.'

The most frightening thing was the way he said it. There was no menace in his voice, just sorrow, regret and absolutely no doubt that it would happen if he so willed it.

Looking at him now, she recalled exactly who and what he was – the mage who had beaten back the greatest invasion of Chaos the world had ever known, who had shackled a continent with his power, whose will, even in death, preserved the spell that preserved the world.

Gazing upon the ancient ghost, Morathi discovered, much to her surprise, that there was still a being in this world capable of frightening her. She awoke covered in cold sweat, her scream awakening the barbarian lovers who shared her bed.

CALEDOR PICKED UP the piece that represented Morathi and removed it from the board, then slumped forwards in his chair. His confrontation with the sorceress had left him feeling weary. It had been a task of near-insuperable difficulty to penetrate the wards surrounding her dreams. Talking with her had been worse.

Death looked at him and smiled. 'An excellent move. I thought your bluff about destroying the Vortex was masterful.'

'It was not a bluff,' said Caledor. 'I never make a threat I am not prepared to keep.'

'Interesting,' said Death. 'I will remember that.'

Caledor feared he had revealed far more than he had intended to or was wise. Death reached down and lifted another piece.

'YOU ARE DOING what?' Malekith bellowed, barely able to restrain himself from rising from his throne. In the mirror, his mother shrugged. She looked pale and dishevelled and there was something in her expression at odds with her normal perfect poise and self-possession.

'I am leaving for Naggaroth.'

'You cannot do that! I forbid it!' His mother looked frightened, but not of him.

'I think you will find I have already done it.'

'Leaving our northern allies leaderless.'

Her smile was full of sweet malice. 'They are not exactly leaderless. They never were. They follow their own chieftains and warlords.'

'What new treachery is this, mother?'

'No treachery, my son, I swear it.' She sounded completely sincere, but then she always did when she wanted to.

'Then why abandon our human catspaws now and retreat when everything is going well?'

She gazed around nervously, that alone told him that something was wrong. Under normal circumstances, she would never allow the slightest trace of weakness to show. 'Caledor has spoken to me.'

'It must have been quite a conversation.'

'He told me he will kill me, if I proceed.'

'And you are still frightened of that ancient ghost?'

'You did not see him, my son. He has changed. I think he is mad.'

'And who would not be, imprisoned within the Vortex for six millennia?' His mother smiled ironically. She was clearly thinking that he had been imprisoned within his armour for almost as much time, although she did not say it. She did not need to. He knew her that well.

'You do not understand, Malekith. He spoke to me. While I slept. While my dreams were warded, through my strongest protective spells.'

That was troubling. The defences his mother had woven around her were every bit as strong as his own. 'He has not taken the trouble to appear to me. Are you implying he considers you more important than me?' There was a dangerous edge to his voice now.

'No. Who knows why he does anything? He defied your father when it suited him. Even in life he was a law unto himself. In death…'

Malekith considered her words and suddenly he understood. He knew why the ancient mage would threaten his mother and not him. 'Mother, if you have been tampering with his work, I swear to you that if he does not kill you, I will do it myself.'

'You may find that more difficult than you imagine.'

'And yet clearly you do not think that Caledor would have any trouble with that.'

'You do not yet have the power he has.'

'And what would that be?'

'The power to destroy everything that exists.'

Malekith slumped back into his throne and considered what she had said. It was true. He lacked the power of that ancient wizard, and while he did it would always hang over his head. He refused to acknowledge that anyone had that right, even the gods. And yet that was a problem for another day.

'Flee back to your kennel then, mother. When I have completed the conquest of Ulthuan, you and I will have words.'

'I wish you luck with that, my son, but I fear there are older and stronger powers working against you.'

The mirror went blank, leaving Malekith contemplating his own massive armoured reflection. He feared his mother was right. Everything was starting to unravel, all of his carefully woven plans. The question was, why? Who stood to gain from that? And what could he do in response?

Malekith faced the mirror for a long time, brooding. His mother's defection was an immediate problem. Without her to restrain them, her barbarian horde would fragment and rampage across northern Ulthuan. In itself that was no great problem, as he had once told her it would simply make it easier to deal with them permanently when the time came. However, that time was not here yet. He still needed their massive manpower to tie down the asur armies in the north. As things stood it was perfectly possible they might turn on his own troops and he would be facing a double threat.

Beyond that, he had no idea what their daemonic masters would put them up to. They needed to be restrained and either brought to heel or destroyed. There was only one person who was capable of doing that, who had the power and the charisma to force them to obey, and that was himself. He would need to gather his force, leave a garrison in Mancastra and head east to take control of the situation. N'Kari would open the gate to take his army there.

It niggled at him, being forced to abandon his carefully laid plans, and yet he had always known that such a situation might arise. No plan ever survived contact with the foe.

He summoned aides and began bellowing orders for departure. He would bring the rebellious barbarians to heel, then hunt down the Everqueen if need be.

# CHAPTER SEVENTEEN

'BE STILL!' TYRION said. Alarielle froze in place, becoming just another shadow. Tyrion listened – he could hear soldiers moving all around, but that was not what he was seeking. He knew there would be others out there, assassins, scouts and dark elf warriors, all capable of moving silently through the night. They would be the real danger.

He gestured with his left hand for Alarielle to start to move again. She did so slowly, like a hunter stalking a dangerous beast. He did the same, moving as cautiously as he could, paying as much attention to his surroundings as his senses would allow. She was keeping an arrow nocked in her bow. He could understand the reassurance that having a ready weapon brought. He dared not draw Sunfang in case the sudden blaze of light drew attention to them. Instead he kept a long hunting knife available in his right hand.

The woods around them were thick. The undergrowth was dense. He gestured for Alarielle to start moving through the undergrowth. He followed her, wriggling on his belly, pushing aside twigs and leafy stalks to keep them away from his eyes. The heavy tread of moving soldiers passed nearby. They were so close that Tyrion could hear them talking.

'I don't think they came this way,' said one voice.

'That would be our bad luck,' said another, obviously more authoritative. 'We could live on the bounty for the rest of our lives if we are the ones who find them.'

'I am never that lucky,' said the first speaker.

'Perhaps you should both be more attentive,' said a third voice, more sinister and quiet. What was startling was the fact that it had come from a point where Tyrion had not expected to hear anyone speak. Its owner was obviously capable of moving with great stealth. How long had he been there? Had he seen the fugitives as they took cover?

'Someone has been this way,' it said. 'Look at these tracks!'

'I don't see any.'

'You've obviously never stalked wolves in the wastelands of Naggaroth.'

'No, Kalysar, I was too busy fighting Chaos warriors.'

'These tracks were not made by Chaos warriors. They were not made by dark elves either. You can see these were made by leather moccasins, the sort that the natives of Avelorn wear.'

'Maybe they were made by hunters. Maybe they were made by scouts.'

'In that case you'd better keep your eyes open, hadn't you? And maybe, just maybe, they were made by the people we are looking for.'

Tyrion lay so close to the Everqueen that he could feel her heart pounding. He realised that they were not in a good position. It would be difficult to rise and fight while concealed in the undergrowth. He was lying flat on his belly. There was no way he could dodge if someone decided to put his spear through him.

'Maybe you should show your skill as a tracker, Kalysar,' said the second of the speakers, whom Tyrion was starting to believe was an officer. 'Maybe you can help us all get our hands on the general's gold.'

'I'll do just that if you give me some space and stop yakking. I need to concentrate.'

Tyrion tapped the Everqueen on the shoulder and gestured for her to move. Every wriggle, every furtive movement that they made sounded as loud as the blare of trumpets in his ear. It seemed impossible that the dark elf soldiers could not hear them as they moved. Behind him he could hear the faint ring of metal on metal as armoured soldiers moved around.

'Idiot!' Kalysar said. 'You've obscured the tracks with your booted feet.'

'At least we know someone passed this way,' said the officer. 'We should report that.'

Tyrion felt some relief. He felt his muscles begin to loosen and only then did he realise how tense he had been. He and Alarielle kept moving through the undergrowth and eventually emerged from the bushes, onto another game trail.

'That was a little too close for comfort,' Alarielle said with a tentative smile. She was trying to conceal her fear and doing it better than most.

'Best keep moving,' Tyrion said. 'There will be plenty more of the sons of Naggaroth about. We may not be so lucky next time.'

Alarielle nodded and started to lope along the trail, moving as quickly as was compatible with being quiet. She was definitely better at this than he was, Tyrion thought. It was an unusual sensation, meeting anybody who was better at anything. He was glad of it at that moment.

TYRION CROUCHED IN the bush, watching another company of dark elves pass. There were dozens of the tall warriors, garbed in mail, clutching crossbows and longswords. They moved through the woods with the swaggering ease of conquerors.

Over the past few days, as they had followed the trail eastwards, it became obvious how lucky they were. They had to move very carefully, keeping always to the undergrowth for fear of daemonic birds. The woods were full of dark elves. They were thrown around the Winterwood Palace in a wide net. There were scores of companies amounting to thousands of elves. There seemed to be no doubt that the druchii had well and truly found their trail. A whole army had been deployed in pursuit of them.

He felt oddly vulnerable crouched down here in a hollow between the trees, with only a thin shield of leaves between him and detection. It seemed impossible that one of the druchii would not sense the pressure of Tyrion's gaze upon him and look round and give the signal that would result in his death and Alarielle's capture.

Several times they had turned at bay and attempted to double back through enemy lines, but each time the enemy had swept forwards and they had been forced back onto the eastward path. If this kept up they would eventually be forced out of Avelorn entirely. With no trees in which to hide, it would not take long for the dark elves to find them.

In the distance he heard the roar of a Cold One. They needed to get moving again soon, before the great lizard got close enough to catch their scent. Alarielle gestured for him to remain in place. It would not do to move now and attract the attention of the passing soldiers.

Tyrion's side ached. He was petrified that he would fall into another feverish faint while there were enemies close. There were times when he was barely strong enough to draw Sunfang, and the intervals of strength and ease of movement came and went with worrying rapidity.

He felt his fingers drumming against the hilt of the blade. It was a nervous tic that had emerged more and more often recently. Cold sweat ran down his forehead. He fought down the almost irresistible urge to cough. His throat felt dry. He wanted to unscrew the top from the flask of brackish water on his belt and drink it all down. Perhaps that would relieve the irritation in his desert-dry throat.

The Cold One's roar sounded again and was answered from a spot to the south of them. They had best not go that way then, he thought. A few moments later, he felt a hand shaking him.

'Tyrion! Tyrion!' Alarielle's voice held a hint of fear. 'Wake up. Move! They've gone and we need to do the same.'

Tyrion realised that he had been lost in a reverie of thoughts and plans for their escape. He had lost contact with his surroundings and he had no idea for how long. It was only going to get worse.

'Leave me,' he said. 'You will have a better chance on your own.'

It came to him then that this had been true for a long time. He was nothing but a liability to her. She might even have been able to escape by now if it were not for him. She was surely much better at woodcraft than any dark elf they had met.

'We will both get out of this together,' she said. 'We started it together and we will finish it together.'

He wanted to tell her to move, that she was not being sensible, but he could not find the energy. He understood why she was doing this as well. He would not have abandoned a comrade either. He forced himself to rise to his feet. The ground rocked. It felt like an earthquake.

'It's like being on the deck of a ship in a storm,' he said, then realised that she was not having the same difficulty. It was the fever, the wound and the fever.

Just put one foot in front of the other, he told himself. Ignore the movements of the earth. This will pass.

'THERE IS A strange stink in the air,' Tyrion said. It was true too. It was the sort of smell he associated with old, damp houses in Lothern, with sickness and plague among humans, with rot. It was like the scent of waste composting in rubbish heaps in a human town mingled with the rotting jungle smell of a Lustrian swamp. He wondered for a moment whether it was the fever. The air seemed to be getting hotter, and there were more biting insects present. There was something else too, something that made his skin tingle in an unwholesome way.

A frown crossed Alarielle's face. 'We don't have much choice,' she said.

'Much choice about what?'

'We need to go on. The druchii are too close for us to go any other way.'

'I know. What has that got to do with the smell, or the bugs in the air for that matter?'

'If we follow this path we will come to the Darkwood.'

'I am guessing it is not called that because it is a place where flowers grow and baby deer frolic through sweet-scented glades.'

'Perceptive as ever, Prince Tyrion. It is a place where the taint of Chaos and the old dark magics are still strong. There are parts of Avelorn that have been that way since the Great Chaos Incursion in the time of Aenarion.'

'It sounds… interesting,' he said.

'Most people would say fearsome.'

'We are heroes, you and I, your serenity. We shall dare these dark lands.'

She smiled wanly. 'As you say.'

* * *

'WHAT IS THIS?' Tyrion asked. He glanced around at the forest with dazed eyes. The pain in his side was getting worse again. The poisoned wound that the witch elf had given him was getting far worse. He felt as if soon it would be impossible for him to go on. He gritted his teeth and forced one foot in front of the other. He was not going to give up. Not now. Not ever.

There was something about this part of the forest that daunted him, though. The trees were older and larger. Some of them were as thick around the bole as the tower of an ancient castle. Many of them were taller than any trees he had seen since he left the jungles of Lustria. Moss covered all of them like a thick fur. Thick vines dangled from the branches. Enormous mushrooms crowded the shadows beneath the ancient leaves. Some of them even clung to the sides of the trees parasitically. Over everything hung an aura of vast age. The air seemed thick and close. It felt damp and fusty. In the distance, the leaves and branches seemed to sway even though there was no wind. It was as if some vast invisible monster was making its way through the ancient forest.

'This is the oldest part of the forest of Avelorn,' Alarielle said. She looked thoughtful. 'There are many strange stories about this part of the wood. Even my people shun it. Not much has changed in there since ancient times. Since the first wars with Chaos.'

'Is it haunted?'

'Who knows. Powerful magic scorched these woods once. In some parts, ancient evil clings even to this day. The taint of Chaos causes mutation. Monsters are often born in these parts. They come out and hunt sometimes and it often takes a great effort to drive them back.'

'I have heard much of the great hunts of Avelorn. I was wondering what you used for prey.'

'Manticores, hippogriffs, half-dragons and other strange things.'

'It does not seem as if we have much choice though. We're going to have to enter these woods if we are to escape our pursuers.'

'Unfortunately, Prince Tyrion, you are correct. I would have preferred to avoid this part of the woods if we could, but we have no choice.'

'Then we had better hope that the monsters are all asleep or hunting for dark elves in other parts of the woods.'

'I suspect that we could not be that lucky,' Alarielle said. Tyrion did not doubt that she was correct in this.

They followed the path deeper into the woods and the taint of old, wild magic became even stronger and more obvious. Even Tyrion could sense it in the air. It went a long way towards explaining the feeling of closeness. He found that he had difficulty in breathing. When he listened closely he could hear a sound that was like the distant buzzing of a huge cloud of flies. Sometimes, he could have sworn that he was surrounded by them. He felt as if their tiny wings were tickling his face, but there were no flies or any other insects that he could see.

Alarielle looked as if the weight of the world was pressing down on her shoulders. There was something in the air that made her look as nauseated as Tyrion felt. He did not doubt that it was the aura of corrupt magic that surrounded them. If it could affect someone even as normally insensitive as he was, what must it be like for she who was a natural sorcerer?

He reached out and touched her shoulder and she flinched a little but did not draw away. 'What is wrong?'

'This part of the land is very sick,' she said. 'And it affects me.'

'Perhaps we should not have come here. Perhaps we should go back.'

'If we did that, we would merely be running into the arms of Malekith and his followers. There would be no escape for either of us then.' Tyrion knew that she was correct and that there was nothing he could say that she had not already thought about.

As they pushed on deep into the forest, the pain in his side intensified. It was as if something in the wound was drawing strength from the corruption of their surroundings. He mentioned his suspicions to Alarielle.

'It is possible,' she said. 'It is not mere poison that is in that wound. There is ancient dark magic. I curse the person that made that blade. What sort of smith would forge such a weapon?'

'A druchii one,' Tyrion said.

'It was a rhetorical question, Prince Tyrion,' Alarielle said.

'It deserved an answer. I have seen Naggaroth. I have fought against its people. I don't think they are sane as we measure sanity.'

'You're not the first to say this.'

'Nonetheless, it is the truth. Think about those witch elves that we met. They were mad.'

'They are the worst of their kind,' Alarielle said.

'Far from it. In them the madness is merely more obvious. In the others, it runs deep and strong.'

'Perhaps they shall find these woods more to their liking than I do,' she said. She meant it as a joke, but her glance flickered around nervously.

'We can't go back,' said Tyrion, glancing over his shoulder. Perhaps it was a trick of the shadows or his own feverishness, but he thought he saw someone moving there. 'We need to move on.'

'Yes,' she said. She raised the Moonstaff of Lileath. A faint aura of light played around it. 'I wish I could use this properly.'

'If I get to feeling much worse, I can use it to lean on.'

Something padded along softly in the shadows behind them.

# CHAPTER EIGHTEEN

SLIME OOZED FROM the bark of the trees. In places it formed bubbles inside of which huge mutated woodlice twisted and fretted. Large, segmented, multi-legged creatures scuttled through the branches above them. The shape of their bodies flowed to conform to the surface they moved over. They were eyeless, with long twitching feelers. So far they had not attacked, but their presence made Tyrion feel uncomfortable. It was like turning over a huge log and having elf-sized monsters scuttle out.

Alarielle followed a path that was invisible to him. 'How do you know where we are going?' Tyrion asked.

'The rangers have left signs.' She pointed to a small mark chipped in the trees. 'These paths are safe, or at least they were when my people last passed this way.'

'That could have changed then?'

'Almost certainly. Not many people come here.'

Tyrion looked at what seemed like a huge spider web, draped between branches. Something large twitched inside a cocoon of silk. It was trapped up there. 'Why would anybody come here?'

'There are certain herbs that can be sold to Lothern merchants for great sums of money. I understand they have alchemical uses.'

'I can't imagine any medicine made from this stuff would have a beneficial effect.'

'I don't think they make medicine from it. I think it is used for sorcery and certain unclean rituals. The rangers try and stop people taking it. That is why they come here, and to hunt the monsters that emerge from the place.'

Tyrion glanced around again. 'That sounds exciting.'

'Perhaps too exciting for me,' she said. A growl sounded somewhere in the distance. It bore some resemblance to the sound made by the big cats Tyrion had heard in the jungles of Lustria.

'As I was saying,' she said. She stowed the staff on her back and took up her bow.

'It sounds like a jaguar,' Tyrion said.

'We never see those in Avelorn,' she said. 'If we are lucky it will be a ghost panther or a sabretooth. If we are not…'

'What?'

'Some mutant monster tainted by old magic.'

They advanced. The trees closed in overhead. The fungi grew taller than Tyrion's head and began to emit an eldritch, spectral glow like the ghostly lights that lead travellers astray in marshes.

'I always pictured Avelorn as a land of beauty and glory and brilliant sunshine,' Tyrion said. 'That's how the legends always portray it.'

'The legends usually miss out the darker parts,' she said. 'But they have always been here, for as long as I can remember, and those memories go very deep.'

The growling sound came again, but this time the note had changed. There was a yammering quality to it and what might even have been words chanted by a madman, as if some odd hybrid of maniac and predatory beast was giving vent to its hunger.

'I don't think that's a cat,' Tyrion said.

'We shall make a woods ranger out of you yet,' the Everqueen replied.

'IT'S FOLLOWING US,' Tyrion said.

'Yes,' Alarielle said. 'And it is not making any effort to cover up the fact.'

She was right. They could hear the massive creature passing through the woods behind them, grunting and grumbling and growling to itself. Occasionally when Tyrion turned, he could see a monstrous form pushing through the undergrowth. There were times when he thought he caught sight of a leonine head with human features and hair like a mane. Its eyes caught the light like those of a cat. It might have been a giant crawling very quickly, or a massive beast, or a creature that was some combination of both.

'What is it waiting for? If it is going to attack, why does it not do so?'

'I would imagine that our rangers have taught it to be wary of armed elves.'

'Not too wary. Otherwise it would not be on our trail.'

'Perhaps it is waiting for us to make camp, to fall asleep.'

'It would have been cleverer for it not to show itself then.'

'No one ever said manticores were very bright.'

'That is what you think it is then?' Tyrion said.

'Yes. With that body and that face I don't think it could be anything else.'

'Will it have poisoned spikes on its tail that it can fire like a mangonel?'

'It might. It's a mutant, a creature of Chaos. For all we know it might squirt intoxicating wine from its tail.'

'That seems a tad unlikely.'

'My basic point stands.'

'We shall soon know if it plans on attacking us when we make camp. It is getting dark.'

'Yes, and none of these trees look particularly homely.'

Tyrion looked at the twisted and mutated plants surrounding them. Slime coated many of them and dripped in webs from their branches. From some of them depended globes of mucus within which things wriggled. All of the undergrowth had a blotched unhealthy look.

'This looks like something you would expect to find in the Chaos Wastes,' Alarielle said.

'The Wastes are not so fertile.'

'You have been there?'

Tyrion nodded, distractedly. He was looking for a place to make camp that was not too close to the loathsome trees. He did not fancy sleeping anywhere near them.

'You have travelled far, Prince Tyrion.'

'My home is Lothern,' he said. 'From there fleets sail to every corner of the world.'

'I have never left Avelorn.'

'You are young. More so than I.'

'The Everqueen leaves Avelorn only under the most desperate of circumstances.'

'Is there any reason for that?'

'Her power is tied to the place. The farther from it she goes… I go… the less it becomes. And at the moment, the power is not too great anyway.'

'I did not know that.'

'It is not something that is made common knowledge. And anyway, when does the Everqueen ever need to leave Avelorn? Who would have thought a day like today would come?'

Alarielle had found a spot in a hollow. It was barren and dry and the plants looked less unwholesome than the others in the neighbourhood. There was even water gathered in puddles along the bottom.

'I would not drink any of that water,' she said. 'It is most likely tainted.'

'I think I might have worked that out for myself,' said Tyrion.

'We need a fire,' Alarielle said. She had already begun to gather wood. Tyrion stood guard, in case anything should come upon them suddenly. A pair of feelers poked over the edge of the small depression. One of the giant woodlouse creatures scuttled in. Tyrion drew Sunfang and advanced upon it. It turned and rippled away.

'I do not like those things,' he said, turning to see Alarielle confronted by the manticore. The great beast moved forwards. It seemed impossible that anything so large could move so quietly. Close up, Tyrion could see it was bigger than a mountain lion. Its body was the size of a horse although lower and much more cat-like. This one had a tail tipped with a scorpion-like sting. Vestigial wings, not large enough to let it fly or glide, emerged from its back. The face was humanoid but might have belonged to an idiot or a madman. The expression on it was one of slack-jawed lunacy, mingled with hunger. For all that, its inhuman eyes were not without a certain cunning.

It growled again and the air seemed to vibrate. Curved claws sharp as sickles emerged from its paws. The tail lashed the air.

Alarielle continued to move back towards Tyrion. The elven warrior swung his sword in a great figure of eight to get the manticore's attention. The passage of air made the flames on the blade roar and flicker. The great head jerked to one side, and it studied Tyrion as a cat might study a particularly foolish mouse.

Tyrion knew that on the best day of his life this creature would over-match him, and he was weakened now by his poisoned and infected wound. He needed an advantage. The only one he could think of was the power that he knew lay dormant within Sunfang. He pointed the blade tip at the manticore and willed it to blast the creature with fire. Nothing happened. He sensed something within the blade, but he could not bind it or make contact with it.

Desperately he tried to remember what had happened when he had blasted the Cold One riders. Perhaps if he could replicate that trick, he would know the sword's secret. He knew from his long talks with Teclis that part of the secret of magic was connected with mood and the manipulation of mental imagery. He never had possessed any talent for such things though. He was not a sorcerer.

Of course, the blade had been intended to be used by one who was not a sorcerer. Perhaps he was over-thinking what needed to be done. Perhaps it was all much simpler than he had imagined. He tried to imagine the flame blazing brighter in his mind.

Had it responded? Had the runes along the blade got ever so slightly brighter? The manticore growled. It carried its weight low to the earth and seemed almost to undulate as it slunk closer. Tyrion could see the great muscles gather in its haunches as it prepared to spring.

Tyrion imagined a ball of flame emerging from the tip of the blade and arcing towards the manticore, just as he had seen it do previously. Something happened. A faint blast of heat singed the hairs on the back of his hand as a small ball of light emerged from Sunfang and wobbled through the air towards the manticore. It exploded at the creature's feet. A smell of singed fur filled the air. The manticore let out a faint bleat and turned and sprang away over the edge of the crater. Its faintly acrid animal stink hung in the air along with the stench of sulphur.

Alarielle looked over at him. 'You surprise me, Prince Tyrion. I thought mastery of the blade was beyond you.'

'I have not mastered the blade. I think I have merely worked out how to make it work. It may be some time before I can harness its full power.'

'Nonetheless, I think you have done enough to save us from that Chaos creature.'

'Let us drink that toast after that particular tournament is won,' said Tyrion. He moved to the edge of the glade, but there was no manticore in sight. The beast's tracks ran to the edge of a deep thicket and then vanished from sight.

Tyrion felt Alarielle move up beside him. She had her bow in her hands now and an arrow nocked and ready to fly.

'Are you going to go hunting?' Tyrion asked.

'The thing is no good for meat,' she said.

'I thought you might like to try it for the sport.'

'Let's put your sword to good use and get a fire going. If nothing else it ought to help keep such monsters at bay.'

Tyrion was glad that Sunfang still possessed enough power to get the fire going. They settled down to a long night with nothing to eat but waybread, and nothing to drink but the last remains of their brackish water.

'WHAT WAS THAT?' Alarielle asked. Tyrion stirred feverishly. He pushed himself upright. Four strangers were approaching the fire. Something about their manner and their garb marked them as druchii although these were not common soldiers.

'You have led us a merry chase,' said one of them, a tall, slender elf who carried a bow as if he knew how to use it. It was nocked and the arrow pointed directly at Tyrion's heart. 'It is over now.'

'We were sent to capture you, your serenity,' said a lovely female in a soft husky voice. 'I think there might be a bonus for us if we take your handsome friend back alive. Our ruler will be most anxious to meet the elf who has caused us so much trouble.'

'He does not look as if he will live that long,' said a huge brutish-looking elf who carried an axe with a blade at each end of its shaft. 'That wound has been infected by poison out of Har Ganeth, unless I miss my guess. I am surprised he is still alive. He should have died a long time ago.'

'Unless you have been keeping him alive with your magic, your serenity,' said the final elf, who bore no obvious weapons at all, which made Tyrion suspect he was most likely the most dangerous of them.

'Who are you?' Tyrion asked. He kept his tone polite and conversational even as he tried to work out a way of killing them.

'We are but humble servants of Malekith,' said the debauched-looking one, whom Tyrion suspected was a sorcerer. His twin had worn similar amulets under certain circumstances. 'I am Khalion. The winsome lady is Amara. The primitive with the bow is Vidor. The large and forceful-looking chap is Balial.'

'You talk too much, Khalion,' said Balial. His voice was

deep and rumbling. He was scarred like a pit fighter. From the way he held the axe Tyrion could see he was enormously strong. The dislike in the voice was obvious. There was some rivalry between these four, that was obvious. Doubtless they would have to split any reward between them. If any of their companions were to suffer an accident it would be all the more for the survivors. It was something to bear in mind.

'At least I am capable of intelligent conversation,' said Khalion. 'And I am not an unmannerly boor, like some I could mention.'

'That is debatable,' said Vidor. He looked directly at Tyrion. 'I confess I am disappointed. I was expecting an epic battle when we found you. Your exploits have already made you quite famous. What is your name?'

'I am Prince Tyrion.' Vidor nodded.

'The reaver who assaulted the coast of Naggaroth. I remember seeing some of your handiwork then. You killed a lot of people, Prince Tyrion, and burned a lot of warehouses.'

'I regret to inform you I would do it again.'

'I doubt you will be given the chance. Our ruler's hospitality makes it hard for his guests to leave.'

'I will see that you are made comfortable,' said Amara, smiling. It was the sort of smile Tyrion was used to getting from women, and its sincerity just made him trust her less.

'Be careful of him,' said Khalion. 'He carries a powerful magic weapon.'

'I don't doubt it,' said Amara.

'That is interesting,' said Vidor.

'I found it first,' said Khalion.

'Of what possible use is a sword to you, mage?' asked Vidor.

'It can always be sold, if it does not prove useful for research.'

'The bounty belongs to our master,' said Balial. 'He shall decide who it belongs to.'

'Doubtless our good Balial hopes it will be awarded to the most faithful lapdog.'

'Once our mission is done, wizard, you and I will discuss manners.'

'I will be only too glad to give you a lesson in etiquette.'

'Take it,' said Tyrion, struggling feebly to unbuckle his sword belt. 'I would hate to be the cause of any falling out between such good friends.'

'Carefully, Prince Tyrion,' said Vidor, keeping the arrow sighted on him. At that moment a low growl sounded behind him. The manticore had returned. Tyrion whipped the blade from its scabbard. Vidor turned and put an arrow through the manticore's eye with an almost lazy ease. He turned back, already putting another arrow to the string.

Tyrion pointed the blade and invoked its power, putting all of his anger and desperation into the summons. If it harmed the trapped elemental, too bad. He could not risk Alarielle falling into the hands of these four.

A blazing fireball arced towards Vidor. He released his arrow but it passed through the flame en route to Tyrion and was partially deflected, becoming a burning comet disappearing into the trees. The fireball exploded next to

Vidor and Khalion. The blast sent Vidor flying, his hair and clothes on fire. Khalion just stood there, limned by flame. Some sort of protective aura had kept the blast from affecting him. He smirked and pointed a finger. Forked lightning flashed towards the spot where Tyrion stood, but he was already in motion. The smell of ozone warred with the smell of flash-fried flesh.

Tyrion raced towards Khalion, ignoring the stabbing pain in his side from his wound. He knew he needed to finish this fight quickly. Khalion spoke a word of power and Tyrion's limbs became leaden. It was like running through deep mud. He threw Sunfang directly at the mage. It sparked when it hit his protective wards but the metal buried itself deep in his chest.

'Foolish, Prince Tyrion,' said Balial, stepping between them. The strange double-bladed axe whipped towards Tyrion with surprising speed. Balial was a lot faster than his size and musculature would seem to imply. Tyrion only just managed to spring backwards and away.

From the corner of his eye, he saw Amara running towards the Everqueen. Alarielle spoke a word and roots and the stalks of plants erupted from the ground, grasping Amara's legs. The assassin raised her hand and suddenly there was a dagger in it. She drew back her hand and threw it. The blade spun end over end towards the Everqueen, till the heavy-balled handle hit her on the forehead and sent her slumping stunned to the ground.

'Alarielle!' Tyrion shouted, turning towards her. Somehow the roots did not seem to grasp for him, the way they had done her enemies. He reached Amara, who slashed out viciously at him with another knife. He could see the blade of this one was poisoned. He sprang back out of her reach. Still immobilised by the grasping plants, she did what he hoped and threw the knife at him.

It came spinning through the air with eye-blurring speed. It seemed to take forever for the blade to reach him. He plucked it from the air by the handle. With a flick of his wrist he sent it back at her. There was a strange sucking sound as it embedded itself in the jelly of Amara's eye. She screamed and died as the poisoned blade pierced her brain.

A splintering sound nearby told Tyrion that Balial had chopped his way out from the imprisoning roots. He glanced around for a weapon. The only thing he could see was the Moonstaff of Lileath, which lay on the ground near Alarielle. He picked it up, turning just in time to block the sweep of the great axe with it. The wood of the staff caught the haft of the axe. Tyrion found himself breast to breast with the massive dark elf.

Balial pushed and Tyrion was sent tumbling backwards. He only just managed to roll clear as the axe blade chunked into the ground near him. His side felt as if he had been stabbed as he flipped himself to his feet. He gritted his teeth and forced himself to lash out with his staff held at full extension. There was a sound like wood hitting stone when he stuck the nerve cluster in Balial's leg, but the larger elf did not fall, he only grinned. The shock that passed up Tyrion's arm felt like he had just hit armour.

'I am glad you killed them,' said Balial. 'Now all the glory will be mine.'

'You will be joining them soon,' Tyrion said. His tone gave Balial pause.

'You are serious,' Balial said. 'You actually think you can win this. You are an arrogant pup.'

Tyrion lashed out with the tip of the staff again. Balial eluded him easily. His return stroke hit the staff. A normal weapon would have broken, but the Moonstaff was not even chipped. The force of the impact nearly tore it from Tyrion's hand.

Tyrion circled, trying to get to Khalion and Sunfang. The blade stood out of the wizard's chest, still burning. The smell of charred meat filled the air. Balial sprang. Tyrion blocked his blow. The pain in his side was so great he almost passed out. He knew he could not take many more impacts like that. He lashed out at Balial's stomach. The giant ignored the stroke. Again there was a sound like wood hitting rock.

'The Witch King's mages have protected me well,' Balial said. 'My skin is like stone.'

It could not be that way everywhere, Tyrion thought. Otherwise the giant would not be able to move. He eluded another stroke, crouched down, stepped forwards and, wheeling, struck Balial behind the knee. This time the giant fell. Tyrion brought the base of the Moonstaff down on his windpipe. It crunched but Balial did not stop moving. He rose. Still Tyrion thought it would take only minutes for him to suffocate through lack of breath. Lack of air would soon slow him.

Balial brought one blade of his axe slashing across his

own throat. Air wheezed into his lungs through the bleeding wound.

Tyrion aimed a blow at his groin, figuring that would be a part of the body that no elf would want alchemically armoured. Balial parried the blow and lashed out with his booted foot. Tyrion twisted to avoid it, but the kick caught him on the side of his leg and sent him tumbling onto his back. Stars danced before his eyes. The world seemed to turn black. His breath came in gasps.

As if from a long way off, he saw the blade of the great axe come swinging down towards him with all the inevitable force of a meteor strike.

Move, he told himself. His body refused to respond. Pain surged through his side. Waves of nausea and dizziness passed through him. All he had to do was lie here for a few more moments and all that would end.

He began to roll to one side. It was like moving the biggest boulder that had ever existed. It was an exercise in futility. If he dodged this blow there would be another and he would just have to dodge that.

The blade crashed to the ground beside his head, shaving locks of his golden hair. Tyrion lashed out with his boot, catching Balial in the groin. The massive elf groaned and stood still for a moment, paralysed. Tyrion threw himself over to the corpse of Khalion, ripped Sunfang from his charred breast and reeled over to where Balial stood. He lashed out with the blade. Balial parried. Tyrion struck again, knowing he would be parried, but angling his blow so that his burning sword would come down next to Balial's fingers. A look of agony passed over the giant elf's face but he held on to his axe. Tyrion struck again with all his desperate fury.

His blow sheared right through the handle of the axe and hit Balial on the chest. His tunic caught fire but the magically hardened flesh resisted even the bite of Sunfang. Balial was left holding the two bits of the haft. It was as if he was holding two hand axes the wrong way. He tossed one into the air and caught it again so the blade was held outwards. He used the remnants of the other half to desperately block Tyrion's blows. The air wheezed through the great gap in his throat.

Tyrion drove him back, slashing out with desperate strength. Balial reeled back, trying to bring both axe heads into play. Tyrion herded him in the direction he wanted him to go. Balial's foot came down on the corpse of Khalion, sending him stumbling back off balance. Tyrion leaned into a long stroke, sending the point of Sunfang through the wound in Balial's throat and right through the other side, severing vertebrae and nerves. Balial flopped to the ground in his final death spasm.

He looked at Balial, then at Khalion. 'He killed you in the end,' Tyrion said, staggering over to where the Everqueen lay and slumping down beside her.

VIDOR LAY THERE dying. Agony ripped through his burned body. His flesh was blackened and cracked in many places. Pus wept through broken skin. He knew that soon he would join all of those he had killed in death's dark kingdom. There was something he needed to do before that happened. He needed to take revenge on the elf who had killed him. He had one last duty to perform in the service of his master.

He tried to move his blasted fingers. Burned flesh peeled away from the bone. He would have screamed if he could, but the only sound that came out was a whimper. He forced his hand to move despite the pain, and somehow managed to bring it up to the stone amulet hanging from his neck. It was warm from the blast of the fireball with which Tyrion had killed him. He touched it and felt strange magical life within. Some distant spark of the Witch King's magic which would serve his purpose now.

He murmured the words that would bring it to life, forcing them out of his cracked lips with his blackened tongue. He felt the stone move beneath his hand. It grew warmer and more pliant. Within heartbeats, it had become softer. He felt feathers beneath the broken remains of his hand. Even their faint touch sent needles of agony spiking into his flesh. He looked down and saw that where there had been a stone amulet there was now a black raven.

'Vidor. Alarielle. Tyrion. He killed us. Seek your master.' The bird looked at him with preternaturally intelligent eyes, squawked once and then flapped skywards faster than any normal bird should have been able to travel. Vidor lay flat on the ground. He was satisfied that he had done all that he could to take revenge. He would have swapped that and all the gold in the world for a drink of water.

* * *

MALEKITH STUDIED THE raven that strutted backwards and

forth in front of him. The barbarian warlords he had brought to heel looked at him nervously. Enormous anger burned within him. He knew that his assassins had failed, that General Dorian had failed. He knew that one element of his great plan had failed.

The Everqueen was still alive and free. She had been saved by the elf called Tyrion. It was a name he was familiar with. It was a name that most elves of Naggaroth were familiar with. It was a name that N'Kari was certainly familiar with. He sensed a rage even greater than his own burning within the daemon's breast. He knew that if he wanted to, he could put that anger to use. He turned and looked at the Chaos creature.

'Tyrion!' N'Kari said. The venom in his voice could have poisoned an army. Malekith knew that at that moment he and the daemon were totally of one accord.

'You think you could kill him?' Malekith asked.

'You jest. The last time I encountered him only the god Asuryan saved him.'

'He has grown more skilled since then.'

'No amount of skill can save him from my wrath.'

Malekith considered the risks and potential rewards of the situation. If he unleashed the daemon, he was certain that he could kill Tyrion and bring him the head of the Everqueen. On the other hand, if anything went wrong, he would lose the services of the one creature that provided the advantage of mobility to his armies. He would be stuck here on the plains of northern Saphery with only his mirrors to keep him in touch with his distant forces.

It was an enormous gamble.

It would take only a few days for the daemon to hunt down the troublesome elf prince and the ruler he guarded. Everything else was going so very well. His armies were triumphant everywhere. Nothing could stand against them. In the north, the remaining horde of Chaos barbarians was laying waste to an entire kingdom. Nothing could go wrong.

'Go, N'Kari. Use all your power. Slay Tyrion and return with the head of the Everqueen as soon as possible. I will place it on my standard and use it for my war-banner.'

'It will be my very great pleasure,' said N'Kari. For once, the daemon sounded entirely sincere. His shape altered and twisted, becoming once again the monstrous four-armed being that Malekith had first bound into his service. It let out a roar of rage and pleasure and snapped one massive claw together.

'I will take the head of the Everqueen with my own claw.' It turned and loped from his presence without another word. A gate opened in front of it and it vanished.

# CHAPTER NINETEEN

HE WAS ALONE in a darkened land. The sky burned. Strange patterns of elemental fire underlit the clouds. Armies of daemons marched. The greatest flight of dragons ever assembled swept by overhead. Fleets full of mutated monsters ploughed through the dark and stormy seas. From the back of a huge dragon, he watched everything pass.

He was burning up. He walked closer to a flame. He had seen it before. It was the sacred fire within the Shrine of Asuryan. A horde of richly clad elves watched him and laughed. It was odd, he thought. You were supposed to burn when you passed through the flame, not when you reached it.

He was cold, so cold it burned. His teeth chattered. In the distance, the black fangs of a giant mountain range marked the edge of the sane world. Beyond that lay only the Realm of Chaos, a place where daemons walked and the flesh of mortals became warped beyond all recognition. He was marching towards it, a black blade burned on his hip while an army of elves followed. He did not want to turn and look back because he knew he would not like what he saw.

Tyrion sat bolt upright, eyes wide open. Above him the waning moon glared down through the branches of trees. Sweat dripped from his brow. His limbs felt weak. His breathing rasped from his chest.

'What is it?' Alarielle asked, looking over at him. A frown marred her brow. He could tell by the way she stared that she was both worried and frightened.

He tried to rise but his limbs felt weak. He almost collapsed so he let himself slump to the ground again. She moved over to where he lay and placed her hand on his forehead. It felt like it was made of flame.

'You are sick,' she said. 'You are burning up with fever. If you go on like this, it might well kill you. You have put too much stress on your body over the past few days. The last fight was too much. That and the march out of the tainted forest.'

He laughed at that thought. He could not die this way, of a fever in a forest far from the fighting. It did not make sense. Teclis was the sickly one, not him. He told her this.

'Lie quiet,' she said. 'We don't want you raving if the druchii come this way.'

'Maybe they will catch whatever I have and it will kill them,' he said. The thought was oddly amusing.

'Not fast enough,' she said.

'Don't you have any magic for this?' he asked.

'I have been trying to remember, but her memories won't come.'

'Her memories?' Tyrion said. 'Why not yours?'

'We are the same. Sometimes I can remember what she has seen and done. Often I cannot. It takes calm and clarity and time.'

'And you are not calm?' he said, trying to make a joke of it.

'I am alone in a forest surrounded by deadly enemies who want to hand me over to the most evil elf who ever lived. My only companion is sick and raving. Why would I not be calm?'

'Good,' said Tyrion. 'You had me worried for a moment there.'

'Be at peace, Prince Tyrion. I think there may be some herbs around here which will help ease your condition. I will see if I can find some.'

'I am supposed to be protecting you,' Tyrion said. 'That is the champion's duty.'

'So you have finally accepted that you are my champion then?'

'I don't see anyone else here,' Tyrion said. He fell back into hallucinatory dreams.

N'KARI MOVED ALONG the trail away from the tournament grounds, head down, tracking by scent like a hound. It felt good to be wearing something like its normal battle-form again after weeks bound into the form of an elf-maid. The chains were still there, still binding it, but at least it was enjoying some variety. It chafed its protean nature to be confined to one shape for so long.

Of course, it was not as powerful as it should be. The chains bound it to this world but they inhibited its ability to draw on its full powers. It was far stronger than anything it was likely to meet in this pitiful plane, but it had only a fraction of the strength it normally possessed even here. Still, it should be more than enough for the mission it was supposed to perform.

It sniffed again. The trail was an easy one for it to follow. It knew the accursed scent it was following only too well. It was Tyrion, and judging by the faint taint of corruption in it, he had been wounded and poisoned.

Good, he deserved it. Of course, it would be a pity if he died before N'Kari could reach him and enact its vengeance.

There was another descendant of Aenarion with him, a female, one touched by an extraplanar being. This would be the Everqueen. N'Kari had to give Malekith credit for something – this was a task it was truly going to enjoy. It did not mind being bound to complete it in the slightest. The only thing that troubled it was the compulsion to complete the task and return as quickly as possible. This was something it wanted to savour, to derive the maximum possible pleasure from. Well, no doubt it would find a way to do that and still stay within the letter of the command that Malekith had laid down.

For the moment, it was enjoying being free to hunt and prowl. It made a pleasant change from being a mere ferryman for the druchii armies. That thought sent a ripple of fury through N'Kari. At some point, it would find a way to take its vengeance on the Witch King too. With that thought, it bowed down over the trail once more and, scuttling along on multiple limbs, began to follow a trail that might have baffled the most sensitive bloodhound.

'BETTER?' ALARIELLE ASKED. Tyrion nodded and drank more of the bitter tea. The fever had subsided. Strength was returning to his limbs. He felt strong enough to grasp a sword once again.

'You were right,' he said.

'Did you ever doubt it?'

'Yet again, I find myself feeling very foolish,' Tyrion said. Moonlight filtered down through the branches. It was the middle of the night but the drugs in the tea made him feel strangely restless.

'Why?' Alarielle asked.

Tyrion swallowed another bitter mouthful. 'I sometimes think I am very stupid.'

'I don't see it.'

'No? I spent my boyhood thinking I was very stupid,' Tyrion said.

'You?' Alarielle said. 'I find that hard to believe.'

'My father is a mage. My brother is a very powerful and very gifted one. My mother is dead. We lived alone in the mountains except for one old servant. I understood nothing my father and Teclis talked about, and it was so important to them. Nothing I was interested in was important to them.' He smiled a little sadly at the thought. 'I think I was very lonely. It was only when I went to Lothern that things were different. People preferred me to Teclis.'

'Women, you mean.'

'No. I mean people in general. It had never occurred to me that it might be the case. Then my grandfather started talking to me about politics. It was obvious he had ambitions for me. He was one of the Lothern cabal who helped put Finubar on the Phoenix Throne. He thought he could do the same for me. In many ways, he was an evil old elf, but he treated me as if I was someone who mattered.'

'Of course you matter.'

Tyrion looked at her and saw that she was sincere. 'I found out quite young what my real gift was for.'

'What was that?'

'Killing. I have always been good at it. No. I have always excelled at it. And I have always loved it. You were right about that too.'

She looked troubled. 'I was angry when I said that…'

'You were still right. I used to think I wanted to be a hero. I could not be a mage but I could be a mighty warrior. I told myself that many times. The truth was I simply liked killing things. There was a great anger in me, very well hidden. I liked proving I was better, stronger, faster than all the people I killed. It made me feel superior to them. There was no more conclusive proof, was there?'

'I don't know.'

'Believe me, if you stand on a battlefield and look down on the corpse of someone who has tried to kill you, you will be glad, and you will think you were stronger, tougher, or maybe just luckier. No matter. You will never feel more alive. It is certainly how I felt.'

'I think I can understand how you might.'

'And it was a game I was good at. Most of my life has been like that. It's been a game I knew I could win. It stopped being that when the dark elves attacked your court.'

'You have fought them before.'

'I fought them in their own land. I fought them at sea. I helped beat off an occasional raid. I never saw anything like this... I never even believed it was possible.'

'I don't think anyone did. Who would have thought it – druchii in the heart of Avelorn, the Everqueen their captive. Until it happened I would have said it was impossible.'

'I find myself wondering how he did it, how Malekith did it,' Tyrion said. 'He forged this invasion force in secret – he's done that before, it is part of his pattern. He is good at deception. But how is it possible that he managed to infiltrate an army into the heart of our realm without it being detected? I can only think of one instance of this happening before, and...'

The thought hit Tyrion with the force of a warhammer hitting a shield. He had seen something like this before. It had been part of his own life. The sickness and the chase had hidden it from him for a very long time.

'What is it?' Alarielle asked. 'Has the fever returned?'

'I am stupid. I should have seen it before now.'

'Seen what?'

'A daemon once moved regiments of warriors around

Ulthuan. It was hunting me and my brother and others of the line of Aenarion. It laid siege to the Shrine of Asuryan.'

'N'Kari?' she whispered.

'N'Kari.'

Alarielle's face went pale. '*She* remembers N'Kari. The daemon commanded the Rape of Ulthuan in the Age of Aenarion. But surely it must hate Malekith as much as it hates us. He is Aenarion's son.'

Tyrion shrugged. 'I am not sorcerer enough to know what is possible. Perhaps Malekith bound it or made a pact with it. It almost killed me once… it will want to kill you.'

'These are very worrying things, Prince Tyrion.'

'We live in a very worrying world, your serenity.'

They both fell silent for a long time. Tyrion felt tired but could not sleep. Alarielle lay down beside him and closed her eyes. Absent-mindedly he stroked her hair.

N'Kari studied the bodies intently. The corpses were old and they had been left to lie. A few had been bitten and chewed on by massive jaws that N'Kari guessed belonged to Cold Ones. The scent of Tyrion led to this place. It had taken it a little time to pick it up when it crossed the river, but it was using magic as much as its nostrils and it had found the scent again though a hound might not have. It was obvious that Tyrion had passed this way and had been joined again by the Everqueen nearby. It was curious though about what had happened here. It was curious whether the one it hated was even still alive. Fortunately, it knew a way to find out.

It extended a claw and inscribed the sign of Slaanesh in the mud around one of the corpses. It spoke the words of an ancient ritual and felt power flow from it into the body. A sigh emerged not from the mouth but from a gap in the cadaver's chest as the lungs wheezed rotten air. The corpse sat upright and its head swivelled until it looked at N'Kari with empty eye-sockets.

'What do you want with me? Why have you disturbed my soul's dissolution in the realm beyond?'

'I would ask you the three questions allowed by spell and ritual.'

'Ask away then and let me fly back to hell. It is too cold for me here now.'

'Who killed you?'

'An elf with a flaming sword. He stepped out of the night and slaughtered us as if we were children.'

'Why?'

'Because we were enemies, why else?'

'Is his soul with yours in hell now?'

'Not to my knowledge, and I would know for he was my killer.'

'Then go, you are dismissed.'

'I go.'

The corpse slumped and the witchfires died in its eyes. N'Kari laughed long and loud. Its prey was out there still. It was good to know. Now it was only a matter of finding it.

'I FEEL LIKE I have just woken up, like all of my life I have been playing a game and things have only just now become serious.' Tyrion felt the sadness in his voice even as he spoke. He was so weak now he could barely even move. He knew he was dying. He had tried to get her to leave him, but she would not. All he could do now was talk.

'Why? Because you saw your friends killed?' She sounded as if she wanted to sneer or cry or perhaps both. He shook his head.

'I have seen friends die in battle before. I killed one in a duel once. But I have lived in a world where these things have had no real consequence, except to make me admired.'

'I don't follow you.'

'I have raided the coasts of Naggaroth. I have fought against the warriors of Chaos. I have defended our shores against the Norse, but there was never anything at stake before except my own life.'

'Surely that is enough.'

'You would think so, wouldn't you? But it's not.' He paused and stared into the fire for a moment, trying to find the words to say what he meant. They were not easy for him to uncover. 'If Malekith succeeds in what he is doing, our kingdom ends. Our world will be changed irrevocably and not for the better. And his capturing you or killing you makes this more likely to happen. You are the last link to one of our old gods, one of the things that makes us who we are and not druchii. That is why he must destroy you.'

'And why is this important to you?'

'I don't want him to win, and not just in the way I don't want someone to beat me at chess. I don't want him to win because I hate him and his people and what they stand for.'

'And what is that?'

'They are us, without you.'

'And you said you were not a poet. That is a very pretty phrase.'

She tilted her head to one side and looked at him thoughtfully. 'You are not quite what I expected you to be, Prince Tyrion.'

'No one ever is. That is the truth of things.' He started to cough. The world spun. The shadows lengthened, his sight became very dim. He felt as if he had only the slightest grip upon his life, as if the smallest breeze could separate his spirit from his body.

She reached down and stroked his brow. Her hand felt very cold. She pulled it away as if he burned. She seemed to have come to a decision. She closed her eyes and murmured what might have been a spell or a prayer. Her face twisted as if she were in agony or undergoing some great internal struggle.

TYRION LOOKED UP at Alarielle.

She was not there. Someone else was. Someone much older and calmer and altogether more majestic. The spell that normally surrounded her was much stronger. He had the impression of other elf-women superimposed on her, many of them, all of whom resembled her but were not quite the same. When she moved, she moved differently as if a stranger were wearing her body.

'Who are you?' Tyrion asked.

'We are the Everqueen.' He did not need to ask why she used the plural.

'Where is Alarielle?'

'She is with us.'

Tyrion knew he was somehow looking at a composite of every personality of every elf woman who had ever been the Everqueen and upon something more, something tinged with divine power. Even as he watched they seemed to go in and out of focus. An expression of pain flickered across her face.

'What's wrong?'

'Our land is in pain. We feel it. It disrupts the flows of power. It makes it difficult to think. This vessel is unprepared to receive us.'

'Can you help us?' Tyrion asked, thinking that if Alarielle could tap into the power of the goddess for even a moment, she might be able to do something that would aid them greatly.

'The wound,' she said. 'Let us see it.'

She staggered like someone imperfectly in control of her body over to where he stood and reached out to touch the wound. Despite himself he flinched as her fingers found it, but he felt no pain. Her touch was cool and oddly soothing.

'Can you help us?'

'Our daughter is too young and too untrained to take the full brunt of our power. The Cold King has chosen his moment too well.'

'Can you help us?'

'Hush. This wound is a vile one filled with poison and powered by potent runes. The blade that did this was wound round with foul spells.'

The Everqueen closed her eyes. She murmured something. The coolness spread from her fingers. The wound pained him less although it would not close. It became less black. He felt as if he had some more energy.

'It is the best we can do. You must find help soon or you will die.'

The Everqueen slumped like a puppet with her strings cut. 'Alarielle!' Tyrion said. He did not have the strength to catch her as she fell to the ground.

N'KARI LOOMED OVER the dead bodies of the Witch King's chosen assassins. The stink of magic hung over the battlefield. It had been unleashed here and quite strongly by the standards of mortals. It was enough for N'Kari to recreate what had happened. Tyrion had been more than a match for Malekith's pet killers. The boy had improved over the last century. His wound had become worse though. He smelled as if he was rotting away inside. Fortunately, he was close now. It would not take long to overhaul him and the Everqueen.

Tireless as ever, N'Kari put its head down and followed the trail. It moved with the speed of the storm wind. Lust for revenge made its bounding stride all the faster.

TECLIS FROZE. HE suddenly felt the closeness of a being of terrifying daemonic power. He sensed its psychic spoor as it moved past him. In the distance he could hear the panicked shrieks of dark elf soldiers as they too felt its presence. He turned to Alanor and said, 'Run!'

The ranger looked at him, bewildered. 'Get away from me or you will die!' Teclis said. Something in his tone must have compelled belief because Alanor turned and ran. Teclis gathered his power to him and waited for N'Kari to arrive.

It would not take long. He cursed. They had finally made their way through the hordes of druchii. His brother was so close he could feel it. It was all going to be in vain unless he defeated the daemon.

N'KARI LAUGHED ALOUD. It sensed the presence of the wizard who had banished it over a century before. Of course, he would be looking for his brother. Briefly N'Kari considered turning aside and swatting the troublesome mage, but it found the compulsion laid on it by the Witch King was strong. Not that it mattered. It was close to Tyrion now. All it had to do was wait for a few moments and Teclis would come upon his dead twin. Then N'Kari would take its revenge on him.

TECLIS BRACED HIMSELF for an attack that never came. The daemon moved past him and on into the woods, its pace suddenly so slow that Teclis could almost keep up. Teclis understood what that meant. Tyrion and the Everqueen must be close. That was what N'Kari had been sent to find. It was the only thing that made sense.

Teclis limped on, pursuing the daemon as quickly as he could.

* * *

'THANK YOU,' TYRION said. He felt better since the Everqueen had worked her magic on his wound. The pain had lessened and he could move again. It still felt as if his strength was slowly leeching away, but at least he had some.

'I did not do anything,' Alarielle said. 'She did.'

'I thought she was part of you.'

'I think I am part of her. At least that is what it feels like when she manifests.'

She looked a little frightened when she spoke of it. Perhaps because of the lessening of his pain, his mood had lightened. The woods looked bright and sunny. A bright red bird fluttered from branch to branch above them. The sun looked golden. War and death might as well have been a hundred leagues away.

'What is it like?' he asked, genuinely curious.

'Like drowning,' she said.

'That does not sound pleasant.'

'They say a drowning person relaxes and enjoys it towards the end, after they give up the struggle.'

'Is that what it's like?'

'The Everqueen is so big and I am so small. I don't think this was the way it was meant to be.'

'I don't understand.'

'Neither do I. There is a process of transition when the power moves from one Everqueen to the next. It can take years before it's complete.'

'We don't have years,' said Tyrion.

'I know, and it makes me feel so... useless.'

'Why does it take years?'

'I don't know. I don't think the elven mind was meant to encompass what the Everqueen is – a god, a composite being, an elemental power. They are all in there, you know…'

'Who?'

'All of the ones who went before me. My mother. I see her sometimes, in my dreams. Sometimes when I am awake and I feel the power bubbling up in me. I think I am going to go mad…'

She looked very pained now. Tyrion was sorry he had started the conversation. It was not at all what he had expected. He had never thought there would be such a price to pay to become what she was. 'You are not mad.'

'But I may go mad. There are rituals to be undergone when you become the Everqueen. Hundreds of them. They stretch out over a period of years.'

'And you have not undergone all of them.'

'Not even the tiniest fraction.'

'Does it matter so much?'

'Yes. My tutors explained it to me. They are intended to accustom me to being the Everqueen and the Everqueen to being me.'

'I always thought you were one and the same.'

She shook her head. '*She* is a living goddess, a spirit, a power that passes from one host to another. I am a vessel. She is the power that flows into me. When one vessel dies, another one must be found.'

'Or what?'

'We don't know. It has never happened. Not in all of

elven history. The power has always passed from mother to daughter.'

'And all descended from the original Everqueen.'

She nodded again. 'I think I am the anchor. If I die, the power is lost. The spirit will have no way into the world.'

'The Shrine of Asuryan...' Tyrion said. 'You are like the Shrine of Asuryan.'

'What?'

'My brother and I were there once. He reached out and touched the god, or perhaps it touched him, I don't know. He told me that it was the only place in the world where such a thing could happen. That is why the Phoenix Kings have to be crowned there.'

'And you think that the daughters of the line of Astarielle are like the gateway that exists on the Blessed Island, a sort of mobile place of power?'

'I am no sorcerer. I don't know about these things. I am just guessing.'

'You are guessing very well. That is exactly the way it is supposed to work. It is a sacred mystery. You must become my champion now. You know this.' Her voice told him she was joking, but there was nothing here to joke about.

'Malekith knows this too.'

'You think he planned his attack now, knowing I would be weak?'

'If he wanted to ensure the elves had one less god, he is going about it the right way.'

'That is sacrilegious.'

'We are talking about an elf who took it upon himself

to walk into the Flame of Asuryan without any protection, who once attempted to destroy all of Ulthuan. I don't think the idea would trouble him too much.'

'You speak as if you understand him.'

'I am trying to. I am trying to understand what is happening here.'

'It might not be the wisest of things, trying to think like the Witch King. He is almost seven thousand years old. I doubt that he is sane as we understand sanity.'

'A few minutes ago you were telling me that you doubted your own...'

'That is why you should listen to me,' she said, with a strange, sad smile. He thought about what it must be like to share your body with a god.

Something she said came back to him. 'Do you have their memories? All of them, all of the previous Everqueens?'

'*She* has them. I can sometimes remember them. Why?'

'That must be a heavy burden,' he said, not wanting to say what was really on his mind, not yet anyway.

'Prince Tyrion, you sound almost sympathetic.'

'I find you more sympathetic than I used to,' he said. 'And I am grateful to *her*.'

'Don't become like everyone else,' she said. 'I have enough worshippers.'

'What?'

'At least you don't give me *the look* – of adoration.'

'I would have thought you enjoyed it.'

'I did at first, but it gets odd and lonely after a time. I am not *her*. I am just the person *she* speaks through. She weaves her spell around me so that people will listen. For whatever reason, you at least can see *me*... and I am grateful for that.'

She reached out and took his hand. He looked up into her eyes. 'So am I,' he said. She leaned forwards. They were close enough to kiss.

Out of the corner of his eye, he caught sight of something. He pushed her to one side into the undergrowth beside the path.

'Quickly,' he said. 'Get out of sight.'

# CHAPTER TWENTY

N'Kari could sense the presence of more of the blood of Aenarion. One of the scents belonged to Tyrion, the warrior who had done so much to help defeat it over a century ago. The other scent belonged to a female. It was a subtle scent and there was the suggestion of great power to it. Somewhere, deeply hidden, nearby there was a deity. It was not quite as warlike or as potent as Asuryan but it was, or it could be, very powerful.

This made N'Kari wary. It moved carefully closer, adjusting its shape to keep it camouflaged among the dense undergrowth. It padded softly closer, sniffing the air and readying itself for anything. Tyrion's scent was even more sickly and tainted. The warrior was very ill. Of course, it did not matter very much because his life was just about to come to an end.

N'Kari was pleased by the fact that it was not only going to be able to carry out its orders for Malekith but take revenge on its greatest enemies in this world at the same time. It could sense the presence of Teclis close behind it but somewhat muffled as if by powerful, deceptive magic. It seemed that fate or the dark gods had conspired to give it the perfect opportunity for vengeance.

It was close enough now to peer out from the bushes and see the pair as they sat by a fire. They looked comfortable, which was also a good thing. It would take great pleasure in tormenting them; these things always went better if the victims felt secure to begin with.

It listened to the conversation for a while. It was the usual mortal trivia, nothing very interesting to one of its age and predisposition. It knew that it could waste a great deal of time waiting for them to say something that piqued its interest.

Instead it moved farther away into the undergrowth, changed its shape again and went crashing through the bushes as loudly as it could, determined to get their attention and unsettle them before it finally took its vengeance. It wanted to draw this moment out, to savour it and feel the fear building in the minds of its prey. It laughed softly to itself. It had waited for this for a very long time.

'What was that?' Alarielle asked. Tyrion forced himself upright and his head spun, dizziness threatening to overwhelm him. He felt sick as he had never felt in his life. And he felt something else, something that was in its own way as bad as the sickness. He sensed the presence of something evil. A faint, sickly-sweet aroma that reminded him of perfume. It also brought to mind something else that he had scented a long time ago.

'I don't know, but I don't like it one little bit,' he said. He forced himself to his feet and stood there swaying. A worried expression fluttered across Alarielle's face. He knew that he was the cause of it, not whatever she had heard out there in the darkness.

That was wrong. There was something that they needed to be afraid of out there. It worried him that she had sensed that before he did. He leaned forwards and threw some more sticks on the fire although he already suspected that whatever was stalking them was not some beast that was going to be frightened of flame.

The twigs caught fire. The sap inside them sputtered. Sparks drifted upwards. He looked around, trying to penetrate the shadows with his vision. Something big was moving out there in the wood. It sounded as large as a bear and it was making so much noise now that it was almost as if it wanted to be detected. Tyrion turned his head to look at the point from which the sound came, and at that moment all of the noise ceased. Tyrion drew his sword, the flames blazing along its length sending shadows dancing away. It just seemed to make the night all the darker.

The poisoned wound pained him deeply. It was as if his whole side had been sprayed with acid.

'I think it's gone now,' said Alarielle. She sounded more hopeful than convinced. Tyrion shook his head. He suspected that whatever it was that was out there was creeping stealthily closer.

Perhaps though it was watching them and getting ready to spring. He turned around just so that he could be rid of the crawling sensation between his shoulder blades. There was nothing there that he could see. No sound came from the woods. Just the simple movement made him feel even dizzier. Alarielle rose now. She held the Moonstaff of Lileath in her hands, clutching it so tightly that her knuckles were white. She looked around as well in the opposite directions from the ones that Tyrion was looking in.

The sounds started again, receding into the distance, crashing away into the darkness. If he had been healthy, Tyrion would have investigated, but he knew that it would be folly to go out into the darkness and look for a creature the size of a bear in his present condition. He gestured for Alarielle to sit down again, looked around once more, sheathed Sunfang and forced himself to remain upright.

'What will you do once we reach our people?' Alarielle asked. There was an aura of false cheerfulness about her that Tyrion disliked. It was as if she believed that he was not going to live to reach their people and wanted to pretend otherwise. He supposed he could not really blame her for that. Her position was not a cheerful one under the circumstances.

'I think I will have a bath,' Tyrion said. It took all his willpower to stand upright and speak. 'It seems like a lifetime since I've had one. The closest thing I've had to a wash was when I fell in the river when we were swinging over it.'

It seemed like a very long time ago that he had done that. The memory of it made him laugh for some reason. She joined in although her laughter was soft and sad. 'That seems like a lifetime ago to me,' she said. 'I did not really know you then.'

He looked at her across the fire. 'Nor I, you. I thought you were a spoiled princess back then.'

'And you don't now?'

He shook his head. 'Find some noble knight to be your champion.'

'I am not sure a noble knight could have got me this far.'

'It was you who brought me this far,' Tyrion said. 'I would not be here now if it was not for you.'

'We did this together. And we will finish it together.' She leaned forwards and touched his hand. Her touch felt very cold, but that was perhaps only because he felt as if he was burning up.

She leaned closer to him until their faces were almost touching. Her lips were slightly parted. Again Tyrion felt the urge to kiss her.

'That you most assuredly will do,' said a voice from the darkness. 'I will see to it.'

A chill ran down Tyrion's spine. He had last heard that voice over a century before but he could never forget it. It haunted his darkest nightmares. He looked up. Emerging from the forest was a massive four-armed figure. One of those arms ended in a monstrous claw. A faint wave of musk hit him. He realised that it must have been there all the time, and it probably explained Alarielle's actions. He knew the powerful aphrodisiac effect it had on others.

'N'Kari,' he said, forcing himself to hold his blade level, even though he was so weak he could barely stand.

'I am glad you remember me,' said the daemon, beckoning in an awful parody of an exotic dancer trying to entice one of her audience. 'I certainly remember you, blood of Aenarion.'

Tyrion knew that his life was over. Even at his best, he would have been no match for this daemon. Now, as things stood, sick and weary, there was almost nothing he could do that would even slow N'Kari down. Without taking his eyes off the daemon, he said, 'Run!'

'Please do,' said N'Kari. 'I will enjoy it all the more. Once I have killed this one, it will give me great pleasure to hunt you down. I would be very grateful to you if you could prolong this for as long as possible.'

Tyrion drew his blade. The flame burned much brighter than it normally would, as if somehow it recognised N'Kari and what it stood for.

'You're somewhat better armed than the last time I met you,' N'Kari said. 'That should make this slightly more enjoyable as well.'

'I see you are wearing chains,' Tyrion said. 'You were your own master, the last time we met. Now it seems you're someone's slave.'

'I will have my revenge on the one who bound me, just as I will have my revenge upon you,' N'Kari said. 'My vengeance will be as terrible as it is inevitable.'

'What is it like being a servant? I have heard that the

followers of Slaanesh enjoy submission. How do you find it?'

'If you're trying to convince me to initiate you into its pleasures, it will not work. I simply do not have the time. I must kill you and I must kill her and then I must return to plotting my revenge.'

'It seems to me that you spend more time talking about revenge than taking it.'

'And it seems to me that you're very keen to meet your death. Do you really suffer so much? Does your wound pain you so?'

'Run!' Tyrion said to Alarielle. 'I will hold it for as long as I can.'

'I am not going anywhere,' she said. 'I would not give this the pleasure of seeing me run. Nor will I leave you.'

'How touching,' N'Kari said. 'Don't you realise that your lover wishes to die? He cannot live with that wound and he wishes to leave this world heroically. I am almost tempted to let him live and watch him die in slow agony. It has certain advantages. He can witness what I do to you before he goes. Do not be afraid. There will be as much pleasure as there is pain in it for you, and you will come to enjoy both before the end.'

Tyrion sprang forwards. Sunfang flashed through a blazing arc. He put all his remaining strength and speed into the blow. N'Kari evaded it easily and laughed.

'It seems I have touched a nerve,' it said. Alarielle spread her hands and spoke a word. A wave of greenish energy flowed towards the daemon. N'Kari's hands made the gestures of a counterspell and neutralised it.

'Pitiful,' said N'Kari. 'An apprentice could do better.'

Tyrion moved in close and struck again while the daemon was distracted. Sunfang bit into its flesh. There was a sound of sizzling as the skin burned away. A faint sweet aroma filled the air. The daemon lashed out with its fist and batted Tyrion away like an elf tossing a small animal across a room. Tyrion fell badly. Blackness swept over him. He tried to force himself to rise but could not.

He knew that the end had come.

FROM THE SHADOWS of the undergrowth, Teclis resisted the urge to intervene. Striking before he was ready would merely result in all of their deaths. Instead he studied N'Kari. The daemon looked very much as he remembered it. Of course, there was no way that he would ever forget his encounter with the greater daemon of Slaanesh. There was something odd about the creature. It was bound not just by spells but by some ancient artefact grafted onto its wrist, a thing almost as potent as the daemon was.

It radiated an aura of awesome power. Teclis did not recognise the workmanship. He knew it was not made by an elf. Perhaps, judging by the runes upon it, it had been made by a Slann or perhaps even one of the creatures that had ruled the Slann back in ancient times.

All that he knew was that those chains had been made in a fashion that not even Caledor could duplicate. They were not only potent enough to bind a greater daemon indefinitely but they had other effects as well. They helped to maintain the presence of N'Kari in this plane of existence.

Normally, entities as powerful as greater daemons could not maintain a physical form for any great length of time except when the winds of magic blew much stronger than they normally did. Normally, only at times of great peril, such as when the northern warp gates were open, could they do so. The last time that had happened was during the reign of Aenarion.

No, there was something woven into those chains that bound the greater daemon. Perhaps he could use that to his advantage.

If he was going to do so, he was going to need to do it quickly. N'Kari was advancing upon Alarielle with something more than merely killing her on its mind. Tyrion, like the idiot he was, was trying to fight. Both of them were going to be killed very quickly unless Teclis intervened.

The daemon radiated an aura of awesome power, but not quite so much as it had the last time Teclis had encountered it. The wizard was sure that that was not simply his imagination or a bad memory. N'Kari was much weaker than it should have been. Teclis suspected that that too had something to do with those strange chains.

If you're going to bind a greater daemon, it made sense to bleed off some of its power. It would make the act of controlling it much easier. Such a creature would still be powerful enough to make a terrible servant or weapon, even if it was not quite so strong as it would normally have been.

There was something familiar about the spell on those

chains. Something about it reminded him of the locking spell that had controlled the door back at the Slann city of Zultec, where Tyrion and he had found Sunfang. It would be easy enough to undo that spell and release the chains, although that seemed like madness. At that point N'Kari would be completely unbound and able to bring all of its power into focus. There would only be a few moments where the daemon would be vulnerable and perhaps Teclis could banish it.

Even at the best of times though, such a spell was not without risks. All Teclis knew was that it was theoretically possible. He had never summoned a greater daemon. He had never bound a greater daemon. He had never banished one either. He was familiar with the spells. He had studied them in the White Tower a long time ago, when he had first gone to study there. The masters had allowed him, for they had known as well as he did that one day he was going to have to face N'Kari again. Now that day had come. The question was – was he ready for it?

There was only one way to find out. N'Kari had almost reached Alarielle. It had stretched out its huge arms like a lover and was herding her towards a great tree. Tyrion lay on the ground and did not move.

Teclis spoke a word of power. A bolt of magical energy hurtled towards the daemon. It screeched. For a moment, it seemed to be outlined in the fire and lightning. It turned to face Teclis and roared.

'It seems I have got your attention,' Teclis said. 'Depart now and I will spare you.'

The daemon said, 'Little Teclis – my, how you have grown!'

'I see you have not lost your taste for melodramatic dialogue,' Teclis said. He made his voice sounded utterly bored even while he studied the locking spell on the chains. With his magesight he could see the intricate pattern woven into the structure.

'It seems your skill at magic has greatly improved,' N'Kari said. The daemon was coming closer, its movements reminiscent of the stalking step of a great predator. Teclis knew that if it got within springing distance he was dead. He did not have Tyrion's lightning reflexes. There was no way he could avoid the fatal strike of those great claws.

Teclis worked the spell of opening, using his powers to undo the intricate magical locking mechanism on the chains of binding. They fell away to the ground. N'Kari spread its claws wide and laughed. It seemed to expand with a new influx of power and evil.

'You have made a mistake, little Teclis.'

Teclis knew he had only one chance. He spoke the words of banishment. N'Kari's outline wavered. Without the chains to anchor it, it was prey to instability once more. Teclis manipulated the flows of magic around him, adding to the resistance of normal reality, aiding it in its attempts to expel N'Kari back to its natural home.

'No!' it cried, realising what was happening. It strode towards Tyrion, determined to take its revenge on one of the brothers.

Teclis invoked another offensive spell. An enormous blast of magical energy ravened through his body and washed over the daemon, limning it with witchfire.

N'Kari faded away, still screaming.

MALEKITH FELT A sudden pain inside his head. What was happening, he wondered? Had death finally overtaken him in the moment of his greatest triumph? Had the Flame of Asuryan and the spells woven into his armour finally failed? Was this what death was like? He was surprisingly untroubled by it.

The faces of his followers turned towards him. He realised that he was swaying and that he had raised one massive, gauntleted fist to his forehead. He forced himself to stand upright and assume his usual, dominant posture. He was not dead.

It dawned on him what it was. The sense of linkage with the daemon N'Kari was gone. Something had happened. Had the daemon finally broken the spell that bound it? Or was this something else entirely?

He paused to consider these questions. He did not think that the daemon could possibly have broken the spell that bound it to this world. Even if it had, the chances were that instability would cause the daemon to vanish back into the Realm of Chaos.

If not, Malekith realised that he had a very big problem on his hands. An angry Keeper of Secrets was not something that anyone wanted to have hunting them. Which brought another terrifying thought to mind – if the daemon had not managed to break the spell binding it, someone had banished it from this world or suborned it to their own purposes. This spoke of magic of the highest level and the most frightening level of power.

He cursed the Everqueen and the land of Avelorn. It did not seem to matter what he attempted – it foundered among the forests of that dreadful place. Another thought filtered into his mind. Without N'Kari, his armies really were reduced to the same level of mobility as his enemies. He could no longer reinforce them using the daemon's transportation magic. He had taken a gamble by despatching the daemon to seek the Everqueen and it had failed – now he was going to have to pay the price. Swiftly he made a few calculations. The war was still winnable. His forces still enjoyed an overwhelming advantage against a surprised and demoralised enemy.

He had contingency plans. He always did. It seemed like he was going to have to regroup and get ready. The war was going to take longer than he thought, but he could still win it. He was going to have to assemble his forces into one mighty sledgehammer and use it to smash the high elves once and for all. He had his own force. He had these tribes of barbarians. He would hunt down the Everqueen himself.

# CHAPTER TWENTY-ONE

'I AM VERY grateful to see you, brother,' Tyrion said. 'And I'm sure that's not something you hear anyone say very often.'

He looked spent, Teclis thought, hovering on the very edge of death. It was a precipice he could fall over at any moment. It was unsurprising. That last blow from N'Kari would have killed a normal elf. The broken ribs he sensed were easy enough to repair. It was something else that troubled Teclis. A dark and evil magic was present within his twin.

'Hush,' Teclis said.

Alarielle hunkered down beside him. 'Thank you,' she said. Teclis looked at her. She was beautiful and her beauty was enhanced by a variety of subtle and complex magics. He sensed another presence within her. He fought to keep her glamour from swaying him.

Teclis spoke a spell of sleep, and Tyrion closed his eyes.

'How was he wounded?' Teclis asked.

'With a poisoned witch elf blade,' Alarielle said. 'He has borne that wound since we left the tournament grounds. I am surprised he is still alive.'

'Then you do not know my brother. He is too stubborn to die.'

'Yes, he is.' Teclis was not surprised by the emotion in her voice. Tyrion always had that effect on women. It appeared not even the Everqueen was immune. 'I tried to heal him, but my grasp of magic is not sure.'

'You might well have killed him.'

'I did not have much choice. He was going to die anyway.'

She was looking at him warily now, measuring him and judging him. It was something he was quite used to from other elves.

'Let's take a look at this wound,' he said, cutting away the area around the tunic with his athame and removing the improvised bandages. The stink of rotting flesh and something else hit him. He looked at the wound. At its centre it was the colour of raw liver, and it was black round the edges. The smell was enough to make him gag. 'I am surprised he is still able to walk. All most people would be able to do in his condition would be lie on the ground and moan.'

'Can you do anything?' Alarielle asked. A frown marked that perfect brow. Long-suppressed tears glittered at the corner of her eyes.

'Let's see, shall we,' said Teclis. He fumbled in his pack and found the small jar of diamond-glass crystal he was looking for. The contents writhed within it. They were maggots of a very special sort. Teclis took them from the jar and placed them on the wound. They inched their way out onto the poisoned flesh and with a horrible slurping sound began to devour it, turning from a sickly yellow to a rotted black as they did so. They ate their own weight in corrupted meat and grew larger and more bloated as they did so, growing from the size of a pared fingernail to the size of a finger in a matter of minutes. Tyrion groaned and stirred in his sleep, but Teclis's spell held him.

The surface of the wound was soon cleared and the edges eaten away until there was only pink natural flesh and seeping blood visible. One by one Teclis took the maggots away, impaled on the point of his athame. They crawled over the blade and tried to bite his hand with their lamprey-like mouths. He dropped them on the ground and incinerated them with magic on a small bonfire made from the stained bandages. A hideous stench arose that was even worse than the smell of the wound.

The wound looked clear. He invoked a forensic spell and studied his brother. The flow of life energy was weak and there were areas of taint and damage in his aura. Teclis wove magic that would cleanse those areas and start them repairing themselves. He spoke wave after wave of spells intended to neutralise poison and cleanse disease. For hours he worked, minutely, carefully, with total concentration and utter care. When he was certain he had done all he could, he spoke the spells that would cause the wounded flesh to knit and then put new bandages in place.

'The healers at my mother's court could have done no better,' Alarielle said.

'I became something of an expert on medical magic at an early age,' Teclis said. 'I have been my own worst patient.'

'Will he live?'

Teclis considered the matter as dispassionately as he could. His brother was very pale and looked more dead than alive. It was shocking to see someone who had always blazed with health looking so sick.

'I do not know,' Teclis said. 'All we can do is wait.'

TECLIS SAT LOOKING over the fire at the Everqueen. She stared into the flames and then at Tyrion and then back at the flames again. Teclis brewed drugs and medicines that he thought might be needed in a small crucible before transferring them to alembics.

'It was only a few hours ago we were talking about what we would do when we got out of this,' she said. 'It seems like a lifetime ago now.'

'Life is like that,' Teclis said. 'Things that seemed permanent vanish in an instant.'

'Nothing has seemed permanent since the druchii attacked us. We have lived a heartbeat from death for a week.'

Teclis looked at Tyrion. 'I am sure he would have enjoyed that. He always loved danger.'

'Don't talk about him like that. As if he were already gone.'

Teclis simply stared at her. She was not used to being

looked at that way, he could tell. 'You look like him,' she said at last.

'You are the first person ever to tell me that. All my life I have lived in the shadow of his good looks.'

Alarielle laughed softly. 'I meant you look at me like him. As if you see a person and not the Everqueen.'

Teclis cocked his head to one side. 'That is interesting. He never had any gift for seeing through magic. I can see the glamours that surround you. I doubt even one in ten mages could. They are fantastically subtle.'

'I don't think he saw any spells at all. He simply reacted against them. I think they made him dislike me, to begin with.'

'Tyrion never disliked anybody in his life. He was… he is very amiable.'

'I did not think so when I met him.'

'I am surprised. Women usually find him very charming.'

'Lots of women?' She sounded jealous and curious at once. Teclis nodded. He felt oddly touched and he was not sure why. He rose from beside the fire and went to check his wards. When he came back the Everqueen was sitting beside his brother, running her hand through his hair.

'What are we going to do?' she asked.

'We can't move him now,' Teclis said. 'We are just going to have to wait here.'

'What if the druchii come?'

'I will deal with them,' Teclis said.

'Can you deal with an army?' she asked.

'I guess we will find out,' he said.

'You don't lack confidence, do you?'

'It is a recent development. I find I have a talent for warfare. I used to assume he was the only one in the family who did.'

'I can see the power in you. Or the Everqueen can. It blazes like a forest on fire.'

'Let's hope I don't have to do that – set the forest on fire!'

'But you will if you have to, won't you?'

'Indubitably, yes.' Teclis wove spells of concealment around them, and they settled down to wait. 'If it would save you both.'

'I've felt better,' Tyrion said. His eyes were open. His voice sounded weak. He was, however, still alive, and these were the first words he had spoken in days.

'I am glad to hear that you are still capable of complaining,' Teclis said.

'It's odd. I thought N'Kari had appeared. It turned out to be you. Not much difference I suppose.'

'The daemon was here,' said Alarielle. 'Your brother banished it.'

'Not for the first time,' said Tyrion. 'It seems it's becoming a habit.'

'I arrived just as you were preparing to make a heroically foolish last stand.'

'You saved me a bit of effort, but I would have beaten him in the end,' Tyrion said. 'I feel fairly confident in saying that.'

'Illness has not increased your intelligence,' said Teclis.

'Nice hat,' Tyrion said. 'We interrupted you on your way to a fancy-dress party, I take it.'

'It is the War Crown of Saphery, worn by defenders of the wizards' realm since time immemorial,' said Teclis.

'It's the right size for your head, and it hides the point your skull comes to, so I suppose it has some benefits.'

'You don't seem surprised that I found you.'

'You have a habit of showing up when least expected.'

'How did you find us?' Alarielle asked.

'It wasn't easy,' Teclis said.

'Don't ask him,' Tyrion said. 'He's a wizard. He will just look mysterious and talk about divinations and the winds of magic.'

'I followed the trail of corpses you left across Avelorn, if truth be told,' Teclis said. Tyrion had fallen asleep again.

'At least I got the last word,' Teclis murmured. 'That happens little enough.'

'That really is the War Crown, isn't it?' Alarielle asked.

'I am surprised you recognised it. It has not been out of the tower for centuries. Most people think it's a legend.'

'*She* recognises it,' Alarielle said. '*She* has seen it many times. It was always worn by heroes.'

'Not this time, I am afraid,' said Teclis. 'They made the mistake of giving it to me.'

'I don't think they made a mistake.'

'That remains to be seen,' said Teclis, reddening. 'What is that staff you are carrying?'

'It is the Moonstaff of Lileath,' Alarielle said. 'I rescued it from the cache in the Winterwood Palace.'

'I wish I had had it when I was fighting N'Kari,' Teclis said. 'It is a powerful magical amplifier. Do you mind if I look at it?'

Alarielle handed the staff over. It fitted Teclis's hand as if it had been moulded for it. He studied the ancient workmanship and the runes inscribed in the shaft. Power flowed through it and around it and he instinctively knew how to use it. With great reluctance, he handed it back to the Everqueen.

'A wondrous thing,' he said.

'Yes,' she said. 'Although I have not been able to make it work.'

'It was intended for certain types of magic.'

'It carries the blessing of the moon goddess, so that is not surprising. She is a patron of spellworkers.'

Teclis said, 'I could tell.' He settled down again by the fire. He was starting to feel restless, stuck here in one place while all around armies of druchii were on the move. Alarielle watched him thoughtfully across the flames.

TECLIS STUDIED THE chains that had once bound the Keeper of Secrets. They were a potent artefact indeed, ancient, powerful and wrought with complex, sinister magic. Power flowed through them still. There was a sense of presence to them, one not simply associated with the daemon.

He concentrated on them fully, extending his magesight to the point where he no longer looked upon the world of light and shadow, only the flows of magic. He saw the glittering souls of those near him, and the gigantic, deeply hidden power that worked through Alarielle. He saw the whirlpools of magic that vanished into the chains and flowed out again somewhere else. He reached out with a divinatory spell and touched them, and in a lightning-like flash made sharp, shocking contact.

Suddenly he was elsewhere, in a land of cold grey skies, of ice and fire, where glaciers flowed from the north, and lava pits spurted burning rock. Before him stood a massive armoured figure. It turned to look at him with cold, cruel eyes. Teclis knew at once who he faced. He had made a mistake. The chains were still connected with N'Kari's binder, the Witch King of Naggaroth.

Malekith looked at him. Teclis felt himself being judged by a being older than kingdoms, only little less than a god. Malekith had walked the world in the time of Aenarion. He was one of the oldest sentient beings on the planet, perhaps the mightiest. The Witch King's mere presence made Teclis acknowledge his own insignificance.

He forced himself to meet Malekith's gaze and smile.

The eyes surprised him. There was a sadness and a loneliness in them that shocked Teclis, mingled with an astonishing, rapacious lust to dominate was a sense of black wisdom. Most of all there was pride – the pride of one who had sought to emulate a living god and could not admit that he had failed, had been judged and found wanting. Malekith was a titan who had once defied the will of the gods and defied it still even though the struggle was hopeless.

Teclis had expected to feel hatred and fear. What he had not expected to feel was pity.

'You look like him,' Malekith said in a voice like a brazen gong being smote deep underground. There was power and assurance in that voice, a timbre acquired from aeons of chanting time-lost spells and bellowing commands across long-forgotten battlefields. It rang with malice and hatred and something else it took Teclis a moment to recognise – loneliness.

There was no need to ask who *he* was. Malekith could mean only one being, his father, Aenarion.

'You do not,' Teclis forced himself to say. It took an effort of will comparable to invoking the most recalcitrant elemental. He made it sound effortless. Nothing else would do.

Malekith laughed, and Teclis felt himself lashed by the Witch King's bitterness and scorn. 'I can see why Urian liked you, little cripple. You are somewhat alike.'

'Urian?'

'You know him by a different name, but no matter. He told me about you, Teclis.'

'I have banished your daemon,' Teclis said. 'You will no longer be able to move so freely around Ulthuan.' Teclis felt he had somehow caught the Witch King's interest. Malekith was not used to being challenged. His curiosity was piqued. He was like a great cat amusing itself with a small mouse before the kill.

'So you have learned that secret, have you?' Malekith said. 'And defeated the Keeper of Secrets again. Hell will be filled with its screams of frustration this day.'

Malekith sounded amused. Teclis was surprised to

discover he had a sense of humour. He noticed something else in the air, a psychic scent he had encountered before; it came from Malekith. It was the faintest trace of the Flame of Asuryan. Of course, Teclis thought. It still burned within the flesh of the tyrant, must have done so since his attempt at apotheosis all those millennia ago. The merest beginning of an idea occurred to Teclis. Perhaps there was a way to defeat Malekith using magic, if only he could get close enough.

'Leave Ulthuan,' Teclis said. 'You can do yourself only harm here.'

'It is not for you to tell me what to do, little cripple.'

'If you do not, this little cripple will give you a lesson in using magic.'

Malekith laughed. Teclis did not flinch. He had endured a lifetime of mockery from his fellow elves. He had schooled himself to endure it.

'You do not lack for confidence, I will give you that,' Malekith said. 'There is power in you, youth, power such as I once saw in Caledor, but it takes more than power to make a wizard. It takes centuries of experience and a willingness to face the deepest, darkest secrets of the universe.'

That caught Teclis's attention, as any mention of magical secrets always did. He thrust his curiosity to one side. 'Perhaps, but to achieve victory, it only takes knowledge of one spell, if that spell is the correct one.'

'Do not let your triumphs over N'Kari make you overconfident. I am not some bound daemon.'

'Nonetheless, if you face me, you will know defeat.'

Malekith regarded him steadily, as if taking him seriously for the first time. He was looking at him, really looking at him. It was not the sort of attention that was calculated to make anyone comfortable. 'I have known defeat many times,' Malekith said, at last. 'But I doubt you are one to inflict it upon me.'

'Then face me if you dare.'

'That day will come soon enough,' said Malekith. 'When it dawns it will be your last.'

A wave of power erupted from him. The link with the chains that had bound N'Kari was broken. Teclis opened his eyes and looked upon Alarielle and his sleeping brother. It seemed as though his audience with the Witch King was over. It was just as well. Through the link he had sensed that Malekith was much closer than he had expected. It would not take the Witch King long to come find them.

MALEKITH BROODED. THE incursion of the young sorcerer Teclis into his very thoughts was unexpected.

The youth had shown a power that was awesome. It had taken Malekith millennia to become so strong. Teclis had been born into it. Now, Malekith regretted not instructing Urian to kill the mage when he was still a youth. In the course of a century he had become powerful enough to challenge Malekith himself. If he lived, he would become one of the great powers of this world.

It seemed that like his brother, Teclis was destined to be a thorn in Malekith's side, to spoil his plans at every turn. Tyrion had saved the Everqueen. Teclis had saved Tyrion from N'Kari. They were his own kin in a distant way, blood of Aenarion. He supposed that they had some claim to the throne of Ulthuan and Naggaroth too. It was another reason to wipe them from the face of the earth. He would brook no challengers to his mantle of power.

Malekith knew roughly where Teclis was now. The link had given him a sense of that. He lay along the path that Malekith had to take anyway, to find the Everqueen and crush all asur resistance in this part of the world.

When the time arose he would find this Teclis and destroy him. Yet there was something in the youth's confidence that troubled him. Could it be that Teclis knew something he did not? Was he about to endure another setback to his great plan?

No matter, he told himself. Whatever happened, he would endure and ultimately triumph. He summoned Urian and his generals to him. He knew now where Teclis was through the link the chains had given him. He knew he would find Tyrion and the Everqueen there too. It was time for the hunt to begin.

# CHAPTER TWENTY-TWO

CALEDOR STUDIED THE gameboard. So much was happening now, so many pieces were in play, it was difficult to keep track of everything. At least part of his plan had worked, and for that he felt grateful. Tyrion and Teclis were reunited and between them they had saved the Everqueen. Two of his greatest enemies, two of the greatest challenges facing him had been removed from the board – Morathi and N'Kari were both out of play. All that remained now was Malekith, and he was sure to prove the most difficult of all.

A small part of his mind whispered that he could stop now, with the removal of Morathi and the Keeper of Secrets his great work was safe for the moment, but he knew this was a lie. If Malekith ruled Ulthuan, Morathi would find some way to undo his spell, or the secret masters of the Cult of Luxury would, or perhaps even Malekith himself would be tempted. The druchii still needed to be stopped and he still needed to do what was necessary.

All of Ulthuan was a great swirl of confusion. Armies were on the move. Forces from everywhere were being drawn into a great whirlpool of violence, moving through forests, along the coasts, across the Inner Sea. Caledor found his attention inevitably drawn to this great nexus of conflict. His vision settled on the vast flat expanse of Finuval Plain in Saphery. This was the place where the crisis would come, where this conflict would be resolved for good or ill. It was there that the small, embattled force of high elves would make their stand and the fate of the world would be decided.

Malekith was in Saphery, uniting a great force of barbarians with his army. One by one he was bringing their chieftains and warlords to heel. He knew now where Teclis was and Tyrion and the Everqueen, and they were still central to the struggle. Malekith had a huge army of humans and druchii with him, as well as his own not inconsiderable talents as a sorcerer. He could still triumph all too easily.

One by one, forces of high elves were converging together to oppose him, small warbands coming from all over the island continent, drawn by rumours of imminent conflict and the news that the Everqueen was still alive. They were drawn to her banner from every part of the island. Many of them had been pilgrims on their way to visit Avelorn when the invasion came. Some of them had survived the invasion itself. Wizards came from Saphery. Riders from the proud land of Ellyrion. Mountain-dwellers from Cothique and

Chrace. At first they gathered together in their scores, then scores became hundreds and then hundreds became thousands. They went from fighting a guerrilla war to becoming an army, albeit one that was hugely outnumbered in its own homeland.

There was one last thing he could do. He reached out to a small pawn, travelling with a reforged suit of armour across the length of the plain. He nudged its thoughts and dreams in a certain direction. He needed what the figure carried to be in the right place at the right time.

Caledor was at the end of his strength. He knew now that there was very little more he could do to influence events. The fate of the elves was in other hands than his.

DORIAN LOOKED AT the captain. The warrior looked tired. There were dark shadows underneath his eyes and his face was leaner. He did not look like part of the victorious army. He looked like many a soldier Dorian had seen before, one who had been fighting for too long without respite and with too little rest.

'You were attacked,' Dorian said. It was not a question. He could see from the way the elf's arm was bandaged and from the bruises on his face that he had been in a fight. The fact that half the captain's soldiers looked just as battered told the same story. The captain nodded.

'Yes, general.' Dorian realised that he had made another mistake. He smiled sourly. It was just the last of many in a stream that no doubt would put an end to his career once Malekith found out about them.

His army had ploughed through southern Avelorn, meeting no resistance. They had put the few elf villages that they had encountered to the sword or the torch when they had been inhabited. They had been abandoned by those who had lived there in the face of the oncoming dark elf army. He followed up all the reports of trails that might have led to the Everqueen and her mysterious defender. Malckith's assassins had not returned, nor had the sorcerers Morathi had sent. Something told Dorian they never would.

He had kept his trackers out there looking for the Everqueen and hordes of warriors who could be trusted to find their way around in the deep woods. That had been a mistake.

Now at last the asur had begun to organise themselves. At first, the resistance had been almost pitiful. There had been a few ambushes committed by young and inexperienced elves. They had resulted in few casualties. Some of the attackers had been caught and made an example of by the druchii. They had learned though. They had gained in experience and they had been joined by others, silent, grim elves from the deep woods who knew how to track and avoid being tracked, who came and went like shadows in the night, leaving behind them sentries with slit throats and dead dark elves.

They had added hallucinogenic poisons to the food supplies, which left some of the druchii dying, screaming that they were being attacked by ghosts. He had been forced to regroup his forces into larger units, which made progress slower and following the trails harder. There had been more ambushes by larger groups of asur, and attacks that resulted in things that were almost as large as full-scale battles. His forces had taken more and more casualties. The offensive into Avelorn was being bogged down. Resistance was becoming stiffer. Morale was getting worse. The quest for the Everqueen still had not borne fruit.

Things might have become grim indeed had he not received reinforcements from a most unexpected quarter. Humans were starting to find their way into Avelorn in greater and greater numbers. He was not sure where they were coming from. It seemed like entire tribes and warbands had become detached from Morathi's offensive in the north and had somehow drifted south into Avelorn.

He sensed that there was more to this than a simple loss of cohesion in the great invasion force. These humans seemed to have their own agenda although they were not talking about what it was they wanted.

Now they too were stalking the woods and joining with the asur in battle. There were far more of them than there were druchii, it seemed like they were keeping more and more of the high elves busy. His troops were starting to come across battlegrounds where humans had fought with high elves. They had found the bodies of the tattooed invaders and their black-armoured leaders mingled with those of the denizens of Avelorn. Having spent a great deal of his career fighting against the servants of Chaos, Dorian felt a certain satisfaction. He was not looking upon the bodies of dead allies when he saw the worshippers of Chaos lying there. He was looking upon the corpses of potential enemies.

There were tales of some mighty wizard stalking the forest as well. A messenger had reached him from his starting point at the tournament grounds, telling him of a great massacre that had taken place there. It seemed impossible to believe that one magician, no matter how powerful, could have destroyed the holding force he had left behind to guard his evacuation route, but there had been no mistaking the truth in the messenger's words or the fear on his face when he described the massacre this wizard had perpetrated.

Not for the first time, he wished that Cassandra was still with him. She would have been able to advise him on how to deal with this wizard. She had not only been a very powerful sorceress but she had been very skilled in the tactics needed to overcome her fellow mages. He missed her more than he could find the words to say. It was just as well there was no one left for him to say them to.

It was clear that the captain before him was looking to him for orders and encouragement. Dorian could not find the words for that either. Instead he dismissed the captain with a gesture and said, 'Go, get some food and then some sleep. Tomorrow we shall set out and find these ambushers and teach them not to attack our forces.'

Horns sounded. A troop of riders rode up to his tent. One of them was Lord Telmar, a high noble from Malekith's entourage. Dorian was shocked. He knew this druchii should be hundreds of leagues away.

Telmar gave him an ironic salute that revealed the signet of Malekith. 'General Dorian, you are not an easy elf to find. Our king requests your presence, General Dorian, along with all your army. He has work for you out on Finuval Plain.'

Briefly Dorian considered refusing, but it was pointless. The alternative was to remain here until his command was slaughtered by the asur. 'He requests my presence personally?' Dorian asked.

'Oh yes, the Witch King is there himself. Malekith the Great is only a few days' march from here. He intends to do with his own hands what you could not – find and kill the Everqueen.'

Dorian shrugged and began to issue orders. It seemed that he would be facing Malekith sooner than he had expected.

So it was true, Tyrion thought. There was an elven army here. Coming over the rise, walking wearily with his brother limping on one side and the Everqueen on the other, he realised that they had done it. It had taken them long weeks of walking and hiding, of spreading the word that the Everqueen was still alive whenever they met a high elf, but it looked like finally they had reached a safe haven. Over the past few days, he had had his doubts whether they would. It seemed like a vast army of druchii was moving across the plains; they had come close to being captured more than once.

Ahead of them lay a small city of tents that looked far more makeshift than the great tournament grounds ever had. Among the tents were the banners of hundreds of elven noblemen. It seemed as if elves from all over Ulthuan had come to this place. It was as surprising as discovering a great festival in the middle of nowhere. But, at last, he told himself Alarielle was safe.

He felt better now – Teclis had proven what a master healer he was. The effects of the witch elves' poison were completely gone. His enormous vitality had reasserted itself. His side was healed and he was as fit as he ever had been.

It was strange. Over the past few weeks a distance had grown up between himself and the Everqueen. Teclis's mocking and sardonic presence had been part of the cause, but there were other reasons. Tyrion was sick and withdrawn most of the time and Alarielle distant as she communed with the power within her, seeking solutions for the problems of her people. They were no longer as close or as intimate as they had been during their long flight through the woods of Avelorn. Alarielle had withdrawn into herself, as if shrinking from him, becoming daily more silent and thoughtful.

They reached the edge of the great army camp. Elves looked at them with suspicious eyes. Of course, Tyrion thought, they were worried about spies. They were wondering who the strangers were. There was a simple answer for that. He gestured for the watchers to come closer and gather round. Once he had attracted a crowd, he shouted, 'Kneel! The Everqueen is among you.'

Alarielle removed her hood. The spell that compelled adoration radiated out from her. All of the elves present knelt and gave thanks for her delivery. Word of it rippled out through the camp. They were ushered into the presence of the army's leaders, hastily arranged in council to greet their queen.

A great cry went up, 'The Everqueen is saved!'

TYRION LOOKED AROUND at the assembled group of nobles and warriors. He was astonished to see a number of familiar and unexpected faces in the crowd. Korhien Ironglaive was there and so was Arhalien of Yvresse. Tyrion wondered if any others had survived the surprise attack on the tournament grounds. There were clearly stories that he needed to hear as soon as possible, but for the moment he needed to concentrate on the asur army and its leaders.

This was not an army in the traditional sense, he realised. It was a gathering of desperate elves who had come together because there was no place else to go. Now Alarielle was the focal point of their effort, partially because they wanted to protect her but partially because they needed protection themselves. They were huddling together like a herd of wild cattle forming a circle to protect themselves from predators.

He had to admit Alarielle formed an admirable living banner for them to rally to. The spell of the Everqueen kept all eyes focused on her; he knew that there was not an elf present who would not give his life to protect her, with the possible exception of Teclis. He would do it himself, and not because he was compelled by ancient magic. He would do it because...

Looking at those adoring faces, he wanted to punch them for their stupidity. Could they not see she was worth protecting for herself, not because of the spells around her? Was he the only one who understood that?

He forced himself to unclench his fists, to relax. They were not responsible for their actions here, any more than she was. In this, as in so much else, they were the pawns of powers greater than themselves. Speeches were given welcoming the Everqueen. She spoke, thanking Tyrion and Teclis for her deliverance. The brothers were cheered to the high heavens when the tale was told, but business pressed on. There was much to be discussed.

Scouts had brought word that a huge army under the Witch King was approaching. It would be upon them in a few days, maybe less. They were badly outnumbered. The thing to do was flee, a few of the nobles claimed. Their words sounded sensible, but could they not see they were making a huge error? Alarielle must have noticed something written on his face for she said, 'Prince Tyrion, you obviously disagree with what Lord Marin said.'

All eyes shot to him. He stepped forwards, giving them a chance to look at him. He weighed his words carefully, trying to put his objections into words. 'If we flee, our army will fall to pieces. The different components will all move at different speeds. The cavalry will outrun the infantry. The refugees who have joined us will be left behind.'

A tall elf garbed like a lord of the riders of Ellyrion said, 'We will not leave our people to be captured by the Witch King.'

'Then you will be overhauled and destroyed. The druchii have a disciplined army. It can march leagues in a day if it has to and maintain its formations. We cannot. This is not a picked force dispatched on a mission by the Phoenix King. This is simply a ragged assembly of survivors.'

There was a hubbub of voices. Many disagreed with him. A few took his words as an insult. Many of those with military experience knew he was talking sense.

'What would you suggest we do?' Korhien Ironglaive asked. He held up a huge hand for silence. His tone was challenging, but Tyrion knew the White Lion was really giving him a chance to explain.

'Our position here is as strong as it's going to get. We have the advantage of high ground and a flank protected by the Everflow on one side and woods on the other. We can take our stand here. If the gods are with us, we can win. If not, a force of fast riders must be prepared to take the Everqueen away. It would be better if she departed at once and we can hold the ground until she escapes.'

Alarielle shook her head. 'I have run far enough. I will not leave this place unless I have to.'

'But we cannot face the Witch King and his champion, this Urian Poisonblade,' someone shouted. 'He has slaughtered everyone who has faced him.'

'Ah, but we can,' said a sardonic voice from the edge of the council. It took Tyrion a long moment to realise that it belonged to Teclis. His twin stepped up to his side.

'Malekith can be defeated,' he said.

'How?' a voice demanded.

'By magic,' Teclis responded. 'He has a weakness that can be exploited.'

'And what would this weakness be, that no one has been able to discover for six thousand years?'

'I will not say,' said Teclis, 'lest word of it reaches his ears and he takes measures to protect against it.'

'You are seriously claiming you can beat the Witch King?'

Teclis nodded. 'I dismissed his pet daemon. I walked unscathed through his armies. Trust me, I can do this.'

All eyes looked at him, some with disbelief, some with awe, some with hope.

A scout ran up and shouted, 'We have sighted the Witch King's army. It will be upon us by tomorrow evening at the latest.'

Alarielle looked at the council and said, 'What is it to be? Stand or run? For myself, I will stay, but anyone who wants to is free to go.'

There was silence for a long moment, then a roar of affirmation that the army would stay.

'I hope this magic of yours works, brother,' Tyrion said so quietly that no one else could hear him.

'So do I,' Teclis replied. 'Our lives depend on it.'

'More than just ours,' Tyrion replied, unable to take his eyes off the Everqueen.

'TYRION!' HE TURNED to find the source of that well-remembered roaring voice pushing through the crowd, and found himself whirled into the air by the massive, muscular arms of Korhien Ironglaive. 'It is good to see you again.'

'Korhien!' Tyrion shouted. 'I might have known I would find you where the action was thickest.'

Korhien gave a sour grimace. 'That is everywhere these days. It seems like our land is overrun by these pests from Naggaroth.'

He was speaking loudly so that his confident assertion could be overheard. He wanted his contempt for their enemy well known and spread about the camp. He was doing his bit to keep up asur morale.

'How did you get here?' Tyrion asked. 'I would have thought you would have been in Lothern. I hear there has been fighting there.'

'I was dispatched to carry the war torch to our armies, to summon our people to the defence of the land. I was dispatched to the White Tower with messages, and from there was taking the word to Prince Moranion. I fell in with your father. He carries a burden of great importance.'

'My father is here? I thought he would never leave his beloved armour.'

'He has brought it with him. He was plagued by prophetic dreams. It seems half the wizards of Ulthuan have been, and the other half have not been getting enough sleep to do so.'

'How did you get here?'

'Once we were on the road, we just got caught up in the war. I was not jesting when I said those maggots were everywhere. We were chased hither and yon about the plain until I found Lord Marin's force, then we turned and gave those druchii a mauling.'

'I am very glad to hear it and even more glad to see you.'

'We must have a drink to celebrate. Come to my tent and

we shall have some wine and you can tell me lies about your great feats of heroism.' Something about Korhien's expression told Tyrion that he wanted to discuss matters that were not for public hearing. He followed his old teacher through the vast encampment with a growing sense of foreboding.

They took a seat inside an old tent and Korhien rummaged in his pack for a bottle of wine. He pulled out the cork with his teeth and passed it to Tyrion. 'No fine goblets here, I am afraid,' he said. 'Drink it down. You will need it.'

'Why do I have the feeling I am not going to like what you are going to tell me?'

'Because you know me too well.' Tyrion took a swig of the wine. It had been a long time since he had drunk any of the stuff. It went down well but it tasted sour.

Korhien grinned. 'It's useful for washing out wounds as well as giving you hangovers.'

Tyrion handed the bottle over and Korhien gulped it down. 'It does the job,' he said.

'What news of the war?' Tyrion asked.

'Bad as bad can be,' Korhien said. 'The druchii took us completely by surprise. Armies everywhere as if by magic. A dozen towns fell before anyone even knew it. Fortresses were besieged. A horde of barbarians have set fire to the north and are swarming through the rest of Ulthuan like maggots in a corpse.'

'Not a pretty image.'

'It's not a pretty time. The worst of it is not just that we were made to look like fools and half-beaten before the war even started. The worst of it was that we were betrayed.'

Tyrion looked up at the note of bitterness in his old friend's voice. He accepted the bottle and took another swig. 'Traitors? Who?'

'Iltharis for one.' Tyrion felt as if the bottom had just dropped out of his world.

'Prince Iltharis?'

'Do you know anyone else of that name?'

'I don't believe it.'

'I said the same thing, but he was seen giving instructions to a band of druchii sympathisers who tried to open the gates of Lothern to the dark elves.'

'He would not do that. There must be some mistake.'

'No mistake at all. He took a swipe at me en route to attempting to kill Finubar.'

'No.'

'Yes. Walked up to me, greeted me like a long-lost brother and then smacked me on the back of the head with the hilt of his sword. Knocked me out and left me with a bump the size of a peacock's egg. Fortunately my skull is so thick or I would not be here to tell you this tale of woe.'

'He could have slit your throat.'

'But he didn't. He'll pay for that mistake.'

'He did not kill you. Maybe he was being blackmailed or did it against his will.'

'He was changed, Tyrion. I am not sure how or what I can say to convince you, but I don't think he was reluctant about what he was doing. Mad, maybe, the way druchii are mad, but not reluctant.'

'He tried to kill Finubar?'

'He would have done it too, but while he was slaughtering a few White Lions, the Phoenix King escaped through the old secret tunnels in the palace. Iltharis followed him too, knew his way through what was supposedly a sacred, secret area. He must have been scouting out the place for decades.'

'How did Finubar get away?'

'Out into the harbour and onto a ship. Lady Malene was there and a bunch of house archers and enough troops to give even Iltharis pause. He vanished into the night, while the traitors were spreading panic. No one has seen him since.'

'I can't believe it,' said Tyrion, but he found he could. After the events of the past few months, nothing could surprise him.

'I couldn't either at first, but the crack in my skull was real.'

'Iltharis? A druchii spy? It's impossible. Who would have the patience to playact for all those years?'

'He did obviously.'

'Maybe it was magic, a spell.'

'Maybe.' It was obvious that Korhien had already discounted that possibility.

'This is not good news. I doubt a more dangerous elf ever lived than Iltharis – he knows all our secrets. He was part of the Phoenix King's council. He worked out what N'Kari was up to all those years ago.'

'He calls himself Urian now, according to those who have seen him. He leads warbands across the plain and kills all who oppose him. Some say he is invincible.'

'We shall have to put that to the test.'

'At least N'Kari no longer fights against us. Your brother sent it back to hell. He's become quite frightening himself, young Teclis, if the tales are to be believed.'

'They are.'

'What changed him?'

'I think he has discovered that he likes killing elves.'

'If anyone ever had a reason to, it was him. His life has not been an easy one.'

Suddenly Tyrion was annoyed with his old friend. Now that Teclis was a hero, people were beginning to sympathise with him and to understand his pain. They had never managed that before. He managed to keep the smile on his face. 'That is the truth.'

Korhien smiled. 'And you. You have become quite the hero too. Rescuing the Everqueen right out of the middle of a druchii army. It's like something from one of the old legends.'

Tyrion shrugged. 'I was in the right place at the right time.'

'You were also the right elf. That is important.'

'She saved herself really though, and she saved me a dozen times. I would not be here now if it was not for her.'

'Nor she if it was not for you. You've picked a bad time to become afflicted with false modesty, Tyrion. What this land needs now more than ever is heroes.'

'And I look like one, don't I?' said Tyrion sourly. He and Korhien looked at each other for a long moment. There was an odd hostility in the air, then Korhien grinned and said,

'You most certainly do. I suspect you will look more like one before this is over.'

Tyrion wondered what he meant.

'TECLIS!' THE WIZARD looked round to see Belthania waving at him. She was in the presence of a company of Sword Masters from Hoeth. More wizards accompanied her. He limped wearily over to where she stood.

'Hello,' he said, and she surprised him by kissing him on both cheeks.

'You did it,' she said. She was smiling. The Sword Masters were smiling too. 'You saved the Everqueen.'

'My brother did that. I just helped them escape.' He felt embarrassed. He did not like being the centre of attention, or the hero of the hour. He seemed to be recognised everywhere he went now. People pointed at him. He felt self-conscious. For some reason, he limped more.

'You banished a greater daemon. You spirited them out from among the armies of the Witch King. It's like something out of an old heroic tale.'

'I am not a hero,' he said.

'You are to most of us.'

'How times have changed,' he said sourly.

'You haven't,' she said. 'You are still a sour bastard.' She was smiling as she said it though.

'I like to be consistent,' he said. 'Is there any news from Hoeth?'

'The White Tower still stands. No one has attacked it so far though. There is other news…'

'What?'

'Malekith is here on the plain. He has come with his army, seeking the Everqueen no doubt.' Teclis felt cold fingers run up and down his spine. He had challenged the Witch King. Now it seemed he might actually have to face him. He hoped his idea about Malekith's weakness was correct.

Teclis felt a hand on his shoulder. He turned and much to his surprise saw Prince Arathion.

'Father,' he said, 'what are you doing here?'

'I came bringing the armour of Aenarion to where it was most needed.'

'Then you're in the right place.'

'I am not so sure about that.' Something in his father's tone alarmed Teclis much more than it should have done.

'SO, URIAN, WHAT shall I do with this one?' Malekith asked. Urian looked at the elaborately dressed and yet shabby figure before him. It took a few moments to recognise his own half-brother. He had heard word that General Dorian and his force had just joined the great army of humans and druchii surging across Finuval Plain in pursuit of the Everqueen. He had not realised that the general might prove to be his brother.

Dorian had aged greatly for an elf. The last time Urian had seen him he had been relatively young. So this is what I used to look like, Urian thought. He did not doubt that there was a certain resemblance in his brother's features to the way he had once looked. Of course, the Witch King's magicians had changed all of that when they had transformed him into an assassin. His features no longer bore any resemblance to those worn by his family. This did not stop him from feeling a certain nostalgia. In fact, it virtually guaranteed it.

Dorian looked at him, confused. He was obviously wondering why this stranger was being addressed by his brother's name. Was it possible that he did not yet suspect the answer?

Malekith's iron gaze moved from one brother to the other and then to the huge crowd of druchii nobles and human warlords gathered around his throne. Urian knew that he was enjoying this. It appealed to his cruel sense of humour. 'This is a general who failed us. He had the Everqueen in his grasp and he lost her. He made no report to his ruler over many weeks while he sought to rectify his error, or so he claims. And he seems somewhat lacking in fraternal feeling – he has failed to greet his younger brother.'

Dorian's eyes widened. He studied Urian closely and then shook his head, as if he could see no resemblance. In some ways, Urian knew that what was happening here was in some ways a reward for his services. There had never been any love lost between him and his brother when they were younger, which was something of a tradition among druchii siblings.

He was expected to name a punishment for Dorian, the crueller the better. After all, it was what most druchii would do to their elder brother. There had been times when he had dreamed of doing so himself when he was young. He had hated Dorian for standing in his way, for being the heir, for being the eldest. He had disliked his older brother's self-confidence and the way he seemed to feel that he was born to command and that others were born to obey. There was a time when this would have been a reward indeed, and Urian knew that.

He did not feel that way now though. He felt almost nothing. He did not resent this cowed-looking stranger. He did not desire revenge. He did not even desire to be particularly cruel. He knew though that such an admission would be seen as a weakness. It was not something he could afford to let slip before his ruler. He did not want Malekith to know how much he had changed during his time among the high elves. He did not want anyone here to know that or even suspect it.

The prospect of ordering Dorian to be tortured did nothing for him. In fact, he found himself thinking back to the long-gone time when they had been young, and he discovered that there were some points of contact that he did not regret – there were moments of shared experience that he even had rather enjoyed.

He did not owe Dorian anything – no favours but not a cruel death either. He looked around at the faces of the courtiers. All of them were watching him closely, some of them licking their lips in anticipation. No doubt all of them were thinking about what they would do to their own kin in a similar situation.

Urian felt nothing but repulsion for those who surrounded him. He wished most devoutly that he was back among the high elves and fighting on their side. The intensity of that feeling surprised him. He had changed much more than he liked to think and not in a good way as far as his prospects of survival were concerned.

Dorian looked up at him baffled. No doubt he was thinking about what he would do in a similar situation. He was probably working his way through all of the inventive tortures that could be inflicted by the minions of the Witch King if they were so instructed. Clearly he anticipated nothing except a long-drawn-out and painful death.

Urian took another glance at all of those surrounding them and felt the pressure of compulsion upon him.

With one lightning-like move he drew his blade and slashed off Dorian's head, then he picked it up by the hair and presented it with a flourish to the Witch King.

'Failure deserves nothing but swift punishment,' Urian said as loudly as he could.

Malekith looked at him enigmatically. Urian wondered what he was thinking. There was a long moment of silence while the audience waited for the king's response. Malekith reached out and accepted the severed head and studied it for a moment before tossing it away.

'You're correct, Urian,' he said. 'Your efficiency surprises me and rather pleases me. It seems you have learned something during your stay among the asur.' Urian wondered whether anyone else detected the ambiguity in Malekith's words.

'Soon we shall encounter the ragtag army that has gathered to protect the Everqueen. I shall have a new duty for you then,' Malekith said. 'There are several people I want you to kill.'

'I look forward to it,' Urian lied.

# CHAPTER TWENTY-THREE

THE BLOOD-RED LIGHT of the setting sun blazed down on the chaos of the battlefield. The screams of the dying and the hellish clamour of blade on blade echoed in Tyrion's ears. Leaning forwards in the saddle, he rammed his sword into the heart of a howling dark elf foot soldier, smashing him down to be trampled under the hooves of his borrowed steed.

Glancing around quickly, he took in the battlefield.

What a terrible place this Finuval Plain would be to die, he thought: a horrible, empty, dreary moorland that few had ever heard of before today. His small cavalry force was badly outnumbered and surrounded by chanting dark elf infantry, part of the vanguard of the Witch King's approaching army. The dark elves fought with the mechanical discipline of automatons and a cold courage as impressive as it was daunting.

Tyrion turned in the saddle and lashed out with his blade, sending the head of his foe flying among his comrades, leaving an arcing trail of blood in its wake. He let his stroke continue and his blade crunched through ribs. Another dark elf flopped to the earth, his spine severed and his body writhing uncontrollably.

Tyrion raised his shield to deflect a blow he saw coming out of the corner of his eye. He felt the impact all the way up his armoured arm. He brought the edge of his shield down on his attacker's face, smashing nose and teeth, leaving another enemy to be trampled beneath the metal-shod hooves of his steed.

'For Alarielle, for the Everqueen!' Tyrion shouted. Just mentioning the name of his lady gave him new vigour and renewed his determination to fight and win. The tired high elves around him responded, hacking about them with more energy, smashing through their foes and into the clear plain beyond.

Tyrion raised his sword above his head and gestured for them to form up, turn around and charge once more into the foe. They responded like heroes. Their formation tightened, their ranks drawing together with the same precision they would have shown on a parade ground. The gaps in the ranks vanished as the unit's frontage collapsed.

As one the proud cavalry wheeled and trotted forwards, gaining thunderous momentum as they went. Amid the ranks of the dark elves, sergeants bellowed instructions, trying to ready their line to take the shock of impact.

Tyrion sensed there was something wrong here. He

glanced around to see what it was and noticed that from the left, coming down from the nearby hills was a formation of dark elven cavalry. If Tyrion's force kept to the same course, the dark elves would take his warriors in the flank even as they buried their blades in the druchii infantry.

'Wheel right!' Tyrion bellowed, his voice carrying over the oceanic roar of battle. There was nothing else to be done. Charging upslope would put his knights at a disadvantage, but it was better than being taken in the flank or rear. Also they were heavier armoured and mounted on better steeds.

Lesser horse-soldiers would not have been able to respond to his command, but these elves adjusted their course instantly, and tensed as they saw what their leader had seen and the trap they had so narrowly avoided.

Metallic thunder raged as the two lines came together, the heavier high elf cavalry smashing through the lighter dark elves despite the other's advantage of slope and momentum. As the two lines came together, Tyrion was shocked to see a familiar face among the dark elf lines. Fear and hatred warred in his heart. He had been seeking a worthy foe and suddenly he had found one.

'Iltharis! Or Urian or whatever you call yourself! Face me, traitor, and die!' His bellow carried above the sounds of battle, as did the answering laugh.

'Prince Tyrion! This is a not-unexpected pleasure.' Somehow Iltharis's mocking voice carried over the ring of metal on metal. It sounded almost conversational. There was magic in that voice, although the dark elf gave no sign of being a mage. Iltharis carried a glowing runeblade in each hand and he used them to cut his way towards Tyrion, slashing through seasoned elf warriors as if they were no more than children. He guided his black steed easily with his knees, a war-rider with centuries of practice in his art.

Blade rang against blade as steed encountered steed. Tyrion's steed was heavier. He reared and lashed out with its fore-hooves and crushed the skull of Urian's mount. With the grace of a tumbler, the dark elf left his saddle, somersaulted and landed on the ground beside Tyrion. His blades rose and opened Tyrion's horse's belly, sending ropes of gut dripping to the ground. Less gracefully than his foe, Tyrion left the saddle and hit the ground. He tried to roll but the shield strapped to his arm prevented it, and he flopped gracelessly down.

Even as he rose, he felt a blade at his neck. It glowed with evil magic, far worse than anything on a witch elf's weapon. He knew that he was dead if his opponent wanted him to be. His luck had finally run out and he would never have the chance to look upon Alarielle's face again. Everything seemed to slow, as if they stood in the heart of some magical maelstrom, untouched by the battle raging around them.

'Shall I kill you, Prince Tyrion?' Iltharis whispered in his ear. 'Shall I do you that great favour?'

'Do what you wish, traitor,' Tyrion said. 'This is the sort of treacherous attack I am sure you would call a victory.'

Iltharis's laughter was mocking. 'You were unlucky, my prince. I would not claim this as any sort of victory. You are almost worthy of my blade now.'

'A traitor's blade, Iltharis.'

'Alas, though it pains me to contradict you, Blood of Aenarion, a traitor I am not. I have always been loyal to one master. And please call me Urian. It is my name, after all.'

Tyrion lashed out with his elbow, hoping to catch Urian off guard. The dark elf avoided the blow effortlessly.

'I would be doing you a favour killing you, you know,' he said.

'Really?'

'My master holds a grudge against you, you and your brother both. His vengeance will be as terrible as it is inevitable. Take my advice, kill yourself and your brother and your beloved queen. It would be better for all three of you than falling into his hands.'

Oddly enough Urian sounded sincere.

'Is that why you have not slit my throat? Because your master wants me alive?'

'Astute as ever, Prince Tyrion. I knew I could count on that razor-sharp wit of yours.'

'You will forgive me if I do not take your advice,' said Tyrion.

'I fear the day will dawn when you will have cause to regret that. Believe me or not, Prince Tyrion, I have always liked you and your brother, and I am not lying to you now. I never really have.'

'You have a funny definition of the truth.'

'All sentient beings have their own definition of the truth, and it is usually a funny one when you get down to it. Life is a black cosmic joke.'

Tyrion threw himself forwards, rolling, and came to his feet facing Urian. It seemed the dark elf was sincere about not killing him. He had not planted his blade in Tyrion's back although he was more than quick enough to have done so. Tyrion advanced, shield angled, blade ready. Urian stood waiting, blades held negligently in each hand, as if he faced a foe unworthy of real effort.

Tyrion struck. Urian parried. Tyrion unleashed the full fury of his sword arm. Urian parried, slowly at first and then faster and faster as Tyrion's strokes gained momentum. Tyrion had never fought so well. His every movement was eye-blurringly swift, his every blow was struck with a force that would have cut through his target if he had managed to land one.

He never did.

No matter how swiftly he struck, Urian always parried. No matter how cunningly he feinted, Urian always avoided the trap, and slowly, with the effortless grace of a big cat, he began to fight back, working ripostes into his swordplay that Tyrion was hard put to parry, gliding forwards easily, and with such cunning that without really knowing how it had happened Tyrion found himself on the defensive, backing away, taking blows on his shield that fell with all the force of a blacksmith's hammer on an anvil.

Urian grinned. 'You have been practising, prince. I don't believe you have ever fought better.'

Tyrion did not respond. He lashed out with a wild flailing cut that Urian ducked under. In return Urian stepped forwards and sent Tyrion reeling with a blow to the helm with the pommel of his sword.

'Given time, I believe you could almost be as good as I am. Maybe even better. So sad that your time is over.'

One of Tyrion's soldiers, seeing what had happened, let out a war-cry and charged towards them. As the rider bore down on him, Urian leapt, kicking him from the saddle and twisting himself to land on the horse's back. A moment later he raised his blade to Tyrion in a farewell salute.

'Goodbye, Prince Tyrion. We will meet again. Unfortunately for us both.'

He let out a loud whistle and his riders broke off the fight and followed him, not fleeing but retreating in good order, leaving in their wake Tyrion's confused company. The dark elf infantry had already begun a withdrawal, taking their dead with them. Tyrion signalled for his soldiers not to pursue. He was well aware it would lead only to their slaughter.

'What just happened here?' Tyrion's lieutenant asked.

'I just encountered someone I knew.'

'You know a dark elf?' There was horror and suspicion in his voice.

'He was not a dark elf when I knew him.'

'How can that be?'

Tyrion did not reply but stared into the distance, lost in thought. After a moment, he found himself a new steed from among the mounts of his dead riders and gave the signal to saddle up and ride back to camp.

* * *

TYRION STARED INTO the fire, watching the flames dance. From the night sky, the huge white eye of the greater moon gazed down on a vast camp. Banners from all across Ulthuan fluttered above the silken pavilions of elven princes. The clank of metal and the neighing of horses told him that more and more troops were arriving. He could hear words spoken in the accents and dialects of half a dozen elven lands. The sophisticated discussions of Sapherian wizards mingled with the terse banter of Ellyrion horse soldiers. A sad and lovely voice sang an old folk song from Tiranoc telling of a drowned land, a drowned city and a lost love. Tyrion listened to the last few fading notes and felt as if a dagger were piercing his heart.

Life was sweet and he did not want to die. His encounter with Urian had convinced him today that it was all too likely he would when the armies clashed on Finuval Plain.

Suddenly the shadows dancing near the fire warped and clotted. A tall figure stood there. Soldiers scrambled away, reaching for blades and spears. Tyrion looked up from where he sat but did not reach for his weapon.

'You need to work on your entrances, brother,' he said. 'I don't think that was quite dramatic enough. At least half of my warriors were not startled out of their wits.'

Teclis smiled sourly and once again Tyrion was struck by the changes time had wrought in his twin. Gone was all trace of weakness and lassitude. Teclis was still gaunt and pale for a high elf and he walked with a slight limp, but that was the only trace of the illnesses that had threatened his life for as long as Tyrion could remember. His features had taken on a gaunt handsomeness they had never had before.

It was not just Teclis's physical appearance that had changed. Perhaps a mage or someone more gifted with the Sight could have expressed it better, but all Tyrion could say was that his brother was cloaked in mystery and incandescent with power. It blazed within him, more than in any other living being Tyrion had ever encountered. Perhaps Alarielle possessed as much, but in the Everqueen it was hidden, like water bubbling up from an underground lake through a deep still well. Teclis was like a massive river in flood. He behaved now as if he had the power to sweep anything from his path.

It made Tyrion worried as well as proud. His brother was like a young warrior who had suddenly discovered he was strong and takes all sorts of crazed risks to test his own strength. He smiled sourly. That was something he certainly knew all about himself.

'You are troubled,' Teclis said.

'Yes,' said Tyrion, cursing his brother inwardly. Could he not see that this was not the time or the place to discuss his troubles, that these warriors looked to him for leadership, for strength not doubt? He rose from his place at the fireside and clasped his brother by the shoulder, the way he had done from childhood, and began to lead him away from the fire.

'Come, brother, walk with me,' he said. It was not lost on Tyrion the way Teclis shrugged his hand away. He needed to assert himself, to break out of the old pattern of their relationship. Tyrion felt a mixture of hurt and pride. It seemed that he was no longer going to get to play the protective elder brother.

'That was a mistake, wasn't it?' said Teclis when they were out of earshot of the fire. Tyrion looked around. They were still the centre of attention as they walked, which was understandable. They were the two heroes of the moment, who had saved the missing Everqueen from daemons and assassins, who had won most of the few small high elf victories there had been in this terrible war.

Tyrion kept his silence till they reached the edge of the camp, and Teclis had the sense to do the same. Tyrion considered his options. It was pointless explaining to Teclis that his soldiers were unsettled and his appearance in such a manner would only have spooked them more. It was not something that warriors needed on a night before battle. Teclis was clever enough to already have understood that. There was no need to batter the point home with a warhammer.

'How goes it?' Tyrion said at last. 'Are you ready for battle?'

'As ready as I will ever be,' said Teclis. 'I will almost be grateful when day breaks and this matter is settled.' Teclis sounded puzzled and looked at Tyrion circumspectly. This was not what he had come to discuss. It was not what Tyrion wanted to talk about either, but the words for that were not ready to come yet.

'Why do you ask?' Teclis asked eventually.

'Because this is a battle that will be decided by magic. We do not have the numbers to overcome the dark elves by strength of arms.'

'That is not what I hear the warriors say or the princes. They all talk of the certainty of victory.'

'What else can they do? They are whistling in the dark, but in their hearts they all know the same thing as I. We do not have the numbers,  the advantage of initiative and morale lies with our opponents.'

'I will take your word for it. You are the expert on military matters.'

Now that he had started talking Tyrion felt the need to continue. 'If it had been a year ago, when our troops were more confident and we had not lost so many warriors, things might be different, but it has been a season of defeat – many of our best are in their graves. Others are scattered over Ulthuan, defending their homes. The Witch King has gathered his forces here and he intends to land a hammer blow that will shatter us.'

'You think we should not be fighting here?'

'We have no choice.'

Teclis nodded, and seemed more interested now than he had when Tyrion had mentioned troop numbers or morale. Then he said something of a perceptiveness Tyrion would not have expected from him at all.

'You love her, don't you?'

'More than I can find the words to say. If I am to die, I would prefer for it to be at her side.'

'You picked a fine time to fall in love, brother, as our world goes down in blood and fire.'

'I never had any choice in the matter. And whatever comes, I do not regret that it happened.'

'If I did not know better I would say that you were afraid,' said Teclis.

'I *am* afraid,' Tyrion said at last. The words hung in the air for a long moment.

Teclis's laughter was soft but there was no mockery in it. 'So the intrepid hero knows fear at last,' he said. 'I always thought nothing could scare you. Fear was my speciality.'

'I have been afraid before,' said Tyrion. 'Often. I have just chosen never to admit it to anyone. Not even to myself.'

'So why are you telling me this now?'

'Because I think I may die soon, and I feel the urge to confess it. I cannot tell it to the soldiers or to the Everqueen or to anyone else, so I am telling you.'

'What brought this on?'

'I met Urian, as Prince Iltharis now calls himself, while scouting the battlefield today.'

'And?'

'And he was better than me. He has always been better than me.'

'He has never been better than you.'

Tyrion laughed. 'I don't mean morally! I mean with a blade he is better than me.'

'Then don't fight him with a blade.'

'The weapons don't matter. If I fought him with a pig's bladder on a stick, he could still beat me.'

'You might want to keep your new choice of favoured weapon to yourself. I don't think it would hearten your troops. They think you are invincible.'

'I am very, very good,' said Tyrion without any false

modesty. 'But it does not matter how good you are, there is always someone better.'

'You can't be certain Urian is better than you.' Teclis sounded shocked to be contemplating the fact.

'Believe me, brother, I can. Your gift is for magic. Mine has always been to be able to use weapons. And with any weapon Urian will beat me.'

'Then don't fight him with a weapon.'

'What should I use then? My cutting wit?'

'You have a brain, little as you choose to use it. Battles are fought as much with the mind as with weapons. I seem to recall someone standing not a thousand leagues from me now telling me that once.'

'Urian is too quick. The sort of fights you have with the likes of him happen at speeds too fast for thought. It is all down to reflex, training and experience – the last is the thing he has more of than me. He has had centuries to learn his trade.'

'I would submit to you, brother, that you are wrong. That the battle has already begun and it is being fought out in your mind now, and that you are losing it.'

'As ever, you are being over-subtle.'

'Think about it, Tyrion! Do you think it was an accident that you met Urian today? Do you think it just happened? That the fates threw you together?'

'If Urian wanted to kill me, he could have done so.'

'And he didn't. Because that was not his purpose. He did not want to kill you, not today at least.'

'Then what does he want?' Tyrion was aware that his

brother might have caught something that he had missed. Teclis always made him feel slow.

'Think! Who is the current hero of the high elves? Who saved the Everqueen in her darkest hour?'

'You did.'

'No. You are the one who dragged her out of harm's way and kept her free when all seemed lost. Who is known to be the greatest warrior in the high elven host?'

'Korhien Ironglaive.'

'That is not what all the warriors are saying now. They are saying it is you. You have the Blood of Aenarion. You are the hero of this hour. You are the one who can lead us to victory.'

'Even if what you say is true, then why did Urian not kill me today when he had the chance.'

'Because it would not be public enough. Because he wishes to crush you in the dirt and to break the will of our army.'

'You think he means to fight a Contest of Champions?' Tyrion laughed out loud.

'Count on it.'

'There has not been such a duel fought since the time of Caledor the Conqueror. It is not the dark elf way.'

'It will be tomorrow. You could bet our family villa on it.' Tyrion turned the idea over in his head. In a strange way it made sense. If he was challenged and turned the challenge down, it would demoralise the whole high elf army to see their champion refuse battle. If he was defeated, it would have the same effect – it would clearly demonstrate the Witch King's warriors' superiority to the best the high elves could put forward.

Tyrion was enough of a soldier to know that battles were not always decided by strength of arms or force of magic or weight of numbers; they were decided by the courage of warriors, their determination to conquer. Soldiers had won battles before by standing firm when they should have run, by fighting long after the time had come when everyone but them had known they were beaten. They could be inspired to that by their belief in one elf, a general or a hero. But not if that elf did not believe in himself.

'I knew you would see it… eventually,' said Teclis. 'You are not entirely slow of mind.'

'Then why the meeting today?' Tyrion asked, although he already knew what his brother would say.

'To sow the seeds of doubt in your mind. To soften you up. To make you afraid. Fear slows a warrior down. You told me that too, once upon a time.'

Tyrion shook his head. 'Maybe, in part, but I don't think that is all of it.'

'What makes you say that?'

'Urian had a message for me, for you too. He said we should kill ourselves.'

Teclis laughed. 'I hope you do not expect me to take his advice.'

'He seemed sincere.'

'I think he sincerely wants us both dead.'

'He says that Malekith's vengeance will be as terrible as it is inevitable. It would be better to die than suffer it.'

'I do not doubt that he is correct in that. But I am not planning to allow myself to fall into the Witch King's hands.'

'We may not have a choice.'

'We always have a choice. The same choice as the Conqueror had when he threw himself into the sea, but I for one will wait until I am surrounded on a burning ship and about to fall into the hands of my enemies before I make that choice. I suggest you do the same, brother.'

They both glanced into the distance to the camp of the dark elves, where an evil as old as elven civilisation waited, surrounded by its implacable minions. They were both aware of it, Tyrion sensed. They both felt its brooding power and its malevolence. They both knew they were kin to it too, through the line of Aenarion for, like them, Malekith was of his blood.

'How can we beat him?' Tyrion asked at last. 'He is the most powerful sorcerer in the world. He has the largest army assembled by the elves since the time of Aenarion. He has been planning this for centuries.'

'He could not have planned for you and me, brother. And as you said yourself, no matter how good you are, there is always someone better. The same applies to Malekith as it applies to you and me.'

Tyrion looked at his brother as if seeing him for the first time. 'You are planning on challenging him, are you?'

Teclis's cold smile gave him his answer.

'You are mad,' Tyrion said, but there was admiration as well as humour in his words.

'Maybe, but so was Aenarion at the end and he still defeated the hordes of hell.'

'Yes, but at what price?'

'Whatever the price is, we will have to pay it, brother. If our lands are to survive, if our people are to be free, if our world is to avoid destruction. Tomorrow, for better or worse, it will be our names that are written in the pages of the history books. If there is anyone left to write them.'

Tyrion looked at his brother, as if seeing him for the first time. 'You've come a very long way,' he said.

'We have both done that, brother,' said Teclis.

A Sword Master of Hoeth appeared out of the gloom, a massive greatsword on his back. He looked flustered and not a little anxious, which was unusual in one of the legendary guardians of the White Tower. 'Prince Teclis, I have been looking for you everywhere. Your father wishes to speak with you.'

'I will come with you,' Tyrion said.

The Sword Master looked embarrassed and said, 'I was told to bring Prince Teclis alone. It is wizard business.'

Bitterness burned in the pit of Tyrion's stomach. Even here as the world ended, their father could not bring himself to treat him as Teclis's equal.

Teclis shrugged. 'I must go. There are plans that must be set in motion. You were right about one thing, brother. This battle will be settled by magic, but for that to happen our armies will need to stand firm. You can make them do that. They believe in you. Remember that. Good luck on the morrow. May Isha smile on you.'

'May you live a thousand years.'

And in a moment, he was gone, although how he left, Tyrion was not sure. He stood for a moment on the edge of the vast armed camp, staring at the fires of the even larger one where the Witch King and his minions watched and waited. He felt small and lost, a tiny particle of life caught up in a whirlwind, buffeted by forces beyond his control, a pawn of destiny. He felt unsettled by his brother's words. A vast weight pressed down on him now, for he had sensed the truth in them. Somehow, the fate of everyone and everything they cared about rested on their shoulders tomorrow. They had both gone from despised outsiders of no consequence to standing at the very fulcrum of destiny.

How had it come to this, he wondered?

# CHAPTER TWENTY-FOUR

HIS FATHER WAS troubled, Teclis could see that. Of course, who would not be under the circumstances? The old elf had witnessed the greatest invasion of Ulthuan since the first Chaos incursion. He had doubtless seen people he knew killed and entire villages laid waste. Like every other elf who had lived through these dark times, he had reason to be unhappy. Somehow though, Teclis doubted that this was all that troubled his father.

'What is it, father?' He asked. His father simply looked at him. His gaze was bleak. He looked sadder than Teclis had ever seen him look in his life and that was quite a feat. His father shook his head and gestured for Teclis to step within his tent.

Inside was a large wooden box that resembled a coffin. Teclis immediately sensed powerful magic within although it was contained by potent runes inscribed in his father's unmistakable hand. His father went over to the box and unsealed it using a crowbar. As the seals were broken, a blast of powerful magic swept over Teclis like heat coming out of an open oven door. The magic was powerful almost beyond imagining and there was a dark taint to it that Teclis did not like in the least.

Lying within the wooden structure like a corpse within a coffin was the armour of Aenarion. It looked very different now from the ancient, dormant artefact that had lain within his father's laboratory for all those decades. It glittered now. It glowed with magical energy. It looked fresh and bright and newly made. It looked magnificent, a tribute to his father's skill as a wizard and to the skill of the ancient archmage who had made it. It blazed with power and Teclis could see that it would protect any warrior who wore it from harm better than any other armour ever made. Not only that, potent enchantments would enhance the strength, speed and skill of the wearer, making them powerful beyond belief.

It was not this that troubled Teclis. There was something else about the armour, a resonance, an imprint of someone's personality that was troubling. There was a sense of rage, a lust for death, that was almost overwhelming. Just looking at the armour made him want to grind his teeth and shout abuse at his father for the stupidity of what he had done. He was a wizard too and he recognised the magic for what it was. Swiftly, he threw a screen around himself and Prince Arathion. He was relieved to see the look of anger vanishing swiftly from his father's face as well.

'You see it?' his father asked. 'Can you see what I have done?'

'You have recreated the armour of Aenarion,' said Teclis. 'This might be the greatest feat of forensic magic in the history of the world.'

'I do not think it was meant to be this way. I have failed.'

Teclis examined the armour with his magesight. He could see that his father's work was flawless. The spells had been recreated perfectly, lovingly, by a mage who had known exactly what to do and have done it. His father had made no mistakes. This was something else.

'Your spellwork is perfect,' Teclis said. 'Whatever happened here is not your fault.'

'I do not think the armour was meant to be like this,' his father said. 'I have read every primary source in existence and there is no reference to something like this.'

'I think what we are seeing is the influence of Aenarion,' Teclis said. 'He was so full of power that he left his mark upon the armour. I suspect also that the Sword of Khaine may have left its mark as well. He carried that blade for a good deal of the time that he wore this armour. It may have affected Caledor's creation as well as Aenarion himself.'

'Such were my thoughts too, my son,' said Prince Arathion. 'The question is what effect will this have on the person who wears the armour.'

'You saw the effect that simply looking upon it had upon you and me. I would imagine that wearing the armour, being connected to it by the web of spells inherent in it, would be much worse. It might affect the personality of the wearer, twisting it and altering it unless that person was very strong-willed indeed.'

'You don't think there is any way that we could cleanse the armour?'

Teclis considered this for a moment. The imprinting was very strong and the effect was potent. He knew next to nothing about the Sword of Khaine's magic and he could not calculate the effects of it. He had made contact with the Flame of Asuryan himself and he could sense a great similarity between the resonance of the flame and the magic that was on this armour that had not been put there by Caledor. He suspected that that was the effect of the flame that had burned inside Aenarion after he had passed through the sacred fires in the shrine. Perhaps what they were seeing was the shadow of Aenarion cast by the flame onto the armour. It was hard to tell. He could not see any way of purifying the armour at this moment. Of course, that did not mean that there was not such a way. It just might take an age to find. He said as much to his father.

'I had feared that this was the case,' Arathion said. 'I am not reassured. It is a pity. I spent so much time recreating this armour and so much effort bringing it here, and now it might be useless.'

'The armour itself will perform all the functions it was intended to,' Teclis said. 'It is a mighty weapon, a great artefact, and these are desperate times. The fate of the elven people hangs in the balance and anything that gives us even the slightest of advantages is to be seized upon.'

'That is what the council of princes says. They say that the armour may be needed to give our champions a fighting chance on the field of battle. They say that the power of Malekith is overwhelming and that we need to grab every opportunity presented to us with both hands.'

'And they are correct,' said Teclis. 'If we do not win here, darkness may eclipse our people and Ulthuan may fall forever.'

'I agree with you,' said his father, 'and still my heart misgives me.'

'You're afraid to ask someone to wear this armour?'

'Wouldn't you be?'

'I would wear it myself if I thought it would help,' Teclis said.

'I know you would, but you are unlikely to be asked to wear it.'

Suddenly Teclis understood who was likely to be asked and he understood his father's misgivings. 'They want Tyrion to take this armour?'

His father nodded. 'The Everqueen is going to present it to him before the battle. They say it will hearten the troops and be very good for morale.'

'They are right and I suspect that the effect is carefully calculated. Tyrion looks like Aenarion, so everybody says, and to see him wearing this armour would be like having Aenarion fight on our side.'

'So you agree with the princes? You think that Tyrion should do this?'

'It does not matter what I think,' Teclis said. 'If he is asked, he will do it. That is the sort of fool he is.'

'Then what can we do?'

'We can try and see whether we can come up with some way to mitigate the effect of the armour's aura.'

'We don't have much time,' said his father.

'Then we'd better get started,' Teclis said.

TYRION INSPECTED THE armour of Aenarion. It looked different. He had seen it almost every day during his childhood, and very often in the years of his adulthood. It had never looked then the way it did now, alive, malevolent and full of power. There was a shadow in it that he could sense and that shadow called out to something in him.

Suddenly a moment from his childhood came back to him. He remembered standing in the chill of the night in his father's alchemical laboratory inspecting the armour. His father and Korhien Ironglaive were somewhere in the house, talking about the old days. Lady Malene was in her chambers writing something. He was standing in his bare feet, looking at the armour and half-fearfully, half-hopefully waiting for something to happen, for some sign to be given, for the same supernatural power that had touched Aenarion to reach out and touch him. Of course, back then, nothing had happened and he had been glad of it.

But something had happened now. The armour was not the same. His father had succeeded in his long labour and finally repaired this ancient artefact. He finally had something to show for squandering the family fortunes, neglecting his family and letting his life fall into ruin. The armour was alive. That was the only thing that could be said about it. It was like a living thing, with a personality of its own.

No. That was not right. It held the echo of a personality, of the elf who had worn it so long ago, of Aenarion. Now, Tyrion had a sense of what his ancestor was like. He did not like what he was seeing. The armour gave off an air of malevolence, of rage, of an anger so great it might consume the world. Aenarion had left something of himself in it, and his father had succeeded in awakening it.

Do I want to be like this, Tyrion asked himself? Do I have a choice?

Someone is going to have to wear this, to inspire our troops, to give our warriors some hope. He knew that if he put on the armour, he would never be the same afterwards. All of his life he had wanted glory, to be a hero. He was surprised to discover that he did not want it so badly that he was prepared to subsume his own personality to another's, to sell his soul for it.

Or was he? He already knew the answer to the decision he had to make.

He sensed Alarielle's presence in the tent. He turned to look at her. She was beautiful in the lantern-light. It had been a while since he had seen her. She had been very busy, talking with princes and wizards.

'What are you thinking?' she asked.

'I was remembering looking at this armour when I was a boy,' he said. 'It always seemed so much larger than it was. As if the wearer was a giant, much bigger than me.'

'It looks as if it was made for you,' she said. 'And you for it.'

'Aenarion wore it. It seems somewhat presumptuous for me to.'

'Tomorrow will be the greatest battle the elves face since his time,' she said. She walked over to him and took him by his hand. 'Someone needs to wear it, to give our people hope.'

'And you think it should be me?' For a moment, something ancient, powerful and unforgiving looked out of her eyes. It was the pitiless presence of the Everqueen. She was here and Alarielle was not.

'I can think of no elf better suited to wear it.' She squeezed his hand gently.

'Aenarion,' Tyrion said.

'He is not here. You are.'

'It's always the way,' he said. 'Heroes are never around when you really need them.'

'You are here.'

'I am just an elf who likes to kill. I am not a hero.'

'You are the only person who thinks that.'

'Doesn't my opinion count?'

'I do not think you see yourself as we see you.'

'I see myself as I am.'

She shook her head. 'I had never thought you so modest, Prince Tyrion.'

'I am not modest. I am just not Aenarion.'

'Has it ever occurred to you that that might be a good thing? We do not need another Aenarion.'

Tyrion smiled. 'It seems most of my life people have been comparing me to him, because I look like him.'

'You do more than look like him. You have something of his power and his grace. Believe me, *I* remember Aenarion. He was not an elf you could forget.'

'That is a chilling thought.'

'You are not him though. I think you are someone better.'

Tyrion laughed.

'You do not have his cruelty. Or his despair. Or his titanic arrogance.'

'They made him what he was, the saviour of our people.'

'Caledor saved our people. Aenarion almost destroyed them. We do not need another Aenarion. We need you.'

'And yet you want me to take up his mantle, don his armour.' Suddenly the sense of ancient presence was gone.

'I want you to wear his armour because it is among the most powerful protective artefacts ever made. I want you to come back to me. Tomorrow there will be a battle. I want you to live through it.'

She looked as if she was going to cry. Tyrion reached out and stroked her cheek. 'We've come a very long way, you and I,' he said.

'Let us hope we have a long way further to travel.'

She reached out and took his face in both her hands. He leaned forwards and kissed her gently. The armour of Aenarion watched over them, brooding in the background.

From outside there came the sounds of an army preparing for war.

# CHAPTER TWENTY-FIVE

THE SUN ROSE as if it was the last day of the world. Red light blazed down upon the two vast armed camps that sat on the edge of Finuval Plain. Tyrion stood upon the small rise and looked aghast at the size of the Witch King's army. It was plain that the high elves were hugely outnumbered. There were not only dark elves over there but a high proportion of humans, followers of Chaos, dedicated to the dark gods.

The assembled asur army looked at the Everqueen. They were drawn up as if ready for battle. In the distance, the horns of Malekith's army sounded but no one was distracted. All of the asur present looked upon their living goddess with reverence.

Alarielle smiled at them and Tyrion thought she had never looked lovelier. Something old and primal in her was responding to the presence and adoration of those present. She was the focus of every gaze, beloved in every eye, and suddenly he felt jealous in a way he never had before of anyone or about anyone.

He actively resented the way all of those elves looked at her, and he realised that for the rest of his life he was going to have to compete with that untiring, relentless torrent of adoration, and that there was no way he could. The sensation was a sour one, made all the more so because it was the last thing he had expected to experience at this moment.

He knew that he should be proud of her courage and her beauty and her gift for inspiring others around her, but instead he found a small, mean thing that wanted to hide her away and keep her for himself. She was revealing to him that he was smaller than he thought he was, and he resented her for that. He told himself it was unfair and unworthy, but unfortunately it was the way he felt.

She seemed unaware of it too, unaware of him. Her attention was focused on the crowd of elves whose attention was focused on her. It was like the relationship between an actor and his audience but multiplied a thousand times by the force of her magic. He was fooling himself if he thought he could compete with that. No living thing could. He might as well slink away now and leave her to her adoring worshippers.

Then she looked at him sidelong and with a small secretive smile. It was aimed at him alone, as if there was some shared joke or knowledge that lay between them and existed only for them – he saw the other side of what being the

Everqueen meant. He was her friend, possibly the only one she was ever likely to have now, the only person to whom she was not the avatar of a living goddess but who saw her as a person.

It was a thing that would make a goddess lonely, he thought.

Good, he thought, the small, twisted jealous side of his nature responded. It would make her all the sorrier when he was gone. But he smiled himself now, understanding that what he was feeling was not the sum total of all his feelings for her, only part of them and not the better part either. It was something he was just going to have to get used to, much as he resented it.

'MY FRIENDS, WE are gathered in very dark times,' Alarielle said. Her voice was one of those magical ones that would have carried to the furthest corners of the assembled throng even if she was talking in a whisper. There was something in it that commanded respect and belief as well.

Teclis recognised the sorcery but it was so subtly done that even he had trouble identifying quite how. 'Our enemies are mighty and our allies few. We have suffered defeat after defeat and loss after loss. I would not blame any of you if you had lost all hope of eventual victory.'

She paused to give her listeners a chance to absorb what she had said. Teclis was no great expert on public speaking but he thought that perhaps her message was somewhat too downbeat for this audience.

'Nonetheless, you have not done so. You have not given

up even in the face of a foe who delights in displaying his cruelty and power. You have not admitted defeat even in the face of overwhelming odds. You stand before me ready to fight and die for your homeland, and that makes me proud of each and every one of you.

'I would not have been here to tell you this if it had not been for two brothers. They saved me from the servants of the Witch King and they are here now to fight alongside you in battle tomorrow.

'I owe them my life and I wish to repay them. Teclis, step forwards.'

Teclis was surprised to be summoned, and embarrassed. He did not like limping forwards to be greeted by the Everqueen in front of the whole army. He would have remained where he was had not Tyrion pushed him forwards.

He limped up and was surprised to hear his name roared in acclamation by the assembled warriors. Alarielle gestured for silence. 'It has been said that you may turn out to be the greatest wizard since Caledor. I truly hope this is the case, for we have need of great wizards today. As a token of my respect and esteem, I give you this staff.'

She held aloft the Moonstaff of Lileath. It glowed in the moonlight, looking more than ever like an artefact of the ancients. Even those with the poorest magesight could see it radiated power. Teclis was stunned. He barely found the words to say, 'It is a queenly gift, your serenity.'

He accepted it from her, and it felt right in his hand, perfectly balanced, augmenting his power in a way that few things could. She leaned forwards to kiss him on the cheek. He was touched by that gesture and bowed to her, before backing away.

As he returned from the rise, he felt hands reach out to touch him and slap his back. He was unused to such gestures of affection or respect. He realised that many of those present were in awe of him. It was intoxicating and disturbing at the same time. He did not like being the centre of attention.

Alarielle continued to speak.

'If it was not for Teclis's brother, Tyrion, I truly would not be here today. He saved me from the midst of a druchii army when all hope seemed lost, and he stayed with me until I found safety among you, despite taking terrible wounds from the poisoned blades of the followers of Malekith.'

She gestured and heralds brought forward a covered wagon. 'Recently, the greatest artefact of our greatest hero has been restored to its full power by the father of these destiny-touched twins. He has spent a lifetime reforging the work of the master-mage Caledor…'

She paused to give her words time to sink in. A silence like that before the breaking of a storm settled upon the army. Teclis knew everyone present was wondering what she was going to say. It was more than magic that compelled their attention now, it was a genuine curiosity. She sprang onto the back of the wagon and stood beside an object covered by a tarpaulin. Teclis knew what was coming, but he still found himself holding his breath as she pulled the cover away.

In full view, on the great stand Teclis remembered so well,

stood the armour of Aenarion. It looked new. It was burnished till it shone and it glowed with awesome power. His magesight allowed him to see deep into the intricate web of spells overlaid on it. Even he was awed by the power and complexity of them though he had added to them himself in an attempt to protect his brother from the armour's power.

There was something else about the armour that compelled attention, a sense of awesome, ominous presence, of a magic that dated back to an earlier, darker, more primitive age. It stood there like a god emerged from the red murk of that ancient era. No one who looked upon it could doubt what it was.

'This is the dragon armour of Aenarion,' Alarielle said. 'And I can think of no one more worthy to wear it than my champion, Tyrion, son of Arathion.'

Tyrion stepped forwards and raised his arm to receive the army's acclamation. He looked the part, Teclis thought, as if he had been born to wear the armour and lead this army to victory.

They cheered him as if he could do it, and it was then that it sank in to Teclis exactly how desperate they all were.

'Let's get this over with,' Tyrion said quietly. He knew that the army was waiting to see him in the armour.

His father and Teclis nodded. They looked more serious and more worried than he could ever remember them doing in his entire life.

'Cheer up. We're not dead yet,' he told them. No one else

was close enough to hear his words.

'Only a matter of time,' said Teclis, ignoring the annoyed look his father shot him. Tyrion understood what his brother meant.

'It happens to everybody,' he said.

'To some sooner than others,' said his father. He looked lost and a little gloomy. Tyrion was reminded of the human explorer Leiber after they had found the treasure house of the lost city of Zultec. He would have expected his father to be more excited. Instead he seemed more than a little depressed, seemingly unaware that there was an entire army waiting expectantly.

'I did not expect to live forever,' Tyrion said.

'You always behaved as if you did,' said Teclis. Again Prince Arathion looked annoyed. He did not seem to be able to realise that Teclis had a different way of dealing with tension than he did.

'Are you sure you want to do this, my son?' he asked. There was genuine concern in his voice, and Tyrion was touched. The elf he remembered from his childhood would have been in a hurry to see him in the armour to make sure that it worked as he expected it to. Perhaps his father had changed.

'I am ready,' Tyrion said. He glanced from face to face and saw only concern there.

'I am the one who should be worried,' he said. 'All you have to do is get me into the suit.'

'It's the first time anyone has worn this armour in over six thousand years,' said his father. He glanced from Tyrion to the armour. A troubled expression flickered across his face. 'This is not without risks.'

'The time for worrying about those risks is long since passed,' Tyrion said. 'We will all die here if Malekith has his way. Some of us more painfully than others.'

Teclis nodded. His father sucked in his cheeks and made a clicking sound with his teeth. 'There is no need for this bravado, Tyrion. No one doubts your courage.'

'I am starting to. Please begin before I have second thoughts.'

His father nodded. He took the armour piece by piece from the stand and placed it reverently on the ground around Tyrion. He strapped the chestpiece into place. It was, for some reason, heavier than Tyrion expected it to be and colder, as if the metal had lain in snow for a long time. He rapped its surface with his knuckles. It rang. It was a strange thought that the last person who had done this was Aenarion, before setting out for the Island of the Dead. Tyrion wondered if he was going to his own death too. There were those who might see it as a fitting punishment for his presumption.

His father put on the armguards and the gauntlets while Teclis helped him into the greaves and leg-pieces. He stepped into the boots. At last, Teclis placed the helmet on his head. It shut down his field of vision and muffled his hearing. There was a certain finality to the act, like the closing of a door. Tyrion could feel the power in the armour. It was heavy and magic flowed through it; there was something else, a sense of anger and power and... resentment there, as if whatever was in it did not wish to see him wearing the armour.

'This is not the most pleasant sensation,' Tyrion said.

'It's about to become less pleasant,' said Teclis. His father nodded. Teclis raised the Moonstaff of Lileath and began to chant the words of an incantation. His father joined in, singing a counterpoint. As they did so, Teclis touched the runes on each section of the armour one at a time with the staff. Power seemed to flow out of him and into the armour.

Tyrion could feel it becoming lighter, or perhaps it was him becoming stronger. The sense of another person being there became more intense too.

He felt a great rage start to settle within him, a bloodthirsty desire to stride out of the tent and face his enemies, to slay them, to tear them apart with his bare hands. It was the sort of rage he had never felt before, but he knew that it had always been there, deep within him, part of his ancient bloodright.

Teclis touched his arms and he felt as if he could lift a horse. When the enchantments in the legs were activated, he felt as if he could run for miles. The activation of the helmet made his senses seem suddenly much clearer. He regained all the keenness of vision and hearing it had cost him, and more besides. He had a sense of *awareness* of what was going on all around him. It was not like anything he had experienced before. He felt those around him as a *pressure*. He knew that if Teclis stepped behind him he would know exactly where he was.

Teclis touched the centre of the breastplate and the armour

blazed to full life. For a brief ecstatic moment, power and energy and a sense of something else flowed into Tyrion. He felt stronger and faster than he ever had before. He knew that great wards had slid into place around him, protecting him from magic and harm. He felt for one brief moment like a god.

Both his father and Teclis stepped back from him with looks of awe and something like fear written on their faces.

'It worked,' Tyrion said. His voice had a booming quality to it and he knew somehow that when he spoke on a battlefield his words would be heard and understood by his warriors no matter what the din of arms was like around him. 'I am ready.'

Teclis held up his hand in a gesture of warning. Prince Arathion walked around him, inspecting him, and then emerged into Tyrion's field of vision exactly when Tyrion expected him to.

'It is done,' his father said. 'The dragon armour of Aenarion has been re-made. The gods help us all.'

Tyrion did not feel like he was wearing heavy armour, more like a suit made from the lightest cloth. He felt as if he could run and jump and fight completely unencumbered, and fight was exactly what he wanted to do. The spirit in the armour demanded it of him.

Tyrion fought down the rising tide of bloodlust. He did not want to be anyone or anything's pawn. He was himself and he intended to remain that way, even if it meant whatever was present in the armour would not help him to the fullest of its abilities.

Slowly his rage subsided a little. He drew Sunfang. It blazed more brilliantly than it ever had before, as if the presence of the armour had lent it new strength. He took another deep breath and raised his burning sword. The watching army roared its approval at the sight of him.

'PRINCE TYRION!' A group of strange elves walked towards him out of the crowd. They led the largest warhorse he had ever seen. It was armoured with heavy barding which it bore as if it were a saddle blanket.

He did not recognise any of them. They were garbed in thick leather armour and they had a peculiar, slightly bowlegged way of walking. Some of them still had spurs attached to their riding boots that clinked as they walked.

'I am Prince Paelus of Ellyrion,' said the leader of the newcomers. 'I wish to thank you on behalf of my people for all you have done. If it were not for you, we would be without a queen at the moment.'

Tyrion knew exactly what the hero of the hour was expected to say. 'I only did what any loyal elf would have done,' he said.

'I'm sure you did what any of us would have liked to do but which very few would have been capable of. You saved the Everqueen from the clutches of the druchii, and we would like to present you with a token of our appreciation.'

'That will not be necessary,' Tyrion said.

'Necessary or not, it would be ungracious of you to refuse us,' Prince Paelus said. 'This is Malhandir of the line of Korhandir, Father of Horses,' Prince Paelus said.

'We were bringing him to the great tournament to be the mount of the Everqueen's champion. Of course, we came too late and were caught up in the great war against the Witch King.'

Malhandir ambled towards Tyrion and nuzzled his shoulder. Prince Paelus laughed.

'It seems Malhandir has already made his choice,' he said. 'Once such a beast chooses a rider, he will never take another.'

Now that Malhandir was near, Tyrion sensed the strangeness in the horse. It was clear even to one as magically blind as he was that this was no normal beast. Malhandir radiated power, intelligence and a potent burning magic.

He was larger, more graceful and stronger than any horse Tyrion had ever seen and there was a wisdom in his eyes worthy of a scholar. Instinctively, he found himself reaching out to stroke the horse's muzzle.

He felt a great affection for the horse, such as he had never felt any moment before. There was a bond between them even after only a few heartbeats. The horse whinnied as if it was laughing at him and then shook its head and Tyrion found himself laughing too. His laughter echoed through the assembled ranks of the elven army.

Tyrion was glad. He truly wanted to be the rider of this steed. It was a warhorse that could carry him through any battle, he felt. Malhandir moved its head in a way that told Tyrion that it was time to mount up. Tyrion vaulted onto the great horse's back.

'Now I am ready to do battle,' he said. The army cheered.

The set of Alarielle's face told him she was worried, but she kept the glorious confident smile on her face.

# CHAPTER TWENTY-SIX

'So it begins,' Malekith said. His huge army was already in position. It looked ready to sweep forward and destroy the asur where they stood. Before that happened, there was something else that needed to be done.

'I am ready, sire,' Urian said. Malekith had reinforced the already potent magic in his armour with still more powerful spells. The magical blades blazed in his fist.

'First you will destroy their champions and then I will destroy their army – then I will have all of Ulthuan under my boot.'

Urian nodded. How many of those people down there faced their last day? How many would be dead before this day was out so that Malekith could realise his mad ambition? For a moment, he was tempted to take his sword and bury it in the Witch King's back. Only the knowledge that it was almost certainly not powerful enough to penetrate that almost-indestructible armour stopped him.

He told himself that today the Witch King would triumph and he stood at the Witch King's right hand. Somehow that knowledge did not make him as happy as it should have.

TYRION REINED MALHANDIR to a halt and watched the army move around him.

Even now in the face of that enormous and seemingly invincible enemy horde, it stirred his heart. He had always loved this time before the blood, the mud and the chaos of battle overwhelmed everything. The formations were drawn up. Everything was in order. There was this sense of being part of something much larger than himself.

Being part of this crowd was something that spoke to something deep within him. He could smell the oiled weapons, the leather and steel of the armour and the animal stink of the cavalry horses.

He felt like he was one very small part of a very large living thing. When he breathed, it breathed. When it spoke, he was part of its voice. Perhaps this was what it was like to be a god. Or perhaps part of a god.

He felt as if he was enormously strong, as if he could do anything, as if all he and all of the other soldiers round about him needed to do was will something to be done and it would occur. He was part of this vast hydra-headed entity that was far greater than the sum of its parts.

Of course, over there, on the other side of the battlefield, was another colossal entity, equally strong, if not stronger, that felt itself to be invincible. Soon these two huge monsters would come crashing together like stegadons in the jungle of Lustria. Then they would rend each other with their sword-like claws until great chunks were ripped bleeding from the flesh of the monsters and the army would lose all cohesion. In some ways, that would be a bit like dying, Tyrion thought.

All around him voices rumbled. The air vibrated as with the droning of a vast hive of bees. The earth shook beneath the tread of the marching army. He felt like a tiny particle being driven before a huge storm wind. It was as if somehow his life had taken on the momentum of the army and it had transferred some part of its vast purpose to him.

Looking at the faces of those around him, he could tell that they all felt the same way. They had a bemused, inebriated look written on them as if the owners of those faces were sodden with drink or under the influence of some potent drug that deadened their sense of individuality and made them less than individuals and yet greater.

He took a deep breath and allowed himself to luxuriate in the sense of being part of a greater entity, then he focused his concentration on his own body and became Tyrion once more, a small mote of life being driven before the vast hurricane of the army's purpose.

He urged Malhandir forwards to the place where the two armies would meet.

TECLIS HATED THIS. He hated the way the army marched together like one monstrous automaton. He felt more alone than at any time since he had begun his quest to find his brother. He could not be part of this. He could not join in.

He disliked the idea of being one mindless creature in a herd of mindless creatures. He disliked the way all of the faces around him showed one fixed purpose: unquestioning, obedient, willing to kill at the orders of someone else. He knew then exactly how different he was. It was simply part of his character that he could not be part of this huge, violent, unthinking community.

It was not that he was incapable of violence or indeed lack of thought – it was simply that he could not lay down his sense of self, subsume it to the will of the crowd.

He was not a leader but he was not a follower either. He was something different, alone, isolated, not part of this vast strange thing that was happening around him.

He was glad of that. Crowds were less than the sum of their parts. For some elves, there was a temptation in that. Perhaps it would be nice to stop thinking for himself for a moment, to suspend his judgement, to not look at the world through his own solitary eyes. He simply was not capable of doing that though. There was no temptation because there was nothing in him to be tempted.

He looked at the faces around him and he felt nothing but contempt at their slack-jawed acceptance of what was going on round about them. He was glad he was not like them.

He was not a sheep. He was an individual. His life had been a lonely one but it had prepared him for this moment, it had prepared him to stand apart and maintain his own critical faculties and be prepared to look with his own eyes upon what was going to happen.

Perhaps if all elves were capable of this, or all sentient beings, wars would not happen. Perhaps this loss of the sense of being an individual was a necessary precursor to mass violence. Perhaps one had to lose one's sense of self in order to become capable of killing.

He knew though that he was deceiving himself. He was certainly capable of killing. The question was whether he was normal, and he knew the answer to that already. He kept walking, carried along by the flow of the army.

Ahead of them a vaster force waited. He sensed the magical power summoned in its midst. Overhead dark clouds flowed, driven by cold winds. There was a storm coming. He could feel it.

THE ARMIES HALTED just out of bowshot of each other. They halted as if a signal had been given, and glared at each other.

A dark elf herald rode right up to the front of the asur force. He was accompanied by a few bodyguards, carrying the flags of truce. He smiled mockingly, confidently, with contempt. He looked perfectly at ease, as if he had nothing to fear, which was nothing less than the case. No one was going to attack him while he bore that flag.

'Malekith the Great, king of all the elves, commands you to listen!' The herald's voice was clear and ringing, some trick of magic allowed his words to carry to the furthest edges of the high elf camp. 'If any of you have the courage to face his champion in single combat, present yourself on the plain between the two armies and allow yourself to be slaughtered. He doubts that any of you will dare do so. He believes that none of the children of Ulthuan have the courage of their ancestors.'

'I will fight!' Someone shouted. Tyrion recognised the voice as belonging to Arhalien of Yvresse. 'I will show you that we do not fear your pathetic master.'

The herald laughed outright. 'You shall pay for the disrespect you show. Still, present yourself! Your death shall be a swift one.'

Tyrion wondered if Arhalien was being wise. Doubtless, Malekith was confident that his champion would be victorious. There was no reason for calling this challenge otherwise. It was meant, as Teclis had claimed last night, simply to give him one more advantage in the coming battle. It was intended to drive another nail into the coffin of high elf morale. On the other hand, Tyrion was not sure it would have been wise to turn down that challenge. To do so would simply be to admit that there was no warrior in the high elf army willing or able to accept the challenge.

He could see that a number of eyes were on him. It was true that he was looked upon as a hero in this army. They had expected him to speak up. It was too late now. Arhalien had spoken. He must be allowed to fight.

Arhalien came riding over to the rise upon which Tyrion stood. The pavilion of the Everqueen was behind him. It was obvious that Arhalien felt himself to be the true champion of Alarielle and this was his way of proving it.

'I have come to ask for the Everqueen's blessing and her favour before I ride out on her behalf,' he said.

Tyrion winced. This truly was playing into Malekith's hands if Arhalien should be killed. That a warrior carrying both Alarielle's favour and blessing should be slain was the worst of all possible omens for the army that represented her.

Did Arhalien not realise this? Did he even care? Or was he so wrapped up in his own personal quest for glory that he was willing to have that happen? It did not matter, Tyrion thought. He had already done it.

Alarielle looked as radiantly beautiful as ever, the expression on the faces of all the watchers changed to reverence by her mere presence. Tyrion wondered if he would ever get used to it. Why was he incapable of feeling that level of reverence and respect? He cared about the woman, but nothing about the goddess touched him at all.

'My blessing you may have,' she said. 'But my favour is reserved for Tyrion, son of Arathion.'

Arhalien accepted her words with a graceful gesture. 'Your blessing is enough for me, your serenity,' he said. 'I accept your decision.'

He rode forth to the centre of Finuval Plain. The soldiers of the high elf army left their camp behind him, just as the dark elves were doing on the far side of the plain. It was a mistake, Tyrion could see that. It meant that if battle erupted after the single combat, the high elves would not be in a good formation. It mattered less to the dark elves that the same would apply to them. They had the advantage of numbers. Tyrion wondered if Malekith had planned it this way all along.

LEADERS BELLOWED INSTRUCTIONS trying to hold formations together. The princes sent messengers everywhere, telling them to hold their formation. It was like watching a rout in reverse. It was as if the army was losing all coherence in its quest to get close enough to watch the champions fight. Tyrion kept close to Alarielle. He noticed that those assigned to protect the Everqueen were doing the same. It was good. If Malekith planned any treacherous attack upon her, she would at least have bodyguards. Somehow, Teclis emerged from the crowd.

'I told you this would happen,' he said.

'As ever, brother, your gift for prophecy is impressive,' Tyrion said. 'I don't like this. I don't like it at all.'

'That's why I decided to join you. This might be cover for something else.'

'What frightens me is the idea that it might not be.'

'What do you mean?' Teclis asked.

'This might be exactly what it appears to be. Malekith may be so confident of victory that he merely wants to put on this little show to damage our morale. This might be the only point of this exercise, as you suggested last night.'

Teclis nodded. 'If any wicked magic is attempted, I will at least be here to counter it.'

'I find your presence oddly reassuring, brother,' Tyrion said.

'As I find yours,' Teclis replied. They moved closer to

Alarielle. She reached out and squeezed Tyrion's hand.

'What is going on?' she asked.

'Apparently Malekith wants to be entertained by some gladiatorial combat before he puts the rest of us to the sword.'

'Do you think Arhalien has a chance?' Alarielle asked.

'I think we shall soon find out. Here comes Malekith's champion now.'

Urian Poisonblade moved exactly the same way as Prince Iltharis moved. He looked exactly as Prince Iltharis looked. It came to Tyrion that that was because he was Prince Iltharis in truth. There could be no mistake about that. He was garbed all in black armour, with two blades strapped to his side. He walked with a certain jaunty confidence that had always been Prince Iltharis's.

'I wish I had killed him back in Lothern,' Teclis said.

'You never had that chance,' Tyrion said. Teclis looked at him coldly.

'You might have it now,' Tyrion told him, 'but you were not capable of killing him in the past.'

Teclis shrugged. 'You might well be right, brother.'

Korhien Ironglaive walked up to the brothers. 'It is all so easy for him, isn't it?' he said, indicating Urian. There was admiration as well as cold hatred in his voice.

'He always was an overconfident bastard,' said Teclis.

It seemed that they were not the only ones who recognised Prince Iltharis. Loud booing emerged from the ranks of the high elves. Urian drew his blades and raised them in an ironic salute. He seemed not in the slightest daunted by the hatred that the massed army expressed towards him.

Tyrion admired his coolness. Prince Arhalien rode up towards Urian. He vaulted lithely from his saddle, looking every bit the poised and polished hero. Behind them, officers still called orders to the army, trying to restore some semblance of discipline and formation.

Tyrion noticed that the druchii were drawn up in ordered ranks. They were already in battle formation. The barbarians were not and they moved restlessly as if they were prepared to attack treacherously at any moment. It was entirely possible that they might – perhaps this was what Malekith was counting upon to give him an excuse to break the truce when he needed to. Equally though, Tyrion felt certain that the time was not upon them when the Witch King would do that. He wanted Urian to fight against Arhalien. He wanted his champion to demonstrate his superiority.

Having fought them both, Tyrion knew that Urian was almost certain to win. The only thing that was likely to save Arhalien would be some stroke of luck of the sort that could never be relied upon but sometimes happened in combat. It was not something Tyrion was counting on seeing. Fighters like Urian made their own luck.

Both of them turned and raised their weapons in salute to the respective armies. Arhalien raised his blade to Alarielle. For once, Tyrion did not look at her. He looked in the direction that Urian raised his blade. He looked upon Malekith, Witch King of Naggaroth, for the first time in his life as he emerged into full view on the cold hillside overlooking the field of combat.

Malekith was a fearsome figure, as terrifying in his own way as a greater daemon. He towered over those around him, a giant among elves. It was the armour, Tyrion told himself. That was what did it. It made him look bigger than he was. There was magic in it that did that and more.

He was not fooling himself. Malekith was bigger than any other elf. Tyrion had no idea why that should be. Perhaps it had something to do with having lived for millennia. Perhaps it had something to do with what had happened to him when he had passed through the sacred Flame of Asuryan and been rejected by the god. Or perhaps it was something else entirely.

All Tyrion knew was that Malekith looked like a giant. There was a sense of terrifying power and strength about the Witch King that was palpable. It radiated out from him. He seemed like a monster made of metal, indestructible, invincible and utterly confident of victory. He raised one gigantic armoured hand in response to Urian's salute.

The two warriors leapt together. Blades flashed too fast for the eye to follow. A flower of blood blossomed on Arhalien's chest and he fell to the ground dead. The high elf army groaned. No one seemed able to believe that the fight was over so quickly.

Tyrion could. He knew exactly how good Urian was.

'Perhaps I should challenge Urian myself,' Teclis said. 'I could probably blast him with a lightning bolt from here.'

'That's not very sporting.'

'What he did to Arhalien was not exactly fair either.'

'Arhalien knew what he was letting himself in for. He chose to do it anyway.'

Teclis looked hard at Tyrion. 'He is going to challenge you next. That is the point of this whole exercise.'

'This is not looking good,' Korhien said.

Tyrion looked at the older warrior. He understood at once. If the battle broke out now, the dark elves would be at a high in their morale. The armies were so close together and so disorganised that they would roll over each other.

Urian brandished his blade over his head. He moved like a showman playing to his audience, walking along the front of the druchii line, punching his fist triumphantly in the air, accepting their cheers like a pit fighter accepting the plaudits of the crowd.

'Is that the best you can do?' he shouted into a momentary silence. His words sounded clear after the oceanic roar of the druchii and the Chaos worshippers. He was staring directly at Tyrion. 'Pitiful! Do the asur have no better warriors than that?'

Tyrion was about to step forwards but Alarielle's hand on his arm restrained him for a crucial moment, and Korhien stepped forwards. 'I will fight you, traitor!' he shouted.

Urian looked off to one side for a moment, and Tyrion thought he saw something like a look of shame pass over his face. For whatever reason, the traitor did not seem all that keen to face his old friend. Korhien strode proudly towards the druchii force. He did not seem in the least afraid and such was his presence that they fell silent.

'A representative of the Phoenix King will be the next to fall before our champion,' the herald of Malekith spoke. Urian glared at him. The herald fell silent.

Korhien and Urian came face to face and exchanged words. Tyrion would have given a lot to know what they said. After a moment they stepped apart and Korhien unlimbered his axe. Urian raised his blade in salute.

Tyrion glanced along the front line of the asur force. The units were falling back into formation. It looked as if Korhien had bought them some time.

The horns sounded. Combat began. Axe and sword clashed, glittering in the sun. All was silence. Korhien lashed out. Urian sprang back and then forwards and his blade passed through the body of his old friend. Tyrion shrugged off Alarielle's hand and stepped forwards.

He was not striding towards a fight, he was rushing to see to his old friend.

'Wait, Tyrion,' said Alarielle. He ignored her cry.

# CHAPTER TWENTY-SEVEN

TYRION WALKED FORWARDS through the ranks of the asur army. All eyes were upon him. Elves stepped back to get out of his way. Something of the power and the terror of the ancient armour was felt by all of the observers. One by one the soldiers began to chant his name, taking it up until it became an awesome, ominous, thunderous roar.

The armour felt as light as cloth now he was wearing it and he himself had never felt better. He felt strong. He felt ready for battle, in some ways too ready. He burned to get to grips with the foe, to lash out with his blade, to bury it in flesh. He felt a low simmering anger deep within his soul, which kept bubbling up and threatening to become stronger.

He tried telling himself that it was not his anger, it was something alien, external, part of the magic bound into the armour itself. He knew that this was not true. Something deep within him responded to the rage that the armour of Aenarion embodied. The magic called out to some deep-rooted part of his being, and that part responded.

He was angry with himself because of this. Some echo of the mighty personality of Aenarion sought to use him as a vessel for its wrath, to turn him into an engine of rage. Much as he wanted to give way to it, to revel in that awesome molten anger, he refused to do so.

He was himself. He was not the tool of some ancient godly ghost. He would, as he always had, make his own decisions, fight his own battles, remain himself, even if it meant he could never tap into the deeper powers of the armour. He did not want the magic so badly.

Even as that thought ran through his brain, he realised that in some ways the armour had already changed him. He sensed the presence of magic as he had never done before. He felt the presence of dozens of magical weapons all around him borne by asur and druchii. He sensed wizards weaving spells, and the simply potent presence of the mages themselves.

More than anything else, he felt the chill and awesome presence of Malekith, Witch King of Naggaroth, as he would have felt the presence of a cold wind blowing out of the north. He could have closed his eyes and pointed to Malekith as surely as if he could see.

He sensed another nearby presence, almost as potent, and far more familiar. It belonged to his twin. Teclis had grown strong indeed, he realised, rivalling the force of that ancient evil entity with a cold, brilliant power of his own. Beyond Teclis he sensed Alarielle and the ancient slow entity that worked through her.

The thought struck him – it could not be chance that brought so many powerful magical beings here today, or so many potent ancient artefacts. Something else was at work, destiny, fate, the will of the gods. It did not matter what you called it. He sensed that he and everyone else here was caught in some great web, woven by beings more powerful even than Malekith.

The last of the high elf army had parted before him now and he walked out onto the open field between the two great elven forces. Ahead of him stood Urian. He wore armour of a strange and alien design. For the first time in his life Tyrion could see the spells woven into it. In their way, they were as awesome and complex as the ones woven into his own. He sensed an evil presence there, a powerful dark magic that drew on the energies of Chaos, that was semi-sentient. There was a daemon bound into it, he realised, a slumbering evil being that powered it and gave it strength beyond any mortal.

In each hand, Urian held a greenishly glowing blade. They radiated a curdled, malevolent energy that seemed to suck the life out everything surrounding them. Black blood dripped smoking from channels in the metal and where it spattered the ground, the grass withered and died and the earth itself cracked as if unable to bear the touch of the poisonous fluid.

Urian wore a great helmet, moulded into the shape of the visage of some daemon prince. The visor was lifted to reveal his pale features. They were sunken and gaunt, and his eyes were tormented and strangely horror-filled. He raised his blades in mocking salute but Tyrion's gaze was drawn beyond him to the real enemy.

On a bleak low hillside overlooking the battleground, Malekith lounged on a great metal throne set atop a huge metal shield. A score of enormously muscular male slaves held that shield aloft. They must have been strong indeed to do so, for Malekith must have weighed far more than any mortal elf. He was more than a head taller than Tyrion and the armour encasing his body must have been inches thick. From within a helmet that might have encased the head of a giant, a cold gaze blazed.

An aura of immense, ageless strength radiated out from the Witch King. Tyrion felt the malevolence and power in it and something else as well, curiosity and… recognition. He gazed right at Malekith, meeting those ancient eyes, and was surprised to see something like shock in them.

It took him a moment to realise why.

Tyrion was wearing the armour of Malekith's father. Perhaps, at this moment, it appeared to the Witch King as if that potent ancient had returned from the grave to judge him. Tyrion certainly hoped that Malekith felt that way. He drew his own sword. It caught fire. He raised it in grudging salute in the direction of Urian and his master. This was a formal duel, the most important of his life, and the proprieties must be observed.

Then he looked at the one who lay on the ground at Urian's feet.

Korhien sprawled, blood pouring from his chest. He looked pale and it was obvious he was on the edge of death. 'Well, doorkeeper, it looks like this is farewell. Kill him for me.'

'I will,' said Tyrion.

Urian raised both blades above his head, acknowledging the applause and cheers of the dark elves who watched, while never taking his eyes off Tyrion.

'Prince Tyrion, it seems we are to duel again,' Urian said. His smile was friendly and mocking, if not for the presence of that huge army of dark elves and Chaos worshippers behind him, they might easily have been meeting in the old practice ground in the Emeraldsea mansion.

'For the last time,' Tyrion said. There was something about the armour of Aenarion that altered his voice, made it more resonant and powerful. At least that was the way it seemed to him. Perhaps it was merely his own hatred that lent his voice such power.

'Sadly, that is true,' Urian said. 'Of all the fights I have had in my life, this is the one I regret most.'

'I don't,' Tyrion said. 'I am going to kill you.'

'That remains to be seen,' Urian replied. 'You'll forgive me for saying that you have never had the skill to do that in the past.'

Tyrion let a cold smile touch his lips. 'I never had the will to do that in the past, or the need.'

'Neither will nor need count as much as skill.'

Tyrion spoke slowly and calmly. 'I am going to kill you.'

'Many have tried,' Urian said. His voice was casual,

uninterested. 'They are all dead.'

'You do not understand me, Urian, Iltharis, whatever you call yourself now. I am going to kill you, if I have to throw myself on your blade and tear out your throat with my teeth. It is going to happen.'

The anger and hatred in his own voice were corrosive. The determination in it reflected exactly how he felt. In that moment, he knew he was capable of it too. For the first time he thought he saw something like fear in Urian's eyes.

He held the killer's gaze and it was Urian who looked away first. Urian took a step back, before realising the error of doing so. The watching dark elves murmured among themselves when they saw what was happening. Urian made another mocking salute and made it look as if the step backwards was simply part of that.

It was a nice recovery.

'I see you have acquired new armour,' he said. 'It seems somehow suitable for one of the blood of Aenarion to be wearing it. At least you will make a pretty corpse.'

'They will not be able to say the same about you,' Tyrion said. Once again, he was surprised by how flat and cold his voice came out. There was an eerie quality to it, as if the ghost of Aenarion was speaking through his lips.

'It pains me that we will not part as friends,' Urian said.

'If you had not betrayed our people, we would be fighting on the same side.'

'They were never our people. They were your people.'

'Are you sure about that?' Tyrion said. His instinct for

going for the jugular told him that was the correct thing to say. Urian shrugged.

The sound of murmuring from the dark elf army was increasing. They were growing restless. They did not like to see the two champions speak. It was not what they expected. It was not what they had come here for. Tyrion and Urian looked at each other warily. It seemed to Tyrion that Urian was reluctant to start fighting. He felt as if there must be some way that he could turn this to his advantage.

The longer he drew things out here, the better it would be for his own side. It would give them more time to get back into formation and recover from the shock of seeing its two champions cut down.

Of course, all of that would mean nothing if Urian killed Tyrion here. Seeing three champions defeated in succession would most likely prove too much for high elf morale, particularly since Tyrion was wearing the dragon armour of Aenarion and carrying his sword. It was impossible to imagine a worse omen than Tyrion being defeated here as far as they were concerned. It came to Tyrion then that his threat to Urian had better prove true. He needed to kill Urian here no matter what it cost – that was the only way to restore the balance even if it cost his own life.

There had been a time when he could have made the decision to do that without a single regret. There had been a time when he was truly fearless. That time was in his past. He did not want to die now. He wanted to live and be with Alarielle.

Of course, that did not really mean anything. If the dark

elves won here, they would have no future anyway. It was not that he was afraid to die, he realised, it was that he wanted to live with her. If that was not possible, then he did not have anything to live for. If by his death here he could save her life, he was prepared to do that too. Not because it would help the elven nation but because it would help her. He wished that he had taken the time to tell her this before it was too late, and it came to him now that he had missed the opportunity to do that, perhaps forever.

He looked across at Urian and wondered if the dark elf had similar regrets. Somehow, he doubted that. Anyone who could do what Urian had done must be completely without conscience.

'The audience is growing restless,' Urian said, pulling down the visor of his helmet and turning himself completely into a metal-faced daemon. 'Let us give them a show.'

'I will give them your death,' Tyrion said.

URIAN ADVANCED LIKE a big cat. His strangely glowing green blades left odd afterimages on the retina.

Was it his imagination, Tyrion wondered, or was the dark elf champion advancing more slowly and cautiously than he normally would? The two sickly emerald blades slashed towards him almost tentatively. Tyrion took the impact of one on his shield and parried the other with Sunfang. He launched his own counter: savagely, swiftly, surely. The high elf army roared, seeing the speed of his response. Urian danced away, not even attempting a counter at this stage.

What was going on here, Tyrion wondered? He had never known his opponent to be so cautious previously. Perhaps it was all part of some new strategy that Urian was using to toy with him. Or perhaps it was something else – perhaps he really had worried his opponent with his threats. Knowing how fearless Urian was, Tyrion somehow doubted that.

It didn't matter – he was committed. He was going to kill Urian, no matter what it took. Sunfang blazed in his hand, almost dazzlingly bright. Its glow was stronger than Tyrion had ever seen it and it radiated heat.

Perhaps this was what had Urian worried. He had never faced Tyrion with this magical weapon before and perhaps he was cautious, not knowing its abilities. Tyrion could not blame him for feeling that way.

Sunfang was a legendary weapon. No one really knew what it was capable of except perhaps Malekith or Morathi. Tyrion wondered if he could summon the fire from within the blade that he had used to kill the four assassins back among the woods of Avelorn. It did not seem either honourable or sporting, but now was not the time for such considerations. All that really mattered now was victory.

Almost as if he sensed the thought, Urian came gliding back in. The two blades flickered towards Tyrion like the forked tongue of a serpent. This time they came in with Urian's accustomed speed and Tyrion was hard put to defend himself, back-pedalling away clumsily, taking blows on his shield and looking for an opening through which to drive Sunfang that never appeared.

For all their speed, Urian's blows were driven with

enormous force. Tyrion felt as if his arm was becoming bruised with the force of the impact and he would not have been surprised to see the shield itself being dented and knocked out of shape. He did not have time to check. The dark elves were cheering now, certain that their champion was on his way to victory.

Why should they not be, Tyrion thought? Urian had easily dispatched the previous two high elf champions and they were among the greatest warriors in Ulthuan.

He felt as if, if he allowed this to continue, he would be ceding entirely the advantage to Urian. If he allowed that to happen, his threat would seem to be hollow. It was not the case. He sprang suddenly forwards, driving towards Urian, ignoring those deadly blades.

Driven by all his weight, he knocked Urian off-balance and slashed out with Sunfang. Lightning-quick, the druchii ducked beneath it and drove his sword forwards. Tyrion flinched as it struck home. He felt a surge of pain in his side and wondered if it was all over. He did not look down. He did not allow himself to be distracted. Instead he brought Sunfang down in a mighty arc, hoping to split his opponent's head with a reflexive death strike.

Urian's blades crossed as he parried, catching Sunfang between them. Tyrion tried to press home but he was only using one arm and his opponent was using both. Urian slowly but surely managed to push himself upright. Tyrion struck at him with the edge of his shield, catching him among the ribs and sending him reeling backwards.

The two armies were silent now as the champions leapt

apart. They stood glaring at each other like maddened wolves. All appearance of civilisation, of urbanity, had dropped from Urian now. He glared at Tyrion in fury, knowing that he was fighting for his life as he had never had to fight before.

'I see your armour is everything the legend said it was,' Urian said. His voice sounded level but there was an undercurrent of menace in it that had not been there before. This pleased Tyrion. It meant that he was getting to his foe, that Urian was worried. He wondered what Urian was talking about then he realised that he did not feel any blood flowing where his enemy had struck him. He felt some pain but no more so than from a normal bruise. Given how powerful those magical blades were, it was a testimony to the work of Caledor and Teclis and his father that he was still standing.

Tyrion sprang forwards, slashing with Sunfang. Urian jumped backwards. The two blades slashed into action once again. One of them cut high, aiming at Tyrion's head, the other was aimed at his leg, at the weakest point in the armour where it guarded the knee.

Tyrion stepped away from the low blow and parried the high blow. It was what Urian had been waiting for; he brought his left-hand blade upwards and slashed at Tyrion's throat. Tyrion raised his shield to block it, partially obscuring his own field of vision.

If it were not for the awareness of magic that his armour had given him, he would not have sensed Urian shifting his position to come in from the side. As it was, he was able to circle and face him, striking out once more and catching Urian on the side of his head.

Urian staggered backwards, taken off guard for once. The dark elf army groaned. Tyrion was surprised. His blow would have beheaded anyone else. He'd put all of his strength behind it. It seemed that the armour that Malekith had given his chosen champion was every bit as good as the armour Tyrion himself wore.

Tyrion felt something new. Cold magic flowed over him, slowing him down. He risked a glance at Malekith from the corner of his eye. He knew the Witch King had cast some sort of spell, invisible to others, that was affecting him even through the armour. His timing was off. He could not press home quickly enough to take advantage of Urian's weakness.

His heart sank. He was not fighting against just Urian now. Malekith himself had entered the fray on behalf of his champion. It seemed like the Witch King was taking no chances. He fully intended that Tyrion was going to be beaten.

TECLIS SAW TYRION slow. He sensed the flow of spellwork coming from the Witch King. It was so subtle that he doubted that anyone else present could perceive it, let alone counter it. It was not a very powerful spell. It did not have to be. In a contest between two warriors so closely matched, even a spell that slowed a combatant just slightly would be enough to secure victory.

What was worse was that if Teclis tried any overt

counterspell, it would look as if he was the one trying to influence the outcome by magic. It was a strategy of daemonic wickedness. Even if Tyrion won, the Witch King would have achieved his purpose. The only way the asur could be seen to win was by treachery.

Teclis closed his eyes and studied the near-invisible gossamer web that Malekith had woven. He would need to be as subtle as Malekith. He extended tendrils of his own magic, reinforcing some of the ancient protections of the armour, one by one unknotting the tendrils of Malekith's spell. He prayed that he would be quick enough.

SUDDENLY, THE FIT passed. The feeling of lassitude lifted. Tyrion felt his body respond with its accustomed speed. Mere heartbeats had passed but it had been enough for Urian to regain his balance.

Tyrion struck again, hoping to take advantage, but Urian countered with his left-hand blade and slid a blow over the top of Tyrion's shield. The poisoned blade glowed where it hit Aenarion's ancient armour and threatened to pierce it. Tyrion stepped away so that it glanced off. Urian landed another blow on Tyrion's shield. The clamour rang out across the field like a daemonic blacksmith striking an anvil in hell.

Malekith had risen to his feet now, apparently to get a better view of the battle. In reality his burning gaze contained potent magic. Something was countering it now. Tyrion suspected his twin was working counterspells. Nonetheless the Witch King's looming presence distracted Tyrion for a moment and Urian struck once more, his blade aiming for his throat. Tyrion parried. Sunfang blazed dimly against a background of infernal green.

'You have improved greatly, Prince Tyrion,' Urian said. His voice was so quiet that Tyrion knew only he could hear it.

'You have not.'

'It is impossible to improve on perfection.'

Time seemed to slow for Tyrion. Everything narrowed down to his awareness of his enemy, of his flashing blades, his constant attacks. He had no idea how long they fought, only that he existed in the middle of a storm of violence, parrying an endless series of subtle and deadly attacks, replying in kind with volcanic onslaughts of violence.

All around them, quiet deadly magic flowed as Teclis and Malekith strove to influence the battle. Tyrion's limbs ached. His breathing was laboured. Even the armour of Aenarion was starting to feel as if it was made of lead. Lifting Sunfang was like trying to lift a tree trunk.

Urian gave no sign of any slackening of his technique. He seemed to fight with the same polished precision as he had when they started, but Tyrion could see sweat rolling down his chin and noticed that he too was breathing hard.

He sensed that despite appearances, his foe must be as weary as he. If he were not, then things were going to end very badly. Tyrion started to limp a little, to slow his parries. Under normal circumstances such a stratagem would not have fooled Urian, but these were not normal circumstances. His enemy must be as tired as he was. Urian sent a sledgehammer blow smashing into Tyrion's guard. Tyrion did not have to fake the slip. His leg gave way and he fell to the ground. Urian raised his blade, going for the final, flashy finishing blow.

'Now you die,' said Tyrion. Leaving himself completely open, trusting to his armour and not caring whether he died as long as he killed Urian; he struck the most brutal, simple and direct stroke he could, aiming upwards for Urian's groin. Urian partially deflected it and struck home with his own blade, a stroke as simple and direct as Tyrion's own. The armour of Aenarion held although the force of the impact was brutal. Sunfang pierced the armour of Malekith and came out the other side. Urian's eyes widened in surprise.

'Well done,' he said, and slid to the ground. Tyrion rose, spat in the direction of the Witch King and then turned and raised his burning blade in salute to the Everqueen. For a moment there was a terrible silence, then from the ranks of the asur a great cheer rang out.

With a bellow of incoherent rage, Malekith signalled for his troops to attack. From the body of the asur forces Malhandir raced forwards, coming for its master. Tyrion vaulted into the saddle even as the steel tidal wave engulfed him.

# CHAPTER TWENTY-EIGHT

WITH A MIGHTY roar the two armies came together. Tyrion rode through the vanguard of the conflict. Malhandir moved smoothly beneath him, sure-footed in the mud and blood. Sunfang blazed in his hand, cleaving through his foes. The armour fed him a terrible strength and a rage that drove him forwards like a drug.

He glowed with the joyous rage of his victory over Urian and the knowledge that he had given hope to an army so close to defeat. It would take more than hope now, he realised.

He fought like a mortal god, killing everything within reach with the sword that had been borne by his famous ancestor. Wherever he rode, his foes fled from him such was the terror inspired by his appearance. The humans would not face him at all, but turned tail as he came closer. He rode them down, and the cavalry that followed him broke them.

The weight of numbers was still on the side of the druchii and their allies, but at least it felt like the asur had a chance, that if nothing else they would make a last stand worth singing about.

TECLIS FELT THE cold power of the Witch King grow. Malekith had begun to summon the winds of magic to him and sculpt them into a massive, cold storm front of power. Gone was all attempt to subtly shape things. Now he was building a spell to smite his foes down with all the force of a hammer wielded by a god. The skies turned black. Strange polychromatic lightning danced along the underside of the clouds. The fingers of the wind tore at Teclis's cloak.

The winds of magic spiralled in around Malekith, forming a cyclone of power. Teclis exerted his will to counter the spell, twisting the currents out of shape, making it ungovernable, poisoning the structure of the spell even as it was created so that it would become unstable. His hope was that Malekith would try and cast the spell and it would run out of control, but the Witch King understood too well the ways of sorcery.

He gave up all attempts at forming the massive attack spell and sent lines of force racing back along the currents of Teclis's own weaving. Teclis had only a few heartbeats to counter them before bolts of scarlet lightning impacted on the wards he had set. He ground his teeth together with the effort of parrying the bludgeoning stroke.

Sweat stood out on his brow. He cursed himself for over-confidence. Until this day he had not encountered a magician who was beyond his strength and skill to cope with.

He had never encountered anyone as powerful as Malekith. He had a real battle on his hands, and he felt certain that if he continued to fight at this range, Malekith would win. The spell that he had been counting on to smite the Witch King with could be used only at close range, and there was a massive army between him and the blasted hillside upon which the Witch King stood.

TYRION SMASHED THROUGH the ranks of black-armoured Chaos warriors, Sunfang burning in his hands. He chopped through the pole holding the obscene banner of a Chaos champion, grasped what remained of it with his shield hand and drove the broken point through the chest of one of his enemies like a spear.

He took in the field of battle at a glance, understanding it in a way that few could. The play of forces was immediately obvious to him. It was like looking down on a chessboard from above. He saw the main lines of advance the druchii army were taking towards the Everqueen's tent. He saw where the forces of the asur were weak and faltering. He understood where they would stand true and hold firm.

Seeing a line of elven spearmen struggling to hold their ground in the face of a tight phalanx of dark elf warriors, he raced forwards on Malhandir, shouting his battle-cry. The mighty armoured steed smashed through the front line of the druchii soldiery. Sunfang arced downwards, splintering the helmet of the dark elf captain. Blades sleeted off the dragon armour of Aenarion and Malhandir's heavy barding. Seeing Tyrion in their midst, the asur took heart, rallying around him, smashing through the broken ranks of their enemies.

From the left, Tyrion saw a company of Cold Ones approaching. They were about to take his own force in the flank. He wheeled Malhandir and charged towards them. For any other elf, it would have been a suicidal attack, but Tyrion was mounted on the greatest warhorse Ellyrion had produced in five thousand years, encased in the dragon armour of Aenarion and equipped with a blade forged by Caledor in the dawn ages of the world. He was among the Cold Ones in an instant, burning sword beheading the first. Malhandir rose on its hind legs and with a massive blow of hooves it crushed the head of a Cold One to pulp.

Unflinching, the remainder of the druchii cavalry closed in and Tyrion found himself surrounded by snapping jaws and hostile blades.

A MASS OF druchii infantry hurled itself at the rise on which Teclis stood. Crossbow bolts turned the air black around him, but so far his warding charms had held good. He wondered how well they would do when the druchii were upon him. He did not intend to find out.

He spoke the words of a powerful incantation, and a blast of lightning smote the dark elf ranks, overloading the warding spells around them, leaping from metal spearpoint to metal spearpoint, jumping from armoured form to armoured form. A score of druchii died in the first blast. More died with his second. Again and again he sent the lightning smashing into them, until it was more than even druchii flesh could bear and the surviving warriors turned and fled.

Teclis's heart leapt with momentary elation, then he shivered as he realised that the attack had distracted him from Malekith, and that the Witch King had prepared a new abomination. From the midst of the enemy ranks a bubbling, boiling cloud of poisonous, putrescent magic emerged. Teclis wracked his brain for a counterspell to this ancient evil sorcery, but nothing came.

The asur screamed as tentacles of the poisonous cloud descended among them. Where it touched, skin sloughed from bone, flesh rotted in a moment, bone turned from yellow to white. In the distance he heard gigantic evil laughter as if the Witch King fed upon the death and could not contain his mirth. The cloud stretched out its monstrous arms, reaching for Tyrion.

TYRION SMASHED HIS way through the riders surrounding him, and found himself confronted by powerful evil magic.

Tyrion saw the elven spearmen start to die as the evil magical cloud settled on them. The asur were not the only ones to die. The druchii infantry they engaged died just as harshly. Clearly the Witch King did not care too much who got killed by his magic as long as his foes were smashed.

Tyrion realised at once that Malekith was concentrating on him. Perhaps this could be used to his advantage. He pulled Malhandir round and moved towards the cloud, veering at the last second to race ahead of the poisonous mist that reached out for him with ghostly tentacles.

The Cold Ones pursuing him were not so lucky. They raced through tattered streamers of mist and where it touched them, scales fell off to reveal the diseased flesh beneath. Where it touched riders' armour, metal corroded and flesh turned to a loathsome, stinking pus.

He only hoped he could outrace it.

TECLIS SUMMONED AN enormous wind to him. He drew it down from the skies, shaped its cyclonic force and then sent the hurricane ravening out over the battlefield. It smashed into the monstrous poisonous cloud pursuing Tyrion and rent it asunder, driving small ribbons of mist back into the druchii ranks, where they killed as they went until the storm force of the wind dissipated them entirely.

Teclis knew that Malekith could keep this up all day and that it would only work to his advantage. His army had the greater numbers, could afford to take the greater casualties. It did not matter how brave the asur were, they would be defeated unless something was done. He needed to get across the battlefield now and get close enough to the Witch King to work the spell he had planned.

He cast his mind back to his first flight on Silver Wing's back, when he had tried to derive a spell of levitation from first principles. It was time to put that spell to the test. He summoned more power to him, and stepped upwards as if walking on an invisible stair.

One step at a time, he walked upwards into the sky above the battlefield and saw all of the carnage laid out beneath him. He saw the thin lines of the asur being overwhelmed. He saw Tyrion rally the high elves again and again, his blade a burning banner, the dragon armour of Aenarion terrible to his foes. He knew that given the weight of numbers, eventually even his twin would be pulled down.

If he was going to do something about that, he had better do it now. He kept walking across the face of the sky, towards the distant figure of Malekith.

TYRION LOOKED UP at the sky, realising that victory or defeat did not lie in his hands any more but in the frail form of his brother, whose magic carried him overhead towards a confrontation with the greatest enemy of their people.

He offered up a prayer and returned to smiting his foes, determined if he could to carve a way to the throne of the Witch King himself.

AS HE STEPPED onto the ground before Malekith, Teclis was shocked by the sheer presence of the Witch King.

It was not just the magical energy which radiated from him like a blast furnace, Malekith possessed an aura of power that had nothing to do with his strength in magic. He gave out a sense of physical might that struck Teclis with the force of a blow from a mailed gauntlet. This massive metallic form was capable of breaking the mightiest of warriors with his bare hands.

Not for the first time, Teclis questioned the wisdom of

the course of action he had chosen for himself. He pushed his doubts aside – the time for having them was long since passed. Now he had to concentrate all his faculties simply on completing the task at hand.

'You should go home, mighty prince,' Teclis said. 'You are not welcome here.'

'Welcome or not, I am home,' said Malekith. 'This is my land and I am its rightful king. Soon all will acknowledge that, or die.'

'You will be king of the dead then in a land of ruins, even if you succeed.'

'If that is how it must be, then so be it. Lands can be repopulated, ruins rebuilt.'

'Not if Caledor's ley lines are destroyed and the world unmade. That is what your mother plans if you are successful.'

'I will deal with my mother.'

'She might prove stronger than you.'

'Do you think you are stronger than me?' Malekith asked.

Teclis knew he was not. At best, he was Malekith's equal in power and he was far inferior in knowledge and skill. All the things Tyrion had said when comparing himself to Urian were just as true for him when he compared himself to the Witch King. More so. Malekith had had millennia in which to perfect his arts.

'You cannot survive this,' Malekith said. He sounded almost sorry.

'I do not need to survive it,' said Teclis, smiling brightly. 'I just need to make sure you do not survive as well.'

'I think that is beyond your skills, little cripple.'

'I must beg to differ,' said Teclis.

'Are you really willing to die?'

'Are you, mighty prince? That is the real question here. I have not found life so much to my taste. If I die here, they will say of me that I died slaying the greatest evil in elven history. If you die here, they will say *he was killed by a crippled boy*. Which of us comes out of that better?'

Teclis held his breath. He was close enough to Malekith to sense the fires of Asuryan that still burned within him. He had touched those fires in the past, had woven them to his will when he had faced N'Kari. The question was, would he have time to do so now?

'Do you really think you can hurt me?' Malekith asked.

'We both know the answer to that.'

'I suspect we do,' said Malekith. His fingers traced a pattern in the air. Teclis could not be certain what he was attempting, but he sensed immense force gathering in response to the Witch King's will.

Teclis invoked the power of Asuryan. He reached out with his will and called upon the flames that burned within the Witch King's body. They blazed up in response to his spell. The wards woven into Malekith's armour could not protect him against the attack from within.

'No!' Malekith's voice boomed across the battlefield. Teclis called upon the full power of the Moonstaff of Lileath, using it to sculpt all of his power into one massive bolt of ravening destruction, knowing the pain of the awakened flame within his body would keep Malekith from countering. Malekith however surprised him.

As the titanic bolt smashed home, he spoke a potent spell. The massive armoured form vanished, leaving an outline limned in fire and the web of energies collapsing around him. Teclis was not sure what had happened. Had the Witch King been destroyed? Had he managed to escape by using some sorcery of translocation or displacement? One thing was certain: his baleful presence was gone, and Teclis knew he was alone on the hilltop.

He was not the only one who knew that.

Beneath him the entire dark elven force let out a great roar of horror and despair. They had seen their king and their mightiest champion destroyed before their eyes – at this moment they did not share Teclis's doubts as to his fate. They only knew that they faced his vanquisher and that thought was not at all to their liking.

TECLIS DREW UPON the winds of magic again. He leapt upwards into the sky above the army, his aura glowing around him like that of a god.

Teclis began to weave spells of destruction, drawing upon all the grim knowledge he had acquired in the library at Hoeth. He felt mad exultation build within him and knew that once more his soul was in danger. He did not let that stop him.

Great clouds swirled over the ranks of the Naggarothi, rains of green acid showering down on them, burning their flesh. Bolts of chromatic lightning stabbed down from the sky, searing flesh and cutting great swathes from their ranks.

Thunder so loud it burst eardrums and caused blood to gush forth made them cringe in terror.

For long minutes an unleashed tide of destruction played over the battlefield such as few had ever witnessed or ever would again. There were times when Teclis thought it was all going to slip beyond his control and the powers he had so rashly thought to bind to his will were going to break free and destroy as much of his own side as they were destroying his enemies.

Somehow, by dint of desperate effort, and mighty exertion of skill and will, and through not a little luck, he wrestled the forces under control, and the great storm of unleashed energy passed, leaving him standing alone on the hillside: drained, elated and empty.

Slowly the magnitude of his triumph sank in. He had beaten the Witch King. He had routed the druchii army. Victory was his. Already the army of Malekith was in retreat and Tyrion and his warriors were riding them down.

DEATH TIPPED THE piece representing the Witch King to one side, signalling his resignation. He raised his pale hand in ironic mocking salute.

'Well played,' he said, rising from his chair with an air of resignation. 'Perhaps next time I will win.'

Caledor felt strangely confused and oddly empty. He knew he was missing something. He knew he had forgotten something. He had a task to do but he could not remember what it was.

'Perhaps next time I will let you,' he said, so softly that he doubted Death could hear.

## ABOUT THE AUTHOR

**William King** is the author of the Tyrion and Teclis saga, the Macharian Crusade trilogy as well as the much-loved Gotrek & Felix series and the Space Wolf novels. His short stories have appeared in many magazines and compilations, including *White Dwarf* and *Inferno!*. Bill was born in Stranraer, Scotland, in 1959 and currently lives in Prague.